COME THE REVOLUTION

BAEN BOOKS by Frank Chadwick

How Dark the World Becomes
Come the Revolution

The Forever Engine

COME THE REVOLUTION

FRANK CHADWICK

COME THE REVOLUTION

This is a work of fiction. All the characters and events portrayed in this book are fictional, and any resemblance to real people or incidents is purely coincidental.

A Baen Books Original

Baen Publishing Enterprises
P.O. Box 1403
Riverdale, NY 10471
www.baen.com

ISBN: 978-1-4767-8095-5

Cover art by Kurt Miller

First printing, December 2015

Distributed by Simon & Schuster
1230 Avenue of the Americas
New York, NY 10020

Library of Congress Cataloging-in-Publication Data

Chadwick, Frank.
  Come the revolution / Frank Chadwick.
      pages ; cm
  ISBN 978-1-4767-8095-5 (paperback)
  I. Title.
  PS3553.H2184C66 2015
  813'.54—dc23
                                                    2015030722

10 9 8 7 6 5 4 3 2 1

Pages by Joy Freeman (www.pagesbyjoy.com)
Printed in the United States of America

For Diana—and a better world for her
than Sasha was born to.

‖‖‖‖‖‖‖‖‖‖‖‖‖‖‖‖‖‖‖‖‖‖‖ ACKNOWLEDGMENTS

Thanks first of all to my many friends and colleagues who read the work and offered both insightful criticism and generous encouragement, especially Jake and Beth Strangeway, Nancy Blake, and Bart Palamaro (still the best freelance editor I've ever worked with). I am lucky to be part of three outstanding writer/critique groups. All of them serve the essential function of listening and criticizing, but most importantly reminding a writer that, no matter how lonely a job writing sometimes seems, he is never really alone. Without in any way detracting from the comments and suggestions of the other members of the groups, I want to single out Elaine Palencia and John Palen for repeatedly providing insights into the story which broadened my own understanding of my own characters. Whenever you guys speak, I listen carefully.

I'm lucky to know some pretty smart scientists. Bob Switzer helped steer me through the treacherous waters of biogenetics and neurotoxins. Rich Bliss and Jim Nevling helped with material science and physics, but also (and more importantly) physics jokes. That said, any implausibility in the science of the story is entirely my own responsibility.

Finally, thanks to the whole gang at Baen, but especially to Toni Weisskopf and to Tony Daniel, whose editorial hand is light, encouraging, and well-considered. The opening of the novel, and general pacing, benefited significantly from Tony's suggestions. I also appreciate Gray Rinehart's thorough and skillful copyediting on this manuscript, as well as his having been the editor who kicked my first novel manuscript for Baen—*How Dark The World Becomes*—upstairs to Toni's desk with a positive recommendation. I still owe you a drink.

SAKKATTO CITY

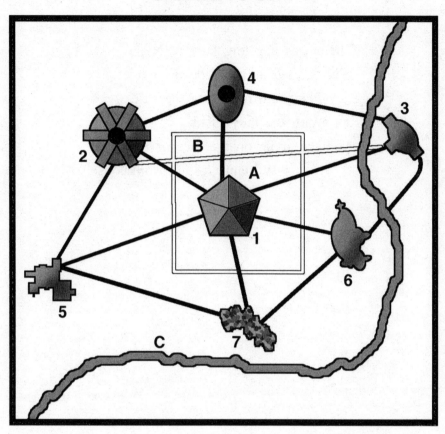

━━━ Maglev Rail Line

═══ Major Street

〜〜 Wanu River

Arcologies
1. Katammu
2. Bannaz
3. Jannu
4. e-Kruaan
5. Kagataan
6. Drak'zanaat
7. Praha-Riz

Other Locations
A. Inter-Arcology
    Park District
B. Sookagrad
C. The Black Docks

There was a young lady of Niger
Who smiled as she rode on a tiger;
    They returned from the ride
    With the lady inside,
And the smile on the face of the tiger.
          —William Cosmo Monkhouse

COME THE REVOLUTION

Chapter One

I killed twenty-two people by the time I died. Hadn't killed any since. Some claimed that was due to a lack of opportunity, but I wasn't so sure.

I was only dead for a couple weeks, and I spent almost all of that cryogenically frozen, so some folks treated the whole thing as just another complicated medical procedure, but I didn't. Dead is dead, and take it from me, it's not for the faint of heart.

After resuscitation there were months of rehab, physical and psychological, but in the two years since my life had gotten back to "normal"—whatever that meant—my existence had been sufficiently nonviolent to satisfy a Buddhist monk. That's exactly what I'd wanted and I wasn't complaining. The problem was, as I looked out the shuttle window at the sprawling night-lit landscape of Sakkatto City, the beating heart of the political and commercial Varoki engines that drove the *Cottohazz*—the Stellar Commonwealth—I had the growing feeling my peaceful interlude was nearing an end. A storm was gathering, had probably been gathering since before I was born, but now it was close. I could sense it, like smelling rain just before it starts to fall.

My parents named me Aleksandr Sergeyevich Naradnyo, but friends called me Sasha.

✧   ✧   ✧

1

Our executive shuttle flew lazy ovals for ten minutes while municipal traffic control figured out which approach pattern they wanted us on. The Wanu River beneath us shone like a silver ribbon in the reflected light of Hazz'Akatu's largest moon.

I'd seen big cities on Earth but Sakkatto was different, dominated by seven enormous arcologies, each of which housed from half a million to over a million people. As we circled the city, the massive, towering structures already glowed from interior lights, washing out the last dull red traces of sunset. Each arcology was unique, built at different times over the last three hundred or so years. Styles changed, material technology changed, but the Varoki desire to live in those giant anthills never did.

Not all of them could afford to, though. Several kilometers separated each of the arcologies from its neighbors. Slums filled the spaces in between, a jumble of lower buildings and twisting streets, at this altitude looking like piled-up refuse that had just blown against the base of the arcs and then settled there. High speed maglev train lines fifty or so meters above the rooftops of the slums linked the arcologies. All of the big cities I'd seen on Hazz'Akatu, the Varoki home world, were pretty much like this.

"Tee-Traak One to Traffic Con, acknowledged," the shuttle pilot said into his commlink, "Inbound for Katammu-Arc on corridor Seven Niner North." He turned in his seat and held up two fingers, visible through the open door to the cockpit, and I nodded. Two minutes to the executive landing pad of the Katammu Arcology, an enormous five-sided metal and glass pyramid almost three kilometers across at the base and two kilometers tall.

"Perimeter team up," I said to my own embedded commlink on the security detail channel.

Our three security people closest to the exit hatch, the three in tactical gear and heavy body armor, checked their Mark 19 RAGs—which stood for *Rifle, Assault, Gauss*—one last time and then slung them and drew their neuro-pistols, nonlethal stun weapons. They'd stay behind with the shuttle once we disembarked and were sure the landing bay was secure. The other six security folks would accompany us to the reception at the uBakai Ministry of Knowledge. I wasn't expecting high-firepower trouble, but it always paid to be prepared. I closed my eyes and leaned back against the seat cushion. What *was* I expecting?

Nut jobs. Angry demonstrators. Lone wolf with a death wish.

Sniper. Those were all in the realm of possibility. They'd never exactly happened to us here on Hazz'Akatu, but they sometimes happened to other "high profiles." The fact that a ten-year-old Varoki girl and my pregnant Human wife were "high profiles" who might need this sort of security was proof enough to any sane person that this world had worms in its head.

But that wasn't exactly news.

Marrissa must have sensed my thoughts. Her hand touched mine and I opened my eyes and smiled at her.

"Hey," I said.

She squeezed my hand. "Everything will be fine."

"I know. Just doing what I'm paid for—worrying."

That's part of what the chief of security for the two highest profile targets in the whole *Cottohazz* got paid for, but not all of it.

I never take anything for granted, but tonight I figured the biggest threats were political, not violent. We were always prepared to deal with direct violence, but so far never had to. The political stuff was unrelenting, though, like mold, like rust. But politics was Marrissa's department, not mine. I reached over and rested my hand on the swell of her belly, felt our future son kick, then kick again.

Sitting on the other side of Marr, Tweezaa leaned forward and looked at me, her face serious, thoughtful. Then she leaned back in her seat.

Tweezaa had just turned ten the week before, which made her about thirteen in Earth years. She'd shot up so fast the last two years she nearly reached my shoulder. When we first met I carried her on my hip with one arm.

Externally, Varoki are a lot like Humans: upright bipeds with a head on top holding a brain and the same sensory organs we have. Their sloping foreheads and lack of a protruding nose, their hairless iridescent skin, the large leaflike ears, and those long slender fingers, made Humans take one look and think *lizard*, even though Varoki have far less genetically in common with terrestrial lizards than we Humans do.

Tweezaa was dark of skin but still richly iridescent, and when the light hit her just right she seemed to glow. Even when she was a little Varoki girl, she'd had an unselfconscious dignity that had me calling her The Dark Princess within a week of meeting her. I still thought of her that way.

Tweezaa e-Traak was heir to probably the biggest fortune in Varoki history, and Marrissa was her legal guardian, and actually sat on the board of governors of AZ Simki-Traak Trans-Stellar, the corporate crown jewel of the e-Traak family empire. She was the only Human ever to have done so, and the only female. The idea of females having that much power in male-dominated Varoki society, and in Marrissa's case a *Human* female, pissed off millions of Varoki in more ways than I could count.

That was one reason I was such a tight-ass about security, that and the fact Marr and Tweezaa were the only family I had still alive.

The shuttle lifted its nose and decelerated, pushing us forward against our seat restraints, but we didn't level to land. I keyed my embedded commlink and pinged the shuttle pilot.

"What's up, Kamal?"

"We've got a temporary hold, Sasha, some kind of disturbance at the VIP landing bay."

"Okay," I answered and looked around the cabin: perimeter team still up at the main hatch, six other bodyguards in formal wear still strapped in, all but one of the team Human, everyone waiting for something to happen.

Something wasn't right about this.

"Kamal, how long does Traffic Con expect us to just hover out here?"

"Um, the flag-off wasn't from Traffic Con. It was on a Munie tactical band."

I felt the adrenaline surge as soon as he said it. "Put us in that landing bay, *now*! Emergency, my authority."

"Yes, sir!" he answered, his own voice rising a note. The shuttle nose tipped down and acceleration pressed us back in our seats just as the missile hit us.

A deafening crack, sparks, whistle of shrapnel, smoke, screams, hiss of air rushing past, screech of metal as we plowed into something and then skidded across it to a halt.

For a moment it was quiet under the flashing overhead orange and blue emergency lights, everyone still alive stunned. The cabin filled with the stench of burning insulation and then the first moans of the injured. I found myself sprawled across Marr and Tweezaa, covering their fronts, although I had no memory of releasing my seat harness. Both of them stirred, eyes opening slowly.

"Marr, are you okay?"

She took a moment to focus on me and then nodded. I touched her stomach, felt both of her hands wrapped protectively over it. She looked down and then back up at me and nodded again.

"Tweezaa, are you—?"

I stopped as she held her right arm up and I saw the shrapnel wound through her forearm. She stared at it, more puzzled than frightened. It only oozed a little blood but that was because of shock. I pulled off my tuxedo tie and wrapped it around her arm.

"Hold that as tight as you can. It's going to start bleeding in a minute, and probably hurt like hell. We've got to get out of here before there's a fire." I triggered both of their harness release tabs and stood up to assess the damage.

We had a fair-sized hole in the forward bulkhead of the cabin on the right side, and a matching one aft. It took me a couple seconds to find the perimeter team, one of them stirring but all of them looking pretty bad. Most of the other six bodyguards were moving. Iris Tenryu, my second in command, popped her restraints and stood up, her tuxedo splashed with blood—someone else's, I assumed. Behind her I saw Hong Lee unhooking as well. There was smoke in the cabin but it wasn't getting any thicker, at least not yet. Liquid hydrogen hissed into the rear of the cabin from ruptured fuel tanks, frosting the walls white.

"Iris, I'm taking the primaries out. Get everyone else organized. Keep away from the deep freeze back there, and haul the injured out before we go up in flames. Hong, can you walk?" He stood up in answer. "Okay, you're my wingman. Grab some firepower."

I got Marr and Tweezaa to the door, mostly under their own power but with one of my arms around each for support. My own knees were wobbly and I wasn't injured or pregnant, so they were holding up really well.

The hatch was sprung and slightly ajar. It didn't respond to the release lever but two good hard kicks sent it clattering to the foamstone landing pad of the VIP shuttle bay. I immediately felt a strong breeze and heard the soft roar of the hangar bay exhaust fans blowing any hydrogen from our ruptured fuel tanks out the open bay door before it could reach explosive concentrations. But it could pocket inside the cabin or machinery spaces, so we still had to get clear of the wreck.

I scanned the bay, which was a good hundred meters wide and

half-filled with other executive shuttles. Ours was the only one wrecked. There were a lot of Varoki as well, at least a hundred of them, starting to stand again after hitting the deck when we made our crash landing. I didn't see any uniforms, though. There were supposed to be Munies—Municipal Police—working crowd control and VIP security. Where were they? I hoped we hadn't landed on them.

Beside me, Hong knelt by the body of one of the perimeter team and unbuckled the ammunition harness. The body was headless, but male, so it was either John Cartwright or Norm Ramirez. Cartwright was new to the team while Ramirez had been with us for over a year. The anonymity of the corpse bothered me, as if somewhere maybe both of them were partly alive and partly dead. Hong buckled on the web harness, picked up the RAG-19 assault rifle, and looked up at me.

"The main exit point is to our left, into the interior of the arcology," I said. "I'm going that way with the primaries and try to find a secure spot away from the wreck. Cover us from here until we're in position, then join us. Got it?"

He nodded and stood.

I jumped down to the pavement, which was less than a meter below the edge of the hatch since the shuttle had come in with its landing gear still retracted. The missile damage didn't look as bad from out here but we'd clipped the edge of the bay door coming in, lost an engine mount, and there were pieces of shattered composite turbine blades all over the floor. I helped Marr and Tweezaa down and then we hustled forward past the cockpit. I saw a maintenance work station, with a heavy metallic work bench bolted to the floor, about twenty meters toward the door. The bench would give us some cover if the shuttle blew so we made for it.

As we trotted, I heard the Varoki crowd to our right start to shout. It was all in aBakaa, which I don't speak, but I picked out a couple words I'd heard often enough to recognize: *heiress*, and *Human*. The tone sounded ugly. I turned and yelled back to the shuttle.

"Warning shots only, Hong, unless they charge."

Gauss weapons, like the RAG-19, don't make much noise, just the snaps of magnetically launched flechettes breaking the sound barrier. I heard Hong's assault rifle stutter a couple three-round bursts, saw the sparks as they hit the ceiling and ricocheted. That put the crowd back on the floor until we made the shelter of the workbench where I found Kamal Darzi, our shuttle pilot, holding his left arm which was pretty obviously broken. His face was lacerated by about a dozen deep cuts and slick with blood. It was a miracle he still had both of his eyes.

"Ah, boss, you're alive!" he said. "Miss Tweezaa, Madame Marfoglia, I am sorry for the terrible landing."

I helped them down behind the bench and Marrissa helped Darzi get his arm wrapped up.

"No apology necessary, Mr. Darzi," she said. "We're alive. I think everyone hurt in back was from the explosion before the crash. What happened?"

"A missile fired from the open bay hatch directly at us. I saw it fire but it hit almost the same instant, came through the windscreen and then the cabin bulkhead behind me, right past my head."

"Hypervelocity kinetic energy missile. They must have figured we'd be armored," I said. "Good thing. That long rod went right through us, did most of its damage with secondary fragmentation and impact. If they'd hit us with an explosive warhead…" I didn't finish the sentence. No point in belaboring the unpleasantly obvious. I looked around. Where were the assassins now? Had they blended back in to the crowd?

I saw Iris and someone else helping our injured out of the hatch and the crowd started finding its voice again, shouting at Iris and the others around the shuttle as well as us. They started edging forward when about twenty Varoki Munies in riot gear showed up, streamed in both entrances to the bay, and fanned out into a control line.

"Cavalry's here," I told the others, trying to sound as nonchalant as I could. Then I sat down because my knees wouldn't hold me up anymore.

Chapter Two

I knelt next to Tweezaa as the Varoki medtech finished apply-ing the spray-on bandage to her right forearm. She still had that eyes-too-wide look that said she was in shock, but she was com-ing out of it. The medtech moved on to have a second look at Kamal. I put my hand on the smoothness of her head and she leaned into me, my arms around her.

"We're okay, Princess," I said. "We're going to be fine."

"Don't call me that anymore," she said softly. "I don't want to be a princess."

I looked over at Marr on the other side of her, saw her eyes fill with tears too. She still held her hands folded protectively over her belly. The medtech had done a couple scans, though, and everything looked good. We'd have our own doctor—a Human doctor—check her out as soon as we got back to our apartment in Praha-Riz, the arcology south of Katammu-Arc.

Hong stood guard over us, his RAG-19 pointed at the hangar bay's ceiling but still ready. He turned to me. "Munie officer com-ing over. Iris sent him here so must be looking for a big shot."

That would be me. I gently untangled myself from Tweezaa's arms and stood up to face him. The Varoki police lieutenant didn't look angry. He looked sheepish, although he probably had never heard of a sheep.

He started and ended with an apology. In between he told me what little they knew.

His detail had been pulled away by fake orders on the same communication band as sent us the wave-off, obviously part of an orchestrated assassination attempt aimed at Tweezaa and Marrissa. That cleared the way for the shooters, who were disguised as maintenance workers. They'd hidden the missile launcher in the very workstation we'd taken cover behind. The Munies knew all that from the surveillance video of the hangar and from what remains they'd recovered so far, and by recovered he meant scraped off the foamstone floor. It seems we'd landed on the missile team and then slid a ways.

How's that for poetic justice?

He also filled me in on the ramped-up security plans for us and transportation arrangements to get us safely back to Praha-Riz Arcology.

"Nothing like this has *ever* happened in Sakkatto City, Mr. Naradnyo. Please be sure the heiress knows we will do *everything* in our power to find any other miscreants involved in this." He shook his head, his expression a mixture of shame and astonishment, his large ears folded back defensively against his skull. "A missile fired at an aeroshuttle *in the city!* I would not believe it were the evidence not in front of me. What is the world coming to?"

He left to supervise the arrest and interrogation of the demonstrators. A cop's instincts, when uncertain or confused, are usually to arrest everyone in sight. He figured they must have been part of the plan, but I couldn't see how. Why stage a demonstration and maybe keep the Munies here when you wanted them to go someplace else? Not the way I'd have run the operation, but I couldn't see a good reason to argue with him.

Iris Tenryu joined me as soon as the cop was gone. Iris was my number two guy, although she obviously wasn't a guy. She was a couple years younger than me, early thirties, very fit, and cute in a lean and scratchy kind of way. She'd been an undercover detective for *Keishicho-koanbu,* the Tokyo Police Security Bureau, before getting into the VIP bodyguard field. I'd been lucky to find her. We'd mostly built the team together.

"How bad?" I asked.

She looked over at the crumpled shuttle where Varoki med techs worked on our injured team mates and two maintenance workers carried a body from the hatch to lay it in line with three others.

"Pretty bad, Boss," she said. "Ramirez, Swanson, Mfengi, and that Varoki kid bought it."

"Jutaant," I said. "His name was Tita Jutaant."

"I know," she said softly. "Cartwright and Gladys Bonderovski got evacuated to a med center here, probably pull through but going to need serious surgery and rehab. Everyone else is banged up, one way or another, but they'll live. You, me, and Hong are the only ones really a hundred percent operational. We got a ride home?"

"Yeah, the Munies set it up—not that I got a lot of faith in them right now, so gather up the RAG-19s and all the extra ammo. I want you and Hong armed to the teeth."

Since we were bound for a lavish state reception, and would be going through banks of metal detectors, only the three members of the perimeter team had been armed and they were all down. The rest of us just carried neuro-wands—painful but nonlethal.

"You want the third RAG yourself?" she asked.

I looked around the hangar bay, choked with Varoki: emergency workers, Varoki Munies, and the Varoki demonstrators, their anger having given way to fear and sullen resentment. We were a human cork bobbing in a Varoki sea—a smaller cork than we had been an hour ago. In two years I'd never lost an agent. Now four of us gone, just like that!

"Bring the extra RAG along," I said. "Hopefully I won't need it."

"Look," she said and nodded toward the crowd of demonstrators. "What's that asshole doing here?"

I followed her gaze and saw a tall Varoki—tall even by their standards, which was saying something. He was expensively dressed, probably for the same reception we'd been heading for. He walked the police line, talking to the detainees on the other side, working the crowd as if he were a politician.

"Elaamu Gaant," I said, "my least favorite Varoki after-dinner speaker. Simki-Traak Trans-Stellar loves to book him for their big conferences. Yeah, what the hell *is* he doing here?"

Gaant saw me, made eye contact, and walked across the hangar floor. Iris left before he got to me.

"Ah, Sasha Naradnyo," he said by way of greeting. "Why am I not surprised to find you surrounded by death and destruction?"

"What do you want, Gaant?"

"When I heard what happened I came to offer advice and comfort to these people, whom the police are illegally detaining following your unfortunate accident."

"*Accident?* Only accident was they missed taking all of us out."

He tilted his head to one side, the Varoki equivalent of a shrug. "It is unfortunate the heiress will be unable to attend the reception. It is in honor of the three hundredth anniversary of the invention of the interstellar jump drive. The fortune you expect her to inherit is, after all, derived largely from that invention and its patents."

"Yeah," I said. "I bet it'll be a swell party. Maybe we'll catch the next one."

"Three hundred years!" he said as if he hadn't heard me. "Three hundred years of star-spanning exploration, commerce, and progress—although your people have only been part of it for, what? Seventy years? Do you know the most remarkable thing about those three hundred years?"

I thought for a moment.

"How little you've accomplished?"

His polite façade suddenly slipped and his face twisted in contempt.

"No! It is that we made the incredible mistake of sharing that discovery with five other races, especially with yours. The discovery which allows travel between the stars in the blink of an eye instead of the passage of a lifetime, the discovery which makes interstellar civilization *possible*, is Varoki. But now the Varoki heiress to that knowledge is being raised and corrupted by an unscrupulous cabal of Humans!"

The iridescent skin of his face flushed orange-pink with rage, his large ears flared wide to the side, and he took a threatening step forward, as if he might take a swing at me, which would have been interesting. But at the moment I had bigger things to attend to. I extended my right arm down and to the side and twisted it so the concealed neuro-wand dropped from my jacket sleeve and into my hand. It shot out to full extension with a hiss.

Gaant saw the movement and froze, ears tight back against his head.

"I got scruples coming out my ears, Gaant. I just don't have many inhibitions."

Gaant took a step back, eyes narrow and teeth showing. "I am not alone in this enterprise, Sasha Naradnyo. The entire e-Traak family, the governors of Simki-Traak Trans-Stellar, and many legislators in the uBakai *Wat* all stand with me. This absurd inheritance will *never* take place, and that is only the first step of many. I have set this thing in motion, *my* hands are upon it, and you will mourn the day you first saw my face or heard my name."

"Oh, I'm already there, Gaant. You know, I liked you better when you were just a two-bit huckster, a motivational speaker peddling dreams of greatness to suckers and losers. But you've been listening to your own bullshit so long you started believing it. You don't scare us, so take a hike."

I lifted the wand a bit to encourage him and he turned and strode away. I'd done him a disservice calling him two-bit; the vidfeeds preaching his brand of Varoki supremacy in the *Cottohazz* sold in the millions. Marrissa stood up from behind the workbench and I turned to her.

"He doesn't scare us?" she said.

"Well, maybe a little. You feel good enough to stand?"

"I don't feel good enough not to. That floor is killing my butt and lower back. The way Gaant talked...could he have been behind the attack?"

I thought about it for a moment but then shook my head. "Anything's possible, but it's not his style. He's all wrapped up in his own political schemes. He's got too much invested in them to risk it all on an attack this messy and dangerous. Besides, if it actually worked he could never take credit for it, and that would drive him crazy."

"So what do we do now?" she asked.

"We got two people in critical condition and they stay here at the med center in Katammu-Arc. The rest of us head back to Praha-Riz Arcology and we'll bunker up in our complex there until we know what's going on. We're going to be real shorthanded in the security detail. *The'On's* still joining us tomorrow, right?"

"His shuttle docked at Old Tower Highstation two hours ago. He'll be here." She looked over at the wreck. "Is a shuttle safe? What if they have another missile?"

"We're going by Maglev train. Munies have arranged a closed car with their people on the exits and our folks will be inside with us."

She looked over at the four bodies on the foamstone landing pad, now covered with dark plastic sheets. "What about them?"

"They ride with us."

She nodded wordlessly, her lower lip quivering.

"Do me a favor," I said. "Next time I have to sit through some Simki-Traak banquet with you, make sure that asshole Gaant doesn't get hired as the keynote speaker, okay?"

She gave me a shaky smile. "I'm not on the program committee."

Chapter Three

The first time I met The Honorable Arigapaa e-Lotonaa, I was in something of a mood—what Marr calls my simmering icono-clasm, which I keep meaning to look up. I'd decided his name was too much of a mouthful, so I'd called him *The'On*—short for *The Honorable*—instead, and that's all I'd called him ever since. Despite that, and the fact he was Varoki, we'd become pals.

The'On was senior staff in the *Cottohazz* diplomatic service but he was between assignments right then, which was good for us. Five months earlier he'd finished his gig as the *Cottohazz* Executive Council's Special Envoy Plenipotentiary for Emergency Abatement on K'Tok. That's five Varoki months, over six months Earth time.

The'On had been called back to K'Tok two months later by some sort of flare-up, and that had nearly ruined our plans, but he'd gotten back to us in the nick of time, just like the U.S. cavalry in those old John Ford flat vids.

I waited for him in the Praha-Riz VIP shuttle bay with one security guy. We were too short-handed and busted up to take a proper detail without leaving security at the family complex light, and the family complex was priority one. Since I only took one guy, I wanted to minimize the chances of someone trying something so I took Baka ah-Quan, one of the two Zacks on our security team. Anyone in their right mind found Zacks physically intimidating and sort of repulsive, too.

14

Zacks, or *Zaschaan*, the Fifth Race, were as tall as Varoki but a lot bulkier. They were known mostly for their sour dispositions, troll-like ugliness (at least by Human and Varoki aesthetic standards), and unpleasant personal habits, many of which had to do with their two mouths. They ate with the lower mouth and spoke mostly through the upper one, which was a highly adapted blowhole. You know how when you talk to someone and they get all excited, you sometimes end up with a little spittle on you? Same with a Zack, except that's not spittle.

They were a rung higher on the economic ladder than Humans, but we were gaining fast. Like us, you saw a lot of Zacks in the military and security details. We Humans were also starting to do well in entertainment and the arts—the Zacks, not so much.

We turned away from the blast of air as the VIP shuttle flared for landing, its ducted fans rotated full down and turbines whining. Almost as soon as the hydraulic landing skids settled under the weight of the flier, the hatch opened and *The'On* climbed down the three folding steps to the pad, ears fanned wide and a broad smile of greeting illuminating his face. He was dressed casually, at least by his standards: a red silk tunic and baggy trousers trimmed in broad black embroidered lace, with two Chinese characters on the left breast. A lot of wealthy Varoki had taken to classical Chinese clothing styles in the last few years but had no idea what the decorative lettering meant. I was pretty sure *The'On* did. It was not something he would take for granted.

"Sasha, it is good to see you alive," he said, shaking my hand. The Human form of greeting had gained popularity among Varoki until the traditionalists like Gaant started raising a stink about anything Human. You didn't see as much of it anymore, but that never stopped *The'On*.

"I'm fine. It's good to have you here. Do you know Mr. ah-Quan?"

"Yes, I believe we met last year. May you and your blood prosper." He didn't offer his hand. Zacks don't like to be touched, at least not by non-Zacks. I'd never heard them say so, but I suspected they found us as physically repulsive as we found them. Maybe that's why they always seemed so cranky.

"Am well," he answered, the voice from his upper mouth strangely nasal and high-pitched. You always expected a rumbling bass to come out of that massive body.

My eyes flicked back to the hatch. Borro, *The'On's* Varoki

bodyguard, filled the opening. He turned his head, taking in the immediate area, memorizing everything just in case. Then his eyes found mine and he nodded, a very slight smile on his lips.

"Come on, let's head to the family complex," I said. "We'll help carry your things."

The'On smiled at that. His profession took him to a lot of residences of the rich and powerful throughout the *Cottohazz*, but I was pretty sure ours was the only one where he got to carry his own bags. Keeping servants to a minimum was good for security. It wasn't bad for the soul, either.

I'd reserved a private autopod which would get us to the main atrium facing the family complex up on level 237. It was more secure than the public elevators and let us talk in private on the way there.

"So how are things on K'Tok? Still the lush green paradise I remember?"

He looked at me, his ears cocked unevenly in a way that made me smile. "The autumn was lovely and no one shot at me this time, if that is what you mean. But there is growing unrest in the old colonies ever since last year, when Humans began illegally settling the western continent and the Utaan Archipelago. At least the Varoki settlers have put aside their animosities, united in their common hostility to their new Human neighbors."

"You can always count on us Humans to bring people together," I said.

Ah-Quan laughed and then belched. You'd never know the Zacks have a sense of humor just looking at them, but they do—a finely honed appreciation for irony. Borro, sitting in the seat across from him, nodded in agreement.

The main entrance to the family complex was off the northwest atrium on what was called the Executive Layer, which was basically everything above Level Two Hundred. From the complex's outer foyer we had to go through an elaborate security routine to get into the inner foyer, and then another different one to get into the main apartment, routines which required not only passwords but also a retinal scan and DNA sample. Tweezaa's late father, Sarro e-Traak, had built this complex six years earlier with security in mind. If he'd have stayed in it, he'd probably be alive today, Marr would still be a market consultant to the rich and powerful, and I'd be dead—or head of the rackets on Peezgtaan and wishing I was dead.

The inner foyer opened onto the suites for the live-in security teams and, past them, the family apartment. Our apartment was open design built around the living room in the middle with the kitchen and four bedroom suites radiating from it. The suites were Marr's and mine, Tweezaa's, and two for guests. Those were empty right now, but we gave The'On one and Borro, his bodyguard, the other. Normally bodyguards bunked with our security folks but Borro was nearly family.

Each suite had a bedroom, bath, office, and den. We'd decorated mostly with soft reddish-tan carpets and furniture, and a lot of bright accent colors. One smart wall in the central living room was set up with Tweezaa's family pictures, school and sports awards, a prize-winning essay, and a bunch of her drawings. A year ago the drawings had been interesting scrawls. Lately they'd started getting pretty good—still very impressionistic, and with some surreal color choices, but I thought she had an eye for important detail. Of course, I was biased.

"So, did Gaant tell you anything useful about the edict?" The'On asked once the new round of greetings were done and he and I, Marr and Tweezaa settled in around the table in the family kitchen.

"He hinted but he didn't mention the edict outright, so as far as they know we're still in the dark," I said. "We know it will retroactively invalidate any will or trust which transfers control—not ownership, but control—of select family assets to a non-family member."

He nodded. "Yes. And since Marrissa is Tweezaa's guardian, and clearly not a family member, the inheritance is forfeit. What a stupid edict! It will also break every charitable trust in Bakaa, don't they realize that? Or don't they care? The *Wat* will be inundated in lawsuits from foundations. Then they will realize their error and try to find a way to exempt everyone from the law but Tweezaa. Imbeciles!"

"No argument from me. Gaant gave us some possibly useful information. For one thing, it's obvious they don't know we've seen the draft. They think they're blindsiding us, so whatever your source was, it's still secure."

"Good," he said, "but after this insane attack against your shuttle, we have to assume Gaant and his political allies will move at once. The situation becomes unstable, hence unpredictable. Do you believe him—that he is behind the edict?"

Marrissa and I exchanged a glance and I shrugged.

"Sasha and I aren't certain," she answered. "He is more inclined to believe the claim than I am. Although I don't know Gaant well, I have met him several times and seen him in meetings, both large ones and small working groups. He never impressed me as a particularly...*deep* thinker. He is the sort of glib spokesperson you expect to see on news feeds and giving keynote addresses, a person most comfortable in a holovid, but not actually working hard behind the scenes. You know exactly the sort I am talking about, Gapa."

Marr had never gotten comfortable calling e-Lotonaa *The'On*, and so she used Gapa, the diminutive form of his first name, Arigapaa.

"Oh, certainly," he said, nodding at her assessment of Gaant's personality. "But that may be a look deliberately cultivated. He moves in the highest levels of society and among many of the *e-Varokiim* there is a stigma attached to having to work *too* hard. Whether Elaamu Gaant is a figurehead, or works on behalf of a political faction, or the other e-Traak heirs, or perhaps follows a personal motivation..."

He tilted his head to the side and didn't finish the sentence. There was no need to. There was no shortage of possible motives for this guy, or for anyone else lining up against Tweezaa and us, up to and including bat-shit-crazy anti-Human. What did their motives really matter? The move itself was important, and what we were going to do about it, nothing else. I'd rather have gone on talking about this Gaant guy all day, but sooner or later we had be adults, had to swallow hard and do what came next.

"You're sure this will work?" I asked him.

He sighed. "Who can really say? It will throw everything into the courts at first, and not simply the uBakai courts. It will almost certainly end up before the *Cottohazz Wat*, unless I am mistaken."

"And what are Tweezaa's chances there?" I asked. Maybe there was an edge in my voice because Marr leaned over and put her hand on my arm.

"Whatever they are, Sasha," she said, "they're better than just taking the uBakai edict as written and giving up." I knew she was right, but I still didn't like it. "I'll still be her fiduciary guardian until she reaches her majority," Marr went on. "We'll still be her *Boti-Marr* and *Boti-Sash*."

All that was true, but it didn't do much for the lump in my throat. I looked over at Tweezaa, the object of this whole exercise, and she looked as miserable as I felt. When she saw me looking at her she looked away, then got up and walked toward the rear of the apartment. After a few steps she began to run and I heard the balcony door slam. The'On's expression suddenly changed to surprised, and then stricken, color flashing across his skin.

"Oh…" he said, and the word had the sound of despair in it.

"I should—" Marr started, but I shook my head and stood up.

"Nope. Better let me."

I found Tweezaa on the balcony, Sakkatto City almost a kilometer below us, sprawling away to the north and east. On clear nights we sat out there and saw the glowing, impossibly thin structure of The Old Tower, the elevator to orbit rising from the southern horizon two hundred kilometers away, rising up and up until it faded into the blackness of the sky. Sometimes we saw the tiny bright light of a capsule climbing the needle to orbit. Now Tweezaa leaned on the railing. She wasn't crying, but she wouldn't look at me. Instead she stared out at the circling birds.

"This sucks, Kiddo," I said in English as a preliminary.

"Why can't I just change my citizenship on my own?"

"You know why. You aren't of age, so Marr would have to do it for you, as your guardian. There's no plausible reason for her to do so except to avoid the effects of the uBakai edict. There's this thing—*deceptive transfer* I think they call it. They could void the change. But if The'On adopts you, you take his uKootrin citizenship as a matter of course."

"They can't say the same thing about that?" she asked, her gaze still on the sea birds way out there over the water. I turned to face her.

"They can try, but The'On's a pretty big guy in the *Cottohazz* executive bureaucracy, and he's been close to you ever since our time on K'Tok." Close was hardly the right word. In truth, The'On loved her like a daughter. That devastated look on his face, that sense of heartbreak when he thought Tweezaa might not want to be his daughter after all, spoke volumes. Tweezaa hadn't seen it, and I didn't tell her now. I didn't want to just beat her down with guilt or pity. This was her life we were rearranging.

"Besides," I went on, "he's been working on the adoption,

quietly, for four months. There's a document trail which predates when they think we learned of the edict." All of a sudden I knew Gaant and his friends had outsmarted themselves keeping the edict secret. Anything we did after they could prove we knew about it would be deceptive transfer, in reaction to the news. They'd have been better off telling us right away.

"Tweezaa, look at me," I said.

She hesitated but then turned to me, her eyes defiant and angry, but only in front. Back behind them I knew she was holding back the tears.

"This edict will invalidate your inheritance."

"Is that all you care about?" she demanded, anger and grief struggling for control of her face.

"No. All we care about is you. Once you're of age, you can do anything you want with your wealth. Give it all away to charity, buy a planet somewhere and turn it into a sex palace, give it to your worthless shit-head relatives who are trying to steal it from you now—I don't care. But it's *your* decision, and it's Marr's job to make sure *you* get to make it, not them.

"The uBakai *Wat* can pass all the edicts they want to about the property of uBakai citizens. If you're an uKootrin citizen before the edict is ratified, they can go pound sand, and it's as simple as that. The paperwork's ready, all three principals are here, and we have a secure link open to the Prefecture of Vital Records. All you have to do is walk back in there and say yes, and all the plans your thieving relatives and that Gaant creep, and whoever else is behind this, have been hatching for the last three months, all that goes right into the crapper."

She nodded and turned back to the ocean, her face under control again.

"Yes, I know," she said. "*Boti-On* is only thinking of me. And you and Marrissa will soon have a child of your own—a Human child. Then you can stop pretending to be parents to the little lizard girl."

The words left me dizzy.

She turned and walked back toward the house. There were only two people left in the world I cared enough about to willingly die for. One of them was walking away from me, and I didn't know how to stop her.

Chapter Four

Three days later, Marr, *The'On,* and I considered our options given a rapidly changing political landscape. Well, they considered the politics. My concerns were more personal.

"I don't want you to go," I said.

"It's my decision to make," Marr answered.

She sat on the living room couch and *The'On* had settled into a formachair beside it. I paced—should have sat beside Marr on the couch, but I was too worked up to sit down, or even stand still.

I looked out the window. Grey skies overhead and whitecaps on the Wanu River down below. To the north the stark, metallic pyramid of Katammu-Arc looked alien and forbidding, like gunmetal in the overcast, slick and shining from rain squalls which had already scuttled off to the east. Good thing the meeting tomorrow was right here in Praha-Riz arcology, just down about two hundred and twenty levels and over to the south.

Our announcement of the adoption three days ago caught Gaant and his allies by surprise. The news feeders didn't even pay much attention until about a half-dozen prominent uBakai *wattaaks* started screeching as if we'd stolen the crown jewels. First they claimed it was illegal, then that it was thwarting the will of the uBakai people, then that it was a naked power grab by the uKootrin, *The'On's* home government. And they'd had a lot of nasty things to say about us.

There were choreographed demonstrations but then things went off-script, turned violent, more than I think anyone expected. There were even a couple full-blown riots, which were nearly unheard-of. Usually Varoki followed the rules pretty well—a habit I figured came from having written most of the rules in their own favor. But now that the factions lined up against Tweezaa's inheritance—mostly the other heirs in her family and the Simki-Traak upper management, along with some anti-Humanist cranks like Elaamu Gaant—had accidentally unleashed this storm of anger and violence, and it looked as if it might slip out of their control, they wanted to sit down with us and talk. *Now* they wanted to talk.

"Sure it's your decision whether or not to go," I said to Marr, "but I'm responsible for security. Any professional security chief worth his salt would resign before he went along with this. It's insane. You know I'm not going to walk away, now or ever. So you want to go over the cliff? I'll be right there with you all the way. But I don't have to lie to you and say it's the best idea you've ever had."

She looked at me hard for a moment but there was thoughtfulness behind the look as well. "You believe this meeting is a set-up?"

"Could be. Even if not, it's a hell of an opportunity for anyone pissed off about the adoption. There were demonstrations in all seven of the arcologies and riots in parts of the Sakkatto slums. Bad riots, Marr—people killed over an *adoption*. That was yesterday and they haven't even got the damned fires out yet."

"That's why we have to meet with them," she said.

"Yeah, I get it, sort of. Sit down with the sponsors of the edict, see if we can work something out to avoid further violence. Except we know we're not going to work anything out."

She sighed impatiently. "No, probably not, but we cannot leave ourselves open to the charge we were unwilling to at least try."

"Okay, but it is *criminally irresponsible* to put you and *The'On*, both of Tweezaa's guardians, in the same room on neutral turf without a platoon of Mike Marines in powered armor with you, along with a couple gunsleds for top cover and extraction. Not to mention you're pregnant with our son, which means it's not the same deal as when we were cutting our way through the jungle two years ago on K'Tok."

"The Munies have guaranteed the security of the meeting," she said.

"Guaranteed it with what?"

She looked blankly at me.

"Come on, you're the economist, Marr. A guarantee is backed by something—replacement of product if it fails due to design defect, double your money back, free trip to Zamboanga—*something*. Otherwise, 'guarantee' is just another empty word bureaucrats use. No offense, *The'On*."

He shook his head but didn't speak, which was smart. This was not a fight he needed to take sides in.

It was Marr's turn to look out the window. "If it is that dangerous, how do I ask someone else to take my place?"

"Why send anyone?" I said. "If they want to talk, we can talk by holoconference. There's no need to put meat in a room."

"Ah, but there is," *The'On* said, "and I think you know it, Sasha. If we are in the same room, our embedded commlinks can all be jammed locally, which means no virtual record of the meeting can be made through our sensory feeds. It is the only way to speak in private."

"If they're ashamed of what they're going to say, the hell with them," I said, but I knew he was right. Record what a politician's saying and he starts speaking for posterity. You want to cut a deal for today, you need to do it in the dark. I shrugged.

"Okay, face-to-face it is. But not *both* of you. Marr, if you aren't both there, it won't be as dangerous for whoever you send in your place, or for *The'On*. Not as inviting a target. Besides, I'll go along."

Her eyes snapped back to mine. "You? Why? Gapa has Borro for security and if I send someone from the Sakkatto office they can bring a security specialist with them."

"*The'On* is Tweezaa's adoptive father. I'm not going to let him go in harm's way and not be there to do whatever I can. If something happens to him, and both you and I sit it out, Tweezaa will never forgive us."

To be honest, I wasn't sure she would anyway. She'd hardly spoken to us since the adoption. But letting *The'On* walk alone into hell and not come back would cap it. Not to mention I wasn't sure how I'd feel about myself afterwards.

Marr's eyes softened and after a moment she nodded. "I'll

have Gaisaana-la attend. She assembled all of the briefing files anyway. She knows who we're dealing with and as much of the legal background as she needs to." She raised her hand to me and I sat down on the couch next to her. She touched my cheek with her finger tips. "Please be careful," she said.

"I am happy to see you both in agreement again," *The'On* said. "But...where is Zamboanga?"

I shrugged. "Some place where the monkeys have no tails."

Chapter Five

Borro, The'On's bodyguard, turned to me in the private autopod the next morning. "Where exactly is the meeting?"

"Chambers of some supposedly neutral counseling house," I answered. "Good-Soul they're called, right here in Praha-Riz, Level Four, South Tower. We'll stop at Marr's office suite on Level Nineteen to pick up Gaisaana-la."

"Why would they consider your home arcology neutral ground?"

"Well, it's a pretty big place and we don't get along with all our neighbors. The *wattaak* from Red Forest Twenty-one is the lead speaker on the new edict."

"Ah," he said and nodded. "And you question whether the counseling house is actually neutral?"

"You know who's neutral, Borro? Dead people."

He smiled his agreement and I settled back to clear my mind.

Praha-Riz arcology—the Red Forest—housed most of the corporate chambers of AZ Simki-Traak Trans-Stellar and two other large merchant houses, but I'd have chosen it as a home anyway, just based on looks. All of the other arcologies in Sakkatto, regardless of the material or design, looked alien: conceived by alien minds, rendered by alien hands. Praha-Riz, on the other hand, looked like an enormous topiary shrubbery, with glass and metallic bits showing here and there from the interior.

The news feed earlier had said the last of the fires from the riots were being extinguished this morning, but from the balcony before we left I saw a lot of smoke still rising from the slums, particularly the Human Quarter south of Katammu-Arc, and this was after rain. The towers of smoke had provided a forbidding backdrop to our upcoming meeting. Borro must have thought the same thing.

"I wonder if the riots have subsided," he said.

The'On's concentration had been on his viewer glasses but now he looked at us and shook his head. "They seem to be spreading."

Ah-Quan, the fourth passenger in our pod, belched.

Gaisaana-la, Marr's senior executive assistant, was a tall, middle-aged Varoki female. Despite a first-class education, she was unprepared for the high-level politics and economics of running an interstellar trading empire—or trying to get a hand on the tiller when the rest of management was trying to make Marr and her staff nonfunctional ornaments. Well, nothing could prepare a Varoki female to deal with a room full of males born to wealth, power, and entitlement, especially since they had also been raised to think of females as not much more than domestic servants. So nothing *had* prepared Gaisaana-la for this life, but she'd taken to it anyway, somehow. I think some people must just be born to punch above their weight class.

"Executor e-Lotonaa, it is an honor to see you again," she said to The'On with a slight bow. To be honest, she didn't look all that happy to see him.

"And I you, Madame Gaisaana-la. I see you are well," he answered but his smile did not draw one in reply. Instead she turned away to me.

Usually folks liked The'On; he had a way about him. He's never run for elective office, which I thought was odd since he would have been a natural at it. Instead, most of his jobs had been bureaucratic, rising steadily through the ranks of the *Cottohazz* Executive Council's administrative and quasi-diplomatic positions. He was what my late Ukrainian father would have called an *aparatnyk*. Maybe that's what Gaisaana-la didn't like about him.

"Mr. Naradnyo," she said to me as we shook hands and she smiled. "Madame Marfoglia told me you would be along as well. I will feel safer with you here."

"I'm unarmed," I said, "so I'm mostly here to spot trouble coming. How's it been this morning?"

She frowned. "Perhaps a third of the staff did not report for work. Many of them are from other arcologies, and transportation has been problematic. Some are afraid."

"Afraid to be caught hanging around us when things get ugly?" I asked, and she tilted her head to the side.

I turned to ah-Quan, who had mostly been absorbed by his own viewer glasses, which were linked into a Munie security feed.

"Do we know what's up with the demonstrations?"

"Riots outside spreading," he said, "farther north, not here. Ground access locked down. Hard for riot spilling over by maglev, air shuttle."

Yeah, if they really were spontaneous, I thought, but ah-Quan continued.

"Municipal constabulary gave access to video feed South Tower Atrium, nearest hub to chambers Good-Soul Counselors. Peaceful demonstrations there yesterday; no demonstration today, but limited information precludes reliable assessment."

"South Tower Atrium. Is that in the Red Forest Twenty-one *Wat* District?" I asked.

His eyes lost focus as he concentrated on his viewer for a moment and then he looked me in the eye. "Yes. Is that significant?"

"Probably not," I said, but it was hard to know. Ah-Quan was right: not enough information to make a good guess, and that made me nervous. There was a time when I'd gladly charged into dangerous situations with less data than this, but ever since I died I'd become more cautious. No matter how bad things get, most people never believe deep down inside they're really going to die. Once it actually happens to you, you know better, and that knowledge changes you.

"Let's get going. The sooner we're done and out of here, the better I'll feel."

The five of us took a private autopod from the office suite to South Tower Atrium. *The'On* and Gaisaana-la spent the time going over the agenda and arguing about our negotiating position, which was bizarre. The position was simplicity itself: we were willing to talk and willing to listen, but we weren't giving a Goddamned inch on Tweezaa's legal rights. They weren't ours to bargain away. But

The'On and Gaisaana-la were arguing about fine points of language so subtle I couldn't even tell the difference between them, not that my aGavoosh was anywhere near as polished as theirs. But it wasn't long before I got the idea Gaisaana-la was just pissed at *The'On* and arguing on general principle. The'On was getting frustrated as well, and this wasn't like either of them. Finally I butted in.

"What's the problem here?"

"I do not know exactly," *The'On* answered, exasperation plain in his voice.

Gaisaana-la sat quietly for a few seconds and then looked at me.

"I was not told in advance of the adoption."

"It was very closely held," I said. "We did not want to put you in a position where you might have to decide between telling the truth and protecting our secret."

She nodded to the side slightly. "I appreciate that. Nevertheless, I have yet to receive any communication concerning the disposition of the office and its staff. It seems logical that Tweezaa e-Traak will live with her adoptive father, presumably in Kootrin, and that Madame Marfoglia will accompany her. One assumes part or all of the staff will either be transferred as well or will be replaced."

"Well...with all that's happened in the last few days we haven't given that as much thought as it probably deserves," I said. "Hopefully this meeting today will help settle things down and then we can figure all the rest of it out as well. I'm sure Marrissa intends you to be part of the transition planning, assuming there is much of a transition. I just don't know yet."

She made that small nod to the side again, her face expressionless.

"Are you offended that you were not included in the planning?" The'On asked.

"I am disturbed by the action itself. Tweezaa e-Traak is uBakai. Saying she is now suddenly uKootrin is...inauthentic. I understand the legal convenience of the move, but I wish it had been possible to negotiate a solution before the adoption was finalized. But that is meaningless now. We are committed to this course of action and I will support it to the best of my abilities."

She sat back and stared straight ahead. I knew her well enough to know that if she said she'd give us her best game in there, she would, or at least I thought so. But she was upset, and that unsettled me.

The'On frowned, partly in embarrassment I think. I resisted

the temptation to argue with her. It's true we'd decided to pre-empt the opposition with the adoption. I didn't think we did it just to take a victory lap. I thought we'd considered the options very carefully and decided this was really our one good play. I had to admit, though, we'd all felt pretty smug about it. We'd all smiled at the thought of short-circuiting all those carefully laid plans by the opposition. I didn't think there was another way, but maybe if we'd thought harder about it we could have come up with one. Maybe, maybe not. In either case it was too late now. The train had left the station.

The question was whether our decision had compromised Gaisaana-la's loyalty, a notion which had never occurred to me or anyone else until right that moment. And if it had compromised it, what did that mean in material terms?

"Atrium still calm?" I asked ah-Quan. He hesitated before answering, studying the video feed through his viewer glasses.

"Still calm, but more Varoki than before. Not moving, just waiting for something."

I glanced at Borro, who had overheard the exchange. He pulled his gauss pistol from his shoulder holster and checked the charge level and flechette magazine.

"They aren't going to let you take that into the council chambers," I said.

"That assumes we actually get there," he answered.

Ah-Quan unholstered his own gauss pistol, which looked about twice the size of Borro's, and checked it as well. I hadn't brought a sidearm, and as I sat there I wondered why.

The autopod decelerated smoothly to a stop and I could see the main atrium through the clear transit tube even before the doors slid open. The atrium was at least a hundred meters tall, lined with open vine-draped balconies from each of the levels above and below us. The tube station deposited us four levels up from the broad plaza. The plaza's floor was an elaborate terra cotta mosaic surrounding a tall fountain, topped by a metallic abstract sculpture, a sparkling, whispering irregular column of polished metal and cascading water which climbed at least fifty meters up the center of the atrium. But the beauty was marred by the hundreds—no, thousands—of Varoki lining all of the balcony railings in the atrium, all the way up to the top, unmoving, silently staring at us.

You know what's scarier than a couple thousand angry people? A couple thousand silent, motionless people—scarier and infinitely more creepy. I was about to get everyone back into the autopod when I saw a familiar Varoki striding down the broad corridor stretching south toward the riverside wing of the tower, none other than my old pal from the cocktail party, Elaamu Gaant, best-selling author of inspirational, motivational, and self-improvement tracts, and self-proclaimed mastermind behind the Edict for the Preservation of Familial Assets.

"Well, well," I said, "look who's here. I didn't see you on the guest list for this sit-down, Mr. Gaant."

"Possibly an oversight," he said. "Ah, and this would be the Honorable e-Lotonaa. It is a pleasure to meet you, sir," he said turning to *The'On,* bowing slightly and raising his open hands to shoulder height, the old Varoki equivalent of a handshake. *The'On* returned the gesture without the bow. More and more Varoki had adopted the Human habit of actually shaking hands, but lately there'd been a growing backlash against borrowed Human customs. Gaant was clearly a traditionalist.

"I have heard of your speeches and recordings, Mr. Gaant," The'On said. "I understand they are quite popular. Allow me to introduce Madame Gaisaana-la, who will speak for Tweezaa's guardian, Madame Marfoglia."

Gaisaana-la bowed but did not offer her open hands. Gaant barely nodded in response. Was that the run-of-the-mill Varoki traditionalist dismissal of a female in a position of responsibility? Or was it an attempt to disguise a relationship or alliance? Or was that just my paranoia talking?

"Madame Marfoglia could not join us?" Gaant asked.

"Security concerns precluded it," I answered. I glanced up and around at the thousands of quiet, staring faces in the atrium. "Pretty good call, I'm thinking."

Gaant smiled and tilted his head to the side. "These people? Why would you fear them? They are residents of this arcology and have the right to travel anywhere in it. They do not create a disturbance and do nothing to threaten you. I think any fair observer would find your objection to them unreasonable."

The smugness in his voice made up my mind.

"Okay, folks, back in the autopod," I said, and turned to leave.

"Wait!" Gaant said. "Please. Lives may be saved by these talks.

I am sorry if your own neighbors frighten you, but I have come to escort you personally to the talks. No harm will befall you while I am with you."

"Yeah? And what about afterwards? What about getting out of this with our skins intact?"

Gaant spread his arms wide. "I will accompany you again, if it will make you happy. Really, Mr. Naradnyo, you have no grounds to distrust me. At our last meeting I was more forthcoming to you concerning my intentions than you were to me."

"Don't pull that crap on me. We were both exactly as forthcoming as served our purposes."

Gaant looked at me for a moment, maybe trying to assess my intentions, then he walked to the nearest railing, raised his head, and called out in a voice which filled the atrium. If nothing else, the guy had a good set of lungs.

"People of Praha-Riz, you know me. These people are my guests. I ask you to extend them the same courtesy you would me. Will you do this thing?"

"*Yes!*" a thousand voices barked in unison like a thunderclap, a solid wall of sound I felt hit me like a tsunami, a wave of sound that made the water flowing down the sculpture spray out from the metal, echoed in the atrium, and made the hanging vines shiver. The hair rose on my arms and neck as a jolt of adrenaline surged through me. Beside me *The'On*'s and Gaisaana-la's ears flattened back and their skin turned pale. Borro's ears and skin remained unaltered, as if he were a statue. That was the result of years of training and probably more violent encounters than I wanted to know about. Behind me, ah-Quan belched again.

Gaant turned back to us, the same soft smile on his face.

"You see? You have nothing to fear here. And I assure you, Sasha Naradnyo, you will find this meeting *enormously* interesting. Others in the meeting will be as surprised as you at the course it takes, and I think you will want to see their surprise with your own eyes."

Something in the way he said that convinced me. He had set some sort of ambush here, but we weren't the targets. The targets were the assholes who had been making my and Marr's and Tweezaa's life one drama after another for two solid years. Would I stick around and watch them brought down a peg? I nodded and we followed Gaant down the south corridor. After about twenty meters or so I heard murmured conversation behind me and turned to see ah-Quan handing his big gauss pistol and spare magazines over to Borro. I stopped until they caught up, then walked beside them and gave Borro a questioning look.

"You will look after *The'On* during the meeting," he said.

Despite the gravity of the situation I couldn't help but smile. I'd never heard Borro call *The'On* anything but his given name or formal title, never the nickname I'd given him. Borro saw my grin and bobbed his head to the side.

"Yes, that little slip will remain our secret, yes?"

"Where you gonna be?" I asked.

"We cannot take our weapons in, and three unarmed security guards will be no more use than two. There is no guarantee that weapons surrendered at the security station will be returned when and if needed. I will stay out here and observe. As a Varoki, I can blend into the crowd. If there is treachery, I will be free to act."

"Yeah, good thinking," I said. I looked back at the silent crowd which now filled the corridor, walking slowly after us. "So tell me—not that we've got much choice now—but is going into this meeting as stupid as I'm starting to think it is?"

"Oh, no," he answered. "*Much* more so than that."

Chapter Six

We passed through a security station manned by Munies and into the chambers of the Good-Soul Counseling House. *Counseling* on Varoki worlds was generally what we called lawyering, although the services offered were a bit broader and usually included legislative lobbying, mediation, financial planning, and astrology.

Varoki astrology was different from the terrestrial version, but most civilizations that start out as agricultural societies—like us and the Varoki—end up pretty interested in the seasons, moon phases, calendars, all that stuff. Early religions get built around the movement of the stars, and when more sophisticated religions displace them, the older ones turn into superstition. Superstition waxes and wanes in popularity, as near as I can tell depending upon how shitty life is. For the last dozen years it had been pretty bad for a lot of folks, and it seemed to be getting worse. The Varoki were on top of the heap and hadn't felt the hard times right away, but they were beginning to. Trade, commerce, all that stuff just wasn't ticking along quite as well as it used to, and it seemed like every economist had a different theory as to why it was happening and what to do about it. Some of them had two theories. I suppose that explained why astrology was a growth industry again, along with charismatic motivationalists like Gaant. It explained it psychologically, anyway. It didn't make it any less stupid.

The meeting room's south wall was floor-to-ceiling composite windows overlooking the Wanu River, about twenty meters down. The water was nearly a kilometer wide here. The south wall of the arcology was almost right on the river, with just a walking path between the building foundations and the bank. A mix of commercial barge traffic and small, fast-looking private boats drew long, fading white lines of wake on the dark river surface.

A smart surface covered the office wall opposite the river windows, with open floor space in front for holographic displays, either for presentations or remote conferencing. The smart surface was a neutral warm gray today, though. This meeting was strictly skin-time.

<Marr, you hear me?> I subvocalized on my embedded commlink.

Yes. Are you there?

<Yeah. Nice view of the river. Not as high up as our place, though. Gaant's full of surprises today.>

We weren't expecting Gaant. Does that mean trouble?

<Probably.>

Silence for a long moment.

Be careful, she transmitted.

Careful? I figured I'd already blown that by not getting back into the autopod.

The polished stone surface of a long table down the center of the room reflected the afternoon sun just starting to emerge from rainclouds and overcast. Twelve chairs lined each side. The side nearest the dormant smart wall already held eleven expensively-dressed Varoki males, most of whom I recognized by sight even though I'd only met two of them. Three wore the ceremonial gray robes of an uBakai *wattaak,* while most of the rest wore colorful and expensive business suits, most of them made of shimmering metallic fabric. Our folks were, by contrast, dressed conservatively, almost austerely, in solid-color suits, gray for Gaisaana-la and *The'On* wearing the dark green of the field service uniform of the Executive Council's Corps of Counselors.

I saw Vandray e-Bomaan, the second governor of AZ Simki-Traak, whom I'd stood five feet from at several corporate functions without him ever giving an indication he recognized my existence. I was surprised to see someone that high up in the official hierarchy. Bringing him in meant they were either confident or desperate, and I had no idea which.

A second long table backed it up with administrative staffers, also mostly male, lining it. On our side *The'On* and Gaisaana-la sat across from the opposition, the other ten chairs empty. Ah-Quan and I stood behind them, our backs to the giant windows. Ah-Quan and I were also the only non-Varoki in the place. The set-up, with all those bodies packing their side of the room, was clearly meant to intimidate us, show us how much combined power and expertise we were up against.

Gaant sat down in the remaining open chair on the opposition side of the table and a Varoki seated at the head of the table spoke.

"Ah, *I* am Counselor Rimcaant, vice-governor of the Good-Soul Counseling House, and I have been, ah, *asked* by the Group of Interest to preside over this meeting. I thank all of you for agreeing to attend. I now advise everyone to power down your embedded commlinks. This is a, ah, *private* negotiating session and the house communication jammers will activate in thirty seconds." He sat back and waited.

<Jammers coming up,> I commed to Marrissa. <Have to power down.>

I love you, she answered.

And then I was alone with the faint background hum of the comm jammers. Jamming meant that no one would be able to communicate, of course, and also would be unable to access their float memory. Everyone had hand readers or viewers with onboard memory, loaded with whatever data they needed for the meeting. But the purpose wasn't to limit access to information, it was to keep it private and unrecorded.

"Mr. Naradnyo, would you and your, ah, *associate* care to sit?" Counselor Rimcaant asked. "There are many empty chairs on your side of the table."

"I did not come here to sit across from a criminal," e-Bomaan, the AZ Simki-Traak second governor, said, his ears folding back against his head. The Varoki to his left, lead counsel for the firm representing the other heirs of the e-Traak family, nodded in agreement.

"Mr. Naradnyo is *not* a criminal," Gaisaana-la said with steel in her voice, but e-Bomaan did not even glance at her.

"That's all right," I said. "I'd prefer to stand."

"What *did* you come here for?" *The'On* asked.

Governor e-Bomaan leaned back in his chair and made a vague hand gesture. "We came to negotiate a compromise." I noticed he didn't look around for approval to speak, so *The'On* had pegged the head guy right out of the gate, and by making it a conversation between the two of them, he'd turned this whole roomful of other folks meant to intimidate us into a bunch of spectators. He was good at this.

"Compromise?" *The'On* said. "Compromise of what? Of Tweezaa e-Traak-Lotonaa's legal rights?"

"You mean you are not willing to negotiate?" e-Bomaan shot back.

"Please," Mr. Rimcaant said from the head of the table, making calming gestures with his hands. "Let us, ah, *proceed* in a polite and orderly manner. I am sure all of us here want the same thing."

I looked at him and about half the heads in the room turned as well, all thinking: *Want the same thing? Is he crazy?* He must have noticed the reaction.

"All of you want an end to the violence, do you not?" he said. "Whatever your goals, they were not advanced by the, ah, *disturbances* yesterday. Sakkatto City is not only the capital city of Bakaa, but also the economic hub of our homeworld, and the Varoki homeworld is the, ah, *epicenter*, yes the epicenter of all major economic activity in explored space. The *Cottohazz* holds its breath, waiting to see what will happen here next."

Well, that was a bit dramatic, I thought. Given the speed of travel and communication, even the closest other planets of the *Cottohazz* wouldn't hear about this dust-up for a week, and it might be a month or more before the news spread all the way to backwaters like Earth. Then maybe people would hold their breath, but whatever was going to happen would probably be over. Nobody contradicted Rimcaant though, and after a pause he went on.

"Interstellar commerce has been weakening for over five years. Capital formation has withered for three years. The continuing, ah, *difficulties* on K'Tok have contributed to *Cottohazz*-wide uncertainties. To that end, I am sure I speak for everyone here in thanking the Honorable e-Lotonaa for his fine work on K'Tok for the *Cottohazz* executive council."

The'On nodded in acknowledgment but e-Bomaan, the Simki-Traak governor, made a disgusted sound.

"If the secret of the K'Tok and Peezgtaan ecoforms had not

been revealed to the Humans," he said, "we would have no trouble on K'Tok today."

The'On tilted his head to the side and spread his hands. "Secrets are revealed," he said. "Wishing it were otherwise accomplishes nothing. Revelation is the destiny of all secrets."

"Not *all* secrets," e-Bomaan said and exchanged a glance with the senior representative from AZ Kagataan, Simki-Traak's biggest rival. The Kagataan governor narrowed his eyes and his ears tightened, as if in silent reproach. E-Bomaan colored slightly and shut up, leaning back in his chair.

Now that was pretty interesting. Those two trading houses were more powerful than most governments, and they did not play well together. Two years ago they had fought a war by proxy on K'Tok, a war Tweezaa, Marr, The'On and I had been caught in the middle of. AZ Kagataan came out a big loser. But they and Simki-Traak Trans-Stellar apparently still shared a secret, and if the shellacking Kagataan took in the war hadn't been enough to make them want to spill the beans out of spite, it must be a real corker. Marr was a Simki-Traak governor, at least nominally, but I wondered if even she knew what that was all about.

"*Capital formation,*" Elaamu Gaant said from the other end of the table, making it sound like a curse. Everyone turned to him. "We formed the Group of Interest, this alliance of uneasy partners, to accomplish a goal of great ideological import, and now we talk of capital formation. What of the principles we share? Do we abandon them because of numbers posted in some money changer's office?"

A stir ran through the Varoki on his side of the table, surprise turning to irritation, then hostility.

"We appreciate the assistance you provided as the, ah, *go-between* assembling the Group of Interest, Mr. Gaant—" Counselor Rimcaant began, but e-Bomaan cut him off.

"I knew it was a mistake allowing you to attend this meeting, Gaant," he said. "Everything you planned has collapsed. You failed, do you understand? This is over your head now, and it is time to let those of us who understand what is at stake here make the best of the situation."

Gaant laughed and stood up from his chair, but not in anger. E-Bomaan had just told him he had no further say in what went on, but Gaant looked to me like a guy who still had an ace up his sleeve.

"*You* have forgotten what is really at stake," he answered, and then he turned to face me. "Sasha Naradnyo, the Honorable e-Bomaan called you a criminal earlier. All of them think of you that way. Do you have a criminal record?"

I looked at him for a moment, now completely confused as to what this had to do with anything. "Not exactly."

E-Bomaan laughed, a nasty little bark, but Gaant ignored him. "What does that mean, please?"

"I was arrested for burglary but the charge was expunged when I volunteered for a hitch with the *Co-Gozhak.*"

"You fought in the Nishtaaka campaign, is that so?" Gaant asked, and when I nodded he went on. "So you have no criminal record, and according to the law itself you have met all your obligations to it. But these gentlemen all still consider you a criminal and I sense you do as well. Why?"

"Well, I guess it has something to do with once having made my living by stealing," I answered, but Gaant cocked his head slightly to the side and smiled.

"I do not think so. The Honorable e-Bomaan and these others all steal, one way or another."

I saw a number of Varoki shift in their chairs and ears twitch over that, anger or confusion flashing across their faces and skins.

"What does this have to do with these negotiations?" e-Bomaan demanded. The voice of Simki-Traak Trans-stellar now took on a harder edge.

"Everything," Gaant answered, and then he turned back to me. "You see, Sasha, these honorables have a philosophy," he said, gesturing to e-Bomaan and the others along his side of the table, "a philosophy which assures them that they are bound by no standard of conduct except *gain*, and of course following the strict letter of the law. Morality and ethics are irrelevant, so long as they follow the law.

"Their philosophy also tells them the best thing they can do for everyone on the planet is to devote their resources to *removing* any legal restraint on their actions, provided they follow the law as they do so. This they do by their support for *wattaaks*, such as the three you see here today, men who share their philosophy and work to implement it.

"They utilize the reduced restraints to extract more money from their customers, from their workers, and from the *Cottohazz* itself in the form of subsidies and reduced taxes. Their philosophy tells them the satisfaction of their unbridled greed is the means for everyone in the *Cottohazz* to prosper, even as they systematically impoverish them.

"Sasha, you are not a criminal because you stole. You are a criminal because you did not have a philosophy."

"What is the meaning of this, Gaant?" e-Bomaan demanded, rising to his feet. I was wondering the same thing, not that I was complaining. "We did not come here to be insulted, or to listen to you flatter this murdering drug dealer."

"No," Gaant said, "you came here to reach an arrangement with the murdering drug dealer. In order to safeguard your own profits, you came here to trade away a part of the heritage which belongs to the entire *Varokiim*.

"For three hundred years you have stolen from the other races, and done so in the name of the *Varokiim*, and you could have done so for all eternity. Instead you stole so much from the others that they are bled dry, but the treasure must still flow, and so now you steal from the *Varokiim* themselves. When I was a child there were no slums between the arcs. Now you cannot see the ground for them, and most of the denizens of that place without hope are Varoki, not the other races. *That is your legacy!* But that stops here. It stops today."

"What are you blathering...?" e-Bomaan started but then faltered. Everyone in the room froze for a moment. Gaant had made a signal to someone, a slight raising of his hand, and suddenly the soft background hum of the local jammer was gone from my ears. I immediately squinted up the access to our local float nexus in Praha-Riz and set up a full-feed recording of my audio and visual input, and locked a coded channel. I snapped to it before the bandwidth got swamped once everyone else in the room figured out what was happening. I must have beaten most of them to the draw because I got my channel up and running. From here on, everything that I saw and heard would be out there on the float memory, and as far as I knew, nobody was good enough to hunt down all those threads and erase them.

Since that was all done with eye movement and pressure, my mind and eyes weren't on the room. As I looked up Gaant gestured again and the wide double doors to the conference room opened. First the jammers, then the door. Whatever cult Gaant was peddling with himself as a leader, obviously someone at the counseling house was on board.

The crowd we saw earlier in the atrium started shuffling in—hundreds of them, silent but curious. Some craned their necks, taking in the occupants of the room and the rich, elegant simplicity of its fixtures. Most of them watched Gaant the way I imagined people look at their messiah.

Chapter Seven

"Shit!" e-Bomaan shouted the English expletive in surprise and anger, which just goes to show he wasn't as much of a traditionalist as Gaant. None of the other five races could swear like Humans, but Varoki weren't above borrowing on occasion. This time I was inclined to agree with the sentiment. I started to reach instinctively for the gauss pistol under my jacket but stopped, because there wasn't one there today.

This must have been the surprise Gaant bragged about earlier. For all these people to make it back to the conference room, they had to have gotten past the entrance security and then through the whole office complex. Since there was no sign of violence, and none of the crowd seemed worked up, somebody let them in—a fair number of somebodies, come to think of it, including Munies at the security station. Gaant had people in the Munies as well as the counseling house? This was a pretty elaborate operation, more than I'd credited him with.

I did a quick scan of the room—no way out. I felt sweat tickle my sides under my armpits. I only saw one possible refuge if things turned ugly, and it wasn't much.

"Ah-Quan, corner to your left, get ready," I said softly in Szawa, the Zaschaan trade language. Ah-Quan would understand but I was betting nobody else in the room would. I put my hands on The'On's shoulders.

41

"If you want to trade away their heritage, you will not do so in darkness," Gaant said to the men at the table, his voice rising in volume and taking on a more dramatic tone. This was probably his motivational speaker voice. He gestured toward the quiet crowd filling the room. "Conduct your dirty business with these people as witnesses, if you have the courage. Let them see the color of your souls!"

I think Gaant had a plan as to what came next. He must have. But no plan survives contact with stupidity, and there was plenty of that going around. One of the Varoki at the back table, one of the staffers, jumped to his feet and pulled a neuro-wand from his under his jacket. So much for no weapons on neutral ground, huh?

"Put that away you moron!" I shouted. As everyone turned to look at him, the guy hit Gaant with the wand. Gaant didn't make a sound except for a sharp hiss of inhaled breath. His whole body spasmed as every nerve in it fired at once and then he seemed to fall in slow motion, the crowd gaping, someone at the table reaching out too late to catch him, until his head clipped the hard stone edge of the table and made a sound like a melon hitting pavement. He continued falling to the floor and then didn't move.

My knees went weak. For what seemed like a very long time but could only have been a second or two nobody moved, nobody said anything. I didn't breathe. I guess I feared—we all feared—the slightest act might break the spell and bring what came next. Then a collective gasp escaped from those at the head of the crowd as they surged forward and some knelt at Gaant's side. Some screamed, some shouted questions from behind, others shouted back.

What happened?

The Guide is dead!

They killed the Guide!

"The corner! *Move!*" I screamed to ah-Quan.

More people surged through the doorway, jostling those in front. Some of those kneeling by Gaant got pushed over and cried out as the mob stepped on them, but a couple big guys managed to lift Gaant's limp body up and over their heads, and soon the crowd passed it back, hand to hand, out of the room, his dripping blood anointing them.

Ah-Quan reached forward and grabbed Gaisaana-la by the

shoulders of her suit, snatching her up and over the back of her chair by sheer brute strength, and then he plowed through the crowd starting to fill the space to our left. I didn't get *The'On* up nearly as quickly and by the time we started after ah-Quan the crowd had closed in.

A female Varoki from the crowd lunged at the staffer with the neuro-wand and he hit her with it, then started trying to drive the crowd back with it, wanding everyone in the front rank, even though they couldn't get away through the press of bodies behind them. Screams of pain and fear and rage. Bodies twitching and falling limp to the floor to be trampled by those behind. Then a growing rumbling chorus of hatred and pent-up rage as the crowd became a mob and then an avalanche under which the staffer with the wand just vanished.

E-Bomaan and the other Varoki across the table from us were all on their feet and pressed back against the stone surface by the pressure of the mob, now tearing and striking at them. The table tipped over on its side and then onto its top and both members of the mob and their targets tumbled over it, the wave of flesh behind them surging over them.

I backpedaled frantically, pulling *The'On* with me, but came up against the smooth, hard composite resin surface of the big window overlooking the river.

The'On started to drop down to the floor but I pulled him up.

"Stand up!" I shouted above the howl of the mob. I turned him so his right shoulder was against the window. "Cover your head! Shoulder against the window, not your chest or back. Otherwise you'll suffocate!"

I saw the panic in his eyes fighting to take control but he nodded. I tried to partially cover him with my own body, my right shoulder under his left armpit, both our arms covering our heads, and then the mob hit us. Someone's fist caught me a good one on the back of my skull that left me seeing flashes of light for a few seconds, but as the mob pressed on from behind, the ones in front lost the ability to do anything but try to stay upright. The pressure grew and in just a few seconds the Varoki pressing against us went from enraged enemies to terrified fellow victims.

A shrill cry of agony sounded to my immediate left and I turned my head. I was face-to-face with e-Bomaan, his chest flat against the window, eyes bulging as the air was forced from his lungs by the inexorable pressure of the mob. His eyes made contact with mine, filled not only with pain and fear, but shock bordering on disbelief. A few seconds ago he had been one of the richest and most powerful men in the *Cottohazz*, and now here he was, losing the fight for life. How had this happened? How was it even possible?

Another surge from behind, even stronger than before, hit us. E-Bomaan's ribcage collapsed against the thick unyielding composite surface of the window, the bones popping and breaking one by one, and his last exhaled groan turned into bloody foam. I turned away, spitting his blood out, and then the surge caught me. For a moment it didn't take my breath because of my position. Then my right shoulder came out of the socket and I screamed in pain as the mass of the crowd flattened me against the window.

With a loud, sharp crack the composite resin of the window finally gave way and I was instantly weightless, surrounded by other screaming, flailing bodies tumbling through the air.

Chapter Eight

Screams filled my ears until we hit the surface of the Wanu River, hit it hard enough to knock the wind from my lungs, almost hard enough to knock me out. Muffled and remote underwater sounds replaced bedlam. Groggy and disoriented, I wasn't sure which direction was up until my feet sank into the weeds and bottom muck. My right arm was useless and I still had the front of *The'On*'s tunic crumpled in my left fist. He floated limp beside me. I couldn't let go, he'd drown. I pushed off from the bottom and kicked with my feet as hard as I could. I didn't seem to be making any progress. I started feeling dizzy from oxygen starvation, could hardly keep my straining lungs from sucking in the Wanu River, when the water around me got lighter and then I broke surface.

Air! I vacuumed in a big, shuddering lungful and my vision cleared, sound came back—people crying for help, screaming in pain and fear, splashing into the water. I looked around, oriented myself. We were close to the river bank, near the base of Praha-Riz, but the river was deep like a canal, so we'd had enough water under us to absorb our fall. Folks after us hadn't been as lucky, and lots were still falling from the shattered windows, tumbling down like an organic waterfall to land with soft thuds among the heaps of still-twitching bodies along the river bank. Only the first of us had been thrown far enough out to reach deeper water and avoid being crushed by the bodies cascading down afterwards.

It was hard treading water with just my legs, but I needed my one good arm to keep *The'On*'s head up. I wasn't sure he was breathing but couldn't do anything about it in the water so I started kicking us toward the bank. I hadn't gone far when one of the Varoki pulling himself up out of the shallows noticed us.

"There, the Human! The one who killed the Guide!"

Killed Gaant! Me? Well, just about everyone who actually saw what happened was probably dead by now, so it made sense to just blame the closest Human. The Varoki groped in the shallow water and came up with a good sized rock, threw it but it fell several meters short. He started looking for another one and a couple of the dazed survivors on the bank started pointing and shouting as well, wading into the water toward us. I kicked harder, now pulling us away from the shore.

The river was too wide to swim this way. As it was I was already tiring and barely making headway, but I had to get away. Reason and calm words weren't going to get me very far with the Varoki survivors on the bank. I stopped for a second and used my good hand to push the back of The'On's collar into my mouth. I held it with my teeth and started kicking again and doing a half-assed back stroke with one arm. I made better progress but I could hardly keep my head above water and was having trouble breathing.

I got another twenty or thirty meters out but my breath came in ragged gasps and my legs were losing power. I needed to take a break, catch my breath, but couldn't with *The'On*. I wasn't sure I could make it back to shore even if the mob weren't there, and I felt panic start to tighten my throat. I got a noseful of water by mistake and started choking. That's when something hit me in the head from behind. Fortunately, it was a rescue float.

I let go of *The'On*'s collar, twisted around, and saw a commercial fishing boat about ten meters away, idling in the channel, with four Humans along the rail yelling in English to me. One of them held the line attached to the float. Problem: I was still coughing, still couldn't manage to gulp down any air, and I'd pass out pretty soon unless I could. I wrapped my legs around *The'On*'s torso and grabbed for the float's handholds with my good hand.

Got it!

I threw my chest over the float and coughed the water out of my lungs as the crew dragged us alongside. A great big guy bent over the rail, grabbed my good arm, and started lifting. He could have managed me, but I still had my legs wrapped around *The'On* and the extra weight stalled him. He struggled for a couple seconds and then growled.

"Let the leatherhead go, yeah?"

Leatherhead. That's what Humans called Varoki sometimes. It's what I used to call them, back before a lot of things happened to me.

"Drop him!" the fisherman repeated.

I shook my head. "He's my friend."

He let go and I splashed back into the water. "Fuck you, then. Drown with your leatherhead friend, yeah?"

One of the other fishermen started pulling in the line to recover the float but I hooked my good arm through one of the flexible loops and held on with what strength I had left.

"Let go!" the big fisherman said.

"Leave me the float," I said. "At least give us a Goddamned chance!"

"I give you boathook is what," he said and turned away from the rail. The fisherman who'd pulled the line taut looked at me, frowning but not angry. When the big guy reappeared with a nasty-looking all-metal boat hook, the three others started talking to him. Up until then we'd been talking English. I didn't understand the language they argued in now, but I recognized it: Portuguese.

After maybe a minute of spirited argument the big guy lowered the boat hook, leaned over the rail, and looked at me. Since my one good arm was tangled in the rescue float and I was mostly out of the water, hanging from the rail by the rescue line, I was about as helpless as I could get. There wasn't any point in giving him a tough-guy glare; I had nothing. But I wasn't going to let go of *The'On*, no matter what. So I just looked back at him and after a couple seconds he shrugged.

He said something in Portuguese I couldn't understand and walked away.

The other three fishermen pulled me and *The'On* over the rail and onto the deck.

I didn't have much strength left but I'd at least recovered my breath. I checked *The'On* for a pulse. It was faint, even for a Varoki, but his plumbing was still working. He wasn't breathing, though, so I started mouth-to-mouth and after about five good puffs he vomited river water and started coughing.

That's about when a stabbing axe blade of pain reminded me how messed up my shoulder was. The fatigue, trauma, and reaction to the adrenaline high all came home at the same time and I passed out. Didn't even feel myself go *clunk* against the deck.

I came to, felt the soft vibration of the boat's electric motors through the metal deck, found my arm strapped against my body and the shoulder packed in ice. Shoulder felt different, too—still hurt, but in a different way. Propped up against a metal locker, I sat up straighter, looked for *The'On*. He was a couple meters away, lying on his stomach, still unconscious. Vomit stained the deck around his face—that alarming orangey-pink Varoki vomit that looks too much like blood—but he was breathing.

I squinted up my commlink and saw I was still recording on the locked channel. I cut it and commed Marr, subvocalizing to keep it private.

Sasha! Oh, thank God you're alive! The feed just went out. I didn't know—

<Yeah, I cut it to comm you. *The'On's* hurt and I'm banged up a little, unconscious for a while, but we're both alive. Have you heard from the others?>

The comms are blacked out in Praha-Riz below Level Two Hundred. You must be outside the effect radius.

<Yeah. My feed came in okay though, huh?>

From when the trouble started, yes. I could hardly watch, and when the window broke...

Her voice faltered and I could hear her crying softly. I tried to imagine what I'd have felt seeing that feed, knowing it was through *her* eyes and ears, and I couldn't. I couldn't imagine it, or what I'd have done waiting to find out the rest. I got choked up myself.

<I'm okay, baby. I'm okay.>

The fishermen noticed the movement and the big guy started walking over.

<Got to deal with this, Hon'. Back soon. I love you.>

I love you, she answered, voice wavering.

I cut the link as he got to me and looked down.

"So, not dead, yeah?"

I touched my ice pack. "Sore as hell."

"We pushed shoulder back in. Not good to leave it out like that. So you the Sasha fellow on the vid feed?"

"Probably."

He looked over at *The'On*'s stationary form.

"So you like the leatherheads, yeah?"

"A couple of them. What's the vid on me?"

He glanced over his shoulder where two of the crew in viewer glasses stood in the lee of the small superstructure. The big guy nodded at them.

"Still coming in, yeah? Different feeds, all show you standing there mouth open and dick in your hand when hell breaks loose. Feed-heads going on about what a mastermind you must be. You know, to arrange the whole thing and then look so stupid-surprised when it happened. You really that smart?"

"Do I look like it to you?" I asked.

"I think maybe I like you better if you did it." Then he shrugged, as if letting go—letting go of the idea he'd rescued a Human outlaw who'd just masterminded the biggest and most brutal mass killing of Varoki big shots in history. Yeah, that'd be something to tell the grandkids someday. "My name—Cézar Ferraz," he said. "Over there is—*Hey! Dado!*"

The brawny fisherman who'd pulled me in on the line looked up and then grinned and waved at me.

"Eduardo Socorro, call him Dado. He pulled you out, yeah?"

I nodded and waved back with my left hand.

"Other fellow's João Pacifico."

The other one, shorter and wiry-looking, glanced up and waved once, as if to say leave him alone, and went back to his viewer.

"Other guy at the helm?" I asked and Ferraz nodded.

"Constancio, my partner. So you're Sasha Naradnyo, yeah? What kinda name is Sasha? Sounds like a girl's name."

"Ukrainian, short for Aleksandr."

"Short for Alexandre? We'd say Xandinho."

"Can you get us back upriver to the Red Forest marina?" I asked. "We got a boat there I can use to lay low until I get a handle on this."

"A boat? That's nice. But no, we're not gonna do that. River Watch already thick in there, diverting traffic. Be asking too many questions, yeah? We gonna get you to shore up here, at the commercial docks is what." He turned back to the other two. "*Joãozinho! Me jogar seu chapéu.*" The short one took off his baggy black wool cap and threw it to Ferraz, who put it on my head and then pulled the bill down over my eyes.

"You're Xandinho the fisherman at the dock, yeah? Mouth shut. One of us asks you a question, just nod. That way nobody wonders about some dangerous mastermind. This one we pulled out of the water alone," he said, hooking a thumb toward *The'On*. "I commed for an ambulance, meet us up there. No drama, yeah?"

I wondered what a bunch of Portuguese fishermen were doing trolling the Wanu River, pulling out longjaws and blacksnaps they couldn't even eat. I didn't ask, though. It would have sounded ungrateful. These guys were getting me and *The'On* out of this, and with "no drama," or at least as little as possible.

"*Obrigado,*" I said.

He frowned. "You know *Português?*"

"Couple words is all. Had a Brazilian girlfriend."

"*Brasileira?* They crazy, yeah?"

"She did try to kill me once," I admitted.

He nodded and looked back down the river at the towering form of Praha-Riz. "She got some company now."

The'On was still unconscious when we got to the docks and I was getting nervous about that. We loaded him into the waiting ambulance, and I rode along to the trauma/med center in Katammu-Arc. Praha-Riz was closer, but the Varoki medic riding in back and working on *The'On* told me both med centers in Praha-Riz were closed to admissions except from inside the arc. They were swamped with injuries. He also said it looked like *The'On* might have a cranial fracture.

I commed Marr and brought her up to date on *The'On*, not bothering to subvocalize. Tweezaa got on the circuit as well.

Boti-Sash! Is Boti-On going to be all right?

"I don't know, Hon'. The medic says he's stable, and his color's good, but I wish he'd wake up."

I saw the video feed of you in the water, the feed from your eyes. I do not...

She trailed off. For a while the three of us just sat, commlinked but silent, overwhelmed by what had happened.

"Is there any word yet on Gaisaana-la, ah-Quan, or Borro?" I asked finally.

No, Marr answered. *No news at all and Praha-Riz below the executive layer is still blacked out.*

That didn't sound good.

I have to go, she said. *I'll have someone waiting for you at the med center. I love you.*

"I love you both," I answered and we broke the link.

I considered my options as the ambulance made maddeningly slow progress through the ground traffic, which seemed thicker and more frenzied that usual. A flyer would have had us to the med center by then, but a call from some Human fisherman didn't rate one. If they'd realized the unconscious Varoki was one of the highest-ranking diplomatic envoys from the *Cottohazz* Executive Council, things would have been different.

All I could see of the traffic was through a small rear window, but the faces on powerscoots and pedcycles looked nervous, frightened. The news from Praha-Riz had folks spooked, and for all they knew this could get worse before it got better.

So what was I going to do? Hiding out was pointless by now; the Munies would have locks on *The'On*'s and my commlinks if they were that interested in us, and it sounded like they might be. I could power down, go black and make a run for it, but how far would I get with a bum shoulder? Besides, I didn't have any cash so I couldn't use any transportation, buy food, do much of anything without using my e-nexus credit line, and then I'd pop right back onto the data grid. So I'd have to face the Munies and see what that led to, but unless they were into manufactured evidence I didn't see they had much on me.

The bigger question was where was all this going and what was I going to do to keep Marr and Tweezaa alive? They were the targets, not me. Folks might not like me much, but I wasn't likely to knock the *Cottohazz* off its foundations. Neither were they, when you got right down to it, but the opposition couldn't count on that, so they were the high-threat targets.

The opposition...who was that now that Gaant, e-Bomaan, and the others were all dead? *Was* there an opposition anymore? Well, Tweezaa's relatives were all still alive, still hungry for her

chunk of the fortune, and a lot of Varoki were scared as hell that
a Human had saved Tweezaa's life and that would warp her or
something. So there'd still be an opposition, but they were going
to have to find a couple new evil geniuses, and that might slow
them down for a while.

That was their problem, not mine. Mine came down to keeping
Marr and Tweezaa—and now *The'On* as well—alive. When you
looked at it that simply, the answer was pretty obvious.

By the time we got to emergency trauma receiving at Katammu-
Arc the Munies were waiting but so was one of Marr's Varoki
counselors-on-retainer. If I'd been an uBakai citizen it would
have gone tougher on me, but since I still held my Peezgtaan
citizenship there were diplomatic niceties to observe. Without a
counselor there the cops might have overlooked that.

Varoki trauma/med centers are different from Human ones:
a lot less clean than the hospitals on Earth, or even the clinic
I used to fund back on Peezgtaan, and sort of cluttered, with
lots of equipment just lying around. To me they look more like
vehicle repair shops than hospitals. The Munies waited outside
the treatment room while a Varoki doc worked on my shoulder:
scanned it and then studied some reference imagery—probably
to brush up on how a Human shoulder was supposed to look
when it *wasn't* all screwed up.

"Oh, I understand!" he said after a couple minutes. "Your
shoulder was dislocated but has been relocated. However, there is
still considerable inflammation there, and your collar thing—collar
bone I mean—is separated from your, um, what is it? That sort
of flat wingy bone?" He consulted the diagram again. "Spacula.
No, *sca-pu-la*. Collar bone and sca-pu-la. What an odd word."

He ended up injecting a pain killer and some NAMS—
nanomachines—programmed to repair the tissue damage and
tamp down the inflammation. Other than that he fitted me with
a sling and told me to try to keep the shoulder immobilized.
Meanwhile Marr's Varoki counselor was giving me The Word.

"Answer every question they pose unless I tell you it is an
inappropriate inquiry. Answer as completely and as cooperatively
as you can. After all, we have nothing to hide."

He said this staring earnestly into my eyes, letting me know
he thought we had *everything* to hide and I should lie my head

off, but since we were being monitored he was speaking for the record. Nice to have people in your corner who believe in you.

"How's e-Lotonaa? Is he conscious yet?" I asked the doc. It was strange calling *The'On* by name.

"I can only share patient information with his family."

"I'm family," I said.

The Varoki doctor looked at me for a long moment, ears spread in surprise. "Not remotely," he said, which I thought was pretty narrow-minded of him.

Once the doc was done the Munies grilled me for almost an hour, asking the same questions over and over but phrased differently. They were trying to catch me in a lie, or maybe they just weren't sure what else to ask but had to put in the time to show due diligence. I'd have felt some sympathy for them if I hadn't been the object of the exercise. After all, they were in a tight spot, no doubt about it. Near as I could tell, everyone in the room before the mob entered was dead except for five people. I was relieved to hear from them that Gaisaana-la and ah-Quan were two of the other three, although ah-Quan was in pretty bad shape. I had to admit, all four of us surviving looked mighty suspicious, especially since only one guy out of probably twenty-five or thirty on the other side had.

The fact that the death toll included three uBakai *wattaaks* and four of the richest guys in the whole *Cottohazz* meant the heat was on the Munies to put somebody's head up on a pike, and I was the obvious candidate. The only thing in my favor so far was that every second of recorded vid of the riot showed me as uninvolved except as a victim. But like Ferraz said back on the boat, that wasn't stopping every feed-head on the float from claiming I had to be behind it all. What would most folks believe: their own eyes or their own prejudices?

I knew where I'd put my money.

Chapter Nine

"Sasha! Oh, thank God you're alive!" Marr said, bursting through the door and into my one good arm, all in one blur of sound and motion. I'd been talking to the Munies nonstop for almost an hour and all of a sudden I couldn't say a word. I just held her, eyes squeezed shut, lost in the touch of her hands on my back, the fragrance of her hair, things I didn't think I'd ever experience again as the mob pushed me against that window.

The Munies started to object, but her counselor was back on the job and by the time Marr and I finished kissing, the three Varoki cops had vanished. In their place, Tweezaa stood with her back to the door, tears staining her face. I gestured to her and she came, arms around us and one of Marr's arms around her, all three of us wordless as we clung to each other.

"How did you get here?" I asked after we'd regained some composure.

"I borrowed the Simki-Traak board's executive shuttle," Marr answered. "It's still in the hospital landing bay."

"Good. Who's driving it?"

I had a plan forming but not everyone would think it was a good idea.

"Mr. Huang," she answered and then she looked at me closer. "Why?"

I moved back a little and looked both of them in the eyes in turn. We didn't have a lot of time to work this out but they had to be convinced, not bullied.

"Because we need a pilot with a flexible approach to the law," I said. "Huang will work. Here's what I think we should do. Tweezaa, you're The'On's legal next-of-kin, which means you'd be responsible for deciding his treatment, except you're a minor. Marr, as her guardian, that puts you in the driver's seat, right?"

She nodded.

"Okay, you can get him released to you and a private doctor. Can you get one here within the hour?"

"If we need to, but why?"

"We get The'On released and we all pile into the shuttle to take him back to the Valley House, north of the city. Only when we get to the Valley House, we keep flying. Huang files an airborne flight plan mod and we firewall the throttle for Kootrin, The'On's country. The frontier is less than an hour from the valley by air. We comm the uKootrin for permission to cross the border with a medical emergency. The'On's enough of a big-shot there they should agree, but even if they get nasty they won't shoot us down."

Her eyes got wider as I explained and she shook her head.

"We can't just abandon our people here."

"Hanging around isn't going to do anyone any good; it just turns up the heat. We aren't abandoning anyone. We'll pick up our security detail. Best thing we can do for everybody else is get the hell out of here."

"There are still things we can do here," she insisted.

"Marr, as long as we're in Bakaa, we're going to be painted as ground zero of the trouble. If we're gone and the trouble continues, they'll find someone else to blame."

She chewed on her lower lip, frowning in thought, reluctant to let go. I let her think. Since I came to on the boat, I'd been working it through, but it was a lot for her and Tweezaa to process all at once.

"We need to pick up Gaisaana-la," Marr said. "She's somewhere in South Tower Praha-Riz."

I shook my head. "Everything in South Tower below the executive layer's locked down, nobody in or out, at least right now. Those cops that just left told me. About three hundred Munie heavy tacticals are getting ready to storm South Tower and start clearing it level by level. They're scared and their blood will be up. Even if we could get down below, if the Munies see either one of us, they're likely to go nuts. The best thing we can do for Gaisaana-la is stay the hell away."

"He is right, *Boti-Marr*," Tweezaa said. "So many people here hate us, want to hurt us. Even before this I could feel it. At school I am afraid, and…I am so tired. So tired of it. Perhaps in Kootrin they will like us." She stopped and looked down. Marr enfolded her in her arms and held her, then turned to me and nodded wordlessly.

Three quarters of an hour later we had Marr's hired doc. Our pilot Huang and I were maneuvering *The'On*'s roller bed into the passenger cabin of the shuttle, up in the med center's hangar bay, when a black-and-red-uniformed Varoki marched purposely toward us across the foamstone hangar floor. For a moment I considered having Huang fire that mother up and make a run for it, but this guy wasn't a Munie. Black and red were the colors of CSJ, the *Co-Gozhak* Provost Corp.

There were one hundred and seventy-two sovereign political entities in the *Cottohazz*, the Stellar Commonwealth. Bakaa and Kootrin were just two of them, but pretty important ones. Still, get across the border and into Kootrin, and Bakaa had no way to get at you other than very complicated legal and/or diplomatic maneuvers, or an act of war. But the *Cottohazz* itself, the actual Stellar Commonwealth government, was different, and as the police arm of the *Cottohazz* the Provosts had jurisdiction everywhere, offices everywhere, operatives everywhere. There was no place in the *Cottohazz* we could run from them.

I touched Marr's shoulder and nodded at the approaching CSJ provost. She stiffened.

"What do *they* want?" she asked.

"We'll see. Don't panic, okay? Everything stays simple. We give them what they want, then we follow our plan."

He came to a halt by the passenger door. I climbed down to meet him and I could feel Marr and Tweezaa's eyes on my back.

"Mr. Sasha Naradnyo?" he asked.

"That's me. And you are?"

"Lance Corporal Kindoon, CSJ. My superior, Captain e-Tomai, requests your presence in two hours for an interview concerning

the events this morning at the Praha-Riz Arcology." He extracted
a paper-thin flexi-card from his uniform breast pocket and handed
it to me. "This has your appointment code and should be pre-
sented at our headquarters complex which is in this arcology.
The card will also provide free automated public transportation
to the complex by passing it over the fare scanner. I am to ask
if this is clear and if you have any questions."

I looked at the card for a couple seconds. All it said was
Captain e-Tomai and the time and date of the appointment.
Everything else must have been chip-coded. I'd met e-Tomai
before, worked with him on some joint security issues. He was
okay, for a provost.

"No questions, Corporal," I said.

"Do you require any further assistance?" he asked.

I shook my head and he turned and marched back across the
hangar floor.

"We'll wait for you here," Marr said.

"Like hell you will. What you will do is stop at Praha-Riz and
pick up Iris Tenryu and as many of our goons as can still walk
to provide security in Kootrin. The executive layer's still open,
so you can manage. No comm in advance though, okay? Just
face-to-face instructions."

"Why are you like this?" she said, her voice rising in anger. "You
almost died! Your arm is in a sling, you're bruised all over, and
you need a Human doctor to look at you. I won't leave you here."

I smiled. "Sure you will. Maybe if it was just you, it would be
different. But there's *The'On*, Tweezaa, and our unborn son, all
of whom are absolutely dependent upon you one way or another.
I'll follow as soon as I can, but you've got to go now. Two hours
from now it may be too late."

"If it's too late for us, then what about you?" The determination in her face flickered and then dissolved into tears. I held
her with my good arm.

"Hey, it'll be okay," I said. "Remember, you guys are the real
targets. I'm just muscle. Maybe they don't like me, but I'm nothing to them. Once you're away, they're not going to care enough
to cross the street to spit on me."

"You lie so convincingly to everyone else," she said. "Why can't
you manage it to me?"

✧   ✧   ✧

Two hours later I showed the flexi-card at the security station in front of the CSJ complex, submitted to the whole-body scan, gave a finger scraping to verify my DNA, and was escorted into the Sakkatto City regional office of *Cottohazz-Gozhakampta Sugkat Jitobonaan*—CSJ for short, or in English the Stellar Commonwealth Armed Forces Provost Corps. Technically they were the military police force of the *Cottohazz*. In reality, they were as close to a secret police as the Commonwealth had, and how close they really were was, of course, a secret.

Five minutes earlier I'd gotten the comm from Marr telling me they had just crossed into uKootrin air space and had picked up a drone escort, courtesy of uKootrin Ground Forces. They expected to be gear-down at the uKootrin capital in another forty minutes. Since CSJ knew pretty much everything going on, I imagined this was going to be part of the subject of my interview.

Back at the trauma/med center I'd finally managed to put Marr a little more at ease by reminding her that she'd never thought of the Co-Gozhak Provosts as essentially evil. For that matter I didn't either. CSJ was just a powerful bureaucracy, a big black-and-red machine that would probably grind you up if you got enmeshed in its gears, but not out of sadistic delight. It just turned the gears and then whatever happened, happened. Hell, one of my best friends in my previous life had turned out to be an undercover CSJ major. A pretty decent guy, too, all things considered.

A Varoki lance corporal escorted me into the large foyer and stood with me as we waited for another guide to walk me to my appointment. The foyer was about three stories tall, mostly glass and polished metal. A very large replica of the CSJ service badge dominated it, hanging from the ceiling and slowly turning, the silver facetted surfaces catching the sunlight and sparkling. I'd seen it a lot of times in my life, usually the ten centimeter version worn on a provost's chest. I realized I hadn't seen one since I became fluent in aGavoosh. I wondered about the three black characters from the Varoki alphabet in the center of the silver sunburst device, characters I'd always ignored as gibberish before.

"J, H, S," I said to the lance corporal. "What does that stand for?"

"*Jiihi, Haramaayi, Sanzaat,*" he answered immediately.

Knowledge, Resolve, Obedience.

I took a deep breath. Just a big bureaucracy, I reminded myself. Just a big bureaucracy.

A junior sergeant showed up and walked me through the internal security checkpoint, which served less to screen people than contain them. The local jammers came up and I turned down the feed volume on my commlink. The dull metal alloy of the sliding door looked like armor plate to me, about two centimeters thick, and it just let us into a holding room. The door on the far side opened as soon as the one behind us closed and clunked like a massive bank vault. Someone could force the security screening stations at the outside doors but they'd play merry hell getting into the bowels of the building.

And once you were in, you'd play merry hell getting out unless they wanted you out.

Although I'd dealt with CSJ liaison officers before, I'd never been to this office. Now I wondered why. This setup gave the guys behind the desks a hell of a psychological advantage. Maybe they didn't want people to get too used to the experience, lest it lose its special luster.

Chapter Ten

E-Tomai rose from behind his desk when I entered. His face was slightly flushed and his ears lay flat against the sides of his head, so when he said he was happy to see me again, I didn't believe him. He offered his hand in a Human handshake, though, and I took it.

"I hope you will not mind if my superior joins us," e-Tomai said once we were seated. "He is visiting and is naturally interested in today's unfortunate events."

I didn't mind, and I realized that was probably why e-Tomai was uneasy. Something to remember when trying to read people: it's not always about you. The door behind me opened and e-Tomai sprang to his feet. I'm not sure I normally would have risen myself but those massive vault doors made me at least open to the idea of respect for authority.

The older Varoki standing in the doorway wore a plain black-and-red uniform, the front adorned only by the silver starburst CSJ badge and two dull metal chest gorgets trimmed in red gold, the rank insignia of a field marshal lieutenant. I felt a little of the blood drain from my own face. E-Tomai had called him his superior. He wasn't kidding. There was only one field marshal lieutenant in the Provost Corps: its commandant.

The officer's face gave nothing away, ears relaxed, skin all but colorless. His head and hands had lost much of their iridescence with age, or perhaps exposure to sun and the elements. He had not acquired the thick midriff common to almost all older Varoki, but he also did not have a lot of muscle mass on his upper body. He had the lean build of an ascetic, not an athlete.

"You are Mr. Naradnyo," he said. "I am Field Marshal Lieutenant e-Loyolaan. Please proceed, Captain." He crossed the room and took a chair where e-Tomai and I could both see him. If he really wanted to spook one of us he would have sat where that person couldn't see him, so that was something.

"Mr. Naradnyo," Captain e-Tomai began, "as you know, we have a very serious situation developing as a result of the Praha-Riz disturbance. It has been only about four hours and we are still trying to assess the cause and extent of the riot. Any light you could shed on the incident would be most appreciated."

"Whatever vid you've seen on the float, I didn't have anything to do with starting that," I said.

Captain e-Tomai exchanged a glance with his boss, e-Loyolaan, before answering. "We have already reached the same tentative conclusion. We have also studied the audio and video feed from your commlink and that of two other witnesses, so we have a fair idea of the sequence of physical events. We are more interested in your impressions."

Impressions? I thought about that for a couple seconds.

"What, you mean like my gut feeling? Some staffer panicked. Gaant caught everyone by surprise, first with the jammers going down and then when the crowd started in. The staffer overreacted, and then everything came apart. I don't think Gaant intended it to play out that way."

"You say it caught everyone by surprise," he said. "Does that include you?"

I noticed e-Loyolaan studying me pretty hard, probably wishing I had big ears to help him tell if I was nervous.

"Good question," I answered. "It sort of did, but in retrospect it shouldn't have."

And then I told them about the whole scene out in the atrium, the creepy mob of Gaant's followers, and what he'd said to pull me into the meeting, that the guys on the other side of the table would be surprised at what happened. At the time I'd thought his little speech about what a bunch of no-good greedy bastards they were was the surprise he had in mind, but he'd meant the whole business of taking control of the meeting, making it public.

"And you believe that is all Mr. Gaant intended?" he asked. "To simply make the meeting public?"

I shrugged. "You want impressions and I'll give them to you, but remember, I hardly knew the guy. I only met him a half-dozen times before today. If I had to guess, I'd say yeah, he just meant to embarrass all those guys, shame them, and maybe stir the public up against them. I think he has this big bunch of followers and he figured to make it even bigger, make some sort of play for political leadership. But what his long-term plans were is anybody's guess. Now that he's dead I guess we'll never know for sure."

"Oh, Mr. Gaant is not dead," Field Marshal Lieutenant e-Loyolaan said, his first comment in the interview.

"Not dead? I saw him..." I stopped. What had I seen? He fell, he hit his head, the crowd moved his body back out of the way, and they *said* he was dead.

"So, just unconscious?" I asked.

E-Loyolaan nodded to e-Tomai and the captain continued. "We located him in the South Tower trauma/med facility. The last report was that he was stable but comatose and under guard by the municipal police, charged with incitement to riot. Communication with Praha-Riz has been temporarily interrupted."

"Yeah, the three officers I talked to in Katammu-Arc said their tacticals were going to clear South Tower. If so, they shut down the comms themselves—standard procedure. But you guys know that, right?"

They exchanged a look and then e-Tomai nodded.

I wasn't sure if Gaant being alive was a good thing or a bad thing. Alive and in police custody he was a living symbol for his followers, and a target for action. Dead he was a martyr, and you can't negotiate with a dead man. I looked at e-Loyolaan, who was studying me again. He cocked his head slightly to the side.

"I do not know either, Mr. Naradnyo," he said.

"Know what?"

"Whether we are better off with him alive or dead."

So this guy was a mind reader too? Or was I just getting that obvious?

"We received word that the Honorable e-Lotonaa, your wife,

and the e-Traak heiress have crossed the uKootrin frontier," e-Loyolaan said. "Do we have you to thank for that?"

Here it comes, I thought.

"Just doing my job," I answered, and to my surprise he nodded.

"Yes, your duty. I understand. And it was the only sensible course of action. I want to thank you for saving e-Lotonaa's life at Praha-Riz and in the water afterwards. You call him *The'On,* I am told, short for *The Honorable.* I do not imagine he enjoys that, and yet he seems to tolerate it from you."

"I didn't know you two were friends," I said.

"Not friends. We are opponents on many matters of policy. But whatever our differences, e-Lotonaa wishes the best for the *Cottohazz,* as do I, and I respect him for that. I respect and value him, regardless of our disagreements."

He said nothing after that, just looked at me. The silence stretched out, but I did not get the sense he was trying to stare me down. He was probably thinking, but I honestly couldn't say for sure. Most people look away from you while they're thinking, so they won't make you uncomfortable, but he was not most people.

"What was it like to be dead?" he finally asked.

Not the question I was expecting.

"I liked it," I said. "You will too."

He leaned back slightly, almost imperceptibly, in his chair and an expression flickered across his face just for an instant, a hint of fear, and then it was gone.

"Were you disappointed to come back?" he asked.

"Little bit. But I had somebody worth coming back to. It makes a difference."

He nodded thoughtfully. "Many say your soul must have left you while you were dead, and that only your body was reanimated. Are you now a soulless creature, Sasha Naradnyo?"

"No more so than ever."

He actually smiled at that and seemed to relax a little.

"Will we soon be seeing mass resurrections of long-dead Humans?"

"No chance. They only managed to get me back because I expired about twenty meters from a starship cold-sleep capsule. They deoxygenated and froze me before morbidity set it. Once you start to rot, I guess that's it."

"That is comforting," he said, leaning all the way back in his chair and folding his hands in his lap. "Please understand I do not share the distaste for Humans many Varoki seem to feel these days. All loyal members of the *Cottohazz* are of equal value to me. But given Human propensity for…*creative* forms of interaction with law and government, there are already more than enough of you to keep me busy."

"Just think of us as job security," I said.

Ten minutes ago I'd never have considered saying anything as flippant as that to the head of the Provost Corps. A lot had changed in ten minutes. Was he my pal? No way. Did I think he was any less dangerous? No, maybe even more so. But I knew that whatever drove him, it wasn't personal insecurity. He wasn't the sort of guy to take a joke personally. I wasn't sure he took anything personally.

"You should know," he said, "that the Sakkatto municipal police have issued a material witness summons for you, which will mean your cross-border travel privileges have been suspended."

Shit! I was stuck. Marr was going to go crazy.

"Are you sure?" I said. "I just talked to them a couple hours ago."

He tilted his head to the side, the Varoki equivalent of a shrug.

"So, are you turning me over to them?" I asked.

"No. The CSJ tries not to interfere in the internal affairs of member polities, so we have no interest in detaining you. Until they are finished with you, however, I do not think you will be able to rejoin your party in Kootrin, and the inquiry into this affair may go on for some time."

"But they'll probably be waiting for me outside," I said.

"Possibly. But the public safety situation has deteriorated further in the past hour and I suspect the police have more pressing calls on their manpower. Shortly before this meeting, we intercepted an order for all investigative personnel to report for riot control duty. I also understand that over seven hundred such material witness summons were issued at first, and more are expected soon. They may consider you of particular interest and assign a higher priority to locating you, but that suggests a capacity for nuance which I have never known the Sakkatto police to display."

E-Loyolaan rose to his feet and e-Tomai jumped up as well.

"I have other work, Mr. Naradnyo, but it was very informative to finally meet and speak with you. Carry on, Captain."

✧　　　✧　　　✧

But there wasn't much left to carry on about. E-Tomai went on for a while, but it was all pretty routine stuff and soon I was on my way out, wondering what the hell had just happened. What did they get from me of value? Nothing I could see. Why had they even wanted to talk to me if they didn't have any tough questions to ask?

An answer came to me, although it seemed highly improbable: that the commandant of the CSJ wanted to sit down and talk to me face to face, to size me up. Why I would even show up on that guy's radar was a different question, and that led to other questions about where his radar was pointed and why.

Then another thought came to me: that the interview wasn't about me at all. Maybe it was really about *The'On*. My friend was a roving ambassador or executive, depending on what was needed when and where, part of the *Cottohazz* Corps of Counselors. From the way he talked in unguarded moments, his outfit locked horns with the CSJ over policy fairly frequently. Maybe this was e-Loyolaan's way of trying to open a back door to someone in the opposition.

And maybe it wasn't just one thing. Maybe e-Loyolaan had more than one ball in the air at the same time. He struck me as someone who usually did.

At the main entrance of the CSJ complex I looked around outside and didn't see anyone waiting to snag me. I did see five uniformed Munies packing assault rifles race by at a dead run, people scrambling to get out of their way. I needed to find a cash station and load up, so I could move quickly and stay off the grid if I had to. Cash made that easier. But first I needed to comm Marr.

"How's *The'On*?" I asked as soon as she opened the connection.

He's conscious and responsive. The doctor says he should recover completely. Where are you?

"The CSJ lobby. They cut me loose but I wanted to call as soon as I got past their jammers."

When will you be able to get here?

"Yeah, there's a problem with that."

She was silent for a moment and if electromagnetic radiation can get cold, it would have.

What do you mean, a problem?

"Municipal cops have lifted my cross-border privileges."

They said they were done with you!

"Well, now it looks as if they're done being done with me."

We should have waited for you.

"No, you—"

We should have waited! Damn you, Sasha, you knew this was going to happen!

I hadn't known, but for the moment arguing was pointless. I could tell her I was going to do everything I could to find a way to duck the border crossing guards, but saying that over an open channel was an invitation to a conspiracy charge for both of us. Once she calmed down maybe she'd figure that out.

If you get killed, I will never forgive you. Do you understand me?

"Yes."

She broke the connection and so I commed Iris Tenryu.

Hey, Boss, I was wondering when you were going to shake loose.

"I'm not loose. Munies need some testimony or something. What's the setup like there?"

It'll hold for a couple days, until the bad guys think through where we are and what to do about it. Then we'll probably have to get creative. Local cops and military are cooperating. None of them can find their asses with both hands, but they mean well. I'm trying to get the rest of our people across the border. We're going to bunker up at The'On's estate and wait for this shit storm to blow itself out.

I had no idea where Iris got her mouth—maybe too many Hong Kong gangster holovids dubbed into English. Marr said she talked just like me, but I don't think Marr had a very discriminating ear in matters of the criminal argot. That's actually what Marr called it, "the criminal argot," which was unfair to Iris, who to the best of my knowledge never broke the law, at least before she came to work for us.

"Okay," I said. "You're in the driver's seat. Try to stay low, but if they find you, make 'em sorry they did."

I'll make 'em cry, Boss.

I powered my commlink all the way down to where it couldn't be tracked and I started to work through whether or not to go underground.

I leaned against a wall, temporarily dizzy and weak in the knees. The sun blasting through the windows at a flat angle made it late afternoon. I hadn't eaten since breakfast, I'd fallen three or four stories into a river where I'd almost drowned, my right arm was crippled, and I was pumped full of pain killers. My leg muscles told me they'd given up their last reserves of energy and from here on out I was on my own. I needed to get a room in a hostel, get something to eat, rest. Otherwise I'd be in no shape to do anything. I looked up at the big rotating CSJ starburst symbol with its three letters in the center:

Knowledge, Resolve, Obedience.

Not *Justice*, I noticed.

Or *Truth*, for that matter.

Chapter Eleven

I woke up in an unfamiliar room and it took a few minutes of shuffling around all the scrambled memories of the previous day before I got them into a sequence that made sense. I was in a cheap hostel in Katammu-Arc. It was charging four times the going rate because of all the displaced people from Praha-Riz looking for a place to flop. I at least blended in with the other Human refugees, especially with my recent injury, rumpled and dirty clothes, and floppy black fisherman cap. I paid cash and when the clerk started ragging me about taking carryout fried tofu up to my room, I shut him up with another twenty *cottos*. Cash is eloquent, more so than me.

I'd gone to my drug-dulled and exhaustion-driven sleep with Marr's words replaying in my head: *If you get killed, I will never forgive you.*

It sounded like the sort of fake-angry threat people make as a token of love—if you die I'll kill you. It sounded like that, but it wasn't. She meant it.

Marrissa was an only child. Her parents both died when she was about seven, leaving her to be raised by polite but unloving relatives. She had never forgiven her parents for abandoning her like that. I know. My parents and my only sister died when I was eight, left me to grow up on my own in the nightmare slums of Crack City on Peezgtaan, and I guess I'd never really forgiven them either. They should have taken more care, been more mindful that their lives weren't just theirs anymore. I wondered if Tweezaa, who had lost both of her parents, would ever forgive them.

The point is, there is a certain type of abandonment for which death is an insufficient excuse. Marr, Tweezaa, and I all knew that, and that common knowledge bound us together in ways powerful enough to transcend blood and even species, but it didn't give any of us a free pass, especially not me.

So I had to get out of Sakkatto City, somehow, and get back to Marr and Tweezaa. The question was, how? I thought that over as I showered and made breakfast out of the cold left-over tofu. I had some cash, I'd gotten a good sleep, and physically I felt a lot better aside from the banged-up arm. Those were about the only assets I could muster, aside from wit, pluck, and boyish charm.

I was in Katammu-Arc, which was in some ways the epicenter of Varoki-dom. It was the largest arcology in Sakkatto City, and held the municipal offices as well as most of the governmental ministries of the Commonwealth of Bakaa. The other six arcologies of the city spread around Katammu-Arc forming the points of a very irregular hexagon, the arcs linked by maglev rails high above the sprawling slums below.

That really wasn't my concern at the moment, though. My target was the uKootrin border, six hundred kilometers to the north. That sounded like an impossibly long distance at the moment, though, since I wasn't even sure how to get out of Katammu-Arc.

My best hope was that a good night's sleep had done everyone else as much good as it had me, that people would wake this morning as if emerging from a bad drunk, shudder at the hangover and at the half-remembered folly of the previous night, and then prepare to go about their business as usual.

I still didn't want to activate my commlink so I used the room viewer to access the public float feed. A note from the management apologized for the smart wall being down for maintenance and offered a hand-held viewer as a substitute. I noticed it was attached to the desk with an antitheft cable, the sure mark of a high-class joint.

The first image I hit on the news feed stunned me: Praha-Riz arcology was burning. The structure itself wasn't flammable, but someone had torched all that beautiful greenery which covered it.

It made me want to cry. Praha-Riz was more than a cool-looking arcology; it was home, and not just because we had one of our residences there. Human and Varoki aesthetics were different, and Praha-Riz was designed by a Human architectural firm thirty years ago. There was just something Human about its look and feel. Maybe that's why they were burning it.

I scanned feed lines, the avalanche of images looking less like news than some nightmare scenario from a bad disaster holovid: Munies in riot gear storming Praha-Riz, shops in the lower levels of the arcologies looted, buildings burning in the slums, and bodies—bodies everywhere. Thugs from one political faction vandalizing political offices of its rivals, Varoki mobs killing Humans, Munies firing on other Varokis—*other Varokis!* I never thought I'd live to see the day Sakkatto City Munies would defend Human slums against a Varoki mob, and do it with live ammo. The entire city had gone mad overnight.

I tried to make sense of the flood of information, all of it distorted through the lens of the panic or rage or political agenda of the freelance feed heads interpreting it all. Everyone called them feed heads because usually all you saw was their head down in a corner of the vid feed, telling you what you were looking at and what it meant. Most of them were Varoki but there were a few other races and even a fair number of Humans.

One thing I knew for sure: until all this bullshit settled down, it would be pretty hard to just slip unobtrusively out of the city. When Varoki mobs filled the streets, a Human like me couldn't exactly blend in.

There was a strain of news feed blaming yours truly for the riot, and that made my chances of slipping away in all the confusion even harder, what with my picture spread all over the feed. They actually had an interesting sliver of evidence: the vid of me yelling at the staffer who drew the neuro-wand, saying, "Put that away, you moron!"

How could Sasha Naradnyo be the only person in the meeting to notice someone drawing a concealed weapon unless he knew of the weapon already?

Would anyone give orders in such a commanding and confident manner to a stranger—or was it to someone in his secret employ?

I'll tell you something, I always know when someone's bullshitting me: they don't tell me what they think, they just ask these leading questions and hope my imagination fills in the blanks the way they want. I figure my imagination's not there to do other folks' work for them, but not everyone sees it that way.

To be fair, there were some skeptics out there, most of them Human but a few Varoki as well. One of the Human feed heads got my attention, maybe because of her intensity, maybe because of her dark good looks, assuming you like your women hard-eyed and tight-lipped. I'm generally open to the idea, but in this case she reminded me too much of me.

There is no real evidence that Sasha Naradnyo was the architect of this riot, and strong reason to believe it was simply a falling out between the mercantile interests of the e-Varokiim, and the Varokist anti-Humanist followers of Elaamu Gaant. But nothing is certain, and if it should turn out that Naradnyo had a hand in this, he bears the crushing burden of guilt for all the Human lives already lost in these riots, and many more to come.

While I wasn't sure that covering all your bets was the mark of courageous journalism, I had to admit she'd summed it up pretty well. Still, she seemed more excited by the prospect of all that crushing guilt than in a less dramatic outcome. It would make a better story, I guess.

There was some feed of Gaant's speech about the über-rich being über-greedy—lots of people hailing him as a genius, although for my money it didn't take a towering intellect to state the obvious. Rich people like money? Wow! What an idea!

Besides, I wasn't sure he was right about this whole mess being about greed, at least on a personal level. I thought it was more about inertia. The plot to strip Tweezaa of her inheritance now, the systematic fleecing of the rest of the *Cottohazz* for the last hundred years—that's just what everyone at the top does. It's not about money in any tangible sense. They do it because that's what they always do—that's what they've been trained to do. That's what's expected. If they don't do it, their friends will look at them funny and stop taking their calls.

Years earlier I'd made the mistake of thinking the Varoki were united in a single-minded quest to screw the living hell out of Humans. Getting caught in the middle of a shooting war between two Varoki nations put that idea to rest, but I still didn't think the differences went any deeper than this nation against that one, this mercantile house against that one. Wrong again, Sasha. There were fault lines in this society which went all the way down, and now I felt as if I was watching them widen before my eyes, like the cracks in an ice shelf just before ten thousand tons of white stuff calve off and thunder down into the ocean. Where was this going to end? I had no idea.

Something bothered me, though—something other than the possible descent into chaos and anarchy of the strongest and most economically important Varoki nation, or even the effect of that descent on my chances of getting away. There was something odd about the vid feed of Gaant's speech.

I watched it again. It was clearly made by someone sitting at the opposition staff table, given the angle. You could see several of the big-shots at the main table and across from them Gaisaana-la and behind her the looming massif of ah-Quan. I played it all the way through and then again, and again. It was just as I remembered it, so what was bothering me?

I played it again, and it was still the same, right up to that little gesture Gaant made at the end, that signal.

The signal that told his accomplice to drop the jammers.

Right. He finished his speech, he gave the signal, and the jammers quit, so everyone could start recording the meeting. So how the hell could there be a recording of his speech, which was *before* the jammers went down?

Interesting as that question was, my problem still came down to getting the hell out of there, and I still wasn't sure how to accomplish that. Assuming things were temporarily calm, I could try to make it to the apartment in Praha-Riz. The fires at the arcology had been external and there was probably a lot of stuff busted up inside as well, but our apartment was in rich folks' country, and the Munies seemed to be protecting that sort of landscape. I had firearms stashed there as well as additional cash, a forged ID, and the access controls to my emergency retransmission sites seeded around the city—highly illegal here in Bakaa, but put in place just for a situation like this, an emergency getaway. The retransmission sites let me use my embedded commlink while making it nearly impossible to locate. It wasn't foolproof, but it would give me enough head start to get out of Dodge. But I had to get there to activate it.

The question was how could I get from Katammu-Arc to

Praha-Riz? With security high, if I took the maglev train or an air shuttle I'd have to do an ID scan, and with the summons out there was no telling what would happen next. Or I could walk. It was only two kilometers, after all, but it was two kilometers through slums which yesterday had exploded with riots, a lot of them directed at Humans. Maybe the rage was temporarily reduced to a low simmer, but I figured the survival time down there of one lone unarmed Human with his right arm in a sling and his pockets bulging with cash could probably be measured in minutes, and that assumed nobody recognized me as that horrible Naradnyo guy everyone on the feed was talking about. I wouldn't have minded having a good skin mask right about then, instead of just a big floppy black hat.

The more I thought about it, the more turning myself in to the Munies seemed like my smartest move. After all, they didn't have an arrest warrant out on me, just a material witness summons. According to the vid feed, the Munies were taking special care to protect the enclaves of the other five intelligent races, like us Humans. The fewer off-worlders that got hurt, the less likely the *Cottohazz* was to get involved in Bakaa's internal troubles, provided all the financial machinery started ticking over again within a day or two. If things got much worse they would probably evacuate the aliens, which if I was included would get my job done for me.

Things could go wrong with that move for sure, but there weren't any perfect choices. I had to play the odds, and, unsettling as I found that fact, the Munies looked like the frontrunners. My only real reluctance was in surrendering my freedom of action. I was used to calling the shots on my own, but right now I didn't see many shots to call.

Someone rapped on the door. I checked the time and it was getting close to checkout. It might be management wondering if I'd cleared out yet, but you never knew. I crossed to the door as quietly as I could and heard a low conversation outside.

"Who is it?" I asked, standing well to the side in case the answer was a burst of smarthead flechettes through the cheap composite door.

"Are Municipal Police. Would like speak Sasha Naradnyo."

Son of a gun! Talk about coincidences. I took a quick look through the peep lens and saw a Munie badge held up by way of confirmation. The English was heavy with the Slavic accent, common to the Sakkatto northside Human slums, but it made sense they'd send some local Human Munies to collect me. I opened the door.

"You know, I was just thinking—" I started, when two Humans in civilian clothes and packing gauss pistols pushed me back into the room.

"Hands up," one of them said.

My stomach tightened in fear and I raised my left hand. I tried to move the right one a little, but nodded to the sling.

One of them handed his pistol to the other and then patted me down, very thoroughly. He dumped the contents of my pockets—mostly cash—on the sleeping pallet then backed away.

"Clean."

"Let me guess," I said. "You guys aren't really Munies, are you?"

"Shut up, traitor," the guy holding the guns said.

Chapter Twelve

One on each side of me, they took me out through the hostel lobby and into the broad, open walkway beyond. We turned right.

"Where are you taking me?"

"Shut up," the guy on my left said. I thought of him as *Lefty.* He was the one who had done all the talking so far, what little there had been, and he looked to be the brains of the outfit. He had one of the local English slum accents, this one kind of a mix between Hungarian and some Slavic languages, which meant he was second-generation and probably hung out somewhere near e-Kruaan-Arc, a couple kilometers north of Katammu-Arc.

Lefty was the larger of the two, although neither one of them was all that big. He had a round face with sharp ratlike features, a scraggly black moustache, and I noticed he was missing the upper half of his right ear. The other guy had two scars on his face, one of which twisted his upper lip slightly. It made him look as if he were sneering all the time. I pegged their ages as mid-twenties. I had a pretty good idea who these guys were—not specifically, but in a general sense. I'd grown up with street toughs just like them. Hell, I'd *been* them.

Not that understanding them made my situation any less dire. In Katammu-Arc I had some measure of security. Praha-Riz would have been better. Outside of either one and at the mercy of two thugs: genuinely screwed. I needed to make some sort of a move and get control.

"Tell me where we're going," I said.

"Shut up," Lefty answered. "or we shoot you here."

"I don't think so. Back in the room, maybe, but out here in a public space? Katammu-Arc, which has the municipal government as well as the national government? Hell, we're only two levels down from the uBakai *Wat* chamber. With the Munies trigger-happy as hell and riots going on all over, you start shooting in here and you'll never get out alive."

The guys exchanged a look before Lefty spoke again.

"So maybe we pull stupid hat off your head and tell everyone here is Sasha Naradnyo. How leatherheads feel right now, will tear you to pieces."

"How many Varoki do you think can tell one Human from another?" I asked.

"Are so mad will not need recognize you," he said. "Take word for it."

I laughed.

"You don't get my meaning. How are they going to tell which of us is me? Once you get them going, they'll kill all three of us, just to be on the safe side."

"Yeah," the guy on my right said in a thick, slow voice, "but you still be dead."

"But I'm gonna be dead either way, right? So why not take you two assholes with me?" It was a bluff, but it hit home. His expression flickered as that sank in. I looked back at Lefty.

"You got no leverage, long as it looks as if you're taking me to an execution. Die here, die there, what more have I got to lose? Any pressure you try to put on me gets you in jail or dead.

"Now, might be I'll go with you anyway if the deal looks right. None of my options sound all that great at the moment, but you gotta make the pitch. There's a food station with tables up ahead, posted as having Human food too. Let's have a tea and talk about this. Otherwise I start yelling, first Munies we see."

He didn't say anything but I could see he was chewing it over. He lifted his right hand and he ran his fingertips absent-mindedly along the scar tissue that formed the top of what was left of his ear, as if checking to see if the other half had grown back.

When we got up to the tables he stopped, looked around, and then nodded toward an empty one a little apart from the others.

"Will not hurt talk," he said. "Pablo, get tea."

"I'm buying," I said. "Just take it out of that cash of mine you pocketed."

Sookagrad was what they called the slum district they came from—which translates as Bitch City in English, probably a comment on the quality of life. I'd been right about it sprawling in the shadow of e-Kruaan-Arc. After about twenty minutes of talking I was reasonably sure of the setup.

They claimed they worked for a Russian thug named Nikolai Stal, who I'd heard of but never met. I tried to keep up on the local criminal underworld but it was hard. There was plenty of information; you just couldn't tell how reliable any of it was.

For all their professed distaste over Human violence, a lot of Varoki found it fascinating, and so there was a thriving fan base for different Human criminal factions in Sakkatto City. Of course the stuff that got on the float about it was mostly made up, but even when the Varoki tried to play it straight and sort it all out, they still couldn't quite get it right. Human organized crime was always simpler than they thought it was, and more complicated at the same time.

So who was this Nikolai Stal? Well, for one thing that wasn't his real name unless his parents had a strange sense of humor. *Stal* was Russian for steel. Nikolai Stal—*nikyel stal*. Nickel steel, get it?

Besides, I'd already figured out these two punks didn't really work for Stal, their big talk notwithstanding. I pegged them as independents who wanted to get hooked into Stal's organization, and they grabbed me on spec, to make an impression on their intended future boss.

I was not clear on why bringing me in would make such an impression. They *said* Stal just wanted to talk to me, because they couldn't say someone wanted me dead. That would not be a very successful sales pitch, would it? They were unimaginative liars. I didn't hold that against them since it was making my life easier. But could I parlay that into my freedom? Maybe so.

I let Lefty talk until he ran out of stuff and was starting to repeat himself. I was careful not to ask any tough questions which would trip him up and make him realize how stupid his story sounded. I just listened and drank tea. When he started running down and his confident façade looked like it might crumble all on its own I came to his rescue.

"Okay, here's the deal. I'll talk to Stal, and I'll let you guys take me there so you get the credit with your boss, but I need to stop at Praha-Riz first."

"Praha-Riz—still locked down," Lefty said.

"I got my own entrance the Munies don't know about."

They looked at each other, suddenly nervous and suspicious.

"What you want there?" Lefty demanded.

"Three things. First, I need to pick up more cash. I got a feeling my negotiation with your boss could get expensive but I can't use a cash station without showing up on the grid. I got about a hundred thousand *cottos* in a safe at home. Second, I want to shower again and change clothes. Looking like a bum puts me at a disadvantage in a sit-down. Third, I need to turn on my remote retransmitters so I can use my commlink without the Munies tracking me. The controls are in my apartment."

"You got equipment can make commlinks invisible to Munies?" Pablo said, disbelief clear in his voice.

"Yeah, don't you?"

They didn't answer. They didn't need to.

"I can fix yours to run through my system while we're up there, if you want," I said, which was total crap but they didn't know. I wasn't sure which would entice them more: the idea of untraceable commlinks or the vision of a safe full of cash, but I figured together they were irresistible.

Lefty tried to keep his face blank, not let me know what he was thinking, but his hand went up to his ear again, stroking that line of scar tissue. "Okay," he said after a few seconds, "we get moving, but not try anything stupid."

"Nothing stupid," I agreed.

They had ground transportation waiting, a beat-up old manual-drive ground car parked in the public garage inside one of the south road accessways for Katammu-Arc. Lefty drove and we all crammed ourselves into the single broad seat. I had the feeling the original plan involved me riding in the baggage locker, but times change.

We emerged from the base of Katammu-Arc into drifting smoke and the stuttering sound of distant automatic weapons fire. My stomach churned in fear. Not your typical day in downtown Sakkatto, even in the slums. The city outside the arcologies was mostly made up of improvised structures with winding streets, some of them too narrow even for Lefty's little clunker.

Some of the buildings were almost substantial: one- or two-story cast foamstone, with the exterior clearly showing the pattern of the improvised mold used to cast it, usually wood planking with gaps between the wood so the foamstone had oozed out a bit in the seams before hardening. A lot more of the structures were discarded metal cargo containers of varying sizes and colors, some with windows and doors cut into the sides, others with flexible plastic or composite sheeting flapping across the original entrance.

Most of the space in between these was filled with shacks, lean-tos, and improvised tents, all of them looking like they wouldn't survive a good strong wind. Building materials were almost all metal, plastic, or composites. No wood—wood was fuel. Thin grayish smoke curled up from cooking fires, from a distance looking like the dirty plumes of a hundred cigarettes.

The ground was covered with garbage and the smell was about as strong as you'd guess. I didn't imagine there was regular trash pickup. In terms of filth and general dilapidation, it was worse than the Human Quarter back in Crack City on Peezgtaan, where I'd grown up, and that was really saying something.

I saw evidence of recent violence: structures gutted by fire, merchandise looted from stores and discarded in the street, and lots of flashing Munie hard posters stuck up on building fronts telling people the curfew hours and which areas were under interdiction, all of which lent a grim postapocalyptic feel to the landscape, made all the more surreal by our having been in the clean and orderly interior of Katammu-Arc only minutes earlier.

Once we had to double back and go around an area completely cordoned off by barricades manned by armed Varoki civilians. The unarmed Varoki we passed looked sullen and ready for a fight. A couple times groups of them started to crowd around the car but Pablo showed them his gauss pistol and they backed off. The farther we went, the more nervous I got, and I could smell both Lefty and Pablo sweating to either side of me, and it wasn't that hot a day.

We passed five Munie checkpoints and I kept the fisherman hat low on my face when we did. Even if Varoki weren't good at telling one Human from another by sight, the Munies' facial recognition programs would ID me and bring up the summons flag, but I needn't have bothered. As soon as they saw the car held Humans, they waved us through. Humans weren't the problem today. That was the oddest part of the entire trip.

We drove through a landscape altered and made unfamiliar, even to Lefty and Pablo, by the growing evidence of mass violence and the responses to it. The situation must have deteriorated just in the time they were inside Katammu-Arc dealing with me. I could tell they were as spooked as I was, although none of us let it show in our faces. We were tough guys, right?

The two-kilometer drive took almost an hour and there were several times I didn't think we were going to make it, but we did. I was right about one thing: I'd have never made it on foot.

Praha-Riz arcology looked desolate from the outside, with much of its foliage burned away and many broken windows, particularly on the lower levels. We parked west of the arc and walked to the maintenance access bay I had an illegal key for. I'd set this up as an emergency escape route, not a way in, but doors swing both ways. The streets were wet and slick with black soot and flame-retardant foam from fighting the exterior fires, but all the streets were nearly deserted, at least on that side.

Once inside we stayed away from the public spaces, instead following the arcology's circulatory system of air and power and fluid pipelines, making our way up through service elevators and maintenance accessways. We saw some damage, but not a lot and most of it was already repaired. A couple Varoki techs we passed looked at us funny but the gauss pistols discouraged their curiosity. I was half surprised we didn't see any Munies, but they apparently had their hands full in the public spaces of the arc.

I wasn't sure what I'd find at the apartment. Our address was public knowledge and I half expected to find it vandalized and looted, although someone would have needed a pretty high-powered pulse laser to cut through the armored door and walls. In any case, the upper levels had come through in pretty good shape. Lots of well-off Varoki lived here and the Munies had protected it, contained the trouble down below.

We had to go through all those layers of security to get it. I doubt that Lefty or Pablo had seen anything like it, even at Munie lockups.

The apartment impressed Lefty and Pablo at first; then it sort of pissed them off. They knew some Varoki lived this well, but the idea that Humans did seemed more unfair, rather than less. That's Human nature for you. Actually, this was very austere by *e-Varokiim* standards, but telling them that wouldn't make them feel any better.

I moved the couch to show them the floor safe and then pointed out the gun safe in the corner. It was all transparent composites so it doubled as a display case. I had a neuro-pistol, a couple very nice gauss pistols—one of them a big Zaschaan model with custom grips—as well as two old-style slug throwers: a little LeMatt 5mm and the Hawker 10mm I used to carry and which Marr had used to save my life after I was already dead. Long story.

"I'm gonna take a shower," I said. "One of you guys want to check out the john before I do?"

Lefty did the honors, leaving Pablo with his nose almost pressed against the clear composite gun safe. The master bath was through Marr's and my bedroom, and I imagine the bathroom itself was about as big as this kid's apartment, which he probably shared with someone, maybe several someones. He checked the shelves and drawers and cabinets, looked for control surfaces, and then just stood looking around for a while, fingering his ear.

"You trying to grow that ear back?"

He scowled at me and dropped his hand to his side.

"Leave doors open, wise-guy, so we see when you get done."

He left and I turned on the shower, waited a minute or two, and then went to the sink.

"Yanni," I said, which was Marr's and my security code for the apartment system. It was sort of a joke between us and usually brought a smile, but given our last conversation it made me feel blue instead, and lonely. A verification square appeared on the mirror and I pressed my left palm against it. The smart wall changed from a mirror surface to the default security screen: a layout of the apartment with thermal tags for the three occupants—me in the john and the two punks in the living room. I brought up the control interface and then closed and sealed all the doors to the living room. As the doors snicked shut I briefly heard Lefty and Pablo yell in anger and alarm. I pumped the living room full of gas and then took my shower.

Chapter Thirteen

It probably frightened Lefty and Pablo to wake up gagged and strapped securely into chairs, and with a tiny comm jammer taped to the back of their necks, but I can't say I had much sympathy for their predicament.

I'd showered and changed while the atmosphere filtration system scrubbed the gas out of the air in the living room. Our security system had an option for lethal gas but it was a lot more trouble to work with. After all, you can't just pump lethal gas through an exhaust duct into the outside air when you're done with it. How environmentally sensitive would that be? So I used a nonlethal gas which promised to knock them out for two hours and leave them weak but clear-headed for at least as long afterwards. I'd never used it before but it performed exactly as advertised.

While I waited for them to come to, I got my retransmitters up and running and then commed *The'On*. I was a little surprised he answered right away.

"Hey, pal, how's the head?" I asked.

Sasha! It is so good to hear from you. Where are you? Are you safe?

"Yeah, I'm fine. No telling how secure this link is so I won't tell you where I am."

Of course. I was not thinking. We were all very worried. And thank you for saving my life yesterday—twice. The vid of you telling the large angry fisherman you would not let me drown, that I was your friend, has made you something of an instant celebrity here in Kootrin. Have you heard from the others?

"I know Gaisaana-la and ah-Quan are alive, or at least they were yesterday. I'm going to try to contact them next. I haven't heard from Borro."

Borro is alive. I received a comm from him earlier. He is still in the city but trying to reach us.

"Well that's some good news. Listen, the situation's pretty bad here in Sakkatto and my gut tells me it's going to get worse. Everyone is losing control. I know you're banged up, but you're the only conduit I can think of to the *Cottohazz* Executive Council. You need to talk your bosses into some emergency abatement, and quickly."

In Bakaa? A frontier world like K'Tok is one thing, Sasha, but Bakaa is the single most powerful political entity in the Varoki circle. The Cottohazz Wat *is itself in uBakai territory, as are the executive offices.*

"More reason to get on top of this," I said. "Face it, pal, when it comes to crises, your Executive Council has a long history of closing the airlock after all the atmosphere's gone. This one's real trouble. I'm not screwing around. You need to break tradition and get out ahead of it, quick."

There was a silence on the line for a couple seconds before he answered.

You may be right. I will speak to my superiors. Politically it will be very complicated.

"Sure it is, but you're my go-to guy for complicated politics. Speaking of which, I ran into an old friend of yours yesterday, guy by the name of e-Loyolaan."

The head of CSJ? Sasha, I assure you Yignatu e-Loyolaan is no friend of mine.

"Yeah, he mentioned that, but I get the feeling he thinks of you as a worthy adversary, something like that. It felt like he was sounding me out, maybe trying to open a direct line to you. Any chance you two can find some common ground in sorting this whole mess out?"

I shudder at the thought, but for your sake I will explore the possibility.

"Last thing, have you seen any vid of Gaant's speech, the one he gave right before the shit hit the fan?"

I have not had much time to watch, but I believe I saw a segment of it. Why? Do you believe it has been altered? I am afraid my own memory of it is incomplete.

"Not altered. The thing is, I don't see how a recording can even exist, since the jammers didn't go down until after he was done talking. I mean, that was the whole point of the jammers, right?"

After? Really? If you are correct then the only explanation is a bio-recorder, a mostly nonmetallic implanted e-synaptic memory system. They are rare but sometimes worn by vid feeders to protect their proprietary content until they can edit and post it with their embedded commentary. Some intelligence operatives are fitted with them as well.

"Bio-recorder, huh? Okay, good to know.

"I'm going to switch to one of my travel cover IDs and try to make it across the border. With any luck I'll see you before too long. Tell Marr and Tweezaa for me, will you? I can't chance too many comms without blowing the encryption ciphers, and I don't know how long I'm going to have to stay down in the weeds. Besides, I think I'm still on Marr's shit list."

I will give them your love. Take care of yourself, my friend. I hope to see you soon.

I broke the connection and leaned back in my chair, letting the news video play across the smart wall opposite me. The Munies were stretched very thin, were spending a lot of time and energy racing from one flash point to another, and their faces in the vids showed the effects of fatigue and stress. Some of them had been at this for thirty hours without a break except for food and stimulants. The strain was showing in their actions, which were becoming more "proactive," a polite word for preemptively violent, often lethally so.

Behind me I heard a chair creak. I turned and saw both my guests were conscious. As I had tape across their mouths, the only sound they made was the rustle of cloth on cushion as they struggled against the broad tape that confined them to their chairs.

I rose and walked toward them.

"Time to talk, boys."

Pablo struggled even harder, rocking the chair from side to side until it fell over, and then he desperately flopped back and forth. Lefty's eyes just got large and he cowered back in his chair, or as much as the tapes let him.

I had already prepped two autoinjectors and now I took them from the pocket of my slacks. I shot Lefty in the neck with one and then leaned down and did the same for Pablo. I tipped him and his chair upright next to Lefty, which wasn't easy with only one good arm, but I managed. After allowing five minutes for the drug to work, I pulled the tape off their mouths.

I always had pretty good results with the interrogation drug I used, nortostecine. It didn't force people to talk and it didn't make them terrified. Instead, it overrode all their fear and inhibitions. It made them relaxed and chatty, and it erased any concern about consequences. No matter what they said, they could not imagine anything bad would happen, which removed their motivation to lie. Its only downside was it made the subject's attention wander.

I liked nortostecine because it was a lot less traumatic than most interrogation drugs. Bizarre as it probably sounds given my history, I had developed an aversion to traumatizing people. It started before I died and had gained increased traction in the two years since my resurrection. That's the real reason I left most of the field work to the kids, and for over six months had managed to come up with one excuse after another for not carrying a sidearm. There they sat over in my gun safe.

"Nikolai Stal going to take your ass!" Lefty blurted out as soon as the tape was off.

"Is he? But you don't really work for him, do you?"

"No...but would, as soon as turn you over. Now you ruin everything."

"Yeah, sorry. So why did he want me? Or was this all your idea to begin with?"

"Nikolai Stal kill you," Pablo said, his first contribution to the conversation.

"We're already past that Pablo. Now, what were you saying, Lefty?"

"Lefty? Name is not Lefty, is Bela Ripnick. Why for you have electric locks and gas in apartment?"

"Bela, don't you think the head of security for the highest-profile nongovernmental target in the entire *Cottohazz* might have extra security in the apartment he shares with that target?"

"Well, yes, makes sense....What you ask me before?"

I pulled over a chair and sat down. This could take some time.

✦　　✦　　✦

It took about two hours, but afterwards I was pretty sure I had everything of value from them, including as much as they knew about Stal's organization. Under the influence of the nortostecine Bela told me why he and Pablo came after me in the first place. A Resistance cell in the Human slum called Sookagrad had a price on my head for "Treason Against Humanity." Long story, but suffice it to say they had most of their facts screwed up, and I'm a much nicer guy than they gave me credit for.

But Bela and Pablo weren't going to turn me over to them. Nikolai Stal, the guy they wanted to impress, was sitting in the back yard of about every law enforcement and military intelligence outfit in the *Cottohazz*, and in addition had to arm wrestle with a local merchants' and citizens' association. Stal couldn't lean on anyone very hard because the citizens' association was backed up by an armed Human separatist resistance cell, the same one that had a price on my head. Politics always gets in the way of business.

Stal wanted to resolve his troubles with the Resistance: either patch things up or eliminate them. Bela figured I'd be the ticket to get either of those jobs accomplished. Stal could offer to hand me over, and either do so as an act of good will if he thought it could smooth over some of the rough spots in the relationship, or he could use the transfer of me to them as a ruse to draw them out and kill them.

That was Bela's idea, and it showed some surprisingly nuanced strategic thinking.

So why did I bother with interrogating Bela and Pablo? It was always good to know what was going on, and at some point I still might have to make a deal with the Munies. Anything of value I could share with them might help grease the wheels of our future relationship. Grease is good.

Once the drug wore completely off, Pablo began crying, a fairly common postinterrogation reaction. Maybe he was crying because of what Stal would do to them once he found out they'd spilled everything they knew about his organization. Maybe he was crying because he figured my best option was to put a flechette in his brain. Hard telling.

"No cry, Pablo," Bela told him, an order rather than an offer of comfort. Bela's voice sounded shaky as well, but the kid kept up the façade. Sometimes that's all you have left. I'll say this:

the kid had guts and brains, maybe more of the former than the latter. I walked around in front of them.

"Look, you two, let's get something straight. I should probably kill you but I'm not going to. I'm twenty-two and zero. That means I killed twenty-two people in my last life but not one so far in this one. You two aren't really important enough to make me break my streak, and you won't be unless you get in my way again.

"I've got some business to take care of here in Praha-Riz and then I'm leaving town. I'm going to leave you tied up for a while but I'll cut you loose before I go."

"How we know that?" Bela asked.

"What choice do you have? But look at it this way: as long as you're alive there's a chance you'll try to escape or do something stupid that could screw up my plans, so if I was going to kill you anyway, believe me, you'd already be in a couple big plastic bags in the back room. So shut up and count your blessings."

I left them with that cheery thought and went into the fabricator room to check on the body armor I was running out. I didn't have a lightweight suit here; both sets were at the valley house. I wasn't expecting any trouble but it pays to be safe and so I'd started the fabricator cranking out a new set before I commed *The'On*.

The shirt was done but the pants were still printing. I ran the vacuum over the shirt and dropped it in the component washer. I'd chosen a lightweight suit designed to be worn under my street clothes, but also one that would print fairly quickly, because I didn't want to hang around here forever. This version would stop a knife and slow down a flechette, provided it wasn't a milspec high-velocity smarthead.

I activated a smart wall in the fabricator room and brought up the software order again just to look at it. A one-time license for body armor, two-part covering torso and limbs, tailored to my laser body scan: three hundred and seventy-five *cottos*, about half of which was the software royalty and the rest was to the distributor, for marketing and product support. This was a fairly low-tech model, moderate protection; a really nice set could run you a couple thousand, not counting the raw material cost to feed your fabricator, and the electricity to run it, but that wasn't much.

Stal was on to something. His racket wasn't just a revenue

stream; it was a worm in the heart of the *Cottohazz*, the whole crooked set-up. The economy ran on decentralized fabrication so anybody could have anything—provided they could pay the design software royalties—with the intellectual property laws rigged so no one could ever get ahead of the Varoki in technology. Anytime anyone needed almost anything anywhere in the *Cottohazz*, all they had to do was punch up the software and fabricate it themselves, and every time they did, the guys on top dipped their beaks. Folks who couldn't afford a fabricator of their own, or wanted something bigger than their fabricator could handle, bought from a store, but most of what they bought was fabricated in the back room and it amounted to the same thing.

Except in Nikolai Stal's neighborhood.

I wondered how he pulled it off. There were two potential ways around the system. One was to disable the purge code which disabled the software in your fabricator after you'd made the items covered by your end user license. The other was to hack the user license itself and change the iteration number. Pay for one item and then convince the software you'd paid for a hundred. Or a million.

But it's not as if that hadn't occurred to the trading houses, and trying to crack that code from the outside was a sucker play. No, Stal must have people on the inside working with him, and that was extremely interesting. The one time I'd tried a really big data mining operation back on Peezgtaan, that's how we'd made it work. After this current emergency was tamped down, I was going to have to figure out a way to meet this Nikolai Stal, some way which would not involve me getting killed.

Before I plunged down into the heart of Praha-Riz, I wanted to take a look around and I was tired of vid feed. I opened the clear sliding doors to the balcony and went out. Right away I caught the trace smell of smoke—not clean wood smoke, but burning garbage, plastic, and something sweet, maybe flesh. Sakkatto City stretched out before me in the late afternoon sunlight, large columns of smoke rising from a dozen or more sites out in the slums and more little smoldering fires than I could count, all adding to a low clinging haze. Maybe because of the elevation I could just see more than before, or seeing it live had more impact than vid, but it looked worse to me, not better.

The arcologies appeared untouched, rising like arcane monoliths

from the clutter of the slums—untouched, unmoving, unseeing—
but the slums looked unsettled. Among the flickering fires and
through an irregular curtain of smoke I saw snatches of movement,
flashing emergency vehicle lights, a waving banner, a sparkling
reflection from a riot shield—movement devoid of clear meaning
but fraught with implication.

I ran my hand along the railing, still slick with fire retardant.
I looked down to the slums directly below Praha-Riz, over a kilometer below me, and I remembered the feeling of vaulting over
the railing of a burglarized apartment in Crack City, fifteen years
earlier, and riding the canyon thermals down on a parawing, with
a rucksack full of treasure—whatever the treasure had been that
night. Did I have a parawing in the apartment? I didn't think so,
but I could whip one up using the fabricator. The problem with
a parawing is you have to come down sometime, and no matter
where I came down, everything was still going to be...*that*.

No, my Peter Pan days were over. If I was going to fly out of
here, it would be by a short-hop turbo-shuttle, and I had a couple
people I needed to take with me on that flight. I owed it to them.

Chapter Fourteen

"Mr. Naradnyo, you should not have taken the chance of coming here. It is too dangerous!"

I flopped down in the chair across from Gaisaana-la and took off the viewer glasses I'd been wearing. I hadn't seen her since ah-Quan hustled her off just as everything had started going to hell and The'On and I flew out a window. She didn't look injured.

"I was already in the arc so it was just a couple express elevators and then a ten minute autopod ride. I wanted to see you but I'm half surprised to find you here at the office. Any other staff show up today?"

"A few. I sent them home at midday. Your arm is injured. I was afraid you and Executor e-Lotonaa were killed until I saw the vid of you in the water."

"We've survived worse. Listen, I need you to get out one of the travel cover IDs we set up for you and book passage for us to Kootrin. We're getting out of here and we'll take ah-Quan if I can arrange it. I think Borro is still in the city as well but when I ping him his commlink doesn't respond."

"Why did you not comm me to see if I was here before coming?" she asked.

"I'd have contacted you if I didn't catch you here, but the less we use the air the better."

She nodded in understanding. She was executive service, not protection detail, but everyone associated with Tweezaa and Marrissa had to be somewhat savvy about security.

"Mr. ah-Quan is in Med South, the same as the others injured from the first riot. I have visited him and he is in grave condition. The medtechs are confident he will recover but the next two days are critical. He cannot be moved now."

"He's that bad? What happened?"

Her face colored and her ears folded back as she remembered. "He picked me up, pushed through the crowd, put me in the corner of the room, and then covered me with his own body. At first the mob tried to beat him to death, then it pushed against him. He wedged his shoulders against the two walls and he continued talking to me until he lost consciousness although I could not understand him. Perhaps he was trying to keep me from fear, or perhaps keep himself from it. Perhaps he was praying. He spoke in a Zaschaan language."

"Szawa?" I asked.

"No, a native language, spoken with both mouths at the same time. It was very beautiful."

She looked away for a moment, maybe remembering that voice.

"He suffered multiple traumatic joint compressions, two spinal fractures, and internal organ damage. He cannot be moved. I will not go either."

"*You?* Look, I know you feel a debt to ah-Quan, but you can't help him by staying here. You're Marr's executive assistant and she's going to need you."

"The Municipal Police have issued a material witness summons for me and frozen my travel privileges."

"Right, same as me. That's why you need the travel cover. If CSJ were manning the checkpoints it might not fly, but with the Munies we'll be fine. Trust me, I just passed through four checkpoints getting here."

I held up the viewer glasses with my left hand.

"These have built-in UV lights that throw off the biometrics of automatic facial recognition scans—not enough to raise a red flag, just enough to throw my eye and nose dimensions out of the program recognition window for my face. If they want a closer scan, my retinas match my travel cover, and you'd need a medtech to tell they're skin contacts. They ran us a small fortune but they work against what the Munies have. You've got the same gear available with your travel cover."

She looked into my eyes and shook her head slightly. "It does not matter. I will not violate the law."

I sat back in the chair and looked at her. "The *law*? Have you looked out a window lately? There's no law out there anymore, just fire and rage and blood, and it's lapping at the foundations of the arcologies. Have you seen the vid of the outside of Praha-Riz burning? That may just be a sample of what's coming."

She dipped her head to the side, and her ears slowly opened up, her skin coloring in a soft hue.

"Mr. Naradnyo, you were born on the uZmatanki colony world of Peezgtaan, of Human parents who had renounced their Ukrainian citizenship. As I understand the law at that time, you were technically a stateless person until Peezgtaan received its independence, about ten years ago. This is correct?"

"Yeah. So what?"

"Believe me, I mean no offense. In the time I have known you I have gained great respect for you. My point, however, is that for most of your life—I think for all of your life really—you have been a man without a country. I do not sense that you understand how this sets you apart from so many of the rest of us.

"I am *uCotto'uBakaa*," she continued, her voice firmer, "a citizen of the Commonwealth of Bakaa. It is my country, Mr. Naradnyo, it is my home, and it is in desperate peril. I do not know that there is anything I can do to wake it from this terrible nightmare, but I cannot abandon it."

I didn't try to talk Gaisaana-la out of her decision. It would have been a waste of time for both of us, and we had a lot to do. She didn't think I understood what she was wrestling with, but in a funny way I did. I might not have a real good handle on nationalism, but I understood abandonment.

I also now understood her ambivalence about the adoption, and I felt small about questioning her loyalty the previous day, even if just to myself. One thing she had plenty of was loyalty, although it must have gotten pretty complicated for her, sorting her loyalties out and remaining true to all of them.

I hadn't had a lot of hope of getting ah-Quan out even before I found out his condition, because we didn't have an elaborate travel cover, or spook gear to back it up, for him. Before this all blew up he was another security guy, one of a couple dozen. Now things were different, but not in a way that was going to do him much good, at least not right away. I wanted to see him, though, say something to him before I went. Med South was not that far below our executive offices so I took another elevator down and watched the crowds of people through the clear composite wall looking out on the wide South Tower atrium shaft. I'd been just a few levels lower in the atrium yesterday morning.

Was that all it was? Just a little over a day?

The meeting had been on Ten of Eight-Month Waning—the tenth day of the second (waning) half of the eighth month in the Varoki calendar. They named their days and months with even less imagination than most of their enterprises. It was no wonder Humans were starting to do well in the arts—the competition wasn't all that tough. I blinked up my personal calendar to be sure I hadn't lost a day somewhere. Nope. Today was Eleven of Eight-Month Waning.

I left the elevator and walked down the broad corridor toward the main entrance to Med South but slowed as I saw a half-dozen Varoki in military uniforms out front, arguing with a couple Munies. There was a time I would have viewed this as an opportunity to slip past all of them while they were distracted, but I have learned from experience that a more likely outcome is for both Varoki parties to find common ground in working their frustrations out on the Human.

I felt as much as heard the repetitive thudding bass of a mech-nod band and altered course, following the sound to a narrower passage. I stopped and glanced at the soldiers and cops, still arguing, and I decided I should kill ten or twenty minutes to give them a chance to sort things out and go about their business.

I followed the passage, which led to a cul-de-sac surrounded by a half-dozen shop fronts. Two of them were shuttered and looked like they'd been closed for a while, and none of the others looked very prosperous, but the music escaped from an opened door leading to a dark room lit only by flickering colored lights. The sign above the door in both aGavoosh and aBakaa read "Koozaan's Beverage Store." Under it a sign in those languages as well as English read "Human's Welcome!"

I resisted the effort to correct the punctuation, wrapped my left hand around the neuro-wand I carried folded up in my trouser pocket, and went in.

Varoki bars aren't like Human bars. For one thing, there's no actual bar, just tables and chairs and a doorway to the back room. Two Varoki in suits sat at one table, already drinking some pastel pink stuff and arguing. I grabbed a table close to the door and punched up the drink options on the smart surface. They had what claimed to be scotch, a label I'd never heard of: *Klan MacKlacklahaan*, which claimed to be "the finest blended single malt scotch on Hazz'Akatu."

Despite some doubts about the existential possibility of a blended single malt scotch, I ordered one over ice. I paid with the fund card associated with my travel cover, just to establish my identity and head off questions. This was the sort of situation where cash would have attracted unwanted attention. I added a nice tip in advance and pretty soon a middle-aged Varoki male server brought the drink, set it down politely, and then returned to the rear of the shop. No small talk but no challenging looks either.

I took a sip and was surprised that it actually resembled scotch after all, and not even the worst I'd ever had. Of course, given what drink fabricators could turn out, there wasn't a lot of percentage in selling rotgut, which would come out of the same fabricator and cost almost as much to make.

Although I preferred jazz, the repetitive pounding of the mech-nod music was strangely relaxing. Instead of distracting me, it cleared my mind. I stirred my scotch with the plastic straw and wondered what the hell I was doing here. Talk to ah-Quan before I got out of town, sure. But why?

I couldn't take ah-Quan with me to Kootrin, so what was the point? He wasn't counting on a visit and it would just endanger both of us. I could send him flowers.

So why was I hanging around in a bar watching the ice in my scotch melt? Why wasn't I already on a shuttle for Kootrin? I was stalling. I was killing time, coming up with excuses *not* to get on that shuttle. I couldn't figure out why, but it had to stop, right now. Get up, book the shuttle, and get the hell out of this mess.

I left most of my drink on the table and walked down the arched passage to the main corridor. When I got there I saw more military types at the main entrance than before. The Munies were gone and a couple high-ranking Varoki officers in the dress grays of the uBakai astro-naval service walked into the hospital like they were in a hurry. Whatever was going on in there, it was more heat than I needed, so I reluctantly turned and headed back to the elevator.

Why reluctantly? That didn't make any more sense than me being here in the first place. I'd already decided to skip a visit to ah-Quan, so why had all that extra security suddenly made going in *more* attractive? Was it the little kid in me, curious about what all the activity was about? Or the adolescent pushing back against all those authority figures telling me what I could and couldn't do? Or the danger junkie, hungry for an adrenaline high? Maybe.

But just maybe it was the loner, looking for any excuse to put off going back to all the responsibilities I'd accumulated over the last two years. Responsibilities I'd never had before.

‖‖‖‖‖‖‖‖‖‖‖‖‖‖‖‖‖‖‖‖‖‖‖‖‖‖‖‖‖‖‖‖‖‖‖‖‖‖ Chapter Fifteen

I got in the express elevator going up and requested Level 237. I shared the compartment with a Varoki couple who moved to one side to give me some space, maybe because I was Human, maybe because of my dark expression.

I loved Marr in a way I'd never loved anyone in my life, in a way that had caught me by surprise because I'd thought it was beyond my capacity. And Tweezaa...sometimes it was hard to believe she *wasn't* my child, my own flesh. And soon there would be a son, one more person to cherish, one more to enrich my life beyond anything I had ever imagined.

One more to let down.

I closed my eyes and just stood there for a while as the floors raced past, faster and faster, and I wondered if these things ever had brake failures, if they ever just kept accelerating until they blew right through the roof and tossed their passengers a thousand meters into the sky, to reach the top of their trajectory, pause there for a moment, and then start that long fall back.

I opened my eyes when the elevator began to decelerate. No brake failure today. It stopped at 200 and the Varoki couple left, silent and avoiding eye contact with me. As the doors closed I blinked up a search for travel services in the city. Marr always booked our travel through the office but it occurred to me someone might be watching for that. I picked the first service that came up and put in a booking for a shuttle departure to Kootrin from the Praha-Riz rooftop terminal, as soon as available.

We Are Sorry But Due To A Defense Ministry Night Aerial Travel Quarantine Over Sakkatto City All Shuttle Departures Have Been Delayed Until Hour Seven, Twelve of Eight-Month Waning. Would You Like To Make A Morning Booking?

"Yes," I answered, confirmed the booking through my travel cover, and closed the connection.

Night? It was only coming up on Hour Fifteen, and this time of year it stayed light at least until Seventeen. Somebody was nervous, not that I could blame them, but it was getting in the way of my efforts to be a responsible adult.

I left the elevator and made my way to the apartment, went in, and paused in the anteroom to check the security monitors inside. Bela and Pablo were still strapped into their chairs, so I opened the inner doors and joined them.

"Change of plans, boys," I said as soon as I got inside. "My shuttle doesn't leave until tomorrow morning, so I'll have to keep you under wraps until then."

"I need go bathroom," Bela said.

"Yeah, not surprising. What I'm going to do is cut you loose and lock you both up in the guest suite until I'm ready to leave. There's a bathroom in there, and smart walls if you get bored. There's also a comm sensor, so if you pull those jammers off your necks and try to call for help, I'm going to have to do something drastic. Understand?"

They both nodded and I traded the folding neuro-wand for a neuro-pistol from the gun safe. I moved it into my right hand, cradled in the sling, and took my old Kizlyar *desantnyk* knife from its scabbard in the safe, holding it in my left hand.

"I'm going to cut your feet free with the knife. Then I want you to get up, carrying the chairs strapped to your backs, and walk to the guest suite, down that hallway. Sit down in there with your backs to the doorway and I'll cut your hands free. Do not stand up until I am out the door or I will stun you.

"This blade is very sharp, so try not to move while I'm cutting the tape. I'm more of a gun guy than a knife guy, so if you try something really stupid, like jumping me, and I have to cut you, I can't guarantee it won't kill you."

"Understood," Bela said. "We do as ask, not cause more trouble.

Most people would kill us. *I* would kill us. Is very good of you not to. I am sorry we try hurt you, Mr. Naradnyo."

"Well, I'll make a deal with you, Bela. If you don't tell anyone I went soft and let you live, I won't tell them about getting the drop on you."

"Is deal. Thank you, Mr. Naradnyo," he said.

All very nice, but I still made them go through every step of the transfer procedure.

Once they were securely locked in I made my way to the living room, poured myself a real scotch, and walked out onto the balcony to think things through. I considered taking along one of the cigars Marr got me as a birthday present but I wasn't in a good enough mood. Cigars should always be celebratory, even if only in some small way, like smoking one with a friend.

I thought for a moment and then went back in and got one, came out, and settled into a lounger. I snipped the end, got it going, and commed Marr.

Sasha? Are you all right?

"I'm fine, Babe. I'm out on a balcony, enjoying a birthday cigar and thinking about you."

Can you get to us?

"Yeah. They shut down transportation for the night, but I have a ride lined up for tomorrow. No details, understand?"

Yes. As long as you're safe you can tell me later. I miss you.

I watched a military shuttle bank and flare for a landing at one of Katammu-Arc's upper bays and I swallowed to relieve the tightness in my throat.

"God, I miss you, too."

I finished my cigar and then showered and packed so I wouldn't have to bother with it in the morning. I warmed up some frozen leftovers, and even made Bela and Pablo dinner, used the intercom to make them move into their bathroom while I opened the door and put the plates on the table, and then gave then the all-clear after I was out and the door locked again. All that took an hour or so and by then the light was fading. It was a beautiful autumn night, though, and I took another scotch out onto the balcony. Maybe things were settling down. I set the internal alarm on my commlink, stretched out on the lounge, sipped my scotch, and eventually drifted off to sleep.

I woke up about Two Hour on the Twelfth and at first I wasn't sure why. I still had almost four hours before I had to leave for the shuttle. Something had changed in the background pattern of noise.

I stood up and stretched, then went to the railing and looked down. The city didn't look much different than it had before except now it was dark, lit by street and building lights, scattered fires, and little patches of twinkling light here and there. It took me a minute to realize the faint sound of automatic weapons fire had woken me, and that's what those little twinkling lights were. The sounds were muted and got to me after the light, so they didn't really seem associated with each other.

The firing wasn't continuous: a smattering here, then it would stop and there would be a cluster somewhere else, going on all over the slums of Sakkatto City. I had a set of long-range vision enhancement goggles somewhere in the apartment and I went in to find them. As soon as I did I heard Bela talking on the intercom.

"Mr. Naradnyo! Are you there? Mr. Naradnyo, better look this stuff on feed. Mr. Naradnyo, where you are?"

"I'm on it," I said into the intercom and opened a vid feed on a smart wall. I didn't have to search for more than five seconds before the images started coming up.

I was looking at a Munie checkpoint which had stopped a military vehicle, a wheeled APC—armored personnel carrier—in uBakai Army urban camo pattern. A dismounted Army officer argued with a Munie in full riot gear.

"This was live just five minutes ago from a municipal streetcam at the intersection of Deliverance Way and the eastern maintenance trunk line," a female Human voice said in English. She sounded short of breath, as if from fear or excitement. I recognized her face in the corner of the picture, the same woman I'd noticed earlier, the one named Aurora.

The Munie in the feed became more heated, shouting at the officer, gesturing wildly. Just watching you could tell the Munies—worn down, jumped back up on stimulants, and scared—were taut as wires stretched right to the breaking point. And then the wire broke.

It was over almost instantly. The Munie pushed the officer back and went for his sidearm, probably a neuro-stunner, but before he even got it out of the holster the remote autogun on top of the ground forces APC punched him with a four-round burst, slammed him back against the police van parked to block the street. He crumpled to the pavement, clearly dead. The other four Munies opened fire with their assault rifles, hit the dismounted officer, and then the APC's autogun went to continuous fire mode and just shredded them, opening up the side of the police van and setting it on fire in the process.

The clip ended. I sat down on the couch and started watching more lines of feed.

At first all anyone had was that one clip, played over and over. Then other streetcam clips started showing up. An abandoned Munie checkpoint, police van still in place. A different checkpoint with a gutted van and dead Munies on the pavement. A clip of Army soldiers pushing disarmed Munies, all of them with their wrists restrained behind their backs, through the rear hatch into an APC. All across the city the Army was moving in and disarming the Munies, except where they resisted, in which case they just cut them down.

I noticed the Army wasn't taking over the checkpoints when they were done with the Munies; they just took off with their prisoners or left the bodies where they fell and moved on. They were creating a vacuum.

I also saw a clip of Varoki troopers loading a dozen panicky Katami, their feathery cranial membranes flaring and swaying, streaked with fear color, their short arms cuffed behind their backs, into the open hatch of an armored carrier. Another feed showed forlorn-looking Buran being herded along by MPs, looking like so many shuffling tree stumps. The Army apparently wasn't crazy about aliens. I didn't see any feed of Human prisoners, but I saw some bodies in very bad shape. No way of telling who'd killed them, but whoever it was, they'd really gotten into it.

Within an hour the feed heads reported military units in most government complexes in Sakkatto City, and then the other cities in the Commonwealth of Bakaa. I saw some fighting in other cities between police and Army units, and even reports of fights between Army units—"rebel" and "loyalist" although I wasn't sure which was which.

Reports started coming that elements of the military high command had taken control of the government to stem the rising disorder and had appointed a provisional government for the duration of the emergency. Back on Earth they called this sort of move a coup. The reports were garbled at first, and sometimes contradictory, but as the sun started coming up, the heads of the provisional government addressed the nation over just about every feed channel. The address coming at dawn must have been meant to be symbolic.

The new head of state, appointed by the military, spoke first. He wore the uBakai astro-naval gray uniform with the rank insignia of a rear admiral, which seemed fairly junior to be the guy in charge. Either he was a figurehead or this was a Young Turk coup.

The feed caption identified him as Provisional President Talv e-Kunin'gaatz. He talked about rampant corruption in the *Wat* and the civilian government, how they no longer reflected the will of the people, how that was why the police, as instruments of the *Wat*, had tried to crush the spirit of the people, had murdered well over a thousand of them.

"As do all members of the armed forces of Bakaa," he said, "I swore an oath to defend the people of Bakaa in time of peril. Whatever we all may differ over, no person within the sound of my voice can dispute that the *Cotto'uBakaa* now face a graver peril than at any time since the dawn of the Stellar Age. If I and other senior officers did not feel that the leaders of the civilian government had dishonored and abandoned their similar oaths, we would never have acted. But they have. So we have taken control of the government in the name of all uBakai. Discipline and values will replace corruption. The Municipal Police, who have shown their brutality and corruption, have been replaced by the Ground Forces Military Police, whom you will find to be stern but principled."

He didn't go on much longer; he spoke briskly and to the point. His commanding presence and self-confidence made him sound like he knew what he was doing, but he was astro-navy, and everything looks easier from orbit. If this admiral thought a bunch of Army MPs could just step in and seamlessly take over the police functions of one of the largest cities on Hazz'Akatu, he was delusional. Whatever lid the Munies had clamped on the Sakkatto pressure cooker had just been removed.

The next guy to speak was the vice-president-designate, none

other than Elaamu Gaant. So that's what all that astro-navy
brass was doing at Med South earlier: chatting up Gaant and
cutting a deal.

Maybe Gaant was part of the government to give it the veneer
of civilian participation, or maybe to let the rioters know whose
side the military was on. His head was swathed in spray-on
bandages and I thought he had sort of a wild look in his eyes
I hadn't seen before. His speech ran longer than the admiral's
and it was...something else—a rambling rant about the destiny
of the *Varokiim*, and the corruption not only of the uBakai *Wat*,
but of the whole *Cottohazz*.

Look at all the Varoki have given the other races of the *Cottohazz*, he lectured: the orbital needle, which enables them to
economically move people and material from planet surface to
space, and the jump drive, which enables them to move between
the stars in the blink of an eye instead of the passage of a
lifetime—the same words he used to me a few days earlier. There
would be no interstellar civilization without the Varoki, he said,
and the idea that the other races of the *Cottohazz* even had a
voice in judging a Varoki nation incensed him.

"It is not for that collection of talking animals," he finished, his
voice rising, skin flushed and ears flared, "which calls itself the
Cottohazz Wat to pass judgment on our destiny. If the *Cottohazz*
does not have the vision to recognize and honor the special place
in history of the *Varokiim*, then we say the *Cottohazz* can rot!"

In the three hundred years since the Varoki had started their
journey into the galaxy, a lot had happened, but never anything
like this, not that I'd ever heard of anyway. A Varoki nation
taken over by a military coup and now telling the *Cottohazz* to
go screw itself? This was crazy talk, deeply and disturbingly crazy.

This new so-called government had taken out the Munies and
didn't have the resources to protect the non-uBakai nationals
and non-Varoki the way the previous administration had. Now
it was pretty clear they didn't have the inclination either, and I
knew from experience that Gaant had an especially dark place
in his heart for Humans.

A military spokesman announced that the Provisional Government had closed the borders and suspended all international
travel for the duration of the emergency. Then all the feeds on
the smart wall went black and I heard the hum of jammers in my

head. I powered down my commlink. Whatever this new government intended to do in Sakkatto City, they didn't want anyone watching, listening, or recording. Gaant might be particularly interested in finding me, and one of the first places he'd have the Army look would be right here. With the Munies all dead or in detention, my range of options had narrowed way down.

How could I have fucked this up so badly? Once I got back to the apartment yesterday and gassed Bela and Pablo, all I'd needed to do was get the travel cover, book a shuttle flight right then, and get the hell out of here. Instead I'd gotten cocky. I'd dicked around with the interrogation, the visit to Gaisaana-la, the hospital, and now my escape window had slammed shut in my face.

My chest grew tight with fear and I started to sweat. I'd thought my situation was bad before but it was nothing compared to this. I'd really put myself in a hole.

I shook my head to clear it. Panic and recrimination weren't going to help anything. Where to from here? Someplace where there were Humans, that's for sure. No way to hide in a sea of Varoki.

Sookagrad.

Of course, nobody on any side of the power struggle there gave a damn about my survival, but two things encouraged me: Stal wasn't particularly set on killing me, and where there was conflict there was also opportunity.

I walked to the intercom and hit the button. "Bela, I'm going to Sookagrad. I need transportation and muscle, and I'm paying cash. You interested?"

Chapter Sixteen

Four eventful and harrowing hours later, I found myself tied to a chair in a room and blindfolded, surrounded by Humans asking me questions—people I couldn't see but, judging from the tone of their voices, pretty pissed off at me. Not sure if it was from the heat of the room or just the situation, but sweat soaked my shirt and stuck it to my chest and back. In one way I was glad I was tied up; it kept these people from seeing my hands shake. On the other hand, while I recognized the irony of finding myself tied to a chair, I didn't appreciate it.

I'd thought I'd have a chance to chat up Nikolai Stal before he turned me over to the "Resistance," maybe change his thinking about that, but no such luck. So now I was being tried by a revolutionary tribunal. No kidding, they really called it that: a *revolutionary tribunal*. It wasn't just the Resistance, but some outfit calling itself the Sookagrad Emergency Citizens' Troika, and I was getting the idea it represented several community groups of one sort or another, and maybe they didn't always get along. I'll say one thing for them: I hadn't been beaten up yet, just bound and blindfolded for a while.

There were three judges on the tribunal, but so far only two had spoken. Both of them spoke English with a standard accent, the sort news feeders and politicians speak, so they either weren't from around here or they were pretty well educated. My money was on the second option. No one had introduced themselves so I tagged the two as Dragon Lady and R.G.—which stood for *Reasonable Guy.* I was starting to suspect Nikolai Stal might be the third judge, but he had kept his mouth shut so far.

"How can you deny you were an undercover operative for CSJ?" Dragon Lady asked. "You were publicly commended for it!"

"Yes, how do you explain the commendation?" R.G. asked. Part of their act was to alternate questions, maybe to keep me off balance.

I took a slow breath to steady my voice.

"A major from the provosts was grateful for me saving Tweezaa e-Traak from assassins, and for trying to save her brother, even though he ended up dead anyway."

I paused to let the lump pass from my throat. I thought about Barraki, Tweezaa's brother, a lot, but I tried not to think about him dying, his blood all over me.

"The major made up the bit about me being undercover," I continued. "I was already in his reports for a bunch of criminal activities. Passing me off to his superiors as an informant was the only way to keep me out of a long-term detention facility."

"He did this because you saved the wealthiest Varoki heiress in a generation," R.G. said. "Why would he need to fabricate such a lie? Surely the CSJ would ignore a few petty crimes in light of a service such as that."

I shook my head. "I don't think e-Loyolaan, the guy running the provosts, is much of a rule-bender. Besides, that CSJ major didn't do it because Barraki and Tweezaa were rich; he did it because he had a soft spot for kids in trouble, and he knew I did too, which is why he sent them to me."

"A leatherhead CSJ officer with a sentimental regard for children?" Dragon Lady said. "Willing to risk his career to repay a debt to a Human? Save your fairy tales, Naradnyo."

I'd been thinking over what Bela told me about the jockeying factions in Sookagrad, and I was mentally penciling in Dragon Lady as the Resistance and Reasonable Guy as the Citizens' League. Of course, they could be playing against role deliberately, but I didn't think so. Dragon Lady's frustration and outrage didn't sound like an act to me.

I looked around, even though I couldn't see any of them, and I shrugged.

"Believe it, don't believe it, that's up to you. But those guys in black and red are people. They are relentless, nearly incorruptible, and usually merciless, and one way or another I think they're always going to be our enemy, but they're people. If you don't understand that, you'll never beat them."

"You mean so we can understand their weaknesses?" R.G. asked.

"No, their virtues."

"Listen to him!" Dragon Lady shouted. "He claims he never worked for CSJ and then lectures us about their *virtues*."

There was something about this whole setup which didn't make sense to me. If this was just the Resistance, I could see them considering offing me, but if there were other factions like the local citizens' league involved, what was their angle?

"I'm telling you the truth," I said, directing my voice toward where I thought R.G. was sitting, "but what if I'm not? What difference does it make? Since when is working for or with CSJ a crime? You guys call yourselves a revolutionary tribunal, right? Who are you revolting against? Everyone?"

"The business of undercover operative doesn't matter," Dragon Lady said, speaking to the rest of the judges, "except for what it tells you about his character. But Naradnyo single-handedly destroyed two Human resistance cells. He can't deny that."

She was right; it would be stupid to deny it. That was all part of the public record as well as being true, after a fashion. I licked my lips and tasted the salt from my sweat.

"Two years ago I killed the two top resistance people on Rakanka Orbital Highstation," I answered. "I didn't set out to do it but they were coming after Barraki and Tweezaa e-Traak, and were going to kill my wife and me in the bargain. Self-defense. Same with Kolya Markov's gang, although talk about fairy tales! You call them a resistance cell? They were hoods. Only one in the whole bunch who could even spell 'politics' was Markov, and all it meant to him was a psychotic hatred of all things Varoki."

"It must be easy to not hate the leatherheads when you live in the luxury their money buys," Dragon Lady said.

"You want to hate the system? Go ahead. You want to hate Varoki who have screwed Humans over just because they could? There's no shortage of them. But if killing a couple Varoki children actually makes sense to you as a revolutionary statement, it's no wonder this half-assed mess you call a resistance movement has never accomplished anything."

"Watch your mouth, Naradnyo!" she barked back.

I knew I was baiting her, but I figured I'd lost her vote before we even sat down here. I was working on the other two judges.

"You still didn't answer my question," I said. "Who are you revolting against?"

"This is *your* trial, Mr. Naradnyo," R.G. said. "We are giving you an opportunity to speak in your defense, but we will ask the questions."

"It's hard to defend myself when I don't know the laws I'm being held accountable to. Is self-defense a capital crime? What am I accused of?"

"Crimes against Humanity," Dragon Lady answered.

"Yeah, but *which* crimes?"

"In the struggle between leatherheads and Humans, you have chosen the leatherhead side," she said, "and your hands are red with Human blood to prove it."

A mutter of angry agreement filled the room until somebody rapped a table to shut them up. There were more than three people here and right now Dragon Lady had them. If she kept them, the other judges would probably go along with her.

"The struggle isn't between all Varoki and all Humans," I said. "Have you been paying attention to what's going on? When the anti-Humanist mobs came to burn this place down and kill everyone here, who kept them off of you? The Munies did, those nasty *Varoki* Munies, and they killed a fair number of other Varoki in the process. Now the Army's taken over, the Munies are gone, and Elaamu Gaant is the number two guy in the new regime. All hell is about to break loose because he despises Humans. Sometimes I think he's right."

I heard another mutter of angry voices.

"Listen to him!" Dragon Lady said. "He condemns himself."

"What do you mean, he may be right?" R.G. asked, ignoring her.

"First time I met him he said the only elements common to every single Human failure are Humans themselves. Now here you are: an avalanche of fire and blood is about to sweep every Human in this district away, and your priority is to waste an hour deciding if some guy hates Varoki enough to be allowed to live. And you're the *brains* of the outfit? Jesus! Just shoot me and get it over with. It'll be a cleaner death than any of you are likely to find."

It was a nice brave speech, but I had to swallow hot spit right after it. Fear does that to you, and I figured throwing up might ruin the effect. Sweating like a pig was bad enough.

"Is right," I heard Stal say, finally breaking his silence. I recognized his voice and accent from our brief meeting right before he hustled me off to the tribunal. "Kill Naradnyo or cut loose. I do not care which, but we have more important things to do."

"You have actually met Elaamu Gaant?" R.G. asked, ignoring Stal's comment. "What do you know of him?"

Sweat burned my eyes and I pressed them closed hard for a moment as I thought about that. It's not as if I knew Gaant all that well. I'd met him a few times and seen him speak on the vid feed, which wasn't a lot to go on, but there was a single hot thread which burned its way through everything I'd seen.

"He's driven by hate," I said, "blinded by it. Something must have happened to him when he was younger, who knows what, but it's left him with overpowering resentment, a sense that even when he's on the top of the heap he's somehow being slighted, cheated. I saw the vid feed of his speech this morning and I don't think getting hit in the head during the riot improved his impulse control any. Most of his hate's directed at Humans, but there's plenty left over for Varoki who don't measure up."

"Why do you think he hates Humans so much?" R.G. asked.

"What matters?" Stal said before I could answer. "Has army behind him. How can we fight?"

"We have weapons!" Dragon Lady shot back. "We fight for every block, every building. We make them pay in blood."

So there was friction between them.

"A revolutionary with a death wish," I said. "Now there's something new."

I heard Stal laugh, a humorless bark.

"We accept the fight that comes to us," R.G. said. "What choice do we have?"

"Sure, the fight's coming to you, and your only options are to resist or to throw yourselves on the mercy of Elaamu Gaant, which is nonexistent when it comes to Humans. But answer the question I asked earlier, if not for me, at least for yourselves: who are you revolting against? Everybody? Proclaim this the People's Democratic Republic of Sookagrad or something and tell the whole *Cottohazz* where to shove it? You'll last a week, tops, and then no one will remember anything about you—except a bunch of crackpots got killed after issuing a political manifesto nobody read."

Stal laughed again.

"And what would you revolt against, Mr. Naradnyo?" R.G. asked after a moment of awkward silence.

"Revolt against the junta and its anti-Humanist mobs. Side with the Munies, with the elected government that was deposed, and with the *Cottohazz*."

"That's what you expect to save us?" Dragon Lady said.

"There aren't any sure things here, only long shots, but at least give yourselves that much. Give the Varoki still loyal to the elected government a reason to make common cause with you. Give yourselves a *chance*. It can't work any worse than suicide by angry mob."

A low murmur of conversation ran through the room, not as angry as before. Frightened. Uncertain.

"Even if we do, what do we lose by killing you?" Dragon Lady asked.

"Your only potential contact to the *Cottohazz* Executive Council, and those terrible Varoki that none of you would dirty your hands with. Do any of you understand who in the *Cottohazz* government you could trust and who would screw you the first chance they got? It's a political minefield, and you don't have a map."

I wasn't sure I did either. Marr and *The'On* were the real masters in that realm. But compared to all the folks in this room I was actually pretty savvy, which said more about them than me.

"Enough talk," Stal said. "Vote now."

"Do you have anything else to say before we do, Mr. Naradnyo?" R.G. said.

"I've never sided with someone because they were Varoki, or against someone because they were Human, only because of who they were as people and what they were doing. That's the truth and I think you all know it. So kill me if you want, but if you do, don't feed yourselves some lie about how this trial was anything but bad theater."

"Very well," R.G. said. "Zdravkova?"

I heard a low murmur of conversation in the room, felt sweat run down my back and tickle the ribs under my arms.

"Life," Dragon Lady said at last, the anger gone from her voice.

"Death," R.G. said.

I felt a surge of fear-driven adrenaline. Boy, had I read him wrong!

"Stal," he said, "it is apparently up to you."

Nikolai Stal laughed.

Chapter Seventeen

"So what you think of two idiots brought you in?" Stal said as we sat in his office an hour after my acquittal. I sipped scotch, my second one. The first one went down in one gulp, but I was feeling steadier now.

Stal sat behind his desk, leaning forward in his chair but relaxed. He smoked a cigar, a damned fine one imported all the way from Earth. I know because it was from the pocket humidor they'd taken from me when I was arrested. The cigars had been a birthday gift from Marr. They were more extravagant than I'd have sprung for, mostly because of the shipping, but maybe that's what gifts are for.

He was shorter than I'd expected and thinner, not all that physically imposing. But I'd known small, wiry guys before you wouldn't want to cross, and he was one of those. You could see it in his eyes, grey and deep-set, guarded, calculating. Someone had broken his nose for him once and it hadn't quite healed straight. His hair might have been brown not long ago but it was sandy grey now, even though I figured him to only be in his early forties. He wore it long, almost to his shoulders, and had a long droopy mustache to match. He had laugh lines at the corner of his eyes and that was usually a good sign. Occasionally it was very, very bad, but usually good.

"Bela's rough around the edges but basically smart and energetic," I answered. "Pablo's stupid and lazy. Both of those are useful combinations, in my experience."

He looked at me like I was crazy. "You *like* stupid and lazy?"

"Sure. You give them a few simple things to do, enough to keep them busy, and you never have to worry about them getting into trouble. They're reliable—no surprises."

He thought about that and his eyebrows clicked up a notch.

"Okay. So Bela make good captain someday?"

I shook my head. "Smart and energetic isn't a good combination for a captain. He'll be a good tactical guy for you, an idea man, but you don't want him calling the shots. You want someone smart and lazy in charge."

He leaned back in his chair, clearly intrigued. "*This* is management philosophy?"

"The personnel end of it, yeah. Smart and lazy guys are always looking for the easiest way to do stuff, which means most efficient and least dangerous. They're the ones you need to rein in the idea guys. They're also a lot better at delegating."

"Huh," he said and frowned in thought. "Okay, so...smart and lazy are leaders, smart and energetic are idea guys, stupid and lazy make reliable followers. Leaves stupid and energetic, *da?* Where they fit in?"

"Oh, they don't," I said. "They're the ones who will screw things up, every single time. I think that's mostly what's wrong with politics and organized religion—like moths to a flame. You need to keep them out of your organization, and if any get in, find a way to deal with them."

"*Deal* with?" he said, and he studied me for a couple seconds. "I heard Sasha Naradnyo *dealt* with over forty guys."

"Well, that's an exaggeration."

Stal's desk beeped and he looked down, for the moment absorbed by the surface set to viewer mode. Despite the army jamming his desk was still live, so it must be hooked to a hard fiber network of some kind. That was an obvious precaution for a hood, since it made it harder for someone—like possibly the police—to do a data capture. I'd done the same back in the old days on Peezgtaan. It also had advantages in an emergency like this, when the wireless links were all down or jammed.

I looked around. His office wasn't what I expected either. I'd never seen a hood with a "love-me" wall before, but he had a whole bunch of group pictures and certificates of appreciation virtually displayed on the smart wall behind him. The smart wall to my left was set to mimic a picture window, while the other two simply showed a pale pastel wallpaper pattern. All the furniture was expensive-looking flexi-units with reprogrammable configurations and surfaces depending on what you felt like that week. Right now it was British Regency. The arms on my chair even felt like wood. Very nice.

Stal tapped a string of entries and keyed two live buttons on his desk. He lifted his eyes to me and took a drag on his cigar.

"Can shoot with arm in sling?" he asked.

I knew that question would come, sooner or later, and I found myself thankful for my injury. I was twenty-two-and-zero, and I was comfortable staying at that score.

"Not if you expect me to hit anything," I answered. "I'm not much of a southpaw."

He leaned back in his chair and gave me an appraising look. "So what good for is Sasha Naradnyo? Aside from maybe feeding to Varoki so kill us later instead of sooner?"

I thought that over for a few seconds. Yeah, what *was* I good for? Things were probably going to turn pretty bad once the mobs out there got organized and started coming after Humans on a methodical basis, and with Gaant behind them, that was almost a certainty. What would these people need, other than rock-steady gunmen?

"Logistics," I answered. "You're going to be under siege here. You know the sort of operation I ran back on Peezgtaan and I also funded a clinic there, handled a lot of its management behind the scenes. In the Army I worked for a while in my cohort's quartermaster shop, learned the four *B*'s of keeping an outfit going: beans, bullets, batteries, and bandages. Unless you already have someone really good to coordinate supply procurement and distribution, you need me for that."

"Citizens' Troika already has guards on two food warehouses in district. What else to do?"

I thought for a moment. They were right: first priority would be just feeding everyone. Since the native life forms on Hazz'Akatu were based on a whole different protein chain than Humans could metabolize, eating almost anything grown locally would kill us, which made foraging pointless. Everything we ate had to be grown hydroponically from imported organic stock.

"Distribution warehouses usually only have a few days of food," I said, "maybe a week's worth, to supply the different food stores in a district, and that's just for your baseline population. If you manage to hold out, you're going to get Human refugees swelling the count, people who don't live in a Human ghetto and start to realize how unhealthy it's going to get for them out there among the Varoki. We need to inventory everything, and it still needs to be guarded, but we need to disperse it some, not concentrate it. Too much chance of one lucky hit taking out half our food.

"But that won't be enough to last long, so we need to find any hydroponic tanks in the district and secure them, make sure they're growing as much protein as we can manage. I don't know what flavoring they'll have, if any, but we can live on plain algae and tofu if we have to.

"There won't be near enough packaged water and sooner or later they'll think to cut off the water mains. We need to set up some reservoirs and draw as much off now as we can."

Stal nodded, eyes on mine, and took another drag on his cigar. I stopped and thought some more, worked out what they'd burn through fastest once the shooting started. I began ticking things off on the fingers of my left hand.

"Drugs and medical supplies: we need a complete inventory, and if one of the local med centers has a drug fabricator—and a good supply of raw organics—we could sure use it. If so, we've got to get it to a secure location as soon as possible.

"Power: we'll need every kilowatt of electricity we can get once they think to pull the plug on us, especially to run autodocs and fabricators, and to charge gauss weapons. We need to pull every LENR generator and solar skin from every vehicle and building roof we can find, get them centralized and redeployed. Wouldn't hurt to identify any electricians and mechanics as well and use them to keep things running.

"Ammunition: no matter what sort of stocks you have, it won't be enough if this turns really hot. We need raw carbon and powdered metallics, and a bunch of fabricators with flechette software loaded. I heard a rumor you might be able to help with the software. I'm not sure what heavier weapons you've got, but—"

"Stop," Stal interrupted, raising his hands to silence me. "Take job."

"You need to clear it with the others or something?" I asked.

He shrugged. "Will go along. Not need gun for job so Katranjiev will like. Do not start now, though. Already dark and most people off streets pretty soon. Get rest. Who knows when next chance?"

"Okay. So tell me, what's the deal with this Citizens' Troika? Is it anything but a funny name?"

"No, but maybe we make it so, *da?* Katranjiev is head of Merchants' and Citizens' Association; I think was formed to protect them from criminals, like me. They misunderstand my motives."

"You just want to shear them, not skin them," I volunteered.

"Precisely! So Katranjiev brings in this awful woman Zdravkova and her revolutionary ideas. Very dangerous. But she has well-armed fighters with hard eyes, and many people listen to her, so to persuade masses has turnip and club."

"What makes you think anyone's going to pay attention to you guys?" I said. "The people I've seen around here so far don't look like they're used to taking orders, and that's on a good day. Hard times coming."

"Food," he answered and took another puff on the cigar. "Once Park Authority Police withdraw yesterday, Zdravkova post guards on food warehouses before smart guys can grab and start black market. Puts out word, bring food in, will guard it."

I laughed. "Yeah, I bet they're lining up to do that."

Stal shrugged. "This morning Chinese gang—*Lěng Nánhái*—from ghetto south of here raid two houses where people have food, kill families. Now many people bring food to warehouse. Troika controls food, Troika controls Sookagrad."

I'd read about *Lěng Nánhái* but never run into them person-ally. They were supposed to be one of the nastier Human gangs in the Sakkatto slums, but you never knew. Anybody posting a feed story wasn't going to get much play by claiming it was "just an average gang," so you had to make some allowance for journalistic hyperbole. Their name meant Cold Boys. Going for the food made sense.

"Grab them by their stomachs and their hearts and minds will follow," I said. "Sounds like Katranjiev and Zdravkova have the bases covered. Since neither one of them cares much for the criminal element, why'd they let you have the third seat? Oh, yeah—*fabrication*."

Stal studied his cigar and smiled.

"Bogo Katranjiev troubled man," Stal said, his voice thoughtful.

"The only one who voted to kill me—not my favorite guy down here."

"What to say?" Stal answered. He settled back again and took a long draw on the cigar. "Katranjiev was married, had little girl. Little girl killed by stray shot when two tough guys had argument. Marriage ended, lost business. So now hate crooks like me—or former ones in your case. Understand?"

Yeah, I understood. There's a cold space in me, though. Well, most people would say there were *lots* of cold spaces in me, but one particular one was for hard luck stories people use to justify acting like assholes. I mean, I get it that everyone acts the way they do for a reason—cause and effect, right? Every asshole I ever knew, once you got to know them, turned out they had a pretty good reason for acting that way. But everyone I ever knew who treated people decently and generously had just as good a reason for taking their pain and disappointment out on the rest of the world, lots of times a better one. They just didn't.

For my money, the important thing which separated folks wasn't how good an excuse they had for acting like a tortured asshole, it was just whether or not they did.

Of course, in Katranjiev's case there was the added complication of him having voted to execute me. My objectivity was probably compromised.

Stal shifted in his chair and frowned in thought, his eyes still on me.

"So tell just me, why you help Leatherhead kids two years ago?"

I shook my head. "Part of it was because they were orphans and alone and on the run, and I knew exactly how that felt. But the other thing was I was tired. Tired of the violence, you know?"

He looked at me, his face carefully blank. If he knew what I meant, he couldn't afford to admit it, not in his position. Some of his people followed him out of loyalty, and some out of enlightened self-interest, but there were some who did so only under the threat of deadly violence, and he could no more admit a reluctance to kill, and survive that admission, than I could have two years ago on Peezgtaan.

He turned to the smart wall to his right, my left, which gave a panoramic view of the northern approach to the district. The setting sun painted the western faces of the buildings orange and red. Smoke columns rose into the sky from a couple fires a kilometer or so away, but it had been worse yesterday. A remote recon hoverplat in military colors made slow orbits around the upper stories of e-Kruaan-Arc, waiting, waiting.

"Heard about what you did on Akampta shuttle two years ago," he said. "Killed Kolya Markov and eight others, hard-core gunmen."

"Actually I only killed Markov and seven others. My wife Marrissa killed the eighth one."

"Wife? Saw picture of her: very elegant, high-class. Does not look type goes around shoot people." He took another draw on the cigar she'd given me and blew a long column of smoke up toward the ceiling.

"Well, you never know, do you?" I said. "She drilled him right through the liver. Took him a while to die."

Stal frowned. "Hard way to go."

"Yeah, sometimes I cry myself to sleep at night just thinking about it. Funny thing is, it never bothered Marrissa one bit." That wasn't really true but he didn't need to know all our personal demons.

He looked at me and the look became something close to a glare. Finally he shook his head.

"Okay. Wife one tough bitch. Sasha one tough bastard. Everybody *tough*, okay? Jesus! Is always same conversation.

"Is funny, you kill all those guys, and ever since I hear that, I want ask, *how*? But you not know how, are you? I mean, you just do, one by one, until are all dead, *da?*"

"Something like that."

"'Something like,'" he said and then frowned. "Now I actually need someone can kill like that, you say, 'Am tired of violence.'"

"Something like that. Besides, I wasn't exactly unstoppable. You might recall Markov killed me the same time I killed him."

He smiled. "Not my problem. Do job, then die on own time. But tired or not tired, arm in sling. So no good with gun...you say. But if mob get past perimeter, then maybe see what Sasha really made of, *da?*"

"You're the boss," I said.

His grin widened. "Famous Sasha Naradnyo calls Nikolai Stal boss? Could get used to that."

"Don't," I said, and his smile became cold.

"Okay, tough guy. And don't make mistake of thinking Sasha and Nikolai same underneath it all. Nikolai Stal not tired. I *love* this."

Chapter Eighteen

What was I good for?

That was a really good question. What I'd told Stal about my background was all true: I was a pretty good administrator, and a good judge of people's abilities, but that wasn't the secret of my success. I had risen as high as I had in the criminal underworld because I could kill without hesitation and without any genuine remorse. That is a much rarer ability, even in violent criminal gangs and the military, than most people imagine. Train soldiers to shoot and stick bayonets in dummies all you want. When it actually comes down to aiming at a living being and pulling the trigger, you would be astonished how many hesitate, or shake uncontrollably, or don't fire, or deliberately miss.

But I never hesitated and I hardly ever missed, and that was my edge. After a while I understood what that meant, that there was something wrong inside me, or something missing, but that realization did not change anything. I wanted to escape that life, wanted to become something different. It wasn't lost on me that my escape from violence involved the single most murderously violent episode of my life.

So I died and I was reborn. Not hard to attach some sort of spiritual significance to that, huh? But now what? What was I good for *now*? The idea of picking up a gun and discovering that

I could still kill without hesitation, that *that* was still what I was good for, would mean it had all been for nothing, wouldn't it? And that thought haunted my dreams like a dark reaper, waiting, waiting.

I was twenty-two and zero.

So far.

Not that I had a wealth of time for introspection. I figured we had maybe a day or two to get ready and at least a week's worth of work to do. Everyone in Sookagrad wanted to do something, but nobody knew where to start, and sure as hell didn't want to take orders, so you mostly ended up with a lot of people standing around talking and waving their arms.

I had an advantage: for that first morning, Nikolai Stal loaned me his personal *shtarker gonef*, a big bruiser of a guy named Petar Ivanov. Ivanov made it easier to get people's attention. At a shade over two meters tall, and well over one hundred kilos of bone and grotesque, bulging muscle, he walked around in no shirt and very baggy pants tucked into low boots. With his oily black hair and swarthy complexion, he looked like something that had materialized out of an old lamp.

I got up before dawn and had an idea. I scrounged a dozen spray bottles of bright yellow-orange glow paint and then, as the district came to life at sunrise, Ivanov started showing me around, searching for people who looked like they knew what they were doing.

At the first food warehouse I visited I found a middle-aged woman of Chinese ancestry, Dolores Wu, arguing with the guards, trying to persuade them to help her move a hydroponics setup to the warehouse. She was painfully slender and took odd little steps from side to side as she listened to the guards, her hands gesturing as if to reinforce or sometimes contradict what she heard. But when she spoke she froze in place, arms slightly out to the side, only moving her head from one side to the other between sentences. I found her physical mannerisms oddly birdlike, but her arguments to the guards were pragmatic, coherent, and forcefully delivered. After a five-minute job interview I sprayed the front and back of her shirt with the big letters "LOG" for Logistics, and did the same for the two armed guards. Ivanov stood with his arms folded staring at them the whole time, so they didn't argue about being drafted.

The spray paint was their uniform and authority: she was acting head of rationing for Sookagrad Logistics, and the guards
were her muscle. I told her to round up a work gang and move
the hydroponics unit wherever she thought best, and then start
looking for more. If she could find a reliable assistant, get him
or her to work on an inventory. The guards at the other warehouse were under her as well. One of the two guards at this
building said he knew them and he'd explain. I gave her one of
the spray bottles to make it official. The sooner people started
seeing a bunch of folks with those markings, the sooner they'd
accept their official status.

There were probably better-qualified people, technically speaking,
than the ones I drafted that morning, but I didn't have a lot of
time. Mostly I concentrated on grabbing people with loud voices
and aggressive attitudes. That's how you fill a power vacuum:
noise and motion.

Within two hours I had a good start on a senior team, all of
them recruiting work gangs to get the most pressing, immediate
needs addressed. Ivanov didn't say much, but when he did it was
worth listening to. He would also take over fabrication himself,
once we finished our morning round of drafting people into the
organization. Despite his looks, he was actually a software guy
and he knew his way around the hardware as well. He didn't
fit my mold of loud and aggressive, but he knew where every
fabricator in the district was, who knew how to run them, what
software was available, and where the raw materials were stored.
I told him to work on finding a loud-mouthed assistant.

I hadn't listed billeting on my original to-do list, but Billy
Conklin, a local building contractor, convinced me we needed
someone to honcho space management. He wore cowboy boots
under his work pants and a cowboy hat so stained, worn, and
crumpled it was hard to tell what it was right away, and he sported
an accent to match. I got the feeling he had a lot of experience
convincing people they really needed things they'd never thought
of before, which was just the sort of skill set I needed, right?
He was smooth, all right, with his feigned bumpkin act, but I
suspected I might have to keep an eye on him. I have an instinct
for guys who are so sure they're smarter than everyone else in the
galaxy, they always have a couple extra things going on the side.

He was right about space management, though; we had too

much critical material looking for a place to live, and would probably have a lot of people fighting for that space as well pretty soon. A couple of the outlying residential buildings would have to be evacuated to make the perimeter more defensible. Where would we put those people? Billy got a spray-painted jacket for his trouble and a new job. He already knew carpenters, welders, plumbers, and finishers he'd hired or worked with. I gave him two spray bottles and told him to draft anyone he needed.

I found our head medic on my own. Dr. Tanvi Mahajan was the director of the community clinic and pitched in with the doctoring as well. Her appearance struck me immediately: well-dressed, trim figure, hair neatly pulled back, and face bearing the prominent scars of childhood acne. If anyone had access to cosmetic surgery, especially something as simple as this, it would be a doctor, but she'd never fixed it. I got the feeling she was pretty comfortable with who she was. She was also the only person I met that morning who didn't seem flustered or a bit overwhelmed. She took five minutes and told me exactly what shape the clinic was in, what she expected would be the things they'd have a hard time dealing with, and what she needed to take care of it all. She got to keep her job with some new challenges. She'd need a lot more space for trauma patients, preferably adjacent to the current clinic. Talk to Billy Conklin about that. She'd also need to secure whatever medical supplies she could, and get Petar Ivanov working on fabricating more.

Moshe Greenwald was my last acquisition that morning. Moshe was short, thick, and balding, at least ten years older than me, and his coveralls stretched taut across his broad belly. A hand-rolled lit cigarette dangled from his lips. The sleeves of his coveralls were rolled up, and I spotted a tattoo on his right forearm: a big gold and red spaceship. Not a real spacecraft, mind you, but what people thought they would look like a hundred or so years ago—a sleek torpedo-shaped hull sporting big swept-back fins and a fiery exhaust. I figured either he had a strange sense of humor or he was drunk when he got that ink.

I found him unbolting the LENR generator from an abandoned Munie van. LENR stood for Low Energy Nuclear Reaction, what they used to call cold fusion. An LENR generator didn't kick out a lot of power, but it was steady and low-maintenance.

"What do you think you're doing?" I asked him.

He looked up and squinted at me over the forward chassis of the van. "I'm paintin' my nails. What does it look like I'm doing?"

"We're going to need that generator you're stealing."

He carefully took his cigarette out and balanced it on the hood of the van, straightened up, hefted the power wrench, and looked at Ivanov. After a couple seconds he put the wrench back down and picked up the cigarette.

"I don't know you," he said, "but I work for Bogo Katranjiev, head of the Citizens' League. He told me to get a working LENR generator and bring it back to his office, which is what I'm doing."

"Can you dismount that thing without screwing it up?"

His face twisted in a sour expression. "For three years I crewed on a deep space C-lighter, engineering department. Then eighteen months I spent grounded here, waiting for another lift ticket. Seven days ago I got one, *seven days!* I was scheduled to ride the needle to orbit *tomorrow*, and then all this *tsuris* breaks loose! Can I dismount an LENR generator? One time I bypassed a burned-out power junction, ran carbon cable by hand to pump a SMESS from a half-gig fusion reactor so we could make jump. You even know what a SMESS is?"

"No."

"Then shut up and let me work." He leaned over and picked up his power wrench.

"You think this is the best use of your time," I asked, "pulling one little LENR generator to run an office suite?"

"Not my department."

"Turn around and put your hands up," I ordered.

He looked like he might argue the point, but when Ivanov took a slow step toward him he laid down the wrench and did as I'd told him.

"You're gonna be sorry," he said.

"Hope not," I answered as I sprayed "LOG" on his back in big bright letters.

"Hey! What the hell?"

"Turn around," I ordered and I did his front.

He touched it with his fingers, looked at the still-wet streak of paint.

"See, now it *is* your department," I said. "You still work for Katranjiev, or rather the Emergency Citizens' Troika, but from now on you report to me. I'm Sasha Naradnyo, head of logistics, and you're now head of the power division. We're gonna need lots of it. There are solar panels, vehicle skins, LENR generators lying around all over. What do we need to do to get them concentrated, secured, and on a grid?"

He thought for a couple seconds, looked around the street half-filled with nervous people hurrying here and there, trying to make their own preparations. He looked back and opened his mouth but I cut him off.

"Not now. Two hours from now at the clinic. Between now and then, recruit whatever technicians you can find. Here's two spray bottles. Have an outline plan of action by then and a list of what resources you need. No telling what I can actually give you, but it'll be nice to have a wish list. You got any questions?"

He looked around some more and then nodded to the LENR generator in the van.

"What about that?" he said.

"It's your call. If you decide that generator needs to be in that office suite, then get somebody else on it. But if I catch *you* turning a wrench anytime in the next two hours, my friend Ivanov here is going to break both your arms, just so you won't be distracted from your real job anymore. Understand?"

To my surprise, he laughed and nodded.

"By the way, what *is* a SMESS?" I asked.

"Superconducting Magnetic Energy Storage System. It's like a big donut only made from superconducting cables. You know, no resistance, so you put electricity in, it just goes round and round until you need it."

"Sounds like maybe we could use one of those. Any around here?"

He just laughed.

Fifteen minutes later I stopped back at the dilapidated wood frame and sheet metal building which housed the offices of the Merchants' and Citizens' Association and was also becoming the headquarters of the Sookagrad Emergency Citizens' Troika, which made sense as, of the three groups that made it up, only the Merchants' and Citizens' Association was actually legal. I wanted to check in before my department head meeting and see how everyone was dealing with my sudden promotion from Traitorous Running Dog to Chief of Logistics. I wasn't sure what sort of working relationship I could manage with Katranjiev, or with Dragon Lady for that matter, but it was time I found out.

As Ivanov and I turned the corner on the winding, narrow street a short block from the headquarters, I saw a sight which excited and scared me at the same time: a group of four Varoki Munies, looking a little roughed up but not really injured as far as I could tell. They still had their sidearms but they hadn't drawn them, and they were under the guard of a half-dozen citizens, assorted firearms raised and pointed.

"Let's not scare anyone," I told Ivanov. "We don't want this to turn ugly. Those four Varoki could be very important to us."

He looked at me. "You like leatherheads," he said, in his rumbling bass voice.

"Most of my life I was a criminal, and I spent most of that time ducking the Munies on Peezgtaan. I got no love for them, but times change. These guys could solve some problems for us."

I tried to find out what was up but the civilian guards didn't know anything useful. They were just covering the Munies until word came back from inside what to do with them. Three of the Munies were patrol officers, looking scared and way out of their depth. The fourth one was older and wore the rank stars of a police captain. He looked more depressed than scared—maybe resigned to his fate was a better description. None of them really wanted to talk to me, at least not yet.

"Keep an eye on things out here, would you?" I said to Ivanov. "Wouldn't want anything stupid to happen."

"Because may be more useful alive than dead," he said.

That was a very utilitarian way of looking at it, and there was a lot to be said for utilitarianism. But there was something to be said for being on the side of the angels as well, not that it was ever easy to figure out which side that was. I sometimes think that the cause you back has less to do with where the angels roost than how you go about backing it. That said, I also think some causes can stain you so deeply that no quantity of good deeds will ever cleanse your karma. So if you're looking for simple answers, some universal formula that will get you through life with your soul intact, try looking where the light's better.

Inside the offices I found Dragon Lady and Katranjiev arguing about what to do with the Munies. They made an interesting physical contrast: Katranjiev tall and skinny, fair-haired and long-faced, the Dragon Lady none of those things.

She was fiftyish—which was older than I'd have thought from her voice—and a little stocky, but she moved as if she was in good shape. She wasn't beautiful, but I'd call her distinguished-looking. "A handsome woman," people might have said once upon a time, or would have if it weren't for her eyes, which were stricken and angry-looking at the same time, as if they had seen too much and now disliked seeing anything at all. Other than being a former legal counselor, the current head of a Humanist resistance cell, and ill-tempered, I didn't know much about her. I'd at least found out her name: Desislava Bogdanovna Zdravkova, which as names go would have been a mouthful if my own folks hadn't been Ukrainian. She was second-generation Bulgarian like Katranjiev and a lot of the folks in Sookagrad.

Between all those Bulgarians, Nikolai Stal the Russian, and me the Ukrainian, this was starting to look like a reunion of the Slavic diaspora.

Zdravkova and Katranjiev both glared at me when I walked in.

"What do you want, Naradnyo?" Katranjiev demanded. "I only went along with Stal's idea of giving you a job because I thought it would keep you too busy to cause trouble."

"Boy, were you wrong."

"I imagine you're here to plead for the lives of those four leatherheads," Zdravkova said.

"As it happens, you're exactly right, although since the Munies haven't done anything but get themselves whacked for protecting us Humans, I'm not sure why their lives would need pleading for. But here's my thing: have either of you given any thought to what's going to happen to us in the unlikely event that we actually survive all this?"

"What do you mean?" Zdravkova asked.

"That would be a 'no,'" I said, and she scowled even harder at me. "I heard you're a lawyer, or at least used to be. We're grabbing everything in the district which isn't nailed down, confiscating supplies, ripping apart cars, demolishing buildings to close routes of approach, knocking new doors—"

"Actually, *you're* doing most of those things," she said.

"A distinction which will be lost on the authorities. My point is, what will the owners say when it's all done? Have we got a legal leg to stand on? Or are we just a bunch of vandals and looters?"

"Legally we're vandals and looters," she said and shrugged. "If we live, we can worry about explaining it."

"By then it will be too late. If we want outside help soon enough to make a difference, our legal status could be the deal breaker. But I got an idea. I know it goes against both of your better instincts, but hear me out on this one. Please.

"I think I've come up with an interesting angle."

Chapter Nineteen

"So, Captain Prayzaat, we're in a tough situation here," I said once the two of us sat down across a small table in a back room. "Much as we'd like to give you and your men shelter and protection, we have no legal authority to resist the Army if they come for you."

"The mutineers," he said without any life in his voice. "Call them what they are."

I had a cup of hot tea and the Varoki police captain had a mug of redroot soup. He'd made sure his three men had theirs before he would take any. That said something about him. I looked at him carefully. He slouched in his chair, worn down, and not just physically but emotionally as well. Even his ears drooped. I think he figured he'd come to the end of his road.

"Army, mutineers: they are whatever they are, and legally that's going to be decided later, after the fighting is all over. What we call them now won't change that."

He looked away, fear and despair and anger all working over his face, sending weak flashes of color across his skin. "We protected you Humans from the mobs," he said without looking at me. "I lost men fighting our own kind to protect your miserable lives. We killed Varoki." He turned and looked me in the eye. "Do you understand? We killed our *own people* to protect you.

If we had not done so, if we had just let them murder you all, I do not believe the Army would have acted against us."

I figured he was right. Hell, I *knew* he was right, and it shamed me to sit there and drive a bargain for his and his men's lives when they'd already paid such a heavy price for us. But theirs weren't the only lives at stake, so I kept my face cold.

His face tightened with remembered pain and he looked away again. "I have no idea how many of my men the army killed, how many are being held, how many are still hiding somewhere out there. All I have left are those three patrolmen out there. My entire life has come down to keeping those three people alive, and you talk to me about legal technicalities."

"Well, they won't be technicalities when the Army comes for us and demands an accounting. But there may be a way."

He turned and looked at me and for a moment his eyes flickered with hope, but then he remembered who he was talking to, and his lips pressed together in distaste.

"I will not break my oath," he said. "I will not break the law. The law and the safety of three patrolmen, these things are the only meaning left to me. For all I know, I am the senior surviving officer of the Sakkatto Municipal Police not in rebel captivity. I will not finish my career, and probably my life, with an act of dishonor."

"I wouldn't ask you to," I said. "Deputize us."

He sat up, looked me in the eye, his own eyes suddenly wide with understanding. The anger and shame colors drained from his face and his ears fanned out wide. "*Deputize* you?" Then he smiled. "Of course! But you understand that would give me direct authority over your armed fighters."

"Well, if you insist on being a hands-on commander, we may have a problem. See, I think you're probably a hell of a cop, but this isn't primarily a law enforcement issue."

He drew back, suspicion replacing the optimism of a moment earlier in his eyes, but I pushed on.

"This is going to turn into a really tough fight, and it's probably going to start any time now. We have a lot of folks here who have actually soldiered. Sometimes, like with me when I was a youngster, it was the Army or a few years in detention over something. Even for more honest Humans, the Army or mercenary gigs are fallback employment. It's second nature for us, you know?"

He nodded reluctantly. Everyone knew about Humans and our

proclivity for violence—ferocious as tigers, but very useful tigers. It was just a stupid stereotype, but right now it might work in our favor.

"Besides," I went on, "I have an idea how we can get communications out of Sakkatto City, even with the jamming. We can tell our story, and that includes *your* story."

That got his attention. "How can you penetrate the jamming? The Army's electronic assets are far more numerous and capable than those to which even we had access."

"I don't think we can penetrate their jamming, but there may be a way to get around it. But here's the problem: if we start broadcasting your appeals to police in other cities to resist the coup, and to foreign powers to intervene against it, and we advertise the fact that you're here with us, the Army is going to throw everything they have at us to shut you down, and we'll just get plowed under."

He leaned back and nodded. "You would not mention this problem unless you believed you had a solution to it as well."

"Yeah, we dummy up an office and have you speak from it, claim it's a remote site. What I've got in mind they won't be able to trace very easily. So let them turn the city upside down. Who says you're even in the city? We'll transmit your messages straight to the e-nexus codes of police, public information sites, and some well-known feed heads outside of Sakkatto, and who knows where they're originating?"

"Yes, that could work," he admitted, "provided you can actually conjure your miracle with the jamming."

"Yeah, but it also means you can't be giving orders here, or even showing your face. This is going to get very scary, and there will be plenty of folks who lose heart. If they think they've got a juicy enough bit of information for the Army, they may try to use it to buy their lives, or the lives of their families."

"You have a low opinion of your own species," he said.

"No I don't. You guys have stacked the deck against us, screwed us over for a hundred Earth years, given us the end of the stick that's so shitty, sometimes the only win that's possible is just staying alive. We were always survivors, but you made us absolute masters of the art. Next time you feel like clucking your tongue at someone about that, take a look in the mirror."

We stared at each other for a few seconds but eventually he nodded.

"Your rather insulting argument notwithstanding, the practicalities of the arrangement you propose are undeniable. I agree, provided you can actually arrange communication with the outside world. How will you accomplish that?"

I leaned forward and put my good elbow on the table. "Can you keep a secret?" I asked in a low voice.

He nodded.

"Good. So can I."

Once the outlines of the deal were firmed up between Zdravkova, Katranjiev, and Captain Prayzaat of the Munies, I headed over to my first logistics staff meeting, a necessary preliminary to getting part two of my plan working.

The meeting was short because all five of my chiefs were anxious to get back to their work. That was encouraging. Each one turned in a resource list and outline plan, but in terms of accomplishments they were mostly still in the staff recruiting phase.

I went through their priority lists briefly and didn't see anything crazy, so I approved them and told them to work on that basis for now and we'd fine-tune as we went along. I'd see what I could do about resources, but for the most part our philosophy would be to take what we needed, so long as we understood that our key goal—only goal, really—was to give the combatants what they needed to fight and give the noncombatants what they needed to stay alive. Nothing else mattered.

Dolores Wu (rations) and Petar Ivanov (fabrication) took off right away, and Dr. Mahajan asked Billy Conklin to stay after and talk about arrangements for an enlarged trauma ward. I buttonholed Moshe Greenwald outside the clinic where he'd stopped to roll a cigarette.

"Greenwald, wait a minute. You were an electrician on a starship, right? You know anything about hard-fiber communication and data transfer systems?"

He gave me a sour look. "*Know* anything? It's my specialty. I ran power lines when I needed to, but that's all brute force stuff. Data flow is art."

"Okay, suppose somebody had a local hard-fiber comm/data system already up and running. How hard would it be to cut it into the city-wide network?"

He finished rolling the cigarette and then licked the paper before answering. "Impossible," he said.

Damn. That wasn't what I wanted to hear, but figured I may as well get all the bad news at once.

"Okay, how come?"

"Encryption," he said and then lit his cigarette with a pocket lighter, drew in and exhaled. "The municipal and national data pipes are encrypted five ways to Sunday, and nobody can hack into that stuff from the outside except in bad adventure holovids. If someone slipped you the security code we could do it, but otherwise you'll never be able to read their feed."

"No, I'm not talking about reading *their* transmissions," I said. "I'm talking about piggy-backing onto their fiber network and *sending* ours."

Moshe shrugged. "Oh. Well that's easy. I mean, it's illegal as hell, but these days what ain't? The utility tunnel with the main data pipe from e-Kruaan-Arc to the capital nexus at Katammu-Arc runs right under Sookagrad." Then he thought for a moment and his eyes got wider. "Hey, that's some idea, Boss! We can get word out about what's going on here. I'm not sure what good it will do us, but if the Army's jamming the comms, it must be for a reason, right? Of course, you know that once broadcasts from Sookagrad start showing up, it could motivate the Army to wipe us out."

"Walk with me. We have to talk to Stal. He's the one with the fiber network we may need to borrow. And I think I have a way around the reprisal thing."

We started walking toward the dry goods store that had Stal's office on the second floor.

"So you crewed on a starship, huh? Why'd you stop?"

He spat out a piece of loose tobacco before answering. "Economy got shitty and the carrier I was crewing for cut back. I ended up on the beach for a year and a half, stuck here. Then a week ago I got an offer. In-system shuttle, back and forth to the gas giant, but better than nothing right? All set to ship out when all this crap hit." He spat again. "Talk about pissed off."

"Yeah, I bet. You know any physics?"

"*Bissel*," Moshe answered. "You know how it is. You work engineering on a starship, you pick some up. You have to or you don't get any of the jokes."

He assured me there were actually a lot of physics jokes, and so I asked him to tell me one. He said I wouldn't get it but I wanted to hear one anyway. He thought for a moment and then nodded.

"Okay, here goes. Heisenberg is driving down the highway and a Munie pulls him over. Munie walks up to the side of his ground car and says, 'Do you know how fast you were going?' Heisenberg says, 'No, but I know where I am!'"

Moshe stared at me and grinned. When I didn't laugh he said, "I told you so."

"So explain it to me."

He shook his head. "Nah, it's stupid to explain a joke. Either you get it when it's told or you don't. If I explain it, it still won't be funny."

I started to argue when we heard the sound of automatic weapon fire. We both stopped and listened, and so did everyone else on the street. The sound came from the north, out on our perimeter, but the intervening buildings made it sound far away and harmless, at least to us.

Moshe dropped his cigarette and ground it out. "So it begins, *nu*?"

I looked around at everyone frozen on the street, their faces made ugly by fear. The hardest thing to get used to in Sookagrad was the unbroken sea of Human faces. Everywhere else we were the exception. We had a reputation for playing poorly by other people's rules. I started wondering how well we could play by our own, how this experiment in cooperative effort was going to work.

I took a deep breath and shouted to everyone who could hear me. "Okay, it's gunfire. Get used to it. It'll get a lot louder soon enough. Anyone with a job to do, get back to it. Anyone without a job, find one."

We started walking again and then everyone did. The firing stuttered, paused, started again, and then faded out. Someone had probably gotten trigger-happy. If there had been a serious push on the perimeter, a few bursts of automatic fire wouldn't have been enough to turn it away.

I realized I didn't know beans about where the defensive perimeter was, and I'd need to if I was going to push ammo forward. It might be a better idea to set up ammo resupply points and have the fighting groups on the perimeter send ammo runners back. I'd still need to know the main concentrations, and what they were armed with. Ivanov might be a software wiz and the right guy to honcho ammunition production, but I had a feeling I was going to have to get personally involved in distribution.

Upstairs from the store, Stal's admin assistant buzzed us into his office. Stal sat behind his desk looking at the smart wall panorama of the northern approaches, smoking another one of my imported cigars. I could smell the cigar: the rich tobacco and just a hint of spice, the scent of the Caribbean. He better be enjoying it.

I glanced at the smart wall. There was a burning ground car down there in a broad street which ran under the maglev tracks high above. A dozen people poked around it—Humans, so they were our guys.

It occurred to me that smart walls in some half-assed poured foamstone building in the middle of all this squalor seemed as out of place as a crystal chandelier in a chemical toilet stall. Speaking of which, I needed to get Billy Conklin to work on setting up a bunch more chemical toilets, and quick.

"Enjoying the cigar?" I asked.

He looked at the ash on the end and smiled. "*Da*," he said slowly. "*Kuba Maduro?* Always wanted know how Cuban cigar taste."

I decided not to tell him they were from Nicaragua. If you need something from someone, don't start by spilling his soup.

He looked as if he'd been deep in a thought trance and was coming out of it slowly. He turned to face us and frowned. "Who this guy?" he asked, pointing his cigar at Moshe.

"Greenwald, my head of power, and an electrical genius. I got an idea."

"*Da?* As good as letting four Munie fugitives hang around in exchange for toy badges?"

So he must already have heard about that deal. Given his line of work I could understand his ambivalence. Well, I was going to have to tell him about it anyway for this whole thing to make sense.

"It's related to the Munies. In fact, it's essential, so if you want to scotch the Munie deal, say no to this, and the whole package goes out the window."

I stopped and felt myself shiver involuntarily. The expression "out the window" suddenly had more significance for me than it used to and I didn't think I'd be using it as much.

"Those Munies aren't anything but a liability," I continued, "unless we have the ability to communicate to the outside world."

"*Da*," he agreed. "And?"

"Earlier I noticed you've got a hard-fiber comm/data network. I got an idea how we can use it to get around the jamming."

He sat for a moment thinking. "Is why electrical genius is here?" he said, nodding at Moshe. He said "genius" the way you'd call someone a "smart guy" and not mean it as a compliment.

I just nodded.

He looked back at the smart wall, at the Humans down around the burning ground car, looking like bugs from this distance. He took a long drag on the cigar and blew a slow funnel of smoke toward the wall, watched it curl and rise toward the ceiling, just like the thicker, blacker smoke from the ground car curled up around the maglev tracks above it.

It wasn't tough to figure what he was thinking. We could play armadillo: curl up, lay low and do the absolute minimum to stay alive, make the fewest enemies possible, and hope things just blew over, got back to normal. Then we could all go about our business same as before.

Or we could play tiger, make something happen to save ourselves, even if that made us a bigger target.

One plan required faith in things just running down of their own accord; the other required faith in the active agency of people and institutions outside of Sakkatto City which had never gone to bat for Humans before. Tough call, and I wasn't positive my idea was the best way to go.

He turned back to us and sighed. "Okay. Explain plan."

Chapter Twenty

"People of Bakaa and the entire *Cottohazz*: I am Captain Arkerro Prayzaat, acting commandant of the Sakkatto Municipal Police. I am communicating from a secret and secure police facility. To the best of my knowledge I am the highest ranking police official who has not been taken into custody or executed by the Army mutineers who violently seized control of the government two days ago."

Prayzaat sat behind a desk backed by a smart wall which was programmed to show a detailed map of the city. We'd put a bunch of arcane and important-looking symbols on it: geometric shapes in different colors and with a four-digit number below each of them. They were randomly placed and didn't actually mean anything. Hopefully a bunch of Army intelligence officers would spend a few sleepless nights trying to decode them, rather than working on something important.

"The mutineers have told the *Cottohazz* they have restored order in Sakkatto City," Prayzaat continued. "There is no order in the city. Aside from a few small areas in some of the arcologies there is only violence and anarchy.

"Hundreds of police officers have been executed by the mutineers and almost all of the survivors of the force have been arrested and are being held at secret locations. Their so-called crime was to use force to protect the lives of non-uBakai citizens of the *Cottohazz* against rampaging mobs. I call on the mutineers to disclose the location and identity of all police in their custody and release them to neutral parties immediately.

"Sakkatto City has been denuded of police and plunged into chaos. The citizen associations of Sakkatto must step into the breach and establish order in their own neighborhoods. To that end, and under my authority as commandant of the Sakkatto Municipal Police, I hereby officially deputize all members of the citizen associations whose names follow this address, and I empower them not only to take all steps necessary to protect the lives and property of their people, but also to resist the illegal gang of thugs who have overthrown our rightful government.

"We face a daunting task, but I call upon all loyal citizens of the Commonwealth of Bakaa to band together and forget whatever differences divided us before. What we fight for now is nothing less than the rule of law. I also call upon the *Cottohazz* itself to recall the pluralistic principles upon which it is based and to aid us in our struggle. This military coup cannot succeed unless the *Cottohazz* so allows it. If you will not stand against this shameful act, what will you stand *for*?"

"That's a wrap," the video tech said after two or three seconds of silence. The seven others of us in the room, who stood outside the arc of the holovid recorder, started moving and talking again. The list of community groups, which we'd culled from the comm lists of Katranjiev's office, included a lot of Varoki groups as well as some of the ethnic community associations. It would scroll on the vid after Prayzaat finished, probably over a frozen ghosted image of him at his desk. That was up to the editor. The citizen groups were listed alphabetically so the Sookagrad Citizens' League was well down the list, nice and inconspicuous—but it was still official.

As calls to arms go, I thought it was okay but nothing special: a bit wordy and long-winded, but that's what a lot of the Varoki are like. I figured it was more important that the speech sound sincere than eloquent, and it did. Those were Prayzaat's words, and he meant them.

The three members of the troika—Katranjiev, Zdravkova, and Stal—clustered around Prayzaat to shake his hand and work out our next move. I slipped out the door and headed toward the clinic, my temporary headquarters. I figured I was going to have to move somewhere else soon, probably into one of the ammo fabrication sites. The clinic was starting to get busy, and things were only going to get crazier there. I already felt like my admin folks were in the way.

I blinked as I came out the basement freight door into the darkness of the empty street, irregularly lit by distant fires and an occasional aerial flare. I heard a lot more small arms fire now, all over the city, but not much near us for the moment. From far off in the distance came the muffled thud of an explosion. So much for the Army restoring order.

In the last twenty-four hours the Varoki gangs had tested our perimeter in three places, tried to bluff or bully their way past the barricades, but so far the fighters had stood their ground and driven them off with a lot of noise but not many casualties. At some point soon that was all going to change, one way or another, and then we'd see.

Someone walked down the narrow street a dozen yards ahead of me, a woman, keeping close by the buildings to her right. People were already learning to stay out of the center of the street, where stray rounds were more likely to fall. Rain earlier had left the pavement wet and shining in the occasional flicker of light, but the clouds were clearing I thought. Maybe we'd have some sunshine tomorrow. I wondered what the weather was like at The'On's place over in uKootrin territory. I wondered if they'd gotten rain, if Marr would feel sunshine on her face tomorrow. I wondered what she was thinking.

At least she knew I was alive. Once Greenwald spliced into the uBakai national data pipe, I'd been able to flash a single message to The'On's residence there: "I am alive. Sasha." No indication of where I was, of course, and no way for them to comm back—too dangerous to everyone else here if anyone figured out where I was in Sakkatto City.

I leaned against the street corner and yawned. I hadn't slept in about two days, near as I could remember, but I'd gone a lot longer than that without sleep before. Of course, I'd been younger then, and the last two days I'd been on my feet almost the whole time. Too much standing around on foamstone pavement was starting to get to me in the joints, especially my knees. I ought to get a little rest, but first I had to get the ammo distribution points reorganized.

Ivanov had placed them where his ammo carriers could get to them, but too far from the perimeter. He was doing fine with fabrication so I let him concentrate on that and I took over ammo distribution myself until I could find some eager beaver to delegate it to. I'd half figured I'd have to step in there anyway so it wasn't a big surprise. Better to get it squared away now than try to shift everything around when the fighting got heavy.

And I needed to get the soup kitchen better organized, with some volunteers to haul hot chow up close to the fighting line. And we still didn't have enough dormitory space for the Sookagrad folks who'd been displaced, let alone for the Human refugees we'd been getting, a trickle at first but more in the last twelve hours.

And I had to convince the perimeter fighters to get a lot more serious about recovering and taking care of the spent magazines from their weapons. Almost every weapon we had was a gauss rifle or pistol of one sort or another. The *gauss* in their name meant they magnetically accelerated a composite metallic flechette faster than the speed of sound, but they needed electricity to do it. The batteries that provided the juice for the system were embedded in the magazines. We could fabricate all the flechettes in the world but if we didn't have magazines to load them into, and recharge with power, we were out of business.

Where to start?

Ammunition distribution. Right. Make the pitch to the perimeter fighters about magazine recovery when I go around with word on the new ammo points. They'd like not having to go as far to get it, so they'd be more disposed to help us on the other thing. I stretched my left arm over my head, twisted from side to side to loosen up my back, and headed on to the clinic. Maybe Doc Mahajan could give me a shot or something for the joint pain.

I heard small arms fire in the distance. I'd gotten used to it lately, but suddenly I realized this sounded like a lot more than usual. The fog of my fatigue cleared and I started trotting. By the time I got to the clinic a couple sets of stretcher bearers were moving through the big double doorway to the trauma receiving station and Moshe Greenwald was yelling at a crowd of guys, trying to get them to do something.

"What's going on?" I said as soon as I got to them. Moshe turned and his face showed relief.

"Boss! Boy, am I glad to see you! Big push at the southwest

barricade. Don't know what's happening except our guys took some casualties and they need ammo and reinforcements."

I looked at the half-dozen guys he had together. "You guys ammo haulers?"

"Yeah, but Zhang here is the runner for barricade four. We got our own guys to haul for, if they get in trouble."

"If the mob breaks through the southwest, we're all going to have a really bad night. Everyone grab one sack of magazines and follow me. Moshe, you stay here. Alert whoever's running the perimeter—I think it's Zdravkova. She might not be back at headquarters yet. We were at that studio you rigged up. But find her and get some reinforcements to barricade four. Then get a work party together and get ready to push ammo wherever it's needed. These guys are now the first echelon reinforcements," I said, pointing to the ammo party. I could see the whites of Moshe's eyes in the flickering flare light. He was excited, keyed up, but his head was still screwed on straight.

"Got it, Boss. Good luck!" Then he was gone, running toward the HQ buildings.

"Saddle up, folks," I said to the other six. "You're all about to become heroes. Do what I tell you and you'll stay live heroes."

"How do we know which bags are which caliber?" the one called Zhang asked. "We need forty-four-thirty pistol, forty-five-forty carbine, and some forty-five-fifty RAG."

"Just grab a bag and haul ass," I answered. I did exactly that and hoped like hell they'd follow me.

Chapter Twenty-One

Twenty minutes later, after most of the excitement was over and I crouched beside a stalled ground car catching my breath, I heard Moshe call out to me.

"Hey, Boss. What are you doing this far forward?"

I turned and saw him emerge from the shadow of a building corner in a low crouch and stop. Four more reinforcements sprinted forward past him and then myself to thicken the firing line, although the Varoki seemed to have lost all their fight for now.

"Come on," I said. "It's pretty clear."

"Fuck that. You come here."

A single round zipped overhead and knocked foamstone chips from a wall. It wasn't anywhere near either of us, but it did remind me that I was pretty far forward for an unarmed logistics chief with one broken wing. I used my good left arm to help duckwalk back to Moshe. We got around the corner and out of the line of fire. Moshe moved the worst of the trash out of the way with his foot and then we both sat with our backs to the metal wall of the shipping container building. Moshe lit a cigarette.

"Looks like the guys held," he said. "How'd it go?"

"Like an Albanian town council meeting," I answered. "Two of them, actually. Fortunately, the one on the other side was even more confused than the one on ours. Much more. But this so-called ammo distribution system we have just isn't going to work. Jesus! Half the guys ended up back off the line rummaging through the bags, trying to find something they could shoot."

I stopped and took a long, shuddering breath. I'd been really scared through the firefight. That wasn't unusual; I'm always scared when there's shooting, especially if I'm unarmed. I keep doing what I need to do, never freeze up, but that doesn't make the experience any more fun. Moshe handed me a glass bottle, about a half-liter. The cap was off and I took a drink with trembling hand. Slivovitz—plum brandy—probably homemade, and pretty stiff.

"Moshe, you are a man of unexpected resourcefulness," I said.

"Is that you, Naradnyo?" I recognized the voice as Zdravkova's and saw her first as movement in the shadows, keeping to the side of the street near our wall. When she got closer I saw she was packing an old Mark 14 RAG.

"Hey, it's the Dragon Lady! Thanks for getting the alert squad up here so quick. Your kids did real good up on the barricade, once they settled down. They had it mostly under control but the bad guys really packed it in when your reserves showed up."

"What are you doing up here?"

I held up the bottle. "You know, having a nightcap, enjoying the evening. Think it's going to rain some more?"

Without a word she stalked past us and dropped into a crouch as she went around the corner.

"If you were a little older and wiser," Moshe said, "you'd appreciate mature women more."

"I appreciate 'em fine," I said and passed him the bottle, "especially when they're packing military-grade firepower." I thought about that for a moment. It was an odd thing to say, given my current elective nonviolent state, but old habits die hard.

"I'm married, though—and never had much of a wandering eye. Wish I was home right now."

"Who *doesn't* wish they were someplace other than here?" Moshe said. "I got an ex-wife on Bronstein's World. Right now even *I* wish I was there. Your wife, she's rich or something, ain't she? Good looking, too?"

"Yup, and a lot smarter than me. Not a bad combination. But we never laugh anymore. We never go dancing, either. We've never danced, do you believe it? You know I can do a pretty mean samba."

"That I'm having a hard time imagining," he said and passed me back the bottle.

"It's true. But all we do is plan and scheme and try to stay ahead of the bad guys, whoever they are today. Saving the galaxy, that's us. Not always sure what we're saving it from, or who for, but by God we're savin' the hell out of it."

I took another drink.

"We're so focused, so single-minded, day in, day out. Everyone needs a laugh once in a while. We used to laugh, until everything got so goddamned serious all the time. Someday some guy's gonna come along and make her laugh again. Then what?"

I took another pull of brandy and handed it to Moshe. The evening had become so quiet I could hear Zdravkova talking to the perimeter guards, maybe a block away, but I couldn't quite make out her words.

"Well, I remembered another physics joke," Moshe said after a while. "This one's great! Einstein, Newton, and Pascal are playing hide-and-seek. Einstein's 'it,' so he closes his eyes and starts counting. Pascal runs off to hide but Newton just stands there and takes out a piece of chalk. He draws a line a meter long on the street, then another one at right angles to it, then another and another until he's made a box. He stands in it and waits. Einstein gets done counting, opens his eyes, and says, 'Newton, I found you!' 'No,' Newton says, 'I am a Newton over a meter squared. You found Pascal!'"

Moshe laughed.

"What the hell kind of joke it that?" I said. "It doesn't even make sense."

"It does if you know physics."

But I obviously didn't. Overhead I saw stars and one of Hazz'Akatu's smaller moons. No clouds so maybe we were going to get some sunshine the next morning after all. We needed it.

What was keeping Zdravkova? I needed to talk to her before I turned in.

"Okay, you know physics," I said. "This is the three hundredth anniversary of the invention of the jump drive. Did you know that? I went to a reception for it a few days ago in Katammu-Arc. I guess you could say we crashed the party."

He offered the bottle but I shook my head. I was already about half-plowed.

"So what's the deal with that?" I asked.

"With the slivovitz? A friend made it over…oh, you mean the jump drive. The deal is it's the only way from star to star and the Varoki own it, *nu*?"

"Yeah, but how does it work? I mean, in general. No equations or my head will explode."

Moshe laughed. "No danger of a head explosion tonight, Boss. I don't have any idea how it works. Nobody outside the research departments of the big Varoki trading houses knows. It's called a proprietary trade secret. It's not even part of the patent description, is what I hear."

"How do you maintain it on a starship if you don't know how it works?"

"The components are black boxes: one jump cortex and from one to ten jump actuator units, depending on how big a ship. You fly with one duplicate of each component. If the component's performance goes subnominal, you install the backup and replace the defective one at your next stop."

"You never look inside?"

"Never, and I mean *never*. They're factory sealed, and they better still be factory sealed when you turn them in. You know, you don't own those components, you just lease them. Mess around with the seals, you violate the lease, get blackballed, and you're done flying. Besides which, its antitamper device is listed as a level five biohazard, which is as bad as it gets."

"*Biohazard?*"

"Yeah, you never heard the story of the *Rawalpindi*? This was about thirty years ago, before I was flying. A Newton tug coming in to dock at Boreandris Highstation had a malfunction. One of the lateral ACTs—that's attitude control thruster—froze in the full thrust position, started yawing the tug. Before they could get it unfrozen, or the pilot thought to just fire the opposing thruster, they hit a maintenance gig and then plowed it right into the side of a Human star freighter, the *Rawalpindi*. Drove that gig through the hull of the freighter like a spike, right into the engineering spaces, and cracked open the jump cortex.

"Two of *Rawalpindi's* engineering crew survived the initial impact, foamed the hull around the breach and got the pressure stabilized enough for the rest of the crew to crack the access hatch and get them out of there. Should have left them sealed in. Whatever was inside that cortex, some sort of neurotoxin they say, once it got out into the air it killed everyone else on the ship, something like twenty passengers and crew, including some rich Varoki who must have been out slumming. Couple of crew suited up but the bug ate through the seals, got 'em anyway.

"No rescue or recovery attempt once the bug was out—not allowed to board it or even take a remote sample afterwards. The *Cottohazz* ordered *Rawalpindi* hauled into a parking orbit nearby and waited 'til everyone died, then had a Newton tug give it a good hard shove toward the local sun. R.I.P."

"Damn," I said.

He nodded and took another sip.

"There was another accident like that, a freak meteor strike, I forget when. Bottom line: nobody outside their labs has looked inside a jump cortex and lived to tell about it."

He screwed the cap on the bottle and stood up.

"I gotta get back to the clinic, look at the wiring on two of the autodocs. You coming?"

"Nah, I need to get this ammo thing worked out and, much as I hate to say it, the Dragon Lady and I need to put our heads together on it."

"Why you call her that?" he said, hands on his hips. I got the idea he felt a little protective about her.

"I don't know. It's a nickname for a capable and dangerous woman."

"Well, try her real one: *Dezi Oobiyets*. See you later."

Now that *was* an interesting nickname. Dezi was obviously short for Desislava, her first name. *Oobivtsya* meant *killer* in Ukrainian. I was willing to bet *oobiyets* meant the same thing in Bulgarian.

Chapter Twenty-Two

I didn't have to wait long for Zdravkova, although I was right on the verge of dozing off when she led a half-dozen people from her reserve squad back down the street.

"Hey, Killer. Got a minute?"

She waved the squad back toward the headquarters and stood facing me, assault rifle's stock balanced on her hip.

"What?"

"Ammo," I said. "This ain't working."

She shifted her weight impatiently. "You asked for the job. *Make* it work."

"Well, it's easy to make it work for *me*. Let me know how many rounds you want, and of which calibers and magazine styles. We'll deliver them to you as soon as possible. The thing is that's not going to work so well for your kids on the firing line. Once the shooting starts, it's too late to screw around with that kind of bureaucratic bullshit. I want to push the ammo to your folks so it's there when they need it, but I can't."

I got to my feet using the wall for support, feeling every stage of the move in my knees and back. I'd already been tired before the firefight, and nothing drains your reserves like a big shot of adrenaline followed by a crash. Also I was a little drunk. Zdravkova slung her rifle over her shoulder and looked at me.

145

"You okay?"

"Sure. I'm just tired, that's all. Little out of shape, too. I gotta take these unused magazines and the empties back. Can't just leave them lying around. Give me a hand?"

I picked up a couple of partially filled bags of magazines with my left hand and Zdravkova grabbed the others. We started walking back toward the clinic.

"Got any more in that bottle?" she asked.

I chuckled. "Sorry, Greenwald's the man with the slivovitz. He was headed back this way to the clinic. So look, I want to push ammo forward to units but we can't because we don't know what they need. We got some different calibers and all, but the real headache with all these different civilian weapons is magazine compatibility. Since the magazine is also the power source, we can't really get around that. Even after sorting out all the one-offs and oddballs, we still have fifteen different magazine styles with only very limited interchangeability."

She looked at me—glared at me is more like—but after a couple seconds her scowl softened and she nodded. "Yes, that's been worrying me, too."

"The supply of magazines is already a bottleneck," I said. "We're trying to fabricate some more of them, but that's harder than just making flechettes, and we're short some of the raw materials we need for the battery components. Turns out it also takes a lot of power to fabricate stuff that complex. We're bumping up against our wattage ceiling already; all this rain means the solar panels haven't done us much good, so we're pretty much tied to the LENR generators.

"As the fighting gets more intense, medical and ammo fabrication are both going to need more juice. Your folks have to get really serious about recovering spent magazines and getting them back to us in good shape."

"Fair enough. I'll make sure they do. But how do we solve the magazine compatibility problem?"

"Well, either reorganize your squads and platoons, or swap the weapons you have within your existing tables of organization. Ideally each squad should have one pistol magazine style and one long gun style. That way we can at least assemble squad packs and make sure they're stockpiled close to where the squad's supposed to fight."

She shook her head impatiently. "I can't limit a squad to one long gun type. I need to spread the RAGs around, put one or two in each squad with the veterans, who are also usually my squad leaders. Without two RAGs up on the barricade tonight, no telling what might have happened."

I thought about the fighting back on the barricade, how the two guys with RAGs had kept firing, spacing their bursts, and telling the others what to do, where to lay their fire. So it wasn't a coincidence those guys had the best weapons. Maybe Zdravkova knew her stuff.

"Yeah, I can see that," I said. "Well, if every squad has a RAG or two, that doesn't really complicate putting together squad packs, since all the RAGs are magazine-compatible regardless of their mark number. At least the Army got that right. We'll just throw RAG mags in each ammo sack and then custom load the rest of the stuff in it. I'll limit our magazine fabrication to the RAGs, too. Sounds like those are the guns we absolutely have to keep fed."

That was as good a solution as we could come up with so we walked on in silence for a while.

"You've been in combat before," she said after we'd walked half a block. "I read that about you."

"Little bit. Not as much as you'd think."

"I'm sort of making all this up as I go," she said, and then we walked on for a few steps. I got the feeling she wanted to ask me something but didn't know how.

"Near as I can tell you're doing fine," I said finally.

"If there's anything you see…well, I'm not touchy about advice."

"Then that must be the *only* fucking thing you're not touchy about."

To my surprise she laughed.

"Okay," I said, "here's my only piece of advice. No matter what's happening, always make sure you're the least excited person in the group. Look around. If anyone's less excited than you, take a deep breath and calm down."

"Always?" she said.

"When people are on the edge of panic, they follow the person who isn't. I know what I'm talking about; I've been scared shitless many times, and I always respected the people whose eyes weren't popping out of their skulls."

She laughed again.

"So," I said, "you get the nickname *Killer* before or after you stopped practicing law?"

She looked at me from the corner of her eye without turning her head. "After. Definitely after."

"Why the career change, if you don't mind me asking?"

Our boots made soft crunching sounds on the carpet of trash underfoot, the sound louder here where the building walls were continuous on both sides and the street narrow. Ahead, over the tops of the buildings to the north, I could see the faint blinking red light of the uBakai Army hoverplat high up in the sky, making its slow transit around e-Kruaan-Arc.

"Oh, I just got tired of being a cog in a machine that eats Humans," she said after a while. "I defended all these people, and eventually I figured out all I was doing was giving the leatherheads an excuse to congratulate themselves on their fair-mindedness. After all, every member of the parade of Humans bound for long-term detention had a Human counselor to argue their case. What more could they ask? So there's that. Then, when my husband left me for a younger woman, I began feeling an urge to blow things up."

I looked over at her, but if she was smiling it was on the inside.

"Well, in my experience, you can get some real growth and progress out of explosive therapy," I said. "Had much opportunity to try it out?"

"Not so far, but the prospects are looking up."

I wondered if her seeing all those clients railroaded by the Varoki had maybe saved my life, made her decide not to participate in one more judicially sanctioned lynching. Sometimes our fate hangs by a strand that slender.

We dropped our bags at the ammo distribution point in front of the clinic. Zdravkova headed inside, I guess to look for Greenwald and his slivovitz, and I walked over to the communal soup kitchen and dormitory, both of which were still works in progress. I needed to get something to eat and then some rack time or I was going to fold up.

I was surprised to see Nikolai Stal hanging around the door.

"Evening, Sasha. Heard was some excitement."

"Yeah. Took a few casualties, too, but I don't think anyone died. What brings you here?"

He smiled. "Oh, couple interesting refugees just come in, look for sanctuary. Do not like dining and sleeping facilities, think should get better treatment because related to very big hero."

"Who?" I asked.

His grin got broader. "Claim to be father and sister of famous Sasha Naradnyo."

I just looked at him for a second and then shook my head. "That'd be a pretty good trick, seeing as how they both died twenty-seven years ago on Peezgtaan."

"*Da*, and these two look alive to me. Since nobody knows Sasha actually here, or even alive, must have believed was easy lie. Like to come along, see faces when meet real Sasha."

He led me across the soup kitchen to a table in back and I saw a man and woman huddled with blankets around their shoulders and bent over their soup. As we approached, the man, sitting across the table facing me, looked up, and then he stood up and let the blanket slip from his rounded shoulders. The room seemed to sway from side to side as I looked at him. His hair was gray instead of black, his face more lined, and he'd put on some weight.

"Hello, Aleksandr Sergeyevich," he said. "Do you remember your sister, Avrochka?"

The woman turned and looked up at me. She was the news feeder I'd noticed earlier, the one named Aurora, now looking dirty and somewhat haggard, but the family resemblance was clear.

No wonder she'd reminded me of me.

"It could be plastic surgery," I said, but Doc Mahajan shook her head.

"The DNA results are conclusive. The man is your father. He is also the father of the woman, and the mitochondrial DNA she shares with you indicates you both have the same mother. As near as I can determine, they are exactly who they claim to be."

"But how? They both died on Peezgtaan in a food riot."

"How do you know that, Boss?" Moshe asked. He offered me the slivovitz but I waved it away. I was punchy enough as it was. Zdravkova took it instead and downed a swallow. The four of us sat in the cramped privacy of Mahajan's office at the clinic, which now also doubled as a supply storage room.

I thought back to that day twenty-seven years ago.

"There were food riots all over the place," I said. "My father, mother, and sister went out to try to find something for us to eat.

I don't remember why they left me in the apartment. Maybe I was sick or too small or something. Hours later my mother came back alone, beat up and in shock. She died in bed a few days later."

"She told you the other two were dead?" Doc Mahajan asked.

"No, she never spoke again. She never even acknowledged my presence after she came back. I'd always assumed the others were dead. Why else would she go into such deep shock and depression?"

There was something more than that, another reason it couldn't be them, but I didn't want to say it. They wouldn't understand.

"Who knows, Boss?" Moshe said. "People do crazy things. Maybe she really thought they were dead."

"Then why didn't they come back? Where have they been all this time? And showing up here the same time I did…that's too crazy a coincidence."

"Perhaps," Doc Mahajan said, "but their being here is not all that unusual. Aurora did several features on Sookagrad within the last year and a multipart investigative series on corruption in the Inter-Arcology Park District. She made a number of contacts here. That she and her father would seek sanctuary here is understandable. Really, Sasha, it is *your* presence which is the anomaly."

"Maybe so, but if they've lived here in the city for a while like you say, and they know who I am, which they clearly do, why didn't they ever contact me?"

—"Go ask them," Zdravkova said and then looked at me with those hard, angry eyes. "Or are you afraid?"

I wasn't about to admit it to her but hell yes I was afraid. If your family's been dead for almost your whole life, see how *you* feel if they start showing back up again one day. What do you say to them? "How you been?"

The thing is, I'd actually *been* dead for a little while, and when I'd been dead there'd been people there—wherever "there" was—who'd welcomed me. All those people had already been dead, including my whole family. It was sort of comforting, and had taken some of the edge off the fear of death since then, knowing that's what was waiting. What I couldn't figure out now was how my father and sister could have been there in dead-people-land if they weren't ever actually dead.

"Okay," I said, getting to my feet, "guess I'll go talk to them."

Moshe offered me the bottle again and this time I took a good slug.

Chapter Twenty-Three

"Okay, they tell me you two really are my father and sister. So what the hell happened?"

They exchanged a guilty look.

Zdravkova had found us a private room, not much more than a big closet, with a light, a table, and three folding chairs. It smelled of mold. The man and I sat facing each other. The woman stood leaning against a wall.

I looked them over. The woman was dressed as I'd first seen her on the vid, four days ago, stylishly but also practical for going out in the streets and looking for news. Four days—it seemed longer than that but that's all it was. The man was dressed expensively, a suit with inset iridescent panels that were popular in the business world these days. It was soiled and one shoulder seam was torn open showing the lining, but he'd clearly had some money before everything went to hell.

"How much do you remember?" the man said.

"The three of you went out. Only mother came back. What happened?"

"What did she tell you?" he asked.

"Just tell me what the hell happened or start looking for a different sanctuary."

"For God's sake, tell him," the woman named either Aurora or Avrochka said.

"Yes, yes, of course," he said, and he rubbed the palms of his hands across his face, either momentarily overcome by emotion and fatigue, or stalling for time, getting his story straight.

He was shorter than I remembered, but all adults look tall to an eight-year-old. He'd become portly, about a hundred kilos, and his hair was thinning on top. He looked scared, scared of me, his son. Of course, if he knew enough about me to claim me as a relative, he knew enough to be scared of me.

"I received word there was a position for me, here on Hazz'Akatu," he said. "You remember, I am a biochemist, a genetic researcher. That is why AZ Tissopharm hired me originally, brought us to Peezgtaan. Now someone else had need for...well, there was a position. But the times were very bad, the riots, so many people trying to get off Peezgtaan after Tissopharm collapsed. There was only passage for two. Later the other two could come, but at first just myself and one other. I chose your sister. She was older, could look after herself while I worked. It was better. Your mother...she and you would come later."

My sister looked at him and I saw contempt in her eyes. Why, I wondered? Maybe just because he'd turned out to be a shitty father, but possibly because he was lying and she knew it. It wasn't all a lie, but something wasn't right. The way he knit his brows, as if in pain, as he told it, the way he wrung his hands, all shouted *liar*.

"Why didn't you send for me?" I said.

Energy flowed into his body and his face lit up, thinking this must mean I believed him.

"Oh, I did, Sasha, I did! But they told me your mother had died and there was no sign of you, not in any of the institutions, no record anywhere. You know how many orphans died, Sasha. You must know better than anyone! They all told me you had to be dead. I'm sorry I believed them."

I believed he was sorry, but more for the fix he was afraid he'd put himself into than anything else. I told them about mother returning home beaten and distraught, how she had never spoken again, gone to bed, and simply died a week later, probably of dehydration since she refused to either eat or drink. The man looked relieved when I told the part about her not talking.

"But you must have figured out I was alive at some point," I said. "Otherwise you wouldn't have claimed to be my family when you got here."

Again they exchanged a look and the man nodded vigorously.

"Yes, Sasha, we heard about you...oh, it must have been just two years ago, when the story of how you saved that Varoki heiress was suddenly everywhere. There were stories about your background, how you were an orphan, survived alone on the streets. We both knew then you must be our lost Sasha."

"That much is true," my sister said, as if to affirm that eventually he'd managed to tell something that wasn't somehow a distortion or outright lie. He shot her a warning frown, quickly replaced by an ingratiating smile as he turned back to me.

"But you didn't contact me then, either. Why not?"

He colored and looked at my sister, then down at the floor. "Yes, you are right. We should have. But...we were afraid it would have compromised Avrochka's journalistic credibility to be the brother of so famous and...controversial a figure. This was especially true when your association with the e-Traak heiress became permanent. A highly political arrangement, you must realize that."

"*My* credibility?" Aurora nearly spat. "You made me swear not to contact Sasha for fear it would compromise *your* position at AZ Kagataan!"

"What do you know?" he shouted. "You know nothing! It was for you. Everything I did was always for you!"

"Tell him the truth!" she shouted, her voice rising toward a scream. "Tell him the truth or I will!"

He jumped up, raised his arm as if to strike her, and I saw her cringe just before I grabbed his belt with my left hand and yanked him back against the table. He lost his balance, fell against the table, it splintered and collapsed and he sprawled across the floor, crying out in surprise and pain. Aurora took a step forward, towering over him.

"You won't tell him?"

When he said nothing in reply she spat on him and then turned to me.

"This is why you were left alone that day. This is why our mother returned home beaten and distraught to the point of suicide. There were not two places on the ship, Sasha; there were supposed to be *three*. Then when there were only two seats, this *thing*, our father, drove the thing that was our mother away with curses and blows.

"They had already decided to abandon you!"

She looked at me and the anger slowly drained from her face, replaced by a deep bitterness, but not directed at me. She flopped into a chair as if much of the life had drained away from her body as well. The man pushed himself up until he was sitting but did not try to stand up. He looked down at the floor.

I sat unmoving, not really thinking about anything, just trying on all this new information for size. Reality had altered, and I was wondering how I felt about that but hadn't really figured it out yet.

"What will happen to us now?" he finally asked, his voice trembling.

"Oh...yeah. Well, you are Human refugees and we don't turn Humans away. You will get the same food and shelter other refugees get. If it's any consolation, I sleep in the common dormitory and eat at the soup kitchen myself. Your accommodations will be every bit as good as those of your famous son and brother.

"Now, I've been awake for over two days and I gotta get some sleep or I'm going to fall over. We're done here, right?"

I remember when I first told Marr about that day I lost my family. Her reaction to my mother giving up and dying was to call her a worthless bitch. It shocked me at the time, but Marr always was a more demanding judge of character than I. At least in this case she was apparently a more accurate one as well.

I kept expecting to feel something really big and important— you know, after finding out my parents had made the affirmative decision to jettison me, an eight-year-old boy, leave me to my fate. I wondered why they did it. I could ask the old man, but I didn't think I could believe anything he said. Had I done something horrible when I was a child that made them suspect what I might grow up to be?

My childhood memories were disorderly fragments, more so than most people's because the brain damage associated with my death two years ago had sort of scrubbed away random bits of the past. I do not recall being particularly happy or particularly sad when I was a boy. I remember being anxious, a reflection I suppose of the constant anxiety of my parents. I don't remember torturing small animals or anything terrible like that, and I don't think that fit my personality anyway. No, I had no clue why they decided to just walk away from an eight-year-old boy.

How did I feel about it? Maybe it was the fatigue, maybe the distraction of the world coming apart around me, or maybe it was just something important missing from inside of me, I don't know. But I didn't feel that different. I mean, I felt surprised, and I felt pissed off, but I didn't feel wounded.

All my life I'd thought my parents died back in 2102 Earth Time. Then it turned out they might as well have, but one of them was still walking around.

Huh.

Moshe shook me awake saying something about ammo and attack. It took a couple minutes before the scrambled synapses of my brain finally started coming back into alignment. I'd left word to wake me in three hours but they let me sleep for five. I think Moshe and the folks who knew what was going on felt sorry for me, which was sweet of them, but we needed me to get the ammo distribution thing squared away before an attack, not during it.

The common dormitory consisted of three really big metal shipping containers welded together side-by-side with wide doors cut connecting them. There were more people sleeping there than when I'd gone to bed, more cots and some folks on the floor wrapped in a blanket or two. Moshe and I had to make our way carefully through the narrow aisles and over tangles of arms and legs.

Outside the sky was beginning to turn from black to gray. I started toward the clinic but Moshe steered me to the soup kitchen, ignoring my protests.

"It'll just be a second. I put in an order on my way to wake you up." One of the cooks was waiting at the door, pushed a plastic cup of hot tea into my left hand and gave a greasy paper bag to Moshe. "Rice balls," he explained as we headed to the clinic.

The tea was sweet. I normally take it without sugar but I probably needed the extra boost.

"Open up," he said and popped a small rice ball into my mouth. I didn't realize how hungry I was until I bit down on it. I tasted some fish oil in the center, maybe on a little tofu, and a delicious piece of pickle.

"Damn, that's good!"

"Ought to be," he said. "Dolores Wu found out the *sous-chef* from Pinnacle came in with his daughter, looking for a place to hide. Now he's the head line cook for the soup kitchen."

"Pinnacle? That Human restaurant over in Arc-Jannu?"

"Yeah. Wait till you taste his faux crab bisque. We could rename the soup kitchen the bisque kitchen, maybe attract a classier clientele. What do you think? Open up again."

He popped another rice ball in my mouth. "Here's another joke I remembered. Two atoms walking down the street. First atom says, 'Hey! I lost an electron!' Second atom says, 'Are you sure?' First one says, 'I'm positive!'" He laughed.

"I'm *positive*, get it?"

"No," I said, still chewing the rice ball.

"Oh, Boss! I mean, that's actually kinda sad."

Maybe so, but two rice balls later I felt like a new man. We were just about to the clinic and central ammo resupply point but I still hadn't heard any small arms fire or seen much frantic activity.

"Where was the attack?" I asked.

"Oh, it hasn't started yet. Dezi's put together a striker squad she's going to use to surprise one of their observation posts, maybe pick up some extra hardware."

"*Dezi?*" I said.

He looked at me. "It's her name, ain't it? Look, you want another rice ball or you want to play wisenheimer?"

Zdravkova waited in front of the clinic with a dozen others, about half of which had RAGs, so it must have been a picked unit. She nodded curtly to me and smiled at Moshe.

"Good, you're finally here," she said to me, and stuffed a paper into my jacket pocket. "That is my new squad list with weapons and their main assignment areas, so you can rework the ammo resupply points. I tried to keep similar magazine types in the same area."

"Thanks. That'll help. Got a party planned?"

"Yes, and we must go before it grows too light. We will be back in an hour if we come back at all."

She waved her squad up and they moved off to the west.

"Treat 'em rough, Killer," I called after her, and then Moshe and I watched them disappear into the shadows. I felt a rain drop, another, and then it began raining softly.

"No solar today," Moshe said, and he sighed. "I gotta scout the east side, see if I can come up with any more LENR generators. Found about fifty liters of deuterium while you were sleeping so I changed out the fuel in our lowest performing plants, but still..."

He squinted up at the now-black sky, the earlier traces of dawn having vanished. "Man, could we use some sunshine."

I felt exactly the same way. I wondered what Marr was doing.

In the distance I heard small arms fire, single shots at first and then the stutter of a RAG on full auto.

Chapter Twenty-Four

Over the next day, Zdravkova led out four different "striker squads" to raid the Varoki observation posts around us. Near as we could tell, the mob had been working itself up to march on Sookagrad before that, but those quick, sharp blows put them back on their heels, made them rethink everything, wait for a while, see what we planned to do next. So the raids bought us at least another day of comparative security, and a fair haul of abandoned weapons, at the cost of two people wounded and no dead.

Humans had a reputation for aggression and violence that was overstated, but for a change was useful. Zdravkova's raids reinforced that reputation, made the Varoki over there start thinking maybe every Human really was as good as two Varoki, or three, or ten. We didn't know what the odds really were, but they were long and probably getting longer every day. Anything that kept the Varoki mentally on the defensive was money in the bank.

It also gave us time to start making reports to the outside world. Our vid tech with the camera had done some promotional work before the troubles—as we were all starting to think of them—and he did interviews with Katranjiev and Stal. Zdravkova begged off and everyone, including me, agreed it would be a terrible idea to let the world in general know that the infamous Sasha Naradnyo was hanging out here. I watched the two interviews and didn't think much of them. Too much like heroic speeches from our fearless leaders. Then it hit me.

"You know, we actually have a semi-famous journalist here," I told Stal. I approached him because he wasn't that anxious to have his face plastered all over, besides which Katranjiev was still likely to call the sky red if I said it was blue.

"You mean long-lost sister? Did not think like each other."

"I haven't seen her since the day she got here, but so what? She's got a following and seems to know her stuff. You ought to get her in on this. Ask Zdravkova, too. Dezi doesn't want her face shown, but being a revolutionary and all she's got to know more about agitprop than some guy who did promotional holovids for Varoki sex aids."

"Leatherheads need love too," he said, but then he nodded in agreement.

So my estranged sister Aurora became the voice of Sookagrad. She ditched the big-shot speeches and that afternoon started doing interviews with ordinary people, finding out their backgrounds, what they'd seen in the last few days. I watched them: good stuff. There wasn't anything weepy about them, if you know what I mean. Just people telling what happened, how they got here, and what they were doing now.

The interviews had a lot of motion, following folks as they worked in the soup kitchen (our former *sous-chef*), swept out a new building for our dormitory expansion, helped mount an LENR generator to power a drug synthesizer. They were all upbeat, smiling at the end as they worked, even if they had a choked-up moment or two when telling their story. Put some of the horrible, frightening things they'd seen together with that energy and optimism at the end and you had a hell of a message without ever having to spell it out or draw pictures.

She didn't mention any of the fighting yet, or what we were doing to defend the district. That would come later, but in the meantime it was nice to give the citizens of the *Cottohazz* a view of Humans doing a whole bunch of different things, none of them violent or illegal. It was a side of Humanity a lot of them had probably never seen.

Katranjiev didn't much like it, whether because his interview had been cut or because Aurora was my sister I couldn't tell.

"You have to show suffering," he said when they held a troika meeting the next morning. I guess I was included because the whole communiqué thing had been my idea originally. "Who's going to come to our rescue if it looks as if we're all happy and healthy here?"

Aurora didn't jump right in to defend her piece. Zdravkova argued with Katranjiev a bit and then asked Aurora what she thought. Waiting to be asked was smart.

"People don't sympathize very much with pure victims, and the *Cottohazz* is tired of Humans complaining about how bad they have it. If we show them Humans taking care of themselves, building a peaceful community in all this chaos, we'll get their attention and grudging respect. And it's better to underplay everything. It must smack of reality, not invented drama, you understand?"

"But there is suffering here, much suffering," Katranjiev countered.

"If what we all think is going to happen comes true," Aurora said, "we will have ample opportunity to show that later. But if you *begin* with suffering now, then later it's just more of the same, like a broken record, and the audience will tune it out. We show them order, community, work, and hope first. What comes later will be more powerful because of the contrast, and it will enrage our audience."

Listening to her sort of gave me a chill. She was talking about a possible nightmare scenario as if it were a video play or an ad campaign instead of something which might engulf all of us. That's how a professional had to think, I guess. A doctor facing vans full of casualties from a major fire thought triage and treatment, not what all those injuries and deaths meant to all those families. A squad leader outlining a mission and identifying where they were likely to take casualties couldn't let himself dwell on how well or how long he'd known the men who were about to get killed or maimed.

Still, hearing it laid out so emotionlessly sent a shiver up my back, but it won the argument.

So the first report went out. It began with a camera shot of Aurora, the soup kitchen in the background with a line of giggling kids going in to get lunch. Her first line was, "This is Sookagrad, calling all the people of the *Cottohazz*. This is Sookagrad calling."

We could send on the fiber cable, but we couldn't receive because we couldn't decode any of the flow in the data pipe, and of course anything broadcast was being jammed, so we had no way of knowing who, if anyone, was actually paying attention, or what anyone thought of it. All we could do was send it out and hope for the best.

I stopped her outside the headquarters building after the meeting, told her that, whatever else there was between us, I thought
the vid report was top-notch, exactly what we needed. She looked
down while I said it and then looked away while she answered me.

"Thank you. I know it must have cost you a great deal to say
that."

Actually it didn't cost me a thing, or at least anything important. If she'd known me at all she'd have known that, but what
was the point in saying so?

"Look, we're strapped for fabricator time," I said, "but I'm
going to try to fit in a special job, some props for one of your
upcoming reports."

"Props?" she said. "I don't know. I like to keep it as authentic
as possible. What kind of props?"

"Munie badges. I can't afford the time to run them off for
everyone hauling a gun, but I can do a couple dozen and you
make sure any fighter on camera has one."

"Badges? Isn't that illegal?"

It suddenly occurred to me that, in all the confusion, not
everyone knew about the deal we'd cut with the Munies.

"Illegal? Oh, boy, you've got a little catching up to do, but
you're *really* going to like what I tell you next. It fits your nar-
rative beautifully."

Two hours later I stood in the cramped workshop Petar Ivanov,
our head fabricator, used as his base of operations. The sound
of humming fabricators and the smells of hot metal, blending
chemicals, and unwashed body odor filled the air in the dimly
lit room. Moshe took a deep drag on his cigarette and exhaled
through his nose.

"Schrödinger's walking down the street with a shoebox under
his arm. A Munie stops him, looks inside the box, and says, 'Hey,
there's a dead cat in here.' Schrödinger says, 'Well there is *now!*'"

He and Ivanov laughed. Billy Conklin, the remaining member
of our quartet, made a sour expression and took a drink of his
tea. I just looked at them.

"This guy Schroder didn't know he had a dead cat?"

"Is Schrödinger," Ivanov said, "and actually, cat not unambiguously dead until Munie look."

I just shook my head. "Don't physicists ever just tell dirty jokes?"

"Oh, sure," Moshe said. "Here's one: why are physicists lousy lovers?"

"I don't know, why?"

"'Cause when they know the right position they can't get the speed right, and when they know the right speed, they can't get the position right."

"I don't get it. Wait...does it have something to do with that guy-on-the-highway joke, about speed and knowing where he is?"

"Amazing! Yes, it actually does."

"Well, I still don't get it."

"No," he said, "but you might not be a *total* shmendrick, much to my surprise."

"Is there some reason I'm here, other than to be insulted?"

"Yeah," Conklin said, "me too. I got some pretty full saddle-bags, you know."

Moshe grinned. "Not to worry, you're both gonna love this, especially you, Billy." He held his hand out to Ivanov, who carefully passed him a small opaque plastic box from the workbench.

"There better not be a dead cat in there," I said.

He opened the lid and showed us. "Don't touch."

A dozen metallic cylinders, about a centimeter in diameter and ten centimeters long, rested on a bed of extruded soft foam with channels cut to hold them and keep them from rolling. They were dull grey but with a red stripe painted around the middle. One end was closed, the other partially open.

"Okay, I give up."

"Blastin' caps," Billy Conklin said. "Right?"

"Mr. Greenwald say need blasting caps," Ivanov said, "so I make."

I looked at Moshe. "And we need blasting caps why?"

"Because I found an industrial storage unit where somebody stashed a bunch of bulk maintenance consumables, including about five hundred liters of a cleaning solvent: CH_3NO_2," he said and then looked directly at me. "That's nitromethane to the scientifically illiterate."

"*Gawd damn!*" Conklin said and nearly dropped his tea.

Given my previous line of work, I knew enough about causing trouble to know where this was going and I started smiling. "What you gonna cut it with? EDA?"

Ivanov shrugged, "Other amines work, but yes, *ethylenediamine—* EDA—is most common."

"Five hundred liters of PLX binary explosive," I said.

"Five twenty-five by the time we add the EDA and mix it," Moshe said, his grin even wider.

I thought that over for a few seconds, and for a change my thoughts were not restricted solely to ways of causing mayhem.

"Billy, you got any people who can use explosives without blowing themselves up?"

"Yup, me for one. Also know a guy, Dhaliwa, been around construction blasting for years, knows his shit. I can probably rustle up a couple more. What you got in mind?"

"We need shelters, as in underground shelters, and we need a lot of them. All these lean-tos and tents—if they start lobbing even mortars in here, it'll cause havoc. We don't have the time or equipment to dig shelters, but what about explosive excavation?"

Conklin scratched his bald spot and nodded. "Sure. I mean, getting cover over the holes is going to be a bitch once we blow them, but even open holes are better than nothing."

"We can maybe do better than that," Moshe said. "The storm sewers run straight to the Wanu River, and they aren't buried very deep. There are some drains from the surface to the storm system, but none here in Sookagrad."

"Gimme a couple kilos of that PLX," Billy Conklin said, "I'll make a connection."

"Yeah," I said, "but with all this rain, won't the storm sewers be full of water?"

Moshe and Conklin both got a little more serious.

"*Oy*, maybe so," Moshe said. "We'll just have to look, right?"

Storm sewers were usually pretty big, so they wouldn't back up in a heavy rain, but if they were even half full of fast-flowing water, it would be somewhere between tough and impossible to use them for shelter. Maybe we were back to explosive excavation, but Billy was right: how were we going to put hard cover over all those holes?

This logistics stuff wasn't as easy as it looked. You knew you had a real problem on your hands if a half ton of binary explosive couldn't fix it.

Chapter Twenty-Five

The days were starting to run together so I sat down and worked out how long I'd been here. This was the afternoon of Sixteen-Day, Eight-Month Waning, the fourth day—fourth day since I'd arrived and also the fourth day since the military coup.

I found Zdravkova in the headquarters building, looking grim. She almost always looked grim so I didn't attach much significance to it.

"Hey, Killer, remember how you told me your secret dream was to blow a bunch of stuff up? I got some good news."

She didn't just look grim, she looked worn down and filthy. I knew she'd gone out with three of the raids on the previous day and had been making the rounds of the perimeter posts since then—at least when she wasn't helping with the training/orientation program she'd whipped up. Try putting an army together in less than a week sometime, see how much sleep you get.

I half expected her to snarl at me, but she just looked up, emotion overwhelmed by fatigue. "I could use some good news," she said, and she nodded toward the back of the office. I saw two Varoki talking to Katranjiev, haranguing him more like. He didn't look happy.

"What do they want?"

"I caught the start of it. They're representatives of the Provisional Government. Seems the gangs around us have been incorporated

164

into a Citizens' Emergency Militia. The government's gotten complaints about unprovoked attacks against them."

"Your raids?" I said. "They must have an interesting understanding of 'unprovoked.'"

"Not that interesting. So pending a complete investigation, they demand we turn over all firearms and that anyone involved in the fighting surrender themselves to custody of the militia."

"Or else," I added. "Is there a time limit on the ultimatum?"

"Twelve hours."

"That means time runs out about dawn." I thought about that for a moment. "You know, if I were a bunch of unscrupulous Human-hating Varoki pricks, I'd think we Humans figured we had twelve hours to get ready, maybe get a last good night's sleep before sunup. I'd think real hard about jumping the gun and launching a predawn attack, catch us napping, maybe finish us off in one big push."

She looked at me. "You are a devious son of a bitch, you know that? I must be too, because I was thinking the same thing. Those negotiators aren't making any bones about the consequences of us turning them down, either. Laying it on real thick, lots of bloodthirsty promises."

"They probably mean every word," I said. "They look plenty pissed."

"Yes," she said, "and that's before they find out we have a hidden camera in the room recording every gruesome and illegal threat, for whatever that's worth."

What *was* that worth? I didn't know exactly, but I knew it was worth something.

After nightfall Zdravkova started moving squads up to the perimeter to reinforce the main accessways. She moved them into civilian-occupied buildings and sent the civilians back to the dormitories. Since there were more civilians out there than reinforcements, the net movement of heat sources would be into the center of the district, assuming the uBakai military was watching us with a recon hoverplat or two and passing the intel to the Militia. We didn't know they were, but it was stupid not to assume that. But if they were, the perimeter would actually look thinner on thermals. If they wanted to screw us, we were bending over for them, or at least it would look that way to them.

Aurora wanted to interview some of the fighters before they moved up to the line so I took her and the recorder guy to one of the assembly areas, and who did I find there but my old pal Bela, now packing a RAG-19 assault rifle. Remembering how he'd carried on once back at my apartment when Aurora came on the vid screen, I pointed him out and suggested she talk to him.

"What did you do before all this?" she asked.

Bela rubbed his deformed right ear before answering.

"Made money here and there. Had trouble with law—nothing serious. But is different to be on side of law. Is good, yes? I think so."

"Why is it good, Bela?" she asked.

He looked up at the stars in the night sky and squinted, thinking.

"When I have no money, nothing to eat, some people help. They don't say, 'Bela, this is what you owe. Pay now!' They just do. Now militia out there, want kill us. Why? We do nothing to them."

He patted the top of his head. "Because have hair? Have little ears? Law says they are wrong." He touched the replica Munie badge on his chest and smiled. "So now help law protect these people. I don't go them, say, 'You owe me. Pay now!'" He shook his head. "Just do." He sniffed and wiped his nose. "Pardon. Have cold."

Behind him his squad started moving toward the perimeter. He slung his RAG over his shoulder and shrugged. "Time for going. Very nice meeting you, Miss Aurora. I watch you much on feed. Be safe." He turned and trotted to the head of the column and fell in beside the squad leader.

Aurora turned toward the vid recorder. "That was Lance Constable Bela Ripnick of the Sakkatto Municipal Police, one of nearly two hundred emergency deputies deployed here to protect Sookagrad's population. As I reported earlier, the Citizen Emergency Militia, or CEM, the paramilitary arm of Elaamu Gaant's Varoki New Dawn Leadership movement, surrounds Sookagrad. It has demanded the Municipal Police in this district turn in their weapons and surrender themselves to the CEM. Of course the police have refused.

"Men and women like Constable Ripnick stand ready tonight to repel any attempt to cleanse the Sookagrad district. This is Sookagrad calling. Good night."

The bit about Ripnick being one of "nearly two hundred" fighters was deliberate deception, a bit of psychological warfare.

We actually had four hundred and seventeen fighters, near as we could tell. Record-keeping was tough with every wireless data device being jammed, but we did have hard-copy muster rolls. Over a hundred of the fighters were purely rear-area security, armed only with an odd assortment of pistols for which we had a limited number of magazines. But we had three hundred front-line combatants.

Assuming we did as much damage to the attacking Militia as we expected to, thinking less than two hundred fighters did it should be an additional blow to their confidence. The people over there already feared Humans. We wanted to stoke that furnace.

I was glad I'd been there for the interview. I'd seen Bela's eyes when he touched that deputy's badge. It was just a symbol, but sometimes a symbol will keep people going when normally they'd pack it in, and this symbol really did sum up what we were becoming as a community. We weren't the rebels, the radicals, the criminals, *they* were. We were…well, whatever we were, somehow it was all tied up with that badge.

So I needed to talk with Ivanov, figure out some way to juggle the fabricator priorities so we could crank out another four hundred badges. They weren't that big or elaborate, and we could use whatever material we weren't short of, provided it was hard and semi-shiny. Didn't want it too shiny.

"I wish you'd let me do a piece on the improvised explosives," Aurora said once the troops had left. "I know we don't want to tip our hand about the implanted minefields Mr. Conklin set up, but we can hold the broadcast until later."

"Too late now. Attack could come in any time and those minefields are right on all the most likely avenues of approach. Besides, do you think something as sneaky as booby traps, especially when we've rigged them to cause maximum mayhem, is the story we want to tell?"

She looked down the street, thinking it over, and then shook her head. "I suppose not. Too bad, though. It's just all so ingenious, and improvised."

It was ingenious. Billy Conklin and part of his crew spent all afternoon and early evening getting the five minefields ready. We had a supply of six-centimeter-diameter composite pipe, about a thirty-five centimeter length of which would hold a liter of PLX. We only had twelve detonators—we'd have more but not until tomorrow—so we couldn't do a lot of individual mines. Instead we made Bangalore torpedoes, although I have no idea why they're called that since I don't know what *Bangalore* means and they aren't really torpedoes. They're basically really long pipe bombs. We made ours two meters long and assembled ten of them, each with a detonator and about six liters of PLX.

The five main avenues of approach each got two of them, one on each side of the street about thirty or so meters past the perimeter barricades. They were laid parallel to the street, one on either side, and offset with a couple meters between them, so they covered a six-meter path. The work crew scrounged as many small rocks, chunks of metal, and pieces of hard composites as they could find and piled then on top of the pipes, then covered the whole thing with trash. There was plenty of that around and it made it easier to camouflage traps like this.

The perimeter barricades would hold unless they got hit with overwhelming force. If so the troops guarding them would withdraw laterally into the buildings to either side of the street and bunker up. Each route had a reserve force back behind the minefields. When the attackers surged down the street into the killing zone of the mines, the local commander would blow an air horn—the signal for his men to duck behind whatever cover they had, then blow the mines using battery-operated detonators Moshe Greenwald lashed together. When the pieces stopped falling, everyone in the reserve force would open fire on whoever was left standing.

I had no idea if it would work that well in practice, but even if it just went *Bang* real loud, it should scare hell out of anyone nearby. Scaring the bad guys in the middle of a firefight is always a good policy.

Aurora looked around the trash-cluttered streets and pursed her lips in thought. "Is there some place I can get a better view of the district? I keep talking about it in general terms, but I don't really understand its layout."

"Yeah," I said, "but we better move fast. No telling when the curtain's going up."

Chapter Twenty-Six

I took Aurora up to the roof of Nikolai Stal's building, since two stories was about as high as anything down here got. I didn't know the district that well so I snagged a local from the soup kitchen, a dark-haired girl, maybe thirteen or fourteen Earth years old, about Tweezaa's size, who had grown up in the district. She'd been washing dishes so she was thrilled to leave that and guide the glamorous feed head Aurora.

None of us looked or smelled particularly glamorous by then, but my sister managed to handle it better than most. Her face was dirty, but almost artfully so. I found out later that before she shot the interviews the day before, she'd used a quarter of her drinking water ration to wash her face, and then had reapplied dirt, almost like makeup I guess. She'd drawn her hair back in a tight ponytail which masked its oiliness. She was a few years older than I was and managed to look at least as many years younger, but I suspected that up until recently my mileage had been a little rougher than hers.

"Ted, we won't be shooting anything from the roof tonight," she said to her vid recorder tech. "I just want to look around. Why don't you get a start on editing the vid from today and then get a little sleep? If there's an attack later, we'll want to shoot some footage and maybe do an interview."

Ted, who had grown a lot quieter since being demoted from producer of the news to Aurora's tag-along recorder tech, left us without a word.

"So what's your name?" Aurora asked.

"Divya, Miss. Divya Jayaraman."

"Call me Aurora. Everyone does. What did you do before all this started?"

"Oh, I was in school. My father got me a position in the Enlightened Technical Preparatory Academy in e-Kruaan-Arc. I am going to be a design engineer like him."

"Enlightened Prep?" Aurora said. "I didn't know they take Human students."

"I am the first one! An experiment, they say." She giggled. "They frown and study me, ask me questions all the time."

"How do the other students treat you?"

Divya shrugged. "At first some of them were mean, but the teachers made them stop. They did not want the experiment ruined, you see. Now they are used to me."

"Your father is a design engineer, you said?"

"Oh, yes, he works at AZ Trimtaax, also in e-Kruaan. He hasn't come home since the trouble started, so he must be staying there."

Aurora and I exchanged a glance and Divya saw it.

"Oh, no, nothing has happened to him, I am sure. My father is very strong."

She said it with such cheerful assurance I almost believed it. And it was possible he was alive but hadn't been able to get back here, was holed up in another enclave or in some sort of protective custody. Maybe his employers had even sheltered him, who knew? I sure wasn't going to be the one to rain on this girl's parade.

Stal's building was pretty much a cast foamstone box, two stories tall, with no holes in the roof except for power lines to the roof-mounted solar skins, ventilator, and a couple clusters of video units which fed the smart walls when they were in window mode. Roof access was by way of a metal stairway bolted to the outside of the building. We clanged up and then had a pretty good panoramic view of the north side of Sakkatto City and the Sookagrad district. Divya began pointing out the landmarks.

"That's e-Kruaan-Arc to the north and see, there's Katammu-Arc almost directly south but farther away. Mmmm, two kilometers, maybe more."

They seemed much closer, but that was because of their enormous size. Katammu-Arc was three kilometers broad at the base and about two kilometers tall. When something is as tall as it is away from you, you feel as if you're in its shadow. E-Kruaan-Arc was closer and taller, I'd say maybe three kilometers high, and it looked even taller because it was so slender by comparison, less than a kilometer at its base and then tapering as it rose.

"You see the broad east-west road between us and e-Kruaan? That's the Avenue of Peace. It is an official thoroughfare, one of the boundary boulevards of the old park district, and the Munies always made sure it was kept clean—no structures and no trash. They would plow the shacks and buildings away once a month, my father told me, although I don't remember anyone trying to live there. That's the northern boundary of Sookagrad.

"You see the other thoroughfares? The broad one cutting straight from e-Kruaan to Katammu, right under the maglev tracks, is The Shadowed Way North. It cuts almost through the center of north Sookagrad. The southern boundary of the district is Grand Vision Way, running almost east-west between Bannaz Arcology and Arc-Jannu. Father says there used to be a maglev line running there before e-Kruaan was built, but that was almost one hundred years ago, before Humans lived here."

She sketched out the less-well-defined eastern and western perimeters, pointed out the important buildings such as they were: the broad metal dormitory, the white clinic building which had acquired two large metal shipping containers attached by composite sheeting walkways as overflow trauma care, the Citizen League headquarters building which now flew a Municipal Police flag provided by Captain Prayzaat. All of those buildings huddled almost in the shadow of the maglev tracks and were close to the Shadowed Way.

The smaller streets wound seemingly randomly, having more to do with where large cargo containers had been abandoned than anything else. Most were little more than pedestrian alleys, but two larger streets, wide enough for vehicles, came into the district from the west and one from the east, in addition to the Shadowed Way which bisected the district north-south.

Divya's act of giving the alleys and buildings names and functions almost elevated them from the squalid shacks and discarded storage units they were to something substantial, something with utility and, by implication, a future. But that was an illusion. Sookagrad was simply the place where a desperate group of Humans had gathered and tried to survive, and that was before everything really started going to hell.

As she talked, I looked at the mountains of trash, the collapsing hovels built on the broken rubble of the previous generation of dwellings, and I knew Sookagrad was finished, no matter what else happened. The idea of Humans, or any race, living like this in the heart of the Varoki home world was insane, and the times which produced the bizarre chain of circumstances and decisions which brought all this about were coming to an end. What was coming next might be a little better, or it might be much, much worse, but in either case there would be no place for Sookagrad. About the best we could hope for was that it not end up a mass grave.

Divya had just begun naming the lesser streets when a flare burst in the sky to the north, over the maglev tracks, and then three more burst in rapid succession. In the flickering light I saw people moving south in the Shadowed Way, lots of them. We all heard the distinctive sound of small arms fire from the north.

"Divya," I said, "get down the stairs and run back to the kitchen. Hurry!" She scampered back to the stairway and then down.

"Come on, Aurora, let's go. There's no cover up here and there will be stray rounds. Not many of those guys can shoot straight."

More aerial flares exploded over the east and west sides as well and a grenade *crumped* down near the maglev tracks barricade. Aurora began walking around the edge of the building, looking at the unfolding panorama of a massed assault.

"Come on, let's go! I've got to start pushing ammo."

"Just a moment," she said, still walking steadily around the edge of the building, looking at the flickering light of flares and burning shacks, the darting shapes of men seen between blowing columns of smoke. Then a thunderous explosion echoed from the Shadowed Way, accompanied by two rising fireballs. She turned and faced it, holding her head steady the whole time. Then she turned to me and blinked.

"Tell me, Sasha, how do you think the fight is going?" She held her eyes open just a little wider than she had before.

I turned my back on her and headed for my main ammo dump, taking the stairs down the side of the building two at a time.

My sister wanted me to like her. I might have liked her a little more if she'd come clean with me about being fitted with a bio-recorder, but not necessarily. You never know.

By the time I got to the main ammo dump, I could hear small arms fire and grenades from the south, which meant they were hitting us from all four compass points. A second minefield detonation made the ground shake and I saw a fireball rise up to the east, which meant there were two places they'd broken through the perimeter. At least two.

My ten ammo runners and my new ammo assistant, Yash Zaradavana, were waiting for me. The runners were armed for self defense, but only with small caliber gauss pistols, and for the most part pistols spared from frontline service by virtue of their poor performance or unusual ammunition or feed system which made supplying them awkward. The men and women detailed as runners were fit enough to haul ammo, and so to fight, but for one reason or another they hadn't found a place in a combat unit. Most of them were happy with that. My point is, their job was to haul ammo, not fight, and that was just as well.

Zaradavana had them organized and settled down, but as soon as I showed up voices rose again. I held my left hand up to quiet them.

"I saw about five minutes of the fight from a rooftop, but I don't know any more than you do. They're pushing all along the perimeter, from all four directions, which means this is a serious and coordinated effort to plow us under. We can't slack off tonight, or there won't be a tomorrow. Everyone clear on that? Good. That said, no heroes tonight, okay? Just do your jobs. People are counting on you, a lot of lives depend on you doing your job, not getting distracted and going off to fight, no matter how much you want to."

I didn't think many of them actually wanted to, but I said it anyway. We did need them to hump ammo, people's lives did depend on it, and they may as well take some pride in it instead of feeling ashamed they weren't doing something more directly violent.

"Near as I can tell, we're engaged on all main axes, so what's our first priority?"

"Feed the RAGs," about a half dozen said at once.

"Right. First runners, one sack of RAG bandoliers each. Push it to your assigned ammo point, make an assessment of what they'll run short of next, and hustle back here. Move now!"

The five "first runners" took their sacks of RAG ammo and trotted off in five different directions. Once they were gone I turned to the "second runners," who would alternate with the first runners or replace them outright if they had to. "You five, give me a security perimeter about thirty meters out, and keep your eyes open. Between the ammo dump and the hospital, this is a key location, and you're just about all there is in terms of firepower."

I could see the fear and excitement in their eyes as they jogged off to take up guard stations with a somber sense of purpose. I didn't expect a breakthrough, but you never knew. The bigger danger was infiltration. We just didn't have the people to cover every little alleyway and back door, and we could have burned half our perimeter force trying and still not gotten the job done.

The wounded started coming in, some walking under their own power, some carried by two-man stretcher teams provided by Billy Conklin's construction gang, and some carried by friends from their squads, even though Zdravkova had given clear orders not to leave the firing line. I became a one-man retreat-blocking detachment, barking the able-bodied troops back to the line. Some went back sheepishly, some sullenly, but they went back. They weren't cowards—most of them weren't anyway—they were worried about their friends. I understood, but this sort of stuff is how wars are lost.

The First Runners started trickling back, breathless with excitement. They'd seen the fighting, seen wounded coming to the rear, heard the zip of flechettes passing overhead. Some of them wanted to make the return trip but I put them on the perimeter and started the Second Runners forward with whatever the Firsts called for—mostly more RAG ammo.

Then shouting, anger, a small crowd of fighters and some of the construction crew arguing, jostling. I trotted over to sort it out and as I got there I nearly vomited. The four fighters were carrying stretchers with two horribly burned Varoki.

"What the hell's going on here?" I shouted. Everyone started talking at once so I waved them quiet and pointed at one of the construction guys.

"We're supposed to be hauling wounded but these jerks stole our stretchers to carry a couple leatherheads. They—"

I cut him off and pointed at one of the soldiers.

"Yes, took them," she said in the thick local accent. "These men not carry and leatherheads burnt too bad to pick up."

"We need those for Human wounded," the construction guy yelled and the argument restarted until I shouted them quiet again.

"They're here now. Let's get them to trauma receiving and see what the docs can do." I looked at them again as the soldiers lifted the stretchers. Much of their skin was burnt black, carbonized, but where patches of it had sloughed off, the exposed meat was the color of blood. Neither of them had ears anymore. Both of them were having a hard time breathing and one moaned in a way that made my skin crawl. I couldn't imagine them surviving, but maybe the docs could give them something for the pain. I walked alongside the lead stretcher.

"The work gang was right," I told the fighters. "Our wounded—your wounded—have to come first."

"Our wounded already back here," the soldier who spoke before told me with puffing breath as she shuffled toward the clinic. "But many leatherheads still there, burned bad, like this. Mines burn them. Platoon leader tell us help them. Those are orders. Work crew not carry them, want to kill them." She spat on the ground.

I didn't have anything to say about that. "How'd the fight go?" I asked instead.

"Stopped assault, drove leatherheads back all way across Avenue of Peace, still running when we stop. Perimeter secure."

We got to trauma receiving and they put the stretchers down by the door. The triage specialist looked at them and shook his head.

"Damn! I don't know...what are we going to do with them?"

"Something for the pain?" I said.

He shook his head, but more in confusion than denial. "I don't know if we've got any Varoki-specific drugs. I mean, yeah, probably somewhere, but—"

"What's the delay here?" I recognized Doc Mahajan's voice and saw her make her way to us. "Oh my God!" she said when she saw the two Varoki.

"Yeah," I said. "And this soldier says there are a lot more just like them, and that's just the north barricade. The mines worked—better than we figured."

"Basil, get them to Krautmann's recovery area," she ordered the triage specialist. "He's worked with Varoki. Have him start them on a saline drip while I see what we've got for pain meds and antibiotics." She looked at them again and shook her head. "Move!"

I walked back to the sullen knot of construction workers.

"Look, nobody expected this," I said, "but we should have. We knew we were going to generate some Varoki casualties and we should have thought through what that meant."

"What's to think about?" one of them asked.

"Shut up, Andy," another muttered.

"Good advice," I said. "There's still fighting at three or four of the barricades. Why don't you link up with one of the other teams, see what you can do to help?"

"We'll need our stretchers," the first guy said.

I turned to look at him.

"Listen, *Andy*, let's get a couple things straight. Those aren't your stretchers, they're my stretchers, and you work for Logistics, which is me, which means you do what I tell you. Right now I'm telling you to get your asses to the south Shadowed Way strongpoint and make yourselves useful."

I took a long breath, tried to get the anger out of my voice.

"Look, all of you. You did a good job getting the mines set up, reinforcing the perimeter strongpoints, and then right away this attack comes. You gotta be tired, but you're doing a great job evacuating casualties anyway. Fight's not over, though, so let's just do our jobs and no drama, okay? The Varoki are giving us plenty of that. Now go, and be careful."

They went, but none of them looked very happy about the whole thing. I wasn't sure how much of that was the fear and fatigue talking and how much of it was a real problem going forward. I liked to think of outfits I ran as one big happy family working together harmoniously toward a shared common goal, and for some reason I was always surprised when it never seemed to work out that way. Despite the evidence of my entire life, I still had this stupid notion that the default setting for everything was "ticking along fine," as opposed to "careening out of control toward disaster." I honestly have no idea why. It had to be some sort of hardwired genetic thing; it couldn't have been a learned behavior.

I turned and scanned the sky above the perimeter. The north should have gone dark again, as there were no flares left, but it glowed and flickered with the residue of fires from the minefield explosion. Most of the aerial flares to the east and west had drifted down to the ground or burned out, although there was a ground fire still going out to the northwest where the second minefield had gone off. Another flare went up to the east, but just one. I heard small arms fire from there but no more grenade explosions. I hadn't seen a mine detonation there either.

Thank God.

"Hey!" I heard someone yell and recognized her as one of my Second Runners, now sprinting flat out down the street toward the ammo depot. "They're breaking through on the east side!"

Chapter Twenty-Seven

An hour later the fighting settled down again and we pushed them back across their start lines in every direction, but it had gotten tense for a while. Our kids had done really well. Mostly they'd followed instructions. The platoon leader covering the eastern approaches had a better idea. He pushed his reserve force forward to reinforce the barricade, stop the assault there. Then when some Varoki infiltrated around him, overran his ammo position and cut him off, he panicked and tried to surrender.

Fortunately for almost everyone involved, the Varoki shot him when he tried to parlay with them. His platoon sergeant stepped up and took over and the platoon kept fighting. When my ammo runner let us know something bad was going on, I got word to Zdravkova and she sent her reserve strikers to sort things out, which they did. In the meantime my ammo runners and I had some anxious moments, but they ended up not having to fire a shot in anger.

It should have calmed down then, but it got worse in a totally unexpected way. The fires our mines started up north and to the northwest got out of control. There was just too much flammable stuff lying around everywhere, including the very trash we'd use to camouflage the minefields. Lean-tos and plastic sheet tents caught and went up, along with clothing, paper, anything in the dwellings that would burn. The only thing working in our favor was the fact that everything was pretty wet from a couple days of rain, but once the fire got into some enclosed and flammable buildings, it got bigger and hotter, and it started drying out the trash around it, adding it as fuel.

The wind was blowing from the west and a bit from the north, so the fire started spreading across the northern half of Sooka-grad, and creeping a bit south toward the clinic and other central buildings. The only water we had to fight it with was our drinking water, and once it was gone, we'd be pretty much finished.

I had Moshe start hooking up a large capacity pump we had to some hoses, although we didn't have very many of them. Meanwhile I got Billy Conklin to start digging down over the trace of a storm sewer, and had Dhaliwa, his explosives guy, go recover one of the unexploded Bangalore torpedoes. My plan was to use it to blow a shaft down to a storm sewer, drop our intake hose down into the flood water, and pump it up to fight the fire.

As it happens, the fire got taken care of for us before we had time to plant and blow the charge. Two big ducted-fan Municipal Fire Service aerial tankers flew over and dropped a couple thousand liters of flame retardant on the fire and then banked away. Later one of our perimeter fighters came in—drenched in flame retardant—and gave us a message she'd seen dropped from the lead tanker. It read:

> Good luck Municipal Police Deputies.
> (signed) Tanker Company Five, Municipal Fire Service.

So somebody out there knew about our broadcast. I wasn't sure how someone in Sakkatto knew, but it meant the soundproof blanket the Army had cast over the city was not one hundred per cent effective.

I wasn't sure what to do about the message. Part of me wanted everyone to know right away, let them know we weren't alone, that at least one Varoki fire service tanker company was pulling for us. On the other hand, that sounded like a good way to get those Varoki in trouble, maybe even killed, if word got out.

The aftermath of the attack...well, we really didn't see all these Varoki casualties coming and we had to do something about them. When Zdravkova tried to parlay at the north barricade a sniper came within a few centimeters of taking her head off. With no way to communicate directly with them, it came down to an emergency broadcast, which was my sister's department. An hour after the fires were put out, she was recording in front of a burned-out, still-smoking building.

"This is Sookagrad calling with an emergency appeal. Before dawn this morning the Municipal Police fought back a concerted attack from the surrounding CEM forces and inflicted heavy casualties on the rebels. However, a large number of critically wounded Varoki have fallen into the hands of the Municipal Police, many of them close to death.

"I am talking to Dr. Boris Petrov. Can you tell us the situation with the Varoki wounded?"

The vid recorder turned to include Petrov in the picture. With wild hair and a dirty white lab coat smeared with dried blood, he looked like something out of a horror vid. In a way he was.

"We have done what we can to stabilize them, but some of them are very badly burned. Our supplies of Varoki-specific antibiotics and pain medication are all but exhausted."

"Won't the CEM provide the supplies you need?" Aurora said. "Surely they understand that Varoki-specific drugs cannot help the Human defenders of Sookagrad."

"We cannot contact them," Petrov said. "Every attempt to parlay has been met with gunfire before we could explain the problem. And medicine isn't enough. Some of these people will die without specialized treatment."

"Thank you, Dr. Petrov. I also have the director of the Sookagrad Citizens' League, Mr. Bogomil Katranjiev, to explain the overall situation." She took a couple steps to her right and the recorder followed her until she stood next to Bogo. "Director Katranjiev, where do the negotiations stand?"

"There are no negotiations," he said with a scowl. "The CEM will not speak directly with us, and with the Army jamming all wireless bands, we cannot communicate with the Provisional Government." He turned to address the recorder directly. "If anyone listening to this bulletin can influence the Provisional Government at all, tell them we have forty-one wounded Varoki, fifteen of them in critical condition. We will post a medical truce flag at the northern entrance to the district. When the CEM posts a similar one, we will transport the wounded across the Avenue of Peace."

"How can you be sure the CEM will not seize or kill the stretcher carriers?" Aurora asked.

"We have enough captured uninjured militia personnel to carry the stretchers, more than enough. We will release them all, subject to their parole not to return to the fight against us. Hopefully the CEM won't fire on their own people, once they know what the situation is here."

Aurora turned back to the recorder. "Amidst the relief of having fought off a major assault by the CEM and having suffered only minor casualties themselves, the defenders of Sookagrad find themselves in the middle of a medical crisis. I toured the trauma ward where the Varoki injured are being cared for and the condition of the seriously wounded, particularly the burn victims, is heartrending. This goes beyond politics and species. Anyone hearing this bulletin, contact the Provisional Government, pass along our appeal, please. This is Sookagrad, calling, and signing off."

She paused a couple seconds then nodded.

"Okay," her vid tech said, "I'll edit in the footage we shot of the trauma ward with your last pitch as a voiceover."

"Ted, let's just get it on the pipe right away," Aurora said. "I don't...their ward is as good as the Human wards, but it still looks like something out of Dante, and those burns! We'll stick with the humanitarian appeal and keep it simple, nothing artsy."

The recorder shook his head. "You're wrong on this."

"Then I'm wrong," she said. "It won't be the first time. Send it out."

"I agree with Aurora," Katranjiev said. "Send it."

I looked at him. Katranjiev agreeing with Aurora? Was he mellowing? Or had he decided she and I weren't exactly pals and so it might be okay to back her up?

Ted shrugged and pulled the data tab from the recorder, then headed for the maintenance access shaft where our illegal transmitter was spliced into the underground fiber network.

I saw Stal and Zdravkova so the whole troika was here for the postbattle executive meeting. They were the executives; I just had to make the report on logistics. Zdravkova looked tired but alert. Stal looked reserved, remote. I wondered where he'd been during the fight. Katranjiev seemed upbeat, maybe from having been in the vid. We walked toward the guarded studio building, the one where Captain Prayzaat now lived, virtually a prisoner of the fiction we had created.

Chapter Twenty-Eight

"So what happened with those mines?" Katranjiev asked as soon as we settled into chairs around Prayzaat's desk.

"It's kind of a long story," I said. "You sure this is what you want to go into first?"

"Don't patronize me, Naradnyo. Just answer the question."

"I would be interested in an explanation as well," Captain Prayzaat said.

I glanced at the others. Stal looked vaguely interested, but also sort of involved in his own thoughts. Zdravkova just looked beat.

"Okay, this stuff we made, PLX? The aGavoosh word for it is *kanaakt'antay*; its main ingredient is what we call nitromethane."

"Yes, I am familiar," Prayzaat said.

I reached in my pocket and pulled out the scrap of paper I'd had Moshe write for me. "Nitromethane's chemical formula is C-H-3-N-O-2. That O-2 at the end means it contains its own oxygen, so you can use it as an explosive in an enclosed space, like a pipe bomb. Gasoline you put in an enclosed pipe with no oxygen, it won't even burn, okay? The thing is, and this is what we didn't count on, that O-2 is only about half enough oxygen to combust all the other stuff in it. So you set it off and half the stuff detonates, which is enough to blow open the pipe and throw fragments all over, but also blow out the unburned part of the fuel."

"Which burn soon as get oxygen," Stal said.

I nodded.

"Crispy critters," Katranjiev said and made a grim smile, and then frowned and colored when he saw Prayzaat's look. I guessed he hadn't visited the clinic, hadn't seen what those poor bastards looked like, but that wasn't really much of an excuse.

"How are the burn injuries?" Prayzaat said.

"Horrible. Doc Mahajan is trying to cope, best as she can, but they need a good Varoki medical team."

Prayzaat nodded and looked away.

"We haven't heard from the CEM yet," I said. "I'm not sure what else we can do until they move."

"Of course," Prayzaat said. "I want to thank you for the appeal which went out so promptly. Hopefully they will respond soon. How many casualties did our forces suffer?"

"We took twelve dead and thirty-two wounded in the fight, and six more burned trying to fight the fire. Nine of the wounded and one burn case are pretty serious. Doc Mahajan says we might lose two of them, and the other eight are out of the fight for the duration. The more lightly wounded will be okay. I think five or six already rejoined their units."

"That's not bad," Katranjiev said. Zdravkova's head came up quickly.

"That's fifty killed, wounded or injured out of three hundred people deployed," she said. "Sixteen per cent losses, perhaps ten or twelve per cent once we got back the lightly wounded, and this was the first serious attack. A few more days like this and we'll be too thin to cover the perimeter."

"I thought your shortage was weapons, not willing fighters," Katranjiev answered. "Can't you use the weapons of the casualties to arm their replacements?"

Zdravkova shot him a hard look but then shrugged. "Willing, yes. Trained and experienced, not so much. We already armed our best prospects, and I lost four squad leaders and a platoon leader—not easy to replace. But yes, you're right, the numeric losses we took have not crippled us. We should be able to improve our firepower on the line with some of the captured weapons. The CEM had a fair number of Army-issue RAGs, and left a lot of them behind." She turned to me. "How many, Naradnyo?"

"Still counting, and we have to make operability assessments since some of them got cooked in the fires pretty good, or just banged around. I've got Greenwald working on it, even though it's not exactly his bailiwick, and we're looking for some qualified armorers. I'm thinking we need an ordnance repair department, but I'll work that out. Ballpark estimate for now, we'll end up with about a hundred more operational RAGs and at least as many civilian rifles."

"*Really?* That many?" she said, and she sat up straighter, energy coming back into her eyes. "Why, I can put three or four more RAGs in every squad! Convert the Strikers to an all-RAG outfit, get rid of all the pistols in the front-line units. If we had the leaders to handle it, and someone to train them, we could raise two more platoons all with long guns. I didn't realize they left so much materiel when they ran."

"Well, they left a lot of bodies, too," I said, and glanced at Prayzaat, "so they didn't exactly all run. I've got some work details out there collecting the corpses for burial or disposal. That may turn into a permanent department, too."

I remembered the line of Varoki bodies I'd already seen, some of them horribly burned, some looking untouched, as if they were just sleeping. I'd seen dead people before, but seeing rows of them all at once is a different matter. Last time I'd seen something like that was over two years ago, on K'Tok. I looked up and saw everyone waiting for me to go on.

"Looks like we've got about a hundred dead Gaantist militia fighters. I'm not sure what to do with them, and they're going to start to decay if we don't burn them or get them underground soon."

"How many prisoners?" Prayzaat asked.

"Forty wounded, since one of them died an hour ago, and thirty-seven uninjured. Our people saw a lot of wounded withdrawing as well. Killer, your kids took a hell of a bite out of them. If I were running that show over there, I'd be wondering how I was ever going to get those guys to make an attack like that again."

"They are fanatics," Katranjiev said. "Do you think losses really matter to them?"

Prayzaat looked at him with an expression of contempt. I hardly knew how to answer that myself. I didn't want to get into an argument right now, but misreading the enemy that stupidly could get a lot of people killed.

"It's easier to be a fanatic when people aren't dying all around you," I said. "You want the rest of the logistics report or not?"

All three Humans nodded. Prayzaat seemed lost in his own thoughts.

"Okay, ammo. Our troops on the line blew through about thirty-five thousand flechettes."

"Thirty-five *thousand*?" Katranjiev exclaimed. "And they only killed a hundred of the bastards? That's insane!"

Zdravkova leaned forward and opened her mouth to fire back but I held my left hand up to stop her.

"Katranjiev, if you keep interrupting with editorial comments, this report is going to take all day. And between the dead, the wounded we recovered, and our estimates of wounded who returned to their own lines or were carried away, I'd estimate over three hundred hostile casualties. That's about one casualty for every hundred flechettes fired. Given the level of training and experience of our people, that is insanely *good* shooting. Killer, you tell your kids I said so."

"I will," she said. "Thanks."

Privately, I figured the high casualty rate was more due to stupid militia tactics than to excellent Human shooting, but better to let our folks feel good about what they did. From what I'd heard from the fighters I talked to, the Varoki just charged, firing their weapons as they came, and then bunched up in the streets once they encountered resistance. Hard not to hit something when your target is a big milling mass of bodies.

"So, back to the hard numbers. We had a total magazine capacity for all our weapons of about sixty thousand flechettes, when every magazine we own is loaded and charged. That means we burned through over half of our ready ammunition in about an hour, maybe a little less. We've got a bunch more flechettes fabricated but it takes time to recover the magazines, reload them, and then recharge them.

"We also suffered some attrition in our magazine supply. We still could use some improvement in how conscientious the troops are about recovering and taking care of their spent mags, but some attrition is inevitable. Here's why that's important. Once we distribute the captured arms, we're going to about triple the number of RAGs we have, but those guys must be having magazine problems too. Most of their fighters only had a magazine or two on them, so I'm guessing we're going to add at most fifteen thousand flechettes to our RAG magazine capacity and less than that to the civilian weapons."

"Get to the point, Naradnyo," Katranjiev said, but Zdravkova frowned.

"I see where you're going, Sasha," she said. "If we ran through over half of our ready ammunition before, if we triple the number of RAGs but only increase the magazine capacity by a half...I'm too punchy to do the math."

"Okay, here it is in simple terms," I said. "We had about fifty RAGs with a total of about three hundred magazines, or six magazines per system, and we burned through over three per system. We add a hundred RAGs to the mix and about a hundred fifty more magazines, and we end up with only three magazines per system instead of six. If each one blows through the ammunition just as fast next time, we're bone dry after about three quarters of an hour."

We sat there in silence for a couple seconds, each of us thinking that over.

"But you said they had a similar problem," Katranjiev finally said.

"They seem to, at least for now, but the Army could solve it for them in pretty short order if they decided to. Now don't get me wrong. A hundred more RAGs is *great* news, not bad. It just doesn't put us on Easy Street, that's all.

"I think ammo is our biggest and most pressing issue for now, so I did that first. Here's an overview on where we stand on the other things.

"Rations. The protein's going to get even more boring before long, but we've got two buildings full of hydroponic tanks and grow racks giving us a good veggie yield, and we haven't had as much of a refugee influx as we figured, probably because of how thick the CEM positions are around us. I'm a little concerned one of our hydroponic buildings is so close to the east perimeter, and we're scouting a site closer to the headquarters cluster. But we've got food to last probably four weeks and can stretch it to six if we have to. After that we're in trouble, but I doubt this mess is going to go on that long."

"What," Katranjiev said, "you still think your precious *Cottohazz* is going to—"

"Shut up and let me finish," I said, cutting him off. He opened his mouth to answer but then glanced at the others and thought better of it. He leaned back and frowned—sulked was more like it.

"We have a big potential fire problem, as I'm sure everyone noticed. I don't think we can count on Municipal Fire and Rescue to save us next time, so we're sinking some shafts down to the storm sewers and will pump waste water up to fight the next fires. We're going to test the water as well. If it's not too bad we may be able to process it to potability, supplement our own supply, and even if it's not quite drinkable we may be able to arrange some showers."

"That would be wonderful," Zdravkova said.

"Yes," Katranjiev said, "it's starting to smell so bad in the headquarters building I can hardly stand going in."

I wondered what he did there. For that matter, what did Stal do all day? I knew what Zdravkova and I did. Something to think about later.

"Power," I said. "We need some sunlight. If we get it, and today looks pretty good in that respect so far, we'll at least keep our heads above water. We've been supplementing the LENR generators with some juice still left in auto and truck battery packs, which is a dwindling supply and not a very efficient use of Greenwald's crew's time, but we really need the wattage, especially with all those magazines to charge right now and the autodocs going full tilt.

"Med looks okay, aside from all those Varoki. We have a couple autodocs which might pack it in, but we're okay on the rest and have a good supply of key trauma drugs. Only thing we can't fabricate is nanites, so that's forcing med to rely on more invasive treatments. The autodocs have the programming they need to do it. We could use another couple surgical techs, but we're squeaking by.

"Facilities and Infrastructure: next big priority is getting some below-ground shelters for our people. We still have some technical issues to iron out, but I want to get going on the initial excavations this afternoon, and we'll work the rest out as we go. We'll be using some of the PLX for that, so I want to have the fire fighting contingency in place first.

"By the way, some of my infrastructure guys working as litter bearers got in a dispute with a couple fighters from the north strongpoint."

"I heard about that," Zdravkova said.

"Yeah, well my guys were in the wrong and yours were right, so extend my apologies."

Her eyebrows ticked up a little in surprise, but she nodded.

The buzzer on Prayzaat's desk sounded.

"Yes?" he said.

"A runner just came for commander Zdravkova," the Varoki patrolman serving as door guard said through the speaker. "He says the militia members are displaying a medical truce panel on the north side of the Avenue of Peace."

Zdravkova grinned and picked up her RAG from beside her chair. "You know what that means? It means our bulletins are getting out there and somebody is not just listening; they're acting."

Prayzaat looked at me.

"What else do you have, Mr. Naradnyo?" he said.

"End of report."

⑉⑉⑉⑉⑉⑉⑉⑉⑉⑉⑉⑉⑉⑉⑉⑉⑉⑉⑉⑉⑉⑉⑉⑉⑉ Chapter Twenty-Nine

"Fire in the hole! Fire in the hole!"

Billy Conklin took one last look around to make sure everyone was clear and then closed the circuit on the detonator. I felt the explosion in the ground under me as much as heard it, saw the force of it blow the narrow shaft Conklin's crew had dug wider, throw earth and pieces of rubble high in the air and then rain it down on the surrounding street and buildings—rain a little farther than we'd anticipated. At least there was no fireball this time. We'd figured out that the best way to use the stuff was to just pour it into the hole and make sure it had lots of air to breathe.

After the chunks had all hit ground but as the dust cloud still drifted over the crater, a dozen of us trotted forward to look at the results of our handiwork.

"Who's got a hand torch?" I said. I couldn't see down the hole but I could hear running water. Someone produced a torch and shined it down the hole, which was now a couple meters across. It took a few seconds for the dust to settle enough to see, but then we made out the surface of flowing water in the storm sewer, sparkling in the light of the overhead noon sun. The work gang cheered and I smiled.

"Nice job, guys," I said. "Drinks are on me, next bar we find."

"Kalabratov, let's get that pump set up," Conklin called to one of the workers, the one I remembered as the loudmouth from the stretcher detail the night before.

"Billy, you might want to let the water flow carry away as much of the dirt and small rubble as you can before you actually start pumping," I said. "We knocked a lot of shit down into there."

"Sure," he said. "don't want to burn out our pump motor. Might have to pry Greenwald off that Bulgarian heifer to get it fixed."

I let it pass. No law against talking behind people's backs, especially since Zdravkova was a member of the Executive Troika. Came with the territory, even if the talk wasn't true, and I didn't figure it was. Most of us were too busy to find the time or surplus energy for the horizontal bop lately.

But I had a feeling the crack was aimed at me, not them, Conklin thinking he'd find a nerve in me and jab it. I didn't like that, which was all the more reason to let it pass. When I didn't say anything for a while, Conklin stole a look at me out of the corner of his eye and crossed his arms.

"You know, Kalabratov's a hell of a metalworker. Kind of a waste having him on work details up close to the fighting."

"He scared?" I said.

"Hell, no! He's a veteran himself, did a hitch with the Bulgarian Brigade in the WEU Army back before he emigrated."

I wasn't aware that the Bulgarian Brigade, or any of the Westeuro military, had seen a lot of heavy action in the last decade or so, but I kept that to myself as well.

"He's tough enough," Billy continued. "I just meant, what if he gets shot? Skilled worker and all."

"Bending metal is more important than saving lives?" I asked.

"Hey, that's not what I said. My guys don't mind humping stretchers for our own kind, but they aren't going to risk their necks for some leatherheads already trying to kill us."

"If this Kalabratov guy of yours ever saw any real action with the regulars, he knows all wounded get taken care of, no matter which side they're on."

"Oh, we'll take care of them," Billy said, and he nodded a couple times for emphasis. "This is war, Naradnyo, not some rumble between two rival gangs. You fight a war to win, and you don't get any points for playing by the rules. You ask most of my guys, they'd say line those prisoners up and kill every fuckin' one of them. Show those bastards who's got more sand in their guts."

His voice had risen while he said all that and I heard muttered agreements from the three men standing nearest us. I looked at them, didn't recognize any of them, but saw Kalabratov put down the portable pump and walk over to the group. A few other men and women from the construction team standing around the crater were listening, watching what would happen, but not part of anything one way or another. So here was my first mini-mutiny.

"This isn't the regular army," I said, "where any NCO worth his stripes would just tell you to shut up and get back to work, and he'd kick your ass from here to Sunday if you didn't."

"Even with one arm in a sling?" one of the men said with a sneer.

"Yup," I answered and looked him in the eye. His expression got hard for a moment, then he blinked and looked away.

"But like I said, this isn't the regular army. It's a real army, just sort of unconventional. So I'll explain why we do what we do, but understand up front, we're not going to have a debate here. You want to know why, and I'll tell you, and then you can agree or not. But all our survival depends on everyone working together, so like it or not, you *will* do what we tell you to, or you'll stop breathing.

"Anybody not understand that?"

I looked around the small circle of faces. They didn't look happy, but I don't think they knew quite what to say.

"Okay, here's the deal. There are over six million Varoki living in Sakkatto City. The Army has moved units into the city as well. We don't know how many soldiers, but several thousand at least. We have about three hundred fighters here with no artillery, heavy support weapons, or armored vehicles. If the Army commits its mech infantry, those guys will at least have ballistic body armor and will be backed up by light armored vehicles and maybe some gunsleds." I plucked at one of their shirts. "That's about as good a body armor as any of us have.

"In other words, we cannot win a protracted stand-up fight. Do you understand that? We. Can. Not. The only hope we have of survival is convincing people outside Sakkatto that not only do we *need* rescuing, but we *deserve* it.

"Execute a bunch of Varoki who have surrendered to us, you not only convince the ones still alive to fight harder, you convince everyone out there that we're just a bunch of bloodthirsty thugs, and if we all get killed, good riddance.

"Conklin here says you fight a war to win. Of course you do. But you don't fight it to win bragging rights, show how tough you are. You fight it to win a good peace for your people, and if that means saving wounded Varoki soldiers, then by God you will hump your asses and risk your lives to do so.

"And that is the *end* of the discussion. Now I think enough of the dirt we dumped into the storm sewer has washed away, so let's drop that hose down there and see how the pump works. Then we can start blowing holes in the ground for shelters."

For the next two days there were no more massed assaults. I guess we cured them of that. We did start getting sniping against our perimeter posts, and we took some casualties before our people got serious about staying under cover. That damned Army recon hoverplat kept hanging around e-Kruaan-Arc, making those slow ovals and looking us over, but there wasn't much we could do about that.

Aurora kept sending out daily bulletins, mostly interviews with folks in the district, trying to put as unique and individual a face on the Humans as possible. She was good at her job, I gave her that. I wasn't sure what the other part of her agenda was, the one which involved a bio-recorder, but my money was on an exclusive long-form feed special when this was all over, assuming we survived. I didn't see anything of my father for a while after that first meeting. I was okay with that.

I still felt as if Billy Conklin and his construction crew were a source of simmering dissatisfaction, but you have to put up with a certain amount of bitching when you're in charge of something. Katranjiev even noticed the bad looks Conklin and Kalabratov gave me behind my back and told me, which surprised me, seeing as how I wasn't exactly his number one boy. Maybe he just wanted to lecture me about his management style, which was to come down hard on anyone who's attitude "wasn't right." I thanked him and went about my business.

Katranjiev seemed to think people's attitude was really important and maybe he was right but I didn't think so. I want people to do their jobs. If they have a shitty attitude about me but do a good job, I can live with that. Besides, if you keep people busy and they do good work, sooner or later their attitude usually comes around.

I sure kept Conklin and his crew busy, mostly digging shelters. He got a laser torch working and used it to cut up a couple metal cargo containers, used the steel and composite components as the braces for the overhead cover, shored them up with lengths of scavenged steel pipe about fifteen centimeters in diameter, and even got some lights and ventilation blowers installed. The "Big Attack," which is what we called it for lack of a better term, had come in during the predawn hours of the fifth day after the coup, Seventeen of Eight-Month Waning. By nightfall on Nineteen of Eight-Month Waning, Conklin had enough shelters to hold five hundred people, with more under construction. If we were lucky, all that effort would end up wasted. I didn't think we were that lucky, though.

Sookagrad mostly shut down at night those days, since electricity was in short supply and not much got diverted to lighting except at the clinic and other work areas. Most folks not working stayed indoors and turned in early, so I didn't see much foot traffic on my way from the building site back to the metal storage unit we'd rigged up as my office and headquarters—another job executed quickly and efficiently by Conklin and his crew. Maybe his plan for getting even with me was to never give me something to complain about.

I had some things to think about on my walk. I'd talked to Doc Mahajan about my postdeath experience two years ago and how it had included contact with dead people, two of whom it turned out weren't really dead. She didn't say anything at first but then told me about the physiology of near-death experiences: oxygen starvation of the brain producing random firing in the optic nerves—the sensation of light and increasing movement along a narrowing tunnel as the peripheral nerves shut down, then a big shot of endorphins to send you on your way happy, along with a lot of other brain chemicals that produce hallucinations and false memories.

"So you're saying it's all bunk?" I asked.

"No," she answered, "I am simply telling you what we know happens, chemically, inside the brain near the final moments of life. I have no insights to offer regarding transcendental truth."

No, she didn't, but I did. In my postdeath world there had been dead people I now knew weren't really dead. Hard taking that as anything but a hallucination.

Low clouds killed any moonlight but numerous fires burned

in the Inter-Arcology Park District—not within a kilometer of
us but the glow from the fires reflected faintly from the cloud
cover and provided enough ambient light for me to find my
way through the twisting, cluttered alleys. Ahead of me I saw
someone talking, I guess to the people in a lean-to. I crossed to
the other side of the alley, such as it was, so as not in intrude
on their conversation, but one of them called out softly to me.

"Excuse me, but could you help us? We're looking for someone."

"Sure," I said, and joined them. I saw the lean-to was empty so
they must have been just talking among themselves. There were
four of them and the guy who called me over had a Standard
accent, so he was educated.

"Who are you looking for?" I asked.

They exchanged a brief glance and one of them turned away,
watching down the alleyway, and another did the same in the
opposite direction, almost as if it was standard drill, and I felt
my heart speed up, blood flow to my face. I took a slow breath
to steady myself. Whoever these guys were, I didn't want to let
them know I was on to them, not that I was really on to anything about them except they weren't quite right.

"We are looking for Dr. Naradnyo. He is here, isn't he?"

Doctor Naradnyo? They were looking for my father, not me.
"Is he looking for you?" I asked.

"We have a message for him," a second guy said, also in a
flawless Standard accent English, "from his brother."

"Wow!" I said. "You guys walked through the Militia lines?
You got more guts than me, that's for sure. Well, let's see if we
can find your friend for you. He'll probably be happy to hear
his brother's okay. I know where to ask. Come on."

Brother, huh? Well, unless I also had an uncle I'd never heard
of, that was bullshit. I didn't know what these guys were up to,
but I had the feeling I wouldn't like it if I knew. Otherwise why
the lies and secrecy? I also wondered if my father would like
seeing them.

The four of them fell in behind me, one to my right, one
behind and to the left, and the other two farther back, all but
disappearing into the shadows. I didn't have a lot to go on so
far, but something in my gut told me they were professionals.
Professionals for whom, though?

I walked them toward the clinic and the main ammo station.

Just as we emerged into the more open and better-lit logistics hub, I felt the barrel of a gauss pistol in my ribs.

"We don't want to hurt anyone, but don't try anything funny or we will kill you."

Zaradavana, the guy I'd made my ammo distribution chief, was sorting magazines under a tarp stretched over his work station. He looked up as I got to him.

"Hello, Sasha, what is up?"

"Have you seen Mr. Greenwald?" I asked.

"Yes, in clinic. You want I get?"

"If you don't mind," I said. Zaradavana showed no interest in the four men accompanying me, which was just as well, and now he trotted over to the clinic entrance and disappeared.

"Very good," the man to my right, who I pegged as the leader, said softly. "We only need to talk to Dr. Naradnyo, then we will go. No one will be hurt, I promise you."

Yeah, and since I know you so well, I'm sure that's a promise I can take to the bank.

Moshe emerged after a few minutes, looked around, and then walked over to join us. Before he could say anything I called out to him. "Good evening, Mr. Greenwald. I hope you and your wife are well."

I was taking a huge chance with that but I didn't see any alternative. I had no idea how smart Moshe was when it came to stuff like this, but I hoped the odd greeting, especially including his ex-wife who lived about a hundred light years from here, would let him know something was up. He didn't disappoint. His eyes flickered for a moment but he didn't break his stride.

"Anya is still sick, all this rain. I should get back to her. What do you want?"

"These men are looking for a friend. I thought you might know where he is staying." I turned to the man on my right. "What did you say his name was?"

"Dr. Sergei Naradnyo," he said.

"Yes, that's it," I said nodding. "I don't know him, but I thought to myself, Mr. Greenwald knows everyone. So I brought them here."

Moshe inhaled and puffed his cheeks out, brow furrowed in thought. "Naradnyo, Naradnyo. It sounds familiar. Where was he? Ah, I know. He's at the Blue Bird House. The main street is closed, though. They are laying a new minefield tonight. Go up

Throat-cutter's Way to the first turnoff on the left past the flop where the Kranski brothers live, you know the one? Then follow that alley until you get to where we used to have the northwest ammo resupply point, before we moved it. Take the left there, and you know what the Blue Bird House looks like."

"Thank you, Mr. Greenwald. Please give my regards to your wife and my hope for a speedy recovery."

"Yeah, yeah," he said, waving me away and heading back toward the clinic.

I led along Throat-cutter's Way, which really was the name of the street which wound past the clinic. Once we left the light of the logistics hub we kept going a dozen paces and then the leader stopped me. He turned and made a hand gesture to one of the men who nodded and slipped silently back to watch the clinic from the shadows. I felt the gauss pistol in my ribs again.

"We'll see if your friend keeps visiting his wife or comes out to run an errand in a few minutes," the one in charge said. "You better hope he stays inside."

Chapter Thirty

I sweated for ten minutes or so, waiting to see if Moshe would hurry out the front door of the clinic, but he didn't and the leader finally nodded to me to lead on. That was another thing I had Moshe to thank for: he had not only played the part well, he had given directions I could follow but which would mean nothing to the others, so they couldn't dispose of me until we got there. Moshe was definitely smarter than he looked.

"Now, let's see," I said, slowing the pace and looking over the shacks and lean-tos filling the long stretch between the foamstone grocery warehouse and the first of the metal buildings that made up the dormitories. "The Kranskis were flopping somewhere in here. Some of these flops have changed."

I made a production of examining a couple of the lean-tos, walking slowly, ostensibly so as not to wake anyone up inside, but I didn't want to stretch it out too much or they'd get suspicious.

"Okay," I whispered, "through here."

We made our way carefully through the piled up refuse that covered the ground between a fairly substantial lean-to on one side and the desolate-looking shredded remnants of an abandoned tent smelling of urine on the other. Once we got clear of that I felt the gauss pistol in my ribs again.

"Hurry it up," he said.

"Sure, sure. We'd be there by now if you weren't so suspicious."

I walked faster down the alleyway, which broadened to perhaps three meters wide for a stretch running straight between two metal container buildings, but then narrowing and starting to meander again after that. I deliberately walked past the turnoff but then stopped twenty meters farther down the alley as it constricted to not much more than a footpath.

"What is it?" the leader whispered.

"This ain't right. We missed the turn."

"If you are trying to stall us—"

"No, no! It's just that everything looks so different at night. It's got to be right back there."

We reversed course and I "found" the turnoff and led them down the alleyway which would take us to the Blue Bird House, a large faded blue cargo container with an AZ Simki-Traak logo on it, stacked on top of a smaller one, so it overhung it in both directions. After twenty meters I could see it ahead, looming over the surrounding shacks, but they didn't know and so I made a production of looking at buildings as we passed, "getting my bearings."

"Multiple thermals up ahead," one of the men said to the leader. The leader squinted and looked, probably kicking in his own thermals. The others scanned the buildings to either side. None of them were wearing goggles or viewers of any type. If these guys had surgically implanted thermal vision enhancement, they were very serious people—not that I hadn't already figured that out.

"Individual signatures to the right, no movement. Probably sleeping," one of them said.

"Same to the left," another said.

"There are a lot of people up in that large building, some moving. What's that?" the leader asked me.

"It's a dormitory. The Blue Bird House is just past it," I said.

Actually, it *was* the Blue Bird House, and since that was where Zdravkova parked her reserve force, the Strikers, there was usually some movement even at night. I wish I'd known these creeps were fitted with thermals. Not sure what I could have done to let Moshe know, but this could really screw up everything.

"Is there another way past that large building?"

I thought for a moment. "Probably, but I don't really know these back alleys all that well."

"Very well, just tell us how far past that building the Blue Bird House is, and what it looks like, and we will go on alone from here. We appreciate your assistance."

I heard blood pounding in my ears as my heart rate surged. I licked my lips. "You'll never find it on your own. I think I know a way. Follow me but be careful."

He looked at me for a couple seconds and then nodded. We started walking but this time the gauss pistol was right in my back. I got us around a low black metal box, half rusted out, and maybe ten meters past it before I knew I had to get us off the main alleyway. We were getting too close to the Blue Bird House. I saw a side pathway up ahead, angling off to the right, and pointed to it. Halfway there I saw a brief flicker of light and then experienced an intense spasm of agony as every nerve in my body lit up simultaneously, followed by blackness.

"Sasha, you okay?" I heard Moshe say, and slowly the world came back, although at first I couldn't remember what I was doing out at night or why Moshe was there.

"Did I fall down?" I asked. I felt bruised all over and my hands and arms shook uncontrollably. "What happened?"

"Dezi took you down with a neuro-pistol."

"Why? What was I doing?" I looked around. The alleyway seemed full of people, which was strange at night. Then I started remembering the four guys. "Oh, there are four men, they're—"

"Don't worry, we got 'em. Dezi stunned you to get you out of the line of fire. She figured putting you down first, they wouldn't shoot you."

I sat up with his help and looked around. All four of the men were down, although one of them was moving. I saw Zdravkova a couple meters away, letting one of the Strikers bandage her right upper arm.

"You stun them all?" I asked.

She turned and looked at me. "Just you and one other. The other three are dead. We only had the one neuro-pistol."

"You should have heard her," Moshe said and smiled. "'Halt in the name of the Municipal Police!'" He nodded toward the corpses. "They didn't halt."

With Moshe's help I got unsteadily to my feet. "You did great, pal," I said. "Saved my life. Thanks."

"Pretty hard not to know something was up, way you tipped me," he answered.

"Yeah, well, important thing is you didn't tip them. Nice acting job."

I hobbled over to join Zdravkova looking down at the one surviving guy, slowly coming to. He'd hit his head going down and there was a fair amount of blood. Head wounds always bleed a lot. The other three, including the leader, lay in awkward heaps, like marionettes someone had cut the strings on. Zdravkova followed my gaze.

"My four best snipers," she explained. "Those three never got a shot off."

"These guys were professionals," I told here, "and they all have thermal implants."

She nodded. "I figured they might. We've run into some night hunters before, but never Humans, only Varoki."

"You know who they are?"

"Probably CSJ," she said and then turned to me with a smile. "Tell me some more about their virtues."

"Provosts, huh? I've never heard of any CSJ operatives with thermal implants, and I've tangled with a couple."

"No offense, Sasha," she said, "but you spent most of your life on Peezgtaan. It's not exactly the center of the universe. We've run into Human CSJ agents before, and Varoki CSJ night hunters, but Humans with thermal implants...that's new."

I'd run into Human CSJ officers as well. After all, CSJ was an all-*Cottohazz* agency, and Humans were part of that. Varoki dominated the service, but you still saw Humans once in a while.

The surviving agent on the ground groaned and tried to sit up, but found his arms held behind him with quick restraints. The two fighters kneeling next to him lifted him up into a sitting position and one of them started spraying bandage on his head.

"How'd you get winged?" I asked Zdravkova. She nodded at the guy sitting up.

"After you went down I switched to this guy, painted his chest with the targeting beam while the pistol recharged. That way everyone else knew not to kill him. He got a shot off before I shocked him. Pretty good shooting, all things considered."

"They know their stuff," I agreed, remembering every move they'd made, the minimum of orders, the constant situational awareness. It was starting to sink in how unbelievably lucky I was to be alive, and that started my knees wobbling and my head spinning.

"Gotta sit down for a minute," I said and sank right down cross-legged in the street. Zdravkova sat down next to me with a bit more grace.

"Why'd you stun one of them?" I asked. "What are you going to do with him?"

"Oh, we have some drugs back at the clinic, or we can fabricate some others," she said and grinned. "Thought I'd find out why he's here."

"You know something I don't about drugging CSJ agents?" I asked.

She looked at me and frowned. "What do you mean?"

"These guys have nanites in their bloodstream. Hit them with any kind of interrogation drug, or just raise their pain to a defined level for a defined period of time, and the nanites put their lights out, permanently. I don't know any way to make them talk unless they feel like it."

"Damn," Zdravkova said. "We've never taken a CSJ prisoner before. Well, one thing's for sure, any hope we had of the *Cottohazz* coming to the rescue just went up in smoke. This tells us what they think of us."

"You're wrong," I said. "I mean, maybe they won't help, but it's not a done deal and these guys have nothing to do with that. The Executive Council will decide whether to get their public hands dirty here. CSJ is playing their own game below the table."

I looked at her and could tell she wasn't buying it.

"Yeah, it sounds screwy, but it's true. The Council mostly listens to the *Khap'uKhaana*, the Corps of Counselors—not lawyers in this case, but diplomats and administrators. One of my best friends, Arigapaa e-Lotonaa, is in the *Khap*, and he can't stand CSJ or its chief. The provosts have power and autonomy, but not as much influence over Executive Council policy. Trust me, we're still in the game."

The guy sitting up a couple meters away was looking at me now. "You feel like talking yet?" I asked him.

He just stared at me, eyes empty. Probably making his peace with whatever he believed in. Then I realized there was another explanation for the way he looked at us.

"You're fitted with a bio-recorder, aren't you?"

He didn't answer at first.

"You know, we can find out easily enough—surgically."

"Yes," he answered after a moment.

"What's a bio-recorder?" Zdravkova said.

"I'll tell you later. You'll love it. But for now keep him away from anything interesting until you figure out what you're going to do with him, and if there's any way to scrub the memory of his recorder. I know someone to ask about that."

I looked the guy over again. I'm not saying he wasn't scared. I think he was terrified, sitting there looking into the abyss. But that terror would not keep him from doing what he believed in, even knowing it was the last thing he was likely to do. I understood. We all die, and few of us get to decide where or how. All we get to decide is how we live. Zdravkova wanted to see virtue? It was right there in front of her.

No, we couldn't make *him* talk, but I knew somebody we could.

"Talk, you miserable son of a bitch. Why were four CSJ agents, loaded for bear, looking for you?"

"I don't know!" my father cried out, but his eyes told me he at least had a suspicion.

"You can't fool me, old man. Were they coming to bust you out of here? Take you off someplace safe?"

"Did they say that? Is that what they wanted?" he asked, and his face turned suddenly pathetic with desperate hope.

"No." I said, and his face fell. I took a step back away from him. So now I knew the answer to my first question, but it raised a different one. "Why does CSJ want you dead?"

I'd made a stir back in the dormitory when I shook him awake then grabbed his shirt front with my left hand and hauled him outside and threw him against a foamstone wall. The cloud cover had thickened, lowered, and now began sprinkling us with a slow, fine rain. My face must have burned with hot pumping blood, because I felt each drop as an icy needle pricking my skin. I half expected it to turn into steam when it hit me.

Moshe stood to one side, arms folded across his chest, just watching. Aurora emerged from the shadows and joined us.

"How do you know they wanted him dead?" she asked.

"The old man knows. But why? Answer me that. *Why?*"

He shivered in the rain, ran the palms of his hands over his face, the same gesture he'd used when we first talked. I slapped his hands away from his face.

"Stop stalling! Stop trying to think up a lie. For once tell me the goddamned truth!"

He looked at me, terrified, but after a moment he shook his head. He might be afraid of me, but there was something he feared more.

Aurora walked forward and looked at him, at the hunched, shivering man who'd raised her.

"I know why," she said.

||||||||||||||||||||||||||||||||||| Chapter Thirty-One

One problem in Sookagrad those days was the lack of privacy. Folks had been pretty packed together before everything started going to hell, and events since then had compounded the problem. Moshe got us the use of Doc Mahajan's office and left the three of us alone there. He displayed more sensitivity to our "family issue" than I thought necessary, but when someone offers you a thoughtful and generous gesture, accept it and shut up.

I sat behind Doc's desk and my father sank into the chair across from me, eyes on the floor. Aurora stood leaning against the wall, full of nervous energy which seemed to keep her from sitting still.

"So what do you know?" I asked her.

"She knows nothing," our father said without looking up.

"How could I live with you, then near you, for a quarter of a century and not know *something*?" she demanded. "You didn't think I was curious? I am an investigative reporter. You never thought I investigated *you*?"

For the first time he looked up and at her. Panic flashed across his face, and then he as quickly looked away. I glanced at her and saw her blink once, slowly, then look steadily at her father as she resumed talking. He wasn't watching, so I don't think he realized that everything from then on was being recorded.

"Peezgtaan was full of biochemists," she said, "all of them suddenly no longer employed by AZ Tissopharm or Simki-Traak. Don't you wonder, Sasha, why AZ Kagataan would single out this one biochemist and offer to rescue him from the chaos engulfing that world?"

"The question crossed my mind."

She looked at our father before continuing. "You published five papers before we emigrated to Peezgtaan, three of them on exotic neurotoxins. Once you were on Peezgtaan, no more publications. Why?"

He shrugged. "All my work there was proprietary."

"Yes, the intellectual property of AZ Tissopharm. But then Tissopharm dissolved, and the research was still in your head. What was it you were working on which AZ Kagataan wanted so desperately?"

He looked up and grimaced. "If they had wanted it 'desperately,' they would have provided four seats, not two. What difference does it make now? There were potential commercial applications from some of the neurotoxins in the Peezgtaan native-form molds—psychotropic drugs."

She laughed. "You haven't been working for twenty-seven years on psychotropic drugs. The CSJ did not send four assassins to silence you over *psychotropic drugs!* I don't know all the details, but much of it began making sense to me two years ago, when it finally came out that the Peezgtaan native mold forms are based on Human-compatible protein. You are developing Human-specific weaponized biotoxins, aren't you?"

I watched his head twitch just a little, his eyes flick up, then to the right, and I knew he was making up a lie.

He blinked a couple times and then nodded. "Yes, I admit it. It is true. We have developed several neurotoxin protein strains which are Human-specific."

So then he told us about how AZ Kagataan had been working on weaponized biotoxins, covertly, for about twenty years, how the psychotropic drug research had mutated into this black op—black because there was a whole string of *Cottohazz Wat* edicts out there banning bioweapon research. He had a lot of detail, stuff which could only be known by someone on the inside, which made the story very persuasive. Aurora listened intently, nodding from time to time, almost glowing with the satisfaction that came from vindication and confirmation after years of growing suspicion.

Back in the old country they had a word: *maskuvannya*—the Russians said *maskirovka,* same thing. It meant deception, a scam to convince someone one thing is true in order to conceal a different, bigger truth. *Maskuvannya* always worked best when you tried to convince someone that what they already *wanted* to believe was in fact true.

The use, by one species, of bugs which killed another sentient species but left their own unaffected could tear the *Cottohazz* apart and lead to a massive interstellar war along species lines, possibly a war to extinction. As much friction as there was in the *Cottohazz*, it never quite broke unambiguously along species lines, which is probably why the ramshackle commonwealth had managed to stagger on for so long. This bioweapon stuff was a really, really big deal, which is what made it such a persuasive *maskuvannya*. Aurora was buying it because she wanted to be right about her suspicions, and it was potentially the biggest story in a generation. I pretended to buy it, but I wondered what it was hiding.

What could be a bigger secret than *that*?

I sent the old man back to Katranjiev's headquarters building along with an armed guard, told the guard to keep him there under restraint. My father was potentially valuable, but I didn't want him under foot where folks were doing important work. That was probably unfair to all the folks working long hours at headquarters, but I couldn't figure out what they were doing or what difference it made. Not their fault Katranjiev had mired himself in bureaucracy, but they could keep an eye on the old man in between processing requests to be added to the official membership rolls of the Sookagrad Merchants' and Citizens' Association, and then updating same. Maybe they'd put him to work collating or something.

I asked Aurora to stay and she finally sat down, as if the old man not being around took away the tension that kept her so wired up.

"This CSJ guy we caught is fitted with a bio-recorder," I said. "I'm wondering if there's any way to erase its memory without killing him."

She kept looking right at me, her eyes not moving. "Why would you ask me?"

We sat there looking each other in the eyes for a few seconds, and then her expression changed from mild curiosity to rueful surrender.

"How long have you known?"

"Since back on Stal's rooftop, the night of the big attack."

She nodded. "Not many people know about bio-recorders, not that they are a big secret. There's just not much interest or demand outside of a couple narrow fields. I'm not recording this, by the way. The agent knows things you don't want to get out, but you don't want to kill him. That's interesting."

"Yeah," I said, "interesting and possibly academic. I may get outvoted, not that I really have a vote, but if we did want to keep him alive is there a way to wipe his recorder's memory?"

She looked down and thought for a few seconds, then looked up again. "You want to wipe my recorder memory as well?"

I didn't actually, but if I said so, there was as much chance she'd take it as a deceptive attempt to manipulate her, and put her on the defensive, as there was she'd believe me. I didn't know her well enough to guess which way she'd break.

"No promises," I said.

She nodded a couple times, thinking that over. Finally she shrugged. "Yes, you can wipe his system memory with a strong electromagnet focused on the memory field, which is usually along the forward surface of the spine, between the third and sixth vertebrae. At least that's where mine is. Your med techs can find it with bio-scanners set to look for silicon. That will also temporarily disable his recorder until he can get it reprogrammed."

"Okay, thanks. And no, I'm not going to scrub your recorder memory. We may need it down the road."

"What do you want here?" she asked. "And I'm still not recording. I just want to know."

I wasn't sure what she was getting at. "What do any of us want? To survive this mess, to get back to our families, to get on with lives."

"The same lives as before?" she asked. "The same shabby dead-end lives as always?"

Good question. Want it or not, I didn't see how life could ever get back to just exactly what it was before, but if not the same, then what? Better or worse? Hopefully better, but how?

"There are a lot of non-Varoki in the *Cottohazz*," I said. "If we can get the bulk of them to see what's going on here, what's going on under all the public slogans about consent of the governed and rights of the races, maybe we'll see some real changes."

She looked away and pursed her lips in thought, but then shook her head. "Hard to see how. I've been covering it for a decade now, all the political wheeling and dealing. The intellectual property covenants are at the heart of the economic stranglehold the Varoki trading houses have over the whole *Cottohazz*, and those aren't changing."

"Why not? The Varoki have fewer than 40 votes out of 172 in the *Cottohazz Wat*."

"The IP covenants are not legislation," she said, "they're integral to the *Cottohazz* charter, and that cannot be amended without a supermajority."

"What's a supermajority?"

"It's an absolute majority of every one of the six circles, the six races. You can't alter that, or any other part of the charter, without getting a majority of the Varoki *wattaaks* to agree."

Huh! Well, so much for plan A. That wasn't going to happen, was it? I figured Plan B was Zdravkova's answer: a revolt, maybe even open warfare between the races. But I was pretty sure we'd get our asses kicked, given the economic and technological differences, and that was even without some Human-specific superbug AZ Kagataan might or might not have perfected. That could leave Humans knocked back to our own world, maybe bombed back to the stone age, and that's if crazies like Gaant didn't get in charge and just solve the "Human Problem" once and for all.

So what was Plan C?

Well, I guessed whatever it was it was above my pay grade. I had a family to survive for and get back to. Unconventional and multispecies as that family might be, as far as I was concerned it was still the only real family I had, these two new strange blood-acquaintances notwithstanding.

"Naradnyo, shake your lazy ass and get out here!" I heard Zdravkova shout to me through the open doorway of Ivanov's main fabrication building, which was starting to look like a mad scientist's workshop. I handed back the long composite penetrator dart with the tungsten tip and walked over to see what was up.

"What?" I said. Brilliant sunlight poured through the open doorway, all but blinding me, as my eyes had adjusted to the dim interior of Ivanov's lair. I stepped out and felt the sun warm my skin, and I smiled. I've always loved sunny days, and now even more so since sunlight meant electricity, electricity to run autodocs and fabricators, cook food and light shelters, charge gauss rifle magazines, and even store up some extra juice in those scavenged vehicle battery packs for a rainy day. *Literally* for a rainy day.

"What's got you so excited?" I asked.

"Some more refugees snuck through the militia lines this afternoon," she said. "I'm damned if I know what to do with them, but they should tickle you."

My eyes were adjusting to the light and I saw a group of tall refugees, about a dozen of them, walking down the street. When I recognized who they were I sucked in a quick breath and felt my skin tingle with the sudden jolt of adrenaline.

"*Varoki* refugees? Coming *here*? Why?"

I walked over and stood beside her as she watched them approach.

"Because they heard we were holding out against the militia," she said. "Because they're loyalists, because the junta was demanding they sign loyalty pledges, taking over their homes, starting to arrest folks. Because somehow they heard about Captain Prayzaat's appeal, and they think we're the closest Municipal Police.

"What the hell do we do with them?"

I looked at her and I saw something shining in her eyes.

"You know what we do with them. We protect them. It's our job. We *are* the police."

She looked at them for several long seconds, then sniffed and shook her head, but in wonder rather than negation. "This is so strange," she said, her voice hoarse.

Yes it was: strange and terrible and wonderful.

I looked back at the refugees, and then I had another jolt as I recognized one of the faces.

"*Borro?*"

The'On's personal bodyguard, who I'd last seen the day of the first riots in Praha-Riz, left the group and walked over to me. He was dirty, clothes torn, and half his face and head was concealed in a bloody bandage. We shook hands.

"Hello Sasha. I had almost despaired of ever seeing you again, but I thought if you were still alive I might find you here. I am afraid I have some very bad news."

Chapter Thirty-Two

My face flushed, I felt dizzy with fear, and a surge of panic constricted my chest and throat, but I swallowed hard and found my voice.

"Marr? Has something happened to her? Is it Tweezaa? Is the baby all right?"

Borro must have recognized the look in my eyes for what it was and he stepped forward, put his hands on my shoulders.

"No, your family is safe and well, Sasha. E-Lotonaa as well. I am sorry if I made you think otherwise. Please put your mind to rest on that score."

Relief didn't exactly flood through my system. The panic which came to visit had been too real, so it hung around for a while, sizing things up. I clenched my fists to keep my hands from trembling, forced myself to breathe slowly and deeply, from down in my belly. That doesn't make you less afraid, but it helps relax your throat and upper body, which keeps your voice from shaking. That's important. When you can't *not* be afraid, all you have is not showing it. I saw Zdravkova beside me, watching me, surprised at what she saw.

"What?" I asked her, and it came out harsher than I intended.

"Nothing," she said, and turned to Borro. "So is the bad news personal for Naradnyo, or do we all get to share the joy?"

"I am afraid the latter," Borro said.

❖　　　❖　　　❖

"This is Borro, the personal bodyguard for The Honorable Arigapaa e-Lotonaa of the Consular Corps of the *Cottohazz* Executive," I said, introducing him to the troika and Captain Prayzaat. I turned to him. "You know, as long as I've known you, I don't know the rest of your name."

"Borro is sufficient, my friend," he said.

"Yeah, it's sufficient for me anyway." I turned back to the others. "I've known Borro for over two years, went through hell with him on K'Tok, and almost got killed with him during the first riot at Praha-Riz. I trust him with my life. You don't know him so I'm sure you're skeptical, and I understand. But for whatever value you place on it, I vouch for him."

We were gathered in Captain Prayzaat's small headquarters, or at least the room dressed as a holovid set to look like one. He'd spent the last few days here, holed up with his three troopers with not much constructive to do. We tried to keep him informed, sought his advice when we had time, but he probably had a lot more influence outside of Sookagrad than inside it. The only people in Sookagrad outside this room who knew he was even here were his three patrolmen and Ted, the vid tech. I think Aurora was beginning to suspect, but she probably wasn't sure yet. Just bringing Borro into the circle required a major leap of faith on the troika's part, but they'd done it without much persuasion once they got a load of what he had to say.

"I appreciate your assessment, Mr. Naradnyo," Captain Prayzaat said. "Do you believe there is a possibility this new intelligence is linked to the CSJ raid last night?"

My initial reaction was to just deny it, but I realized there were a lot of ways they could be related, and I took a little while to think about them, but I ended up shaking my head anyway.

"Not directly. I mean, I don't think CSJ is working with the junta or the militia. Gaant's speech that first day of the coup, the one about how 'the *Cottohazz* can rot' is just the sort of thing to make the provosts roll their eyes back up into their heads and swallow their tongues. Really, I can hardly think of anything more calculated to drive those guys into a seizure than talk like that. The *Cottohazz* forever, that's what CSJ believes. From their point of view, the Gaantists are worse bad guys than we are."

"And the raid?" Prayzaat asked.

"Only reason CSJ would try to kill my father is if he knew

something which, if revealed, would damage or destabilize the *Cottohazz*." I then spent a moment thinking about that. Other than a species-specific superbug, what could a biochemist specializing in exotic neurotoxins know which could destabilize the *Cottohazz*?

"You said no direct relation," he said. "But indirectly?"

Katranjiev jumped into the discussion. "Their raid and the military buildup could be independent responses to a common external pressure. Your appeals and directives, Captain Prayzaat, along with our local bulletins, must be paying off. They must both feel as if the time for action is running out, that whatever is going to get done has to get done right now."

For a change, I thought Katranjiev might have hit the nail on the head. Prayzaat nodded as well.

"Very well, let me hear the details of this buildup."

Borro repeated what he'd already told the rest of us, but in more detail this time. Lots of logistical units, supply dumps, mess facilities, and mobile med units for casualty treatment. Headquarters in place along with laser communication hubs, which would cut through the jamming provided they had a line of sight to their receiver. The logistics people had been showing up all last night and this morning, and now the first combat units were arriving: APCs carrying regular infantry, some light combat walkers, and at least a handful of gunsleds that Borro had seen himself, out west of our lines. He hadn't seen any indirect fire support assets, but he'd been close to our lines when the combat units started showing. The support weapons, if they were there, would be farther to the rear.

This was a real army moving in, not the militia, not a bunch of yokels pumped up on big talk and then slapped down so hard they'd had enough to last them for the duration. This was trouble, probably terminal trouble.

"How soon can we expect an attack?" Prayzaat asked.

We looked around at each other but I was probably the one with the most actual time in service with a combat unit, even if corporal was the pinnacle of my responsibility.

"They brought in the logistical tail first," I said, "so the combat troops should be able to jump off fairly soon after they get here. On the other hand, and not to sound too much like a crazy optimist, the uBakai Armed Forces haven't fought a conventional ground campaign in over a generation. The war with the uZmatanki was mostly fought in space and with surrogate and mercenary forces on the ground. I think the uBakai training is okay, so far as it goes, but it's slanted mostly toward small-scale internal security missions."

"That pretty much sums this operation up too, doesn't it?" Katranjiev said.

"Maybe. The thing is, it looks like they're planning a big coordinated assault from four sides, and they can't afford another fiasco. It's got to go off right. I wouldn't be surprised if they spent some time making absolutely sure everyone was in place and on the same page before they pull the trigger."

"From what I have seen in our joint exercises with them," Prayzaat said, "I am inclined to agree. They could launch an attack as early as sundown, but I think it more likely they will wait until predawn to launch a well-coordinated operation. Do you agree?"

I realized with a start he was talking to me.

"Sure."

"Commander Zdravkova, what condition are our defensive forces in?"

"The six line platoons are up to strength, about three hundred fighters mostly equipped with RAGs. Number Six Platoon, that's the Strikers, is pretty good, mostly combat veterans from before the troubles. The other five have seen an hour of intense combat and come through it smarter than they went in. They can execute very simple tasks. Petar Ivanov has managed to fabricate several hundred two-centimeter grenades for the launchers integral to most of the RAGs. That's a capability the opposition hasn't seen from us before.

"We have five additional provisional platoons, formed in the last two days, armed mostly with civilian rifles and carbines. They're more backup security and to keep out infiltrators, and I don't expect much from them in a hard fight. They don't have any real training, but they have some experienced people running most of the squads, so I'm hoping they'll hang together and generate some fire until they start taking casualties. I wouldn't expect them to last long after that.

"Behind them we have probably two hundred more security guards armed with pistols, not incorporated into tactical units or actually trained to fight."

"You clearly have some familiarity with the military, Commander," Prayzaat said. "Did you serve?"

She shrugged. "I was a major in the Judge Advocate General Corps, if that counts. I never carried a weapon, let alone fired one, in uniform. I've done some shooting since then."

"I see. And what sort of antivehicle weapons do you have? Can you stop a mechanized assault?"

Zdravkova frowned down at the floor before answering.

"If they throw a vehicle or two at us to scare us, we can hurt them. If it is a well-coordinated mechanized assault, with dismounted support, and delivered with determination, we cannot stop it.

"We have about twenty improvised antivehicle launchers Ivanov rigged up. Each one is loaded with twelve long-rod penetrators which are salvoed all at once, propelled by a PLX explosion which will destroy the launcher as well. The twelve penetrators will spread laterally, probably a lot, and I can't guarantee they'll hit anything, but they'll make a lot of smoke and noise."

I remembered looking one of those penetrators over this morning in the workshop. The actual launcher looked like a lashed-together mess to me, but I wasn't very mechanically inclined.

The core of the launcher was a honeycomb of composite tubes, each holding one of those titanium-tipped long-rod penetrators I'd handled back in Ivanov's workshop, where I'd also seen them assembling the contraptions. Behind the tubes was a reservoir of PLX and a detonator connected by a long wire to the electronic trigger. There was a sheet of composite armor behind the charge and four more sheets making up the sides of the box. The space in the box between the launch tubes was filled with foamstone, and there were a couple fiber straps around it, holding everything together.

When the PLX detonated, it would blow the whole thing apart, but the sides and rear would, in theory, contain the explosion long enough for the penetrators to blow out the front, through their launch tubes, and be on their merry way before everything came apart in a giant ball of flame.

"How do you aim the launchers if they blow themselves up?" Stal asked.

"We just emplace them pointing down a street, back off with the detonator wire, and when it looks like something's in the way, light it up. At least that's the theory. We've only test-fired one of them. It didn't work, but we're pretty sure we fixed the problem."

There was a moment of silence as everyone thought about that.

"What about gunsleds?" Borro asked. "I saw four of them before crossing the lines."

She smiled a gallows smile. "We think we can get a pretty good slant angle of attack by propping some rubble under the front of the launcher."

Jesus! I felt the first chill of real physical fear, as opposed to generalized anxiety and dread. They were going to roll right over us. I could see Prayzaat thought the same thing. Katranjiev looked as if he wanted to soil his pants. Stal was as difficult to read as always.

"We have many civilians to think of," Prayzaat said. "It may be time to attempt to negotiate a surrender."

"What about you?" I asked Prayzaat. "If you throw in the towel, a lot of folks are going to think of that as the end of effective resistance."

"It has not rained hard in three days, as I recall," he said, and I nodded in agreement. It had sprinkled a little bit last night, but it ended almost as soon as it started. "You have opened several shafts to the storm sewers, and the water level should be much lower now. I and my men will try to escape that way. From what Mr. Borro said, there are other pockets of resistance still holding out, yes?"

"Yes," Borro said. "One of them is the Black Docks, south of here on the river, a mixed Human and loyalist Varoki enclave. If Sasha was not here, I would have gone there next. But there is a—"

"I believe we will head in the opposite direction, north, and try to get out of the city," Prayzaat said, cutting Borro off. He looked down at his desk, although there wasn't anything there to look at. "It has been an honor serving with you all. I could not ask for a more gallant company with which to share this ordeal, but now I think you should see to obtaining the best terms possible from the Army."

"I doubt that is an option," Borro said. "There is one more thing I have not yet told you."

The meeting broke up and we all headed back to our people to get things moving. We had a whole lot to do and no time

to get it done, but when things get really bad, that's usually the
way. Borro's last information had been a bombshell, and two of
the other Varoki refugees confirmed it. The Army wasn't making
much of a secret of it; uBakai soldiers and militia were openly
bragging about it to the locals.

No surrender. No prisoners. And they weren't just talking
about armed combatants.

I let the others go their own way and stopped in an alleyway
where half a dozen kids were playing with a soccer ball. I looked
up at the clear afternoon sky, felt the sun warm my face, listened
to the voices of the kids yelling after scoring a goal, probably
their last goal ever. What was Marr doing? Was Tweezaa playing
soccer somewhere on *The'On*'s estate? I'd never know.

This was it, the finish. This was where it all ended. We had a
plan, a way of not going gentle into that good night, a plan that
gave some of our people a chance to live, but mostly was just a
way to take a lot of our murderers with us.

The pain of never holding Marr in my arms again and never
seeing Tweezaa grow to an adult lanced through me, a sudden
physical reaction to loss so intense I bit my lower lip. I should
have felt something like that for my unborn son, too, but I didn't
know him. Now I probably never would. I couldn't miss him as
much as the others, but I still felt a burning inside, a mixed-up
ache of unfulfilled yearning and regret over a responsibility not
discharged.

I didn't want him to grow up without a father, like I had, but
he'd still have Marr. She was as strong as most men I'd ever
known, and she'd do the job for both of us. Hard on her, having to do it alone, but she'd do it. And she'd tell him all about
me—the good parts anyway. I guessed my life story could benefit
from a little editing. Or maybe he could learn something from
my mistakes. Either way, I trusted Marr to sort it out for him.
In some ways it would be as good as me being there.

That gave me some comfort, but only for a minute or so. Then
I thought about what that meant.

If he'd really do as well without me as with me, what good was
I? Was I just a sperm donor? If somehow I managed to survive
this nightmare, what difference would it make in his life? What
would I give him? What would I change?

Nothing.

He'd grow up with a good education, enough money to open doors, enough opportunity to follow whatever talents he found in himself, and go as high as a *Human* could go, but only that high and no higher. I'd gone about as high as a Human could go, and I hadn't had any of the advantages he'd have, so what good would those advantages do?

The system was rigged and everyone knew it. We all just made our peace with it, got by as well as we could, and said there was nothing we could do to change it. I'd settled for a place in it for me, and I guess that was my choice. But along the way I'd settled for that place for him, too, and that *wasn't* my choice to make.

I'd spent the last two years worrying about me, about *my* future, *my* soul, and all I could come up with was don't make the same mistakes I made before. Was that it? Sit for the rest of my life at twenty-two and zero and just run the clock out? *That* was my plan? For what? What difference would it make to anyone? What difference would it make to my son?

What difference was *I* going to make?

"Boss, you okay?"

I turned and saw Moshe Greenwald, concern on his face. He had five or six gauss pistols in his arms. We'd gotten some from when the line troops got better weapons but we hadn't distributed all of them yet. This morning we'd decided to.

I looked down the alleyway.

"You kids, something's about to happen, something big. Get on back home, pronto."

They looked at me with resentment at first, but then they saw the yellow-orange LOG on my jacket, waved, and took off. Everybody knew LOG, even when they didn't know it stood for logistics.

I pulled off the soiled grey arm sling and dropped it into the rest of the trash covering the alley. I flexed my right arm, stretched it over my head. It was stiff, a little sore, but the mobility was satisfactory. They must have pretty good nanites in that Varoki med center. I wiped the tears from my face.

"I'm fine, Moshe." I took a deep breath and let it out slowly. "You know, I think I really am. Get all the department heads together at the clinic. Ten minutes. We got a nightmare coming and hardly any time to get ready.

"And give me one of those gauss pistols."

Chapter Thirty-Three

Two hours later I crouched with the troika and a crowd of our troop leaders in the long shadow of a rusty cargo container that smelled of soiled diapers and rotting food. Beyond the shadow, the setting sun turned the tangle of debris and improvised structures soft orange and dull red, like a painting you'd sell to a rich Varoki: a miserable existence scrubbed clean of its despair by cheerful use of color.

Zdravkova, Katranjiev, Stal, Aurora and I faced the eleven platoon leaders and eleven platoon sergeants of our miniature army. Off to one side my six department heads waited for their own final briefing. Aurora was recording everything, although most of them didn't know that.

"Okay," Zdravkova started, "you know this is how it could have wound up all along, and now here we are. We know from refugee reports that the Army has moved in and that their orders are, 'No Human Prisoners.' That means us, and everyone else in Sookagrad.

"We have two objectives. First, find a way to break out of this pocket. Second, and if that fails, hurt them so badly they'll think a truce might be worthwhile after all. But your fighters have to understand that we are against the wall. Maybe nobody wants to be a hero. I sure don't. But today the uBakai Army gives us no choice.

"So, reserve platoons two-one through two-five have completed their relief-in-place, taken over the defensive perimeter, and assault platoons one-one through one-five are back in their assembly areas. When we break up here you five assault platoon leaders have thirty minutes to brief your squad leaders and get your platoons to their lines of departure. It's not much, but we need to move fast and hit hard, before the regulars have settled in. Our guess is the militia has effectively stood down in place, now that they think the regulars are here to protect them, and the regulars aren't expecting any action until *they* start it. Surprise is our secret weapon. Does everyone understand that?"

I saw intensity, excitement, and a fair amount of fear in their faces, but I also saw twenty-two heads nod.

"Here's the mission: each assault platoon pick a quiet route away from the main barricades, advance in loose column of twos, squads stacked one behind another, with scouts out front and flank. Avoid contact for as long as you can. Get deep, find those regulars, and hit them hard.

"Trailing squad in each platoon split off and double back to hit the militia roadblocks from behind: plow the road for the reserve platoons and provide rear security for the assault force.

"Reserve platoons, your main job is perimeter security. But when you hear shooting in front of you, hit the militia as hard as you can. We hit them from both sides, most likely they'll cave. You've got the portable mines. When you move forward and take over the old militia positions, that's where you place the mines. On *their* ground, not covering our approaches. Understand?"

More nodding heads.

"Assault platoons, show me your flares."

The platoon leaders and platoon sergeants of the five assault platoons each held up a hand launcher, designed to fire three yellow flares in succession.

"Okay. You do whatever damage you can, but you also look for a weak spot, a way out. If you find it, you fire those yellow flares. What do you do if you find an open road?"

"Fire the yellow flares," they answered in a ragged chorus.

"Striker Platoon, I'll be with you. There may be more than one open road, so we'll make the decision then, decide where to break out, and we'll punch straight through. When we make the call, we'll fire purple flares at the base of the breakout corridor." She paused and held up her own launcher. "We'll keep firing them as we move into the corridor, but we only have a few, so keep your eyes open.

"Assault platoons, when you see our purple flares, or when it gets too hot out there, break off and fall back, passage of lines through the reserve platoons and to the old barricades. Once you make contact with the reserve platoons, you assault platoon leaders are senior, and in local command. Reserve platoons, if the chain of command is disrupted, wait ten minutes and then break off. Fall back and join the assault platoons. Don't forget to set those remote mines.

"I'll try to get runners to you assault platoon leaders when it's time to collapse the sack and go, but things are going to get very crazy and you may just have to make your own call. Questions?"

One of the platoon sergeants raised her hand and Zdravkova nodded to her.

"Ammo. Can we get any more? We're going to burn through our basic load very quickly."

Zdravkova turned to me.

"You've got every single magazine we have," I said, "loaded and charged. When that's gone, we're dry."

I saw quite of few of them exchange worried looks at that.

"It works out to every one of your troopers having a magazine in the system and one backup magazine, and then you've got a platoon reserve of one more magazine per system. How you want to split that up is your call. But here's what I'd emphasize to your people: there are a shitload of RAG mags out there where you're going, all of them compatible with our systems. Snag as many as you can."

Zdravkova bobbed her head. "Yes, live off the enemy. Take their ammunition. But also remember, we can't get bogged down in protracted firefights. Most of the damage we do will come in the first minute or two of contact. Unless the enemy panics and runs, break off and find another spot to hit."

"What about my reserve platoon?" one of them asked. "Almost every weapon we have is a sporting rifle. Assault rifle magazines aren't going to do us much good."

"If you find RAG magazines, you'll find RAGs with them," she said. "Upgrade. Anything else? All right, assault platoons jump off thirty minutes from my mark...*now*. We'll meet again on the other side of this. *Confusion to the enemy!*"

"Confusion to the enemy!" they chorused, and then they were off, trotting in pairs, each in different directions. They didn't have a lot of time to spare. I waved my department heads forward and with less precision the six of them moved over and sat or squatted on the ground.

"Doc, have you got our wounded ready to move?"

"Those who can move, yes," Dr. Mahajan answered. "The critical cases will stay, and I'll be staying along with a med tech and five volunteer orderlies."

"I'd rather you came with us."

"I know and I appreciate the sentiment, but we've been over this. No matter what happens, not everyone will get out. There will be wounded from the fighting as well. My work is here. We just have to hope they exempt the clinic from the no-prisoner order." She clasped her shoulders with her hands, arms crossed, and shivered, although it was not at all cold.

"We have litter bearers for those who cannot walk but can be moved, with reliefs for each party, so they can keep moving. Both of my doctors and seven medtechs will move with the column and will be available to give first aid along the way. I do not know what else we can do."

"No, I don't either," I said. "Dolores, what about traveling rations?"

"There's not much we can do, given how little warning we had," Dolores Wu answered, her voice betraying exasperation. "We have been cooking riceballs for the last hour, boiling pots of edamame, and we have some sacks with a piece of fruit or two, some pickled vegetable, and whatever else we can find, to pass out to whoever we can get them to. Also we're filling as many people up with miso soup now as we can, but any liquid container we have we will need for potable water. We are passing out tomatoes and peapods to whoever wants them as well. At least there will be something."

"Yeah, I know it was short notice. Tell your crew good work under some impossible time constraints.

"Everyone else, you and your team members all have your assignments—dormitories, shelters, residential blocks. Everyone recognizes these orange-painted LOG shirts. They think we actually know what we're doing, so we're the guides. Your folks will explain the breakout plan to the civilians, get everyone ready to go, but keep them in place until you see those purple flares. Section leaders, it's your jobs to tell them when to start moving. Space the serials. Tell your guides to keep their people together and moving.

"Billy, your construction goons don't have assigned groups to lead. You are the traffic cops along the breakout route. Keep them moving, but moving in the right direction."

"Don't worry about us," he said.

"Okay. Remember, no equipment destroyed. Fabricators, generators, everything left in place and workable. Folks are going to need it later. Although Petar, make sure all the, uh…military software is scrubbed from the fabricators."

I didn't want to say "illegal software" with Aurora's recorder running.

He glanced at Stal, his old boss, and then looked back to me. "Not problem."

"Anyone else want to say anything?" I said to the three troika members.

"Yes," Zdravkova said. "All of you people in logistics have done a wonderful job, I really mean it. The improvisations, the clever ideas, the long hours of work…I'm sorry this isn't ending in a parade, because you earned it as much as anyone. Many of my fighters are still alive because of you. Thank you. Now I've got to go."

She stood and trotted down the street into the lengthening shadows. I looked at Nikolai Stal and Bogo Katranjiev. Maybe Bogo realized there was a recorder running, because he cleared his throat before speaking and managed a hard-jawed look of steely determination.

"What Commander Zdravkova said is true. No one ever thanks the people behind the scene, the little people, but none of this would have been possible without you. My hat's off to you." He reached up but then remembered he wasn't wearing a hat and tried to turn the gesture into an awkward salute. I saw some smiles, but more from gratitude rather than ridicule. Folks might not think of Katranjiev as a dynamo when it came to leadership, but they appreciated the effort. I did as well, insincere as it may have been.

Stal pointed at my crew. "When shit hits fan, stay low, keep moving. Most of you guys too ugly to die, but not you, Dolores, so don't press luck, okay?"

She chirped like a bird and smiled. Dolores Wu was probably pushing seventy and thin as a stick, with graying black hair whacked off in an uneven line across the back of her head and then shorter above her eyes. Maybe she'd been pretty when she was younger. I hadn't expected flattery from Stal.

"Okay folks," I said, "get back to your teams and get ready to move. Our assault teams jump off in about twenty minutes, but if all goes well they'll slip through the enemy lines and there won't be any fighting for a little while. When it starts, sit tight and wait. We don't even know that we will find an open road, but when and if we do, be ready to haul ass.

"Thanks for everything you've done—even you, Billy."

"Eat me," Conklin said, but he grinned past his fear.

As the group broke up, Stal paused next to me and said in a low voice, "You want one of my guys take care of CSJ agent before leave?"

"Already taken care of," I said. He looked at me and his eyebrows went up, but then he just nodded and left.

"You get that last bulletin on the pipe?" I asked Aurora after the others had gone back to their teams.

"Yes," she said. "I told about the refugees bringing us word of the Army's orders, the fear it was causing, the feverish preparations for a last ditch defense. Nothing about our attack, of course.

"Our father wants to travel with us."

She was taking it for granted that the two of us would be moving out together, and she was right. I couldn't trust her survival to chance. I also couldn't guarantee it myself, but what I could do I would. Not for her, for the bio-recorded record she carried of everything all these other people had done here. That story needed to get out. Maybe she was right about the politics. Maybe it wouldn't change everything. But it might change *something*, and that was a start.

"What do you think," I asked her, "about the old man traveling with us?"

She looked down and moved some trash around with her foot. "When there were only two seats, he had to choose between me and our mother. He chose me because of my singing voice. You don't remember but—"

"Yes I do," I said, and I was surprised, because I hadn't remembered until she said that. But then I recalled her singing when our parents had friends over for dinner, a recital at her school, and even her singing me to sleep once when I was sick. Her voice had been like the tone fine crystal makes when it's struck softly.

"Oh," she said. "Well, there was a great deal of talk about me as a child prodigy and Father decided my career was more valuable than Mother's companionship. He remarried here on Hazz'Akatu, once Mother's death was confirmed. It didn't last."

"And your career as a child prodigy?"

She shrugged. "My voice changed when I got tits. I still have okay pipes, but not good enough for Father to retire on. Not in the style to which he always wanted to become accustomed, although the bioweapons career worked pretty well for him until recently."

"He sounds like quite a guy," I said. "I guess that explains where a lot of my personality comes from."

Her head snapped up, eyes narrowed in anger. "Don't say that! Don't you *dare* say that. You were my little brother and there was nothing wrong with you. Nothing! Your only crime was… was not being *marketable*.

"What do I think of him coming with us? He'll just slow us down and the first chance he gets he'll try to sell us out. Leave him to die, like he did you."

I *had* been her little brother, hadn't I? I'd actually lived a fairly normal existence once, had even been loved by my parents, if only in a perfunctory sort of way. I had bits and pieces of memories, just flashes. Some of it was probably suppressed, but some was just gone, physiologically gone due to my traumatic brain injury. But so what? It was so long ago, so fragmentary, it was more like a half-remembered story I'd heard than something that actually happened to me.

But it was real to Aurora. I could tell how miserable she felt about that, and maybe about her whole life. For the first time I felt sorry for her. I thought it would make a big difference to her if I called her *Avrochka* again, like I had as a little boy, maybe let her start forgiving herself for a crime she had no real responsibility for.

But I did not call her *Avrochka*. It would not have been honest.

"This exotic neurotoxin thing," I said. "He called it a protein, right?"

She nodded, brow furrowed in confusion at the change in topic. "All naturally occurring neurotoxins are proteins. That much I found out in my background research. That's what makes them so deadly."

"Okay. The thing is all six races have unique protein chains. That's why we can't ingest the same foods, except some simple sugars and starches, right? We can't break their proteins down. So if neurotoxins are proteins, aren't *all* neurotoxins species-specific? I don't mean really *species*-specific, but specific to some or all the species from one of the six trees of life? Don't they have to be?"

She thought for a moment. "I think…maybe so. What are you getting at?"

"If there are lots of neurotoxins around, and they're all tree-of-life-specific, then why is one more such a big deal? Big enough to make CSJ want to rub out the old man?"

She looked at me intently, thinking hard. "You're saying you don't think he's working on a bioweapon?"

"That's what I'm saying."

"What then?"

"I don't know—yet. And that's why he travels with us. Find him and meet me at the headquarters building. I've got one more thing to take care of."

I found the CSJ agent bound and gagged, and under guard, in a metal locker in the back of Moshe's equipment storage building. I sent the guard to join the rest of his breakout party, told him I'd finish up here. I cut the restraints on the agent's legs and then helped him stand up. He had trouble at first, the restraints having cut off the circulation to his feet. I led him out of the building, talking as we went. His hands were still bound behind his back, which looked odd, but everyone we passed was in a hurry going somewhere else with a lot on their minds.

"The uBakai Army's about to come roaring through here and kill every single Human they can find. Afterwards they'll probably blame it on the mobs, round up a few Gaantist ringleaders and execute them, and express their regrets, but they'll have made their point and no Human will ever feel safe in Sakkatto City again.

"Of course, when they come in here shooting, they aren't going to stop to ask if you're CSJ, and the way they feel about the *Cottohazz* right now I'm not sure it would do you much good anyway. Understand?"

He was still gagged but he nodded.

"Okay. So I can leave you here, in which case you'll die. Or I can take you with me, in which case you'll probably try to kill Dr. Naradnyo, and I want him alive, at least for a while. So what do I do about you?"

We walked on in silence, heading toward the underground shelters we'd never used for anything except overflow dormitory space.

"Something puzzled me at first, because I wasn't using my head. I couldn't figure out why none of you guys knew who I was, but it was because of the Army jamming, wasn't it? You can't access the float out here so your facial recognition software doesn't work."

We got to the first hole we'd blown down to the storm sewers, to pump water in case we needed it for fighting fires. The hole was still there, now with a warning sign and a rigid composite panel across it so folks wouldn't fall in. The pump and hose had been moved somewhere else. People were moving around the shelters, forming up into breakout serials, but we were by ourselves by the hole. Off to the south I heard some single shots, then the stutter of automatic weapons fire. I waited for a moment, listened, but that was all. Maybe just random shooting, maybe the southern assault column running into trouble, hard to say.

I pushed the panel back. I could still hear water running down below, but not nearly as energetically as before. Prayzaat was right about that. I pulled the gag off of his mouth but he didn't say anything. He just looked at me, waiting for what came next.

"Sit down here, legs in the hole with your hands back toward me."

He did it and then just stared into the hole, into his personal abyss.

"In case you're curious, I'm Sasha Naradnyo."

He turned to me and his eyes got larger with surprise, but just for an instant and then his face was under control again. I grinned.

"Yeah, didn't see that coming, did you? Well, you're going to love the next bit. Follow this storm sewer south, which is the direction the water's flowing. It should take you to Katammu-Arc. Not sure how you get out of it there, but you're a resourceful guy. I'm going to cut your hands loose as I push you into the hole, because I still don't trust you not to jump me. But first I've got a message I want delivered to Field Marshal Lieutenant e-Loyolaan. Listen carefully."

Chapter Thirty-Four

Tell me a physics joke I can understand or so help me God I'll kill you.

Sure, Boss. What do you call it when Einstein jacks off? A stroke of genius! Get it?

Yeah. I mean, it's not very funny, but I do understand it, so I guess you get to live.

Gee thanks! If every boss I worked for was as generous as you, maybe I'd still be alive.

"You *are* still alive, damnit! Don't give up on me!" I said that out loud and I guess the other stuff was just in my head because even if Moshe were still conscious, he'd never have told that joke.

I struggled pulling him through the low spots in the rubble with one arm, trying to keep my head down, away from the scattered shots that still zipped overhead. The collar of his overalls was slippery with his blood. My left hand slid off. I flexed it to get some circulation back, tried to wipe the palm clean on my jacket front, and got a tighter hold on him. I kept pulling. Then Borro was by my side, pulling on an arm, and we had him behind a low foamstone wall that used to be part of a building.

"*Medtech!*" I yelled, unsure there was one within hearing range, or even one still alive this side of the flying monster up ahead. Miraculously, one materialized at my elbow, and started pumping A-stop into the spurting chest wound.

227

"Is he going to make it?" I asked, probably yelled.

Without taking her eyes off of him, she said, "If the heart's intact, I can deal with everything else. The entry wound is pretty far to the right, so unless there were some fragments flying around in there, I can at least get him stabilized."

I hovered there, staring at Moshe's face, pale beneath the spattered and smeared bright red arterial blood, until Borro pulled at my shoulder.

"Sasha, he will survive or he will not. We have work to do."

I looked up and then back down the narrow street called Throat-cutter's Way, illuminated in the overcast night only by fires burning here and there and the flickering light of overhead flares. Four or five of our fighters had shot the uBakai soldier at the end of the block, where the street opening into The Shadowed Way. It earned its name tonight—the overhead maglev tracks keeping the flare light from reaching down into the black velvet void underneath. Halfway to the Shadowed Way, with two bodies beside it, lay the salvo launcher Moshe had been trying to set up.

I looked at the long stretch of open ground between me and it, tasted bile and hot spit, but knew somebody had to do this and if not me, who?

"Not us," I said to Borro, "just me. If I go, all I'll have shooting at me is the Army. Everyone's likely to shoot at you."

I stood up and sprinted toward the launcher, trying to stay low and run a zigzag course. I thought the uBakai trooper who had shot up the original crew was down, but he had to have friends nearby. I got to the launcher and crouched beside it, that absurd lashed-together impossibility. Borro was only a few steps behind me.

Moshe and the two gunners had brought a couple good-sized foamstone blocks with them and I remembered that was the plan for how to get some elevation. We'd probably need it because there was a gunsled up ahead which had interdicted movement across the Shadowed Way, effectively cutting our breakout column in half. It had been moving slowly down the Way, supporting infantry clearing the buildings to either side. We'd hammered the infantry, driven them back. Now we wanted the gunsled to come to their rescue so we could get a clear close-in shot at it.

I started trying to tilt the launcher back to get some blocks under it but it was heavy. Borro stood up to get better leverage and rock it back on its rear corner.

"Keep down!" I yelled at him.

"There, slide the bocks under the front. Hurry!"

I managed to get them under it just as Borro let go and let it drop, the same time I heard the snap of a gauss rifle flechette. I looked up and saw Borro pitch backwards. I scrambled to his side but knew he was gone before I got there. The flechette had hit him square in the forehead and hadn't come out the back.

I knelt there looking at him for a moment feeling strange and hollow inside. I'd known him for over two years, but in a way I'd never known him, at least not in the conventional sense. He guarded The'On, but he didn't work for The'On, and I'd never been able to find out who he did work for. Now I never would, but I didn't really care about that anymore. I just wanted my friend back.

Behind me I heard the rising whine of the four ducted fans of a gunsled, knew I had to get off the street now or I'd die here with Borro, and then a lot of other people would as well. I grabbed the trigger assembly, pulled the wire off the spool on the side of the launcher, and let it play out of my hand as I ran for the cover of another low foamstone wall on the south side and about five meters back from the Shadowed Way. I dove over it and then stuck my head up and looked, saw the gunsled ease past the corner, hovering right below rooftop level, the image slightly distorted by the flickering glow of its electrostatic armor field. Its turret swung toward us, as if sniffing for prey. It wasn't quite in the center of the opening, but I didn't want the gunner to take out the launcher box on spec. I ducked down behind the wall and closed the trigger circuit.

Deafening noise. Heat. I felt the wall I sheltered behind seem to give and for an instant I was afraid it would collapse on me. Then I was on fire, or at least the right arm of my jacket was. I grabbed a handful of dirt and trash from the street and rubbed the fire out.

By the time I could look over the wall, most of the fireball from the exploded launcher had burned out and the smoke had drifted up, so I could see the end of the street. I'd actually hit the son of a bitch! I couldn't tell all the damage the launcher did, but it had at least taken out the right rear ducted fan. That side of the gunsled dipped down and the twisted frame of the fan housing dragged along the ground as the other right-side fan whined to high speed to get the sled stable again. Then it slid forward against one of the support columns for the overhead maglev tracks and must have knocked something loose, because the other fan on the near side just disintegrated, sent pieces of blade flashing and sparking off the track support girders, and the sled came down on its belly hard.

It was still dangerous, just sitting there, or it would have been if its weaponry was still operational. The turret wasn't moving and neither the main pulse laser nor the coaxial VRF autogun were firing. I saw evidence of a couple other strikes on the chassis of the vehicle, but couldn't tell if the penetrators had punched the hull or glanced off.

Then one of our fighters was running toward it, lugging one of those portable mines the reserve squads were supposed to seed the perimeter with.

"Covering fire!" someone yelled from behind me and I heard flechettes snap down the street and start taking chips off of buildings, I guess in case the sled's supporting infantry got that close. The guy made it to the crippled sled, but enemy flechette fire started hitting the hull near him. He got the mine up onto the hull of the sled and slid it under the combined weapons mount on the front of the turret before he got hit and knocked down. He got back up, set the timer on the mine, and started running back. More small arms fire from up the street took him down. Then the mine went off and blew the weapons mount right off the front of the turret, and a lot of the unburned PLX must have gotten in the hull breach, because pretty soon the whole vehicle was burning.

I heard the whine of more turbines and a second gunsled came forward, floating over the burning wreck of the first one, its downdraft laying the flames flat against the ground and shooting smoke and burning trash off in every direction. This one started hosing down the alleyway with its autogun right away. The rounds all went over my head but I heard screams of fear and pain behind me, and the sounds of metal and stone structures coming apart. Someone back there was yelling to fall back before the voice was chopped off in midcommand.

I rolled to the right until I couldn't see the sled anymore, then ran back toward the headquarters building through a narrow twisting alleyway that turned to the left and then right a little, hard left, and then I wasn't sure where I was going. I stopped for a minute and tried to get my bearings, but everything looked unfamiliar in the darkness. Finally I got a look at the maglev tracks and oriented myself, started down the alley again and soon found people running in panic the other way.

"Wrong way!" I shouted and tried to stop them, but most of them were beyond listening. Four of them stopped by me, looking nervously back, eyes wide and whites showing in the faint light.

"What's up there?"

"That rapid-firing gun," an old man said. "It's churning the ground, cutting through buildings!"

I could still hear it, firing short bursts now, maybe starting to conserve ammunition. Those VRF autoguns just burned through the ammo. Flechettes weren't that heavy and a sled could carry a shitload of them, since its power plant produced the juice to run the gun system, but there were still limits on how long they could keep shooting. The autogun stopped and I heard a loud sizzling crack, the sled firing its pulse laser.

"Come on. It's doing grazing fire, interdicting north-south movement. We just need to keep to the left."

I got them moving again and a little ways farther we found a larger clump of people, maybe a hundred of them, some wounded or injured by flying debris. There were some fighters with them but nobody seemed in charge.

"Sasha?" I heard Aurora call from the other side of the crowd. "Sasha! Are you here?" Her voice had a frantic edge to it. I hadn't seen her and the old man since the uBakai Army cut the breakout corridor at the Shadowed Way.

"Aurora, I'm over here! Stay where you are, I'm coming to you."

I pushed through the crowd and I asked the fighters I saw who was in charge, where their squad leader was. "Dead," one of them said, the rest just shrugged or looked blank. In the middle of the crowd I found the medtech with a two-man stretcher detail and Moshe.

"How's he doing?"

The medtech nodded and patted him on the shoulder. "He's weak from loss of blood, but I kept most of the blood out of his lungs and did some quick suction. We need a long-term fix to the lacerated artery, but the A-stop will hold it for now. Get us to a med center and he'll make it."

A med center. Yeah, that was going to be a good trick.

By the time I pushed through to Aurora and our father, another party of soldiers emerged from an alleyway behind her. They looked like they were still together as a unit, not just a random bunch of stragglers.

"Who's in charge?" I asked, and the trooper in the lead stepped forward.

"Squad leader dead. Was assistant, so now in charge. What is hold-up?"

"The uBakai cut the corridor. Mech infantry with gunsled support. Hear that firing? They have a solid hold on the Shadowed Way and I don't think we can move them."

"How hard try?" he said, a note of derision in his voice.

I remembered Moshe in a stretcher just hanging on to life, the two guys with him at the launcher who died right there, Borro who died aiming it, the soldier who put the demo charge on the gunsled and didn't make it back. I almost punched the guy standing in front of me, but instead I took a couple slow breaths to calm myself.

"A squad from one-three and parts of two other squads from one-two took a bite out of them and brought down a gunsled, but then got blown to pieces by its wingman. But you want to try, wise guy, go knock yourself out."

"Okay, okay," he said and pushed his cap back on his head. "Be easy. Is just...we did job, paid plenty for it, now everything fucked up."

"Yeah, everything is. We're not getting out to the east with the main breakout, and we can't get north past that grazing fire. Pretty soon they'll move in and cut off the south and west and that mech infantry is going to be on our ass as soon as they sort themselves out. Weren't there some yellow flares fired to the southwest?"

"Sure, road open then. But purple flares come, we fall back."

"You guys found the open road? Can you find it again?"

He scratched his chest through his shirt front and frowned. "Maybe closed now."

"Well it's sure as hell closed here. Come on, corporal, get your guys off their asses." I turned around, not giving him a chance to argue, and I started yelling. "Listen everyone! We can't go north or east. We're walking out to the southwest. Any fighter without a unit, report here to Corporal..."

I turned around. "What's your name?"

"Chernagorov."

"Report up here to Corporal Chernagorov, on the double."

There's nothing like a plan and some clear, simple orders to get people's heads together after a funk. Six fighters made their way to the front and joined Chernagorov's five, so we had about a full squad. He moved some ammo around so the three men who were completely out at least had some, and assigned them as our rearguard. Chernagorov picked one of his own men as lead scout and got him started, then turned to me.

"Ready?"

"Corporal Chernagorov," I said, "lead these people across the River Jordan."

He frowned and shook his head. "Be lucky get to Wanu River tonight."

‖‖‖‖‖‖‖‖‖‖‖‖‖‖‖‖‖‖‖‖‖‖‖ Chapter Thirty-Five

There were still a lot of people in Sookagrad, stragglers from the column, people who didn't believe the Army would really kill them, some who had lived here secretly all along and didn't know why everyone else had left. It sounds strange, but even in Sookagrad there were people living below the radar. Pushing through them sometimes was our main delay, trying to answer their questions, explain. Some of them joined us, so the group grew as we went. Just seeing purposeful action, armed men at the front and rear, was pretty persuasive to desperate people.

Some wanted to argue. One old guy, with about a dozen others with him, mostly women and children, had a petition. He wanted us to turn due south, march along the Shadowed Way to Katammu-Arc, so we could petition the uBakai *Wat*. I just ignored him and we kept marching. He tried to talk some of the others into joining him, but in the end most of his people followed us. I never saw him again.

The fighting to the north grew heavier as the Army closed in on the perimeter. I heard the thud of mines up there, saw more fires starting. There were already plenty of fires and they had started to spread, join together in larger conflagrations, and the flickering light and stark dancing shadows they cast turned Sookagrad's final night into Dante's nightmare.

We came out into the semi-open ground where the shelters were and found our lead scout crouching behind a metal building, waving us to stop. He laid his right arm across his chest, hand on his shoulder, two fingers extended like a pistol barrel—the *Cottohazz* tactical hand signal for armed soldiers, and then pointed around the corner of the building.

"Stay here," I told Aurora and she nodded wordlessly, eyes wide with fear.

Chernagorov moved forward to the scout and I joined him. He looked around the edge of the building, looked for several seconds without moving, then came back, face twisted with horror and rage. I looked.

I saw uBakai troopers, over a dozen of them, executing people, lots of them, all civilians who had taken cover in the shelters.

I turned and waved Aurora forward. "Record this," I hissed, "but don't let them see you." Then I turned to Chernagorov. "Get all your people up here, everyone with a gun."

"What if are more soldiers than just those?"

"Then we die, but those guys go first."

"*Da!*"

It won't go down in history as the best-executed charge ever, but what we lacked in skill we made up for in earnestness. We charged in earnest, and we killed in earnest, and we took them by surprise, still drunk from their orgy of murder, and some of them died without firing a shot at us, staring stupidly at their oncoming doom. One even looked ashamed to have been caught in the midst of this unspeakable act. He dropped his gun and stepped back, as if to distance himself from what he had done.

I killed him.

The first man I ever killed I killed for vengeance, executed for what he had done, but every man I had killed after that I had done only to keep them from doing something else, killing me or someone important to me, never as revenge or punishment. Now I had come full circle, and for this execution I felt no remorse. I stood there in the sudden silence, my nose filled with the odor of ozone from the gauss weapons and then the rising coppery smell of blood, lots and lots of blood. I looked at the silent Human bodies, the hundreds of bodies, the carpet of bodies, and I threw up.

I felt a hand on my arm and I turned suddenly, pistol up, but it was only Aurora. She recoiled in alarm, in fear, and she was right to. I gestured to the killing ground.

"Record this!" I ordered, my voice hoarse. She nodded mutely, and I could see she already was.

There were still people alive, clumps of them, rising from the ground, emerging from two of the shelters, sobbing with horror or relief or emotions they would never be able to put a name to. At my feet I saw a blood-spattered soccer ball. Were those kids I saw earlier here? Who could tell? That wasn't the only soccer ball in Sookagrad, but it belonged to someone, and I couldn't stand to look at the ground anymore.

"Chernagorov!" I shouted. "Where are you?"

"Here!" he answered and held up his arm, maybe twenty meters away.

"Get your shit together. Pull every weapon, every grenade, every round of ammunition off these guys. Reorganize your squad, arm whoever looks like they can use it, and let's get moving."

He gestured to the ground, where many of the people shot now moved, twitched. "Some still alive."

"Medtech!" I shouted, but she'd already come forward, was kneeling by one of the wounded. Behind her the rest of our people were straggling out onto the open ground to see what had happened.

"Medtech, look at me!"

She looked up, face twisted with emotion.

"You have ten minutes to identify people we can take with us who are likely to survive."

"I can't—"

"People are coming who will kill everyone here. *Ten minutes!*"

She looked overwhelmed. Everyone did. Everyone was. I picked up the RAG the Varoki I shot had dropped and then I knelt and stripped his ammunition harness and helmet. The helmet was a little big, but it had a night vision visor and projected a sight picture from his RAG onto it. I adjusted the chin strap so it wouldn't move around too much. Others were starting to strip weapons and ammo as well.

A female fighter walked up to me, looking bewildered.

"uBakai throw grenades into shelter," she said. "Incendiary grenades. Was full of people, uBakai shot as tried coming out."

"Weapons and ammo," I said. "These guys aren't just going to stop on their own, and you can't stop them with an empty rifle."

She nodded and moved off toward Chernagorov.

Aurora walked back to me, her face no longer blank with shock, but determined.

"I can't go yet," she said.

"There's no choice. We need to get out of here. We need to get the story you're carrying to the *Cottohazz*, especially after this."

She nodded. "We need to get it to them, but we need to get it to them *right now*. They need to see it as it's happening, not a couple months from now in a documentary. The access to the data pipe is right over there, not fifty meters south of here. I need a knife, though."

I looked south toward where Moshe had tapped into the data pipe. "What do you need a knife for?"

"I can edit internally, but my bio-recorder normally downloads wirelessly. With the jamming I can't. But there's a subdermal backup link. It's compatible with Moshe's input socket; I saw it before. I've never used it, but I have a tattoo that shows where it is. I have to cut my arm open to get to it."

I told Chernagorov what we were going to do. He wanted to wait for us, but that was stupid. He had wounded to carry, a mob of over two hundred people to keep moving, and he needed to get started. The three of us could move a lot faster, would catch up with him when we were done with our business, and he ended up agreeing. We shook hands and Aurora, our father, and I headed off to find the data pipe. The old man said he would rather go with the column, but his rathers didn't carry much weight anymore.

We found the maintenance shaft without any trouble. The medtech had given me what was left of a roll of surgical tape and a mostly empty bottle of spray bandage, because we were going to have to patch up Aurora's arm when we were done. I used part of the surgical tape roll to secure the old man's hands behind his back, around the base of the stanchion above the maintenance shaft. It wouldn't hold forever, but long enough.

"You don't need to tie me up," he protested.

"Of course not. You'd never go off and leave *me* in the lurch, would you? Now don't go twisting this tape all up. I may need to use it later on Aurora's arm. I'm going to climb down there and help her get started. Then I'll be back up. If you wander off, I'll find you and shoot you in the knee so you can't wander again."

"How will I keep up if you do?"

I didn't bother to answer him.

I climbed down into the shaft first, my night vision helmet letting me see well enough to find the switch for the work light. Once it was on, Aurora climbed down. It was a close fit. She found the download socket and then pulled out the knife I'd given her, rolled up her left sleeve, and held her arm up in the light to see the tattoo. She had to wet her fingers with spit and rub some of the dirt around until she found the mark, just a short blue-black line less than a centimeter long. "Cut here" it might as well have said.

"Where's Ted?" I asked. "Your vid tech guy? He should be helping with this."

"He took the hard recorder and ran off on his own after the last bulletin. I think he wants to make his own documentary."

"Afraid of the completion?" I asked, more teasing than serious.

She pushed the point of the knife deep into her arm and sucked in her breath with pain. Then she shook her head, lips pursed tight.

"No," she said, voice trembling. Blood oozed around the cut, a fair amount of blood. She handed the knife to me and held her arm in her right hand, knuckles white. "That hurt," she whispered.

"No shit. That's too much blood. You must have nicked the vein. The medtech told me what to do if you did. Here, let me hold your arm."

I steadied her arm with my left hand and with my right hand pressed the pressure point near her elbow to slow the blood flow to the cut. "Can you get the jack out?"

"I think so." She bit her lower lip and then probed into the cut with her little finger. I could feel her arm start to tremble in my hand and she closed her eyes and bent her head back, but she didn't make a sound. After what seemed like a long time to me, and which must have been an eternity to her, she pulled the small composite socket and fiber data link slowly out of the wound. Then she slowly exhaled and I realized I'd been holding my breath too. Her head lolled back a bit and then came forward.

"Feeling little woozy," she said, the words slurred. I lowered her back so she was lying in the tunnel and tried to get her knees elevated with one hand, keeping my other on the pressure point in her arm.

"You'll be okay. Just give yourself a minute. I'm going to use a little of the spray bandage on your arm. It's got an anticoagulant that should help. We may have to do it again later. I don't know if you put that thing back or what."

"I don't know either. I knew it was a backup but didn't think I'd ever need it. If I did, it was supposed to be a simple in-and-out procedure at the med center. I guess they'd put it back in, huh? And seal me back up? I'd just say the hell with it and cut the plug off when I'm done, but the damned system cost me a fortune. You think this invalidates my warranty?" She laughed. "Okay, help me up."

I got her sitting and after a quiet moment, waiting for dizziness to pass, she pulled the protective cover from her arm plug and had me connect it to the data jack in the signal splicer Moshe had put in. She closed her eyes and breathed in and out slowly three times, and then opened her eyes and nodded.

"I've got a channel. It will take me about ten minutes to download what I've got. It's rough, wish I could do more of an edit, but..."

"Yeah, but," I said. "You planning on sending that taped confession our father made to bioweapons research for AZ Kagataan?"

"I don't think so."

"Send it," I said.

Her brow furrowed in confusion. "But I thought you didn't believe it."

"Who knows? I've been wrong about a lot of things in my life. I could be wrong about that too. Send it and let the rest of the *Cottohazz* dig out the truth. Here, use your right hand to keep the pressure on the vein. Will you be okay here if I go up and keep the old man company?"

She nodded and I climbed the ladder into the darkness. I made sure our father was still where I left him and then I made a long slow sweep with the thermal viewer. The field by the shelters had a lot of thermal signatures: people too wounded for Chernagorov to take with him, people dying whether they got taken or not, people already dead but not down to the ambient temperature yet—lots of signatures, but none of them moving.

I saw traces of thermal movement here and there around us,

but a ways off. Most of them looked like people wandering lost, not like a military sweep. Nothing looked immediately threatening. I sat down next to our father.

"Are you going to take the tape off? I can't feel my fingers."

"Maybe later. While Aurora's sending she can't be recording, so we've got a few minutes to ourselves. There's something I've been meaning to ask you."

"I'm sorry I left you, Sasha. I wanted to take both the children, but your mother insisted she go instead of you. I know I should have said no, should have stood up to her. I've never forgiven myself for—"

"Ancient history," I interrupted him. "It's not about that. I want to know about neurotoxins. They're proteins, right?"

"Yes," he said cautiously, clearly surprised by the change in subject. "All naturally occurring neurotoxins are proteins." He looked at me as if he distrusted the question, thought it might be some sort of trap.

"So doesn't that make them *all* species-specific? I mean, since the major races all have incompatible protein chains?"

He frowned in thought, I guess trying to figure out what this had to do with his abandonment of me. "Yes."

"So how does a non-species-specific neurotoxin work?"

"We aren't exactly sure," he answered, but as soon as he said it he knew he'd blundered. His eyes shifted up and then to the right, the sign he was lying. "I mean...no one knows, because there is no such thing."

I grinned.

"Sure there is. The neurotoxin used as an antitamper device for the jump drive works on all the races, right? Otherwise it wouldn't be any good. Sell a drive to a Human, he gets a Zack or a Katami to look inside with impunity. But when the drive on the *Rawalpindi* cracked, *everyone* died, Human and Varoki. How did that happen?"

"I'm...not familiar with the particulars of that—"

"Bullshit! You work in neurotoxins for AZ Kagataan. AZ Kagataan is one of the biggest jump patent-holders and drive manufacturers in the *Cottohazz*, second only to AZ Simki-Traak Trans-Stellar. You mean to tell me you don't know *anything* about the universal neurotoxin they use to guard the jump drive?"

"No, I—"

"You're lying. Kagataan and Simki-Traak hate each other, have fought surrogate *wars* against each other, but about a week ago I sat in a meeting with the second governor from Simki-Traak and a third or fourth governor from Kagataan, and I listened to them as much as admit they shared a secret. How big a secret does it have to be for neither of them to spill it, even to screw over their biggest enemy?

"I think you know. I think that's why they want you dead. And I think it's so hot a potato that even CSJ was willing to do the wet work necessary to bury it and you.

"CSJ only cares about one thing: the *Cottohazz*. They guard its future, sometimes with a creepy single-minded devotion. They wouldn't care about this unless revealing it would damage the future of the Commonwealth. So what secret do the jump drive patent holders share, which is big enough to rupture the *Cottohazz*, and which involves you, and so presumably neurotoxins?

"You can tell me or not. If you don't, I'll leave you, just like you left me when I was eight years old. I'll leave you strapped to this post, and you'll die, probably very badly. If you tell me, I'll take you with us.

"Please, *please*, don't tell me."

He sat quietly for a while, maybe a minute, staring out into the dancing light and shadows of burning Sookagrad. When he turned to me his face was twisted in contempt, but right away I knew it was not for me. I'm not sure if he even saw me.

"They think they're *sooo* smart," he said, his voice low and bitter. "They think they're so very smart, but they aren't smart enough to unravel this mystery, and they knew it. Science is sometimes as much art as it is rigor, as much inspiration as procedure, and they are uninspired, worthless artists.

"So they *used* me—me and some other Human researchers, but in the end mostly me. They broke the problem up into little pieces, embedded them in different projects, spaced them out over the course of years—over *two decades!* They didn't think I'd ever see the common thread, ever see the pattern these pieces formed. After all, *they* never would have.

"Yes, I will tell you. I wonder, are you intelligent enough to grasp its significance? I somehow doubt it. You were always a disappointment to me."

And then he told me the secret.

Chapter Thirty-Six

"Sasha, can you help me please?" Aurora's voice rose from the maintenance shaft and sounded weak. I got to the edge and looked down and could see her sitting in the glow of the work light, her arm and upper legs red with blood.

"Shit!" I scrambled down the ladder and knelt beside her. "What happened? Why didn't you keep the pressure on your arm?"

"I'm sorry. I thought I did. But I got so involved with the story, with sending it...I must have been pressing the wrong place. I didn't notice until I finished. I'm sorry. Does this mean I'm not going on?"

"Shut up," I said, and started to work. She winced as I unplugged the data feed, sprayed it with the antiseptic prep spray for the bandage, and pushed it back into the open wound. I put her thumb on the upper arm pressure point and had her push. She still had enough strength to do that. As I worked, she began to talk.

"There's something else. I don't know if I'll have another chance to say this to you."

I sprayed the wound with the last of the liquid bandage solution in the dispenser and made sure it set before I ripped a sleeve off my shirt.

"Back on Peezgtaan, when Father and Mother left you, they told me only the three of us were going. Before we left."

242

I folded my shirt sleeve into a square pad, and taped it over the bandage as a cushion and protection.

"I knew we were leaving you behind. They told me not to say anything, and I didn't. I didn't."

I unbuttoned one button of her blouse and pushed her hand into it, so it would act as a sling. That was the best I could do. I couldn't scoop up all that blood and put it back in.

"Can you climb the ladder?" I said as I put my jacket and ammo harness back on.

"Did you hear me?" she said. "Do you understand what I'm saying?"

"Yes. Can you climb the ladder?"

She looked up without moving her head, as if she lacked the strength to do even that, and then looked back at me with apologetic eyes.

"If I get you up there, can you hang onto the ladder?"

"I think so."

It was hard and awkward work in the narrow shaft, but I managed to get her most of the way up, with her good arm through a rung of the ladder. I worked my way around and past her and out the narrow access hatch, then turned around and leaned in, grabbed her collar with my right hand, and supported her weight while she moved her arm to the next rung up. Then I pulled her up a rung, and we did that four more times until I had her to the lip of the hatch and out, both of us panting and sweating.

"I think someone is moving around out there," our father said. I sat up and did a thermal sweep, and there was some movement to the south, broken up by intervening structures, but it looked like three or four figures moving in formation, not toward us but heading west.

"Aurora, can you walk?"

"Maybe you should leave me here."

"Can you fucking walk?"

She looked at me and nodded. "I don't know how long."

I pulled the gauss pistol from my belt. "Can you use one of these?"

She took it in her right hand and felt its weight. "I've fired one before, but never at a person. I don't know if I could shoot someone."

"Can you shoot the old man if he tries something?"

She looked over at him and her eyes narrowed. "Yes."

I got her to her feet and then cut the tape holding the old man's hands. I'd wanted to recover the tape in case we needed it later but couldn't afford the time. I arranged us in a V formation, the old man in front, Aurora back and left, me back and right, and started us walking slowly north. I figured if we showed up on thermal sensors, we'd look like uBakai soldiers conducting a cautious sweep, not fugitives trying to escape.

North was the wrong direction, but first I wanted to get some distance between us and that patrol to the south. As we approached the open ground and shelters I saw more thermal activity off to our left, the west, including a ground vehicle moving slowly along a side road. That was probably an APC. Too much activity to the west. I wasn't sure how we were going to follow Chernagorov through all of that. I hadn't heard a lot of shooting so he must have slipped through just in time.

The ground ahead still glowed with cooling corpses and some still alive, but I also saw a flicker of shadowy movement in the uneven light of spreading fires.

"Stop." I called out to the others. "Kneel or sit where you are."

Aurora sank gratefully to the ground, the old man somewhat more cautiously.

"Movement up ahead. I'm going to check it out. Aurora, if he decides to run for it, shoot him."

"Avrochka!" he said, pathetic appeal in his voice.

"I will," she answered. "Go."

Time was running out so I covered the ground to the first of the shelters quickly, in a crouching trot. Something about the nature of the movement I'd seen didn't look like a soldier to me. I slipped down into the sandbagged entrance to the shelter for cover and used the RAG's bore-sight picture on my visor to give me a magnified view. The movement had stopped but I still saw a couple bright spots on the thermal.

"Who's up there? Show yourself or I'll throw a grenade over."

"Mr. Naradnyo?" I heard a young voice answer. "Please don't shoot!"

Then I saw movement, half a dozen figures rising up, and leading them I recognized the slight form of Divya Jayaraman, the young design student, the girl who knew every street and alley in Sookagrad by heart.

✧   ✧   ✧

"That is Plovdiv Alley, very narrow, but it empties into Grand Vision Way perhaps fifty meters to the south," Divya said, pointing at a darker part of the hodgepodge of structures and ruins. The two of us crouched next to the sandbagged entrance to one of the shelters which was not full of burned corpses.

"No good," I said. "I can see a bright heat source at the southern end of it, but there's no fire burning there. It's a vehicle with its power plant running, and there's no reason to do that unless it's carrying armament."

"Well, we can go due west for a while but we still have to cross Grand Vision Way if you want to move south. It runs all the way to Bannaz Arcology."

I'd already seen even more activity to the west, and getting closer all the time. We had to move and move now. Our party had grown to about a dozen as some stragglers wandered south, trying to escape the fighting. There was only one alternative really. Little as I liked it, I couldn't put if off any longer.

"Okay, everyone out of the shelter. Come on, form a column of twos, try to make it look military."

The rest of our party emerged from the blackness of the shelter and walked up the packed earthen ramp, singly or in twos. The old man and Aurora led them, father supporting daughter. About half of them were hurt, one way or another. Five of them were kids, not infants but ranging from about eight to twelve. One guy, a fighter named Wilson, had a RAG-14—empty until I gave him one of my two extra magazines.

They formed a ragged column of twos which would not look the least bit military except from a distance on thermals. Then it might. I stood to the side, like a sergeant addressing his squad.

"Okay, here's the deal: we can't go north, south, east, or west, and we can't fly, so we're going down that hole over there into the storm sewer. I'm going first because I have the thermal visor and will be able to see down there. We have two electric torches, but one goes with Wilson and one with Aurora," I said, giving them the lights. "Aurora, I want you and the old man in about the center of the group and Wilson, you bring up the rear. Shine the torches on the ceiling ahead of you, so we'll have reflected overhead light.

"It's a bit of a drop so I'm going first, then you," I said, pointing to a fairly strong-looking guy. "We'll catch, or at least break the fall, of the rest of you as you jump down. You'll move south, which is the direction the water's flowing, ten paces, then stop and wait for me to come up and lead. Any questions?

"Okay. Once we get set, everyone will grab the belt or shirt of the person in front of them. If there's a little one next to you, grab them with your free hand. Those of you helping wounded folks, do the best you can as a team. I won't set a fast pace, but it will be steady and you have to keep up. We'll rest five minutes every half hour."

I looked at the inky opaqueness of the hole, heard the running water down below, and wished I could recall that map of the tunnels Moshe had shown me, but all I could remember were lots of different-colored lines. Which were data, sanitary, and storm tunnels I couldn't tell you. But water flows to the sea, or in this case the Wanu River. I figured if we followed the flow of the water, and bore right whenever we could to avoid Katammu-Arc, we'd hit the river eventually. I wished I had more to go on than gut instinct, though.

"Okay, let's go."

We got down without breaking any bones, got sorted out, and started pretty much as planned. I figured navigation would be the main technical challenge, endurance the main physical one, and panic the big psychological hazard. Mostly that was right, but we'd all figured on being alone down there. Panic loomed much larger as a threat when we started hearing the voices.

They were almost certainly Human voices, but ghostly and distorted by echoing and re-echoing down the foamstone tunnels, mixed in with the omnipresent sounds of running water and our own splashing footsteps. We stopped to listen the first time but couldn't understand what they were saying, couldn't tell the language, couldn't even pick out words, just a general Human babble noise. We couldn't tell if they were close or far, approaching or receding. You could hear the emotions in them, though: panic, rage, protest—things intense and dire.

We listened, then we talked in whispers, but what was there to decide? We could go on, go back, or stand still. We went on. I unslung the RAG I'd picked up from the dead uBakai soldier and checked the magazine: twenty-three smart-head flechettes still in the system and a hundred more in the single magazine in my belt. I made sure the selector switch was on single fire instead of automatic but left the safety on.

We made slow progress, interrupted by fairly frequent slips and falls into the water. The bottom of the tunnel was slimy with mud and algae, and the current made balance tougher, especially for the kids. The tunnels being circular cross-section tubes didn't help. The only place you had much chance to keep your footing was right down the middle, which made it really difficult for those helping wounded. The healthy one had to walk in front, the injured person holding onto their shoulders, sometimes riding piggyback.

We slithered and stumbled and splashed along by fits and starts, nothing like the orderly procession I had imagined. I planned on five minutes of rest every half hour, but after about an hour of walking we needed longer breaks. Not only was trudging through the water exhausting, the air was stale and so humid it seemed thick and heavy, as if it took more effort to force it into your lungs than normal air. The tunnel wasn't sealed, but there was no regular ventilation either, just whatever air happened to drift in the storm drains.

Probably in our second or third hour we encountered the first of the sewer people. I heard the suddenly louder voices up ahead, then the frantic splashing run.

I held my fist up to stop the column, then whispered, "Torches out!" Instantly the tunnel was pitch black.

They came around a bend ten or twenty meters ahead of us and I saw them in green negative images on my visor before anyone else could make them out. There were three of them, Humans, filthy and in rags. I think one of them was a woman. They ran with their arms thrust out ahead of them, used to moving in the dark.

"Halt!" I yelled and Aurora turned on her torch, shining it ahead and over my shoulder. It played across them and they instantly covered their eyes with their hands and screamed in panic, then turned and ran back the way they'd come.

"Wait!" I called out. "We won't hurt you! Who are you?"

They didn't hear me, or didn't believe me, or were beyond understanding.

The encounter left us unsettled, but we kept going.

An hour or two later—it was getting hard to remember how

long we'd been walking down there—five of them ran toward us down a long straight stretch, so I saw them on thermals from quite a distance and they saw our light. For whatever reason, maybe because it was not such a surprise, it didn't frighten them, or at least not as much as what they were fleeing. They ran toward us shouting, all at the same time, the different voices and echoes rendering each other mutually unintelligible. But one word jumped out, over and over again.

"*Gas!*" they screamed. "Run! Gas! The Varoki are gassing the sewers!"

I took a step back in panic but made myself stop. I grabbed the first man as he tried to push past.

"Where? Did you see it?"

He wouldn't make eye contact, struggled to get free, and kept gesturing down the tunnel behind them. "*Gas!*"

He pushed against me and I lost my footing, fell against the tunnel wall and slid into the water, and he was gone past me followed by the others. They pushed Aurora and our father down and the torch fell into the water, making the surface glow and sparkle.

I sat there for a moment, short of breath as much from the excitement as the exertion. I got the RAG out of the water and shook it, then got the electric torch. Both were solid state and designed to take at least this much punishment, but it was stupid to tempt fate.

"Is everyone all right?" I asked, shining the torch back on the others. The gauss pistol I'd given to Aurora had found its way into our father's hand and although it wasn't aimed at me, it was angled in my general direction.

"You better either shoot me or give that back to your daughter," I said, "and do it now."

Something flickered in his eyes, a moment's pause before deciding. Then he made a production of shaking the water from the pistol as I had done and handed it grip-first to Aurora.

I held the torch higher and shined it farther back. I could see a light bouncing up and down, receding up the tunnel. "Wilson, where's your light?"

"Mr. Wilson left with the others," Divya said.

"The others?" I said and played the torch around. Our group had grown smaller. Aside from Aurora, Pops, and myself, there was Divya, a middle-aged woman holding onto her young boy, and three wounded—two men and a woman—slumped in the water where their helpers had dropped them.

"Oh shit."

I walked back to them and sat beside them, trying to assess how bad off they were.

"Can you walk on your own?" I asked each of them in turn. One of the men said yes, he thought so, but the other two shook their heads, their faces lined with exhaustion and pain, eyes wide with fear.

"Aurora, can you walk on your own?" I called to her.

She paused before answering, then said, "Yes, for a while at least."

"I can help Miss Aurora," Divya said.

"No," the mother said. "You mind my Petya and I will help Miss Aurora."

"Thanks. Father-of-ours, you will help this injured lady and I'll try to carry the guy. What's your name, by the way?"

"Konstantine," the wounded man said, his voice weak. His head and left leg were bandaged, both bandages soaked with blood and now muddy as well.

"Okay, Kostya, looks like I'm your ride. Put your arms around my shoulder and hang on."

"I'm an old man," my father said, looking at the woman he was to carry.

"You want to get any older? Help her."

"What about the gas, Sasha?" Divya asked. No one else spoke but I could see in their eyes that all of them were thinking that.

"I don't think there's gas up ahead, or if there is, I'm betting it's a nonlethal riot control agent. Might make us puke and cough, but it won't kill us. If it's lethal, nobody would have gotten away to give the warning, not down here. But I'll go ahead of the group just to be sure. Aurora will keep the light on me so you will know whether or not I fall down. Pretty tough on you, Kostya. You up for it?"

"Better than to stay here," he said.

Chapter Thirty-Seven

I found the switch for the helmet light and turned it on, switching off the thermal viewer. The thermals ate a lot more power and I didn't know how much battery life the helmet had left, and who the hell knew how far we had to go? Every hundred meters of tunnel looked exactly like the last hundred meters and the next hundred meters, unless there was a junction. We came to a couple junctions and had always taken the right branch, so I was pretty sure we'd steered clear of Katammu-Arc.

Kostya and I were still out front. I hadn't sniffed any gas, at least that I could be sure of. A couple times I caught a whiff of something sharp and industrial, something which got my eyes watering, but it had passed. There was enough funky stiff down there, no telling what that was.

First time we got to a rest halt I looked back and saw the torch lighting the ceiling behind me and had called out to Aurora, "Rest break, ten minutes."

"Okay," she called back.

I had a chronometer in the helmet so you'd think I could tell ten minutes, but I kept forgetting when the time started. When it seemed long enough I yelled, "Starting up again," and she yelled, "Okay," and we splashed on down the endless pipe. Aurora didn't answer on rest breaks after a while, too tired I

250

guess, but the light was still there lighting the ceiling, so I knew they were following.

I heard more voices in the side corridors when we passed some of the junctions, but we didn't see any more sewer people. I wondered where they came from and how long they'd been down there. They couldn't have been there the whole time. The rains those first few days would have drowned them, but they looked as if they'd been there forever, as if they'd forgotten any life they'd had above ground.

Kostya wasn't much of a conversationalist, and after an hour or so he passed out, so it was just me, the voices, and the sound of my own splashing footsteps, one after another. There were some small animals in the water too, not at first but later. I wasn't afraid of them. After all, I was a lot more dangerous to them than they were to me. Any local animal, one bite out of me would kill them. Maybe that's why Varoki didn't like us; they couldn't eat us without dying.

The water got shallower and I realized I could hardly see where the helmet light was pointed. Maybe the battery was running down, but I could still see okay, so I guessed my eyes were adjusting to the dark. But when I stopped to catch my breath and looked up, I saw the wall noticeably brighter by the next bend. I lowered Kostya to the floor and leaned him against the wall of the tube. Then I unslung the RAG and clicked the safety off.

"Stay here, pal. I'm going to check out that light." Of course he was unconscious so he couldn't hear me. I looked back and the tunnel was empty up to the last bend. I splashed back to it, where it was much darker, and looked around the corner and up. I saw the glow of the electric torch on the ceiling.

"Aurora," I called in a hoarse whisper, not wanting my voice to carry too far. "Are you there?"

No answer. I looked again at the ceiling and saw the reflection of the torch but it moved when my head moved from side to side, and I realized I was seeing the glow of my own helmet light. How long had I been seeing my own light and thinking they were still behind me? Hours? Days? How long had I been down here?

I sat down in the water and just looked, my mind empty, body spent.

After a while I got to my feet and staggered back toward the lighter end of the tunnel. When I got there I raised the RAG in both hands and walked around the corner. I could hardly see in the dazzling glare, but in a few seconds my eyes adjusted enough that I could see I was looking at daylight, the yellow-white glare of the star Akatu reflected off the rippling surface of the Wanu River. The storm sewer terminated about five meters past the bend.

I walked back and pulled Kostya to the entrance of the pipe where the air was a lot better and the sun would warm him, because he'd gotten pretty cold. I turned his face to the sun and noticed his eyes were about half open. I sat down beside him for a while and looked at the river. I wasn't so far gone I hadn't figured he was dead. It just took me a while. As I sat there, two men with rifles over their shoulders walked up. They had black fisherman caps, just like I used to before I traded it for this helmet. I also noticed they wore Munie badges, just like our fighters had.

"Where you from?" one of them asked.

"Peezgtaan," I answered, and then realized he meant more recently. "Oh...uh, Sookagrad. I think I'm trying to find the Black Docks. Have you heard of them?"

They grinned.

"About two hundred yards downriver is where the docks are. You inside the perimeter right now. We supposed to watch for Varoki infiltrators."

"I'm not Varoki," I said.

They exchanged a look and then the other one said, "You better come with us, we get you fixed up."

"Can't. Eight more people back in there. I gotta go get them."

They looked at each other again, their looks incredulous. "Go? Can you even stand up?"

It took a little work, but I stood up.

"Let Abílo go instead," the first one said. "He's gone in the tunnels, pretty far."

The second guy nodded.

I looked at the sun and felt it warm my face, felt how sweet the air smelled, how easily it filled my lungs after the stale miasma of the tunnel. I was weak, might not even make it back to wherever they were. This guy knew the tunnels, he was strong. I closed my eyes for a second or two.

"He can come along with me."

✧　　　✧　　　✧

"You went back?" Cézar Ferraz said. "So, you crazy, is what. Well, I thought so since I pull you out river. But for family makes sense, yeah?"

I took another drink of the espresso, which was heavily laced with something potent. Whatever it was, it was smoothing out a lot of kinks and bumps.

"My family's in Kootrin. Those people from the tunnel are mostly strangers."

He frowned. "Not father and sister?"

I looked at him for a moment, thinking about my answer. "That's complicated," was all I could come up with.

"Well, two little kids and boy's mother fine. Other five in med center, but be okay."

I finished my cup.

"More?" he said, and I nodded.

As he poured I looked around the bunker built into the riverbank and with a wide view of the river. It was poured foamstone, fairly recent too, the walls still sweating and smelling of catalyst. The main firing slit facing the river was broad but not very high. What looked like a big electrocoil harpoon gun was bolted to the floor, its muzzle poking out of the center of the embrasure. I wasn't sure what it was loaded with, but it sure wasn't a harpoon. Some sort of spigot bomb, it looked like. They had a land line phone installed in the bunker. That was smart. I wonder if we didn't think of it or just didn't have the needed hardware.

I nodded toward the harpoon gun. "Can you actually hit anything with that?"

"Sank militia boat with it, two days ago." He shrugged. "I think lucky shot, but Dado say he always hits where he aims. Same Dado pulled you out of the water."

I took a sip of the fresh cup. "What do you call this stuff? It's pretty good."

"*Café com música*. The *aguardente* makes it sing."

"Sure does." I sipped again and leaned back, watched driftwood slide by on the Wanu. No boats out today—too dangerous. The government was shooting at Human-crewed boats and now Dado was blowing up militia boats with a jury-rigged explosive harpoon gun. It was no more ridiculous than the multiple launchers we'd used to bring down a gunsled.

Cézar had already roughed out the situation for me. The Black

Docks had been under siege as long as Sookagrad. The big difference was the Black Docks people weren't all Human; a lot of stiff-necked Varoki loyalists had stuck around. They helped the Humans fight off the mobs until the initial attacks had petered out.

Now getting rid of the enclave was a little more complicated than Sookagrad had been. After all, the Provisional Government had overthrown the old bosses for killing Varoki citizens. They couldn't very well just kill a bunch of them themselves, and so far all attempts to coax out the Varoki fishermen had failed. The irony of it made me smile.

"So, Cézar, what do you think of leatherheads now, since they're saving your ass?"

"Oh, fishermen are different. All fishermen are brothers, yeah? Besides, maybe not save ass much longer. Army says we keep them here as hostages, is what. Maybe they have to come rescue them."

Yeah, dirty rotten Humans took Varoki hostages, who were tragically killed by their Human captors during the rescue attempt. If you could control the news, control the communications, you could make something like that fly. And they'd finally thought of it, right when we got here.

"Man, I tell you," I said, "lately I am like the cooler in a casino. I show up and everyone's luck turns to shit."

I looked down at the *Café com música,* but all I saw were faces, faces of people I hadn't even known ten days ago, but who had grown large in my life in a very short time. How many of them were alive to see the sun today? Were any of them?

"Has anyone else from Sookagrad come in, other than us?" I asked.

"Not many. Maybe one, two hundred, come in all through the night and morning. Looked like hell of a fight."

"It was a massacre," I said, but the word felt bad in my mouth. "No, that's not right. That's not right at all. A woman named Zdravkova, who commanded the defense force, planned and executed a surprise attack that was a thing of beauty, caught the Army in the middle of setting up shop and spanked their asses good, chewed the militia up and spit out the bones. She put the Army right back on their heels, and then she led the breakout, due east, cracked their line wide open and pushed right through, taking everyone with her: kids, wounded, mothers with babes in arm, the whole outfit."

"What happened?" he asked.

I sighed. "No heavy weapons except made-up crap like that." I nodded at the harpoon gun. "Not enough ammo. No communication except by runner. We still might have pulled it off, but gunsleds cut off the escape corridor. We even brought one of those bastards down, but it wasn't enough. They just kept coming. I don't know how many people got out with Zdravkova, or if she even managed to fight her way free. What came after...well, *that* was a massacre. But Zdravkova and her kids made the uBakai pay for it in advance. They really made 'em howl."

I finished the espresso. "We had a patch into a data fiber pipe, started sending out bulletins. My sister got one last one out about the massacre. I don't know if anyone—"

"*That* your sister? Aurora? Didn't recognize her in hospital."

"Yeah, she's my sister, sort of. But how—?"

"Broadcasts got out, yeah? We see all of them. We made some bulletins, too, like yours but without Aurora, so not as good. 'Black Docks Calling,'" he said in a deep voice.

I opened my mouth again to ask how but he shook his head. "You think you are only smart ones, yeah? All broadcast jammed. Army blocks all uplinks to satellites. Data lines all encrypted. What is left? Oceanic navigation relay towers, is what. Along coast of *Zhak Kakavaan*. From top of Mercantile Building have line of sight, down Wanu River valley, and Army never thinks to block. Navy might have. So can bounce tight beam off towers, send and receive, but we not advertise how, yeah?

"I tell you, things getting bad out there: uKootrin Army has crossed border, occupied everything down banks of *Zhak Kakavaan* to maybe two hundred kilometers north of here."

The *Zhak Kakavaan* was a large inland sea east of Sakkatto City, about as large as Lake Baikal back on Earth. Tweezaa's family had a house on its shore north of the capital.

"Not much fighting yet—disarmed uBakai troops, turned towns over to loyalist officials, but word is uBakai moving troops north for counterattack. Gaantist demonstrations in Kootrin last few days, now in some other Varoki countries too, maybe even riots is what. Somebody don't slap the Army down here pretty soon..." He let his voice trail off and looked down at his espresso.

So the trouble was spreading. At least the last bulletin got out. Everyone saw it. I closed my eyes for a moment and just sat there, feeling one part of the anxiety I'd been carrying for days slip away. Whatever else happened, the *Cottohazz* knew what we'd done, and they saw what the uBakai Army had done.

I pushed my chair back from the table and stood up.

"I'm going to the hospital. Aurora needs to hear this."

"Needs to hear from brother, yeah?" Cézar said. "Okay, go. But then come back, you meet big boss, tell him about fight, what worked and what not, yeah?"

Chapter Thirty-Eight

Aurora seemed to get stronger as soon as I told her the news, and I think the fact I came to tell her personally helped.

She'd lost a fair amount of blood and then had driven herself to exhaustion, as we all had, getting here. They were giving her plasma, and would have done whole blood but there was a shortage of A negative. I offered to give some of mine—no question of compatibility there—but the tech took a look at my veins, gums, and eyes and told me to spend a day getting hydrated and some sleep and decent food first. I didn't know about the sleep, but the food and liquids I could manage. The big question was whether any of us would still be around tomorrow.

Concerning that subject, I had another meeting to get to so I left her to rest.

I remembered the Black Docks district as being a lot cleaner than Sookagrad back before the trouble started, and if it was getting cluttered now due to all these people, it still didn't look like a trash pile. A lot of commercial activity went on here before, and that meant real money flowing in. I didn't see any rich folks, but I saw a lot of working class people who looked as if they ate regularly, had medical and dental care, and bought clothes instead of scrounging for cast-off rags.

I sensed energy as I walked from the med center to the head-quarters bunker back by the river bank. People moved like they

257

had somewhere to go and something to do when they got there. I saw no complacency, and plenty of anxiety, but faces with hope and determination instead of resignation or despair. I also saw a lot of Varoki, many of them with Humans. We'd taken a step toward that a few hours before the end at Sookagrad, but these folks had been doing it all along here, and it probably had kept them alive this long. They certainly hadn't had to do as much fighting.

The headquarters was another bunker built into the riverbank, but bigger and with the northern face slightly above ground, showing some firing slits to landward. They'd piled dirt over the roof to partially conceal it, and unless you looked close it looked like any of a dozen other excavations along there. A guard made me wait until Cézar came and vouched for me, and then I got in to see the "big boss."

He rose to greet me and offered his hand to shake. "Mr. Naradnyo, it is a pleasure to finally meet you. You will appreciate that I have already heard a great deal about you. My name is Ita Maganaan, and I am the executive secretary of our citizens' counsel."

Son of a bitch! He was *Varoki*.

I shook Maganaan's hand and looked at Cézar, who grinned back at me, enjoying his joke.

"Secretary Maganaan, I'm sorry if I look surprised, but our friend Cézar did not tell me you were Varoki. In fact—"

"I understand completely. Cézar was my most outspoken opponent when we had to select a secretary, one might even say my most virulent one. But I think to both of our surprise he has become my closest associate on the counsel. Unfortunately, that means I am required to endure his dreadful sense of humor.

"As you can see, the Black Docks is not a Human enclave; it is a Loyalist enclave. Perhaps seventy percent of our pre-coup population was Varoki. Now the populations are probably about even, as a number of our Varoki residents have left the enclave, out of fear of attack or in support of the Provisional Government, while many Humans have come here for sanctuary. You and the other refugees from Sookagrad are the most recent.

"I would like to tell you more about what we have done here, how we have organized ourselves for everyday sustenance and for defense, but I am afraid time is short. All afternoon Army units have been redeploying south from the Sookagrad area to back up the militia units holding the perimeter around the enclave. They have issued an ultimatum similar to the one Sookagrad received, and I think it almost certain they will launch an attack sometime before its dawn expiration."

"Yeah," I said, and then stopped myself from a comment about how Varoki were not generally very imaginative. "I'm also willing to bet a preemptive attack by your troops will not do as well as ours did. We caught them completely by surprise, and I think they'll be on their toes this time."

"I agree," he said. "In any event, our defense forces are not as numerous, as well-equipped, or as organized as were yours, so far as we can determine. They are enthusiastic, but you seem to have had a number of very experienced fighters and leaders. As I understand, Commander Zdravkova was a former officer in the ground forces."

I nodded, because that was technically true. Better for him to think she learned the fighter's trade in the military than in the anti-Varoki resistance.

"Now, I have viewed the feed clip which shows you destroying a gunsled with an improvised launcher of some sort, the recording made by your sister I understand. We have no time to build additional weapons, but I would like you to tell me every detail you can remember about how the uBakai Army fought and what your soldiers found to work and to fail against them."

I sat for a moment thinking, organizing my thoughts and memories, and finally I shook my head.

"No, there's no time for that. I don't know any silver bullets which can turn the tide here, and the sort of nuts-and-bolts procedures I do know—there's no time to collect, organize, and disseminate them in time to make any difference. If you don't mind some advice, why don't you just have Cézar or someone else take me on a tour of your troop positions? Just talking to the troops, answering a question or two, giving them a piece or advice here or there—that might do a lot more good. If any of our fighters came in, especially squad leaders or higher, maybe they could do the same."

Maganaan exchanged a look with Cézar and then nodded.

"Very well. That may be better. I am afraid our time is very short."

✧　　✧　　✧

Cézar took me off to the far eastern end of the perimeter, where it butted up against the river and I started talking with fighters. The first strongpoint covering the River Road approach had about twenty men and women with an assortment of small arms, mostly civilian sporting stuff, and one of those electrocoil harpoon spigot cannons. It turns out most of them had seen the clip of the destruction of the gunsled and wanted to know how to bring one down themselves.

"I'll be honest, luck played a big role. But you can't get lucky unless you give yourself the chance. Their main vulnerable points are the four lifting fans. The blades are superhard composites, so even milspec smart-head flechettes won't make much of an impression. But that spigot harpoon thing of yours might."

"What about their electrostatic armor?" one of them asked.

"It's designed to detonate an explosive round and vaporize the tip of a solid penetrator, destabilize it. I think we got through by getting a bunch of simultaneous hits, that and the fact that even a destabilized, tumbling penetrator of that size will still mess up the fan blades. The ESA field is in pretty tight. That harpoon thing's got a big enough warhead, if you get it next to the fan assembly and the ESA field detonates it, you'll probably still get pretty good results."

I took a closer look at their harpoon gun, asked them about its effective range, and found out they couldn't hit much of anything beyond about a hundred meters. Fortunately, this one was on a wheeled carriage.

"Here's something you have to do right now," I said. "You've got your gun out here where it's got a field of fire a kilometer long out into the river and nearly as far down the road. Fields of fire work both ways. Once they know it's here, they can just stand back out of range and kill you."

I looked around the nearby buildings.

"Try moving it over by that little building there, right behind that loading dock. You want a field of fire that, as soon as something shows up in it, you can kill it."

I still wasn't sure how much effect the harpoon explosive would have on a gunsled, but giving them something constructive to do, something which made sense and at least increased their chances, seemed to pump their morale.

We continued moving along the perimeter and I said something to every group of fighters, try to give them some sort of little advice that would help their confidence. After about twenty minutes I saw a familiar figure approach us.

"Corporal Chernagorov?"

He smiled. "So, you remember Chernagorov? Very glad see you, Mr. Naradnyo. Was worried when not catch up. Too many soldiers behind for to go back and find."

"Yeah, same guys that kept us from following you. How many did you get through?"

His smile faded. "Not so many as started. Seventy-one I brought here is all, out of maybe two hundred. There was fighting, some got shot, but lost more I think from tired and discouraged."

"I know. Over half the people I started to bring through the storm sewers turned back. I don't think any of them made it out. You did what you could."

I paused before asking the next question. Until I did, Moshe was just missing, but this might make it final. "I don't suppose many of the stretcher cases made it through with you."

"Most, yes. People who carried, maybe they felt not just walking for self, also for someone else to live, so kept on."

I took a breath. "Moshe Greenwald?"

"Yes, your friend! Thought knew, is in med center. I hear be okay."

I felt a wave of relief wash over me, a more powerful emotion than I was prepared for and I couldn't speak for a few seconds, so I nodded my understanding.

Chernagorov had been sent to join us, so he walked with us and added comments to those of mine. His were a lot more specific about small unit tactics, which is exactly what these guys needed. At one stop he also commented on how little ammunition the front line troops had, and wondered what the arrangements were for getting more to them. There were none, because this was all the ammunition they had.

Until then I hadn't appreciated what an enormous difference Nikolai Stal's software pirating operation had given us in Sookagrad. They had almost no ability to fabricate anything here, since the jamming kept them from downloading any fabrication licenses, no matter how much they were willing to pay for them, and they couldn't hack their fabricators' storage memory to get at the programs already downloaded to memory.

The only fabricators which worked were the ones set up for on-demand fabrication of long-term licenses with automatic billing, like drug fabricators in med centers. The bills were building up inside the machines and once the jamming ended there'd be a lot of money sucked out of the district, but in the meantime they could get a few basic necessities made. That included some common types of flechettes, but didn't include rifle and pistol magazines.

So the fighters on the perimeter were really short of ammunition, and there was nothing in reserve behind them. They also weren't as well equipped as the Sookagrad forces had been. I suspected that Zdravkova had something to do with that: her resistance cell must have stockpiled a fair cache of milspec small arms, and that's why I saw so many RAGs at first. Of course, after the Big Attack they were everywhere. Here I hardly saw any at all.

Within an hour the sun dropped below the horizon and we continued the tour in deepening twilight. We were almost to the far west side when a runner found us and told us to get back to the north side right away. Something was happening. The runner was little Divya Jayaraman.

"Why'd they send you?" I asked. "You don't know the streets here yet, do you?"

She nodded. "We used to live here before we moved closer to e-Kruaan for my school. We lived lots of places. But you need to hurry, you too Mr. Ferraz. They say the Army may be getting ready to attack."

We moved pretty fast through the gathering darkness back to a command post about fifty meters behind the positions blocking the main street from the north, the center of the defenses. A soldier directed us up the stairs to the building's roof where Secretary Maganaan and several Humans and Varoki who looked like officers met us.

"Mr. Naradnyo, I am happy to see you," Maganaan said. "Our rooftop observers have seen clear evidence that the militia and regular army units are pulling back from the perimeter all along its length, and are doing so with some dispatch. Did you encounter a similar act as prelude to their assaults on your defenses?"

"No. Nothing like that."

"What do you think it means?" one of Human officers asked.

I thought for a moment. "All I can think of is they are tired of taking heavy losses in frontal attacks without softening things up first. My guess is they plan to pound the perimeter with indirect fire and don't want any friendly casualties."

One of the rooftop lookouts turned and shook his head. "I think they're running, is what. No more fight in them." I started toward him but Divya grabbed my arm and pointed up.

"Look, Sasha," she said, "fireworks in the sky. Does it mean we won?"

I looked up and saw the yellow-red streaks of reentry capsules, hundreds of them, no, a couple thousand, burning in across the night sky at a steep angle from the west. Some would be decoys, but among them...

A few ground interceptor missiles streaked up but remote escorting gun capsules took most of them out, their rocket booster exhausts terminating in bright yellow explosions, followed by soft thuds a couple seconds later. Just like fireworks.

Mike Troopers—Meteoric Insertion Capable—in at least reinforced cohort strength, maybe a full Mike brigade. The *Cottohazz* to the rescue: an opposed meteoric insertion from orbit here, on Hazz'Akatu, the Varoki home world. This was one for the history books. It took me a few seconds to find my voice.

"Yes, sweetheart. It means we won."

Chapter Thirty-Nine

This was the third opposed insertion by Mike troopers I'd seen in my life. The first one was twelve years earlier, on a nasty little world called Nishtaaka. I was a newly promoted (by virtue of my three predecessors all having become casualties) lance corporal in the 2nd Cohort, Peezgtaan Loyal Volunteers. We were strictly a second-string outfit of ground pounders whose job in the Second Battle of Sikander's Mountain was to make a heroic frontal assault and get everyone's attention while an *Azza-kaat* cohort dropped on the main objective. *Azza-kaat* is what the Varoki call their Mike troopers.

Second time was two years ago on K'Tok, when a platoon of USMC Mike Marines dropped to rescue us. That time I was right in the middle of their drop zone: very impressive.

This time the sky was full of them. Each trooper's descent ended with a final glide under a parasail and a landing on their feet with weapons ready. Some of them came down right inside the perimeter, and by the time their boots touched ground, everyone in the Black Docks knew the cavalry was here. There was a lot of cheering.

All of the crew from the roof of the headquarters trooped downstairs to meet them in the street and by the time they landed it was clear they were Human, not Varoki. After my initial surge of relief,

264

I started wondering if dropping Human Mike troopers into the middle of this was the best way to calm things down. Once Humans got a look at what had happened in Sookagrad—and there hadn't been enough time for the uBakai to have sanitized the site—they might just start shooting uBakai soldiers on general principle. Not that that was such a bad idea, I just wasn't sure if Humans doing the shooting would help things in the long run.

The first thing I noticed about the Mike troopers when they dropped their parasail harnesses was the big fistful of black feathers on the sides of their helmets. I'd never seen anything like it, not that my military experience was all that broad. I saw a conference between a handful of Mike troopers and the defenders at the main roadblock down the street and then a party of Mikes started trotting toward us, trotting in step and in formation, no less. We waited for them and when they reached us the guy in front stepped up and gave a really sharp salute.

"Lieutenant Arturo Lorioli, Tenth *Bersaglieri Inserimento Meteorico*, at your service. Who is in command?"

Maganaan stepped forward and offered his hand. "I am the Executive Secretary of the Citizens' Counsel of Black Docks District. We are delighted to see you Lieutenant."

"Secretary Maganaan, I see you in the vid bulletins you file. Good day. My cohort commander, Major Massignani, would like to colocate his command post with yours, for cooperation. Also, if you can give a list of your most urgent supply needs to our quartermaster sergeant, we can have them dropped in one or two orbital transits. Within a day, two at most, we should have air supply available from Old Tower Downstation, but until then..." he pointed upward, shrugged, and smiled.

"Has there been any opposition on the ground?" I asked.

"Not in our cohort's area of operations," he said. "Our task is to secure your perimeter and take over its defense, although we welcome the assistance of your fighters in any capacity they choose. But it is our responsibility now. The uBakai Army has withdrawn, but we will remain alert. There is fighting in the other two cohort zones, I am told."

"You have a working tacnet?" I asked.

"*Sì*. We eliminated the hoverplats disrupting uplink communication, so our command net is functional and civilian service should return within an hour, maybe a little more."

"Where is the fighting," Maganaan asked, "if you are free to say."

"Of course. One cohort dropped to secure the Sookagrad site, prevent destruction of evidence, search for possible survivors, and disarm all uBakai military units—by force if necessary. The other cohort dropped around Drak'zanaat Arcology. Many of the survivors of Sookagrad fought their way there and entrenched themselves in the interior lower levels, where uBakai heavy vehicles could not be used against them. Very resourceful. That cohort rescues them."

"Are all three cohorts Human?" I asked.

He frowned. "No. That is why we are sent here, where there is less chance of fighting. Politics, you see. Major Massignani asked, no, *begged*, for one of the other drop zones, but instead we are here."

He glanced around and looked suddenly sheepish. "I do not mean we do not think this is important. We follow your bulletins, we admire you very much, and are proud to secure your safety. But to hit back, that is what we wanted most."

He might be disappointed, but I was relieved. Somebody up in orbit, or on the Executive Council, had used their head. Well, given the fact that this whole crisis had spooled out in about a week, they probably had to go with what they already had on station here, whatever that ended up being, but it had worked out fine. No Human-Varoki fighting, so less chance of a long-term festering wound. Of course, using troops from a different Varoki country might have its own repercussions.

"The other two cohorts are Varoki?" I asked.

He turned to me and smiled broadly. "No, they are Zaschaan."

The sun shone bright overhead, a cool breeze blew in from the south across the Wanu River, and for the first time in a very long time I laughed.

I found a spot away from all the noise and celebration and just sat quietly for a long time. I turned the power up on my embedded commlink for the first time in over a week and listened to the hum of the jammers. I listened to it for almost an hour before it suddenly went away, and I blinked to send the comm address I'd had waiting all that time. She answered almost immediately.

Sasha!

"Marr, I'm okay. I'm okay, honest, I'm okay and I'm so sorry, so sorry, and I love you so much."

Oh, come home! Please just come home to us.

"I will, I promise. As soon as I can get transportation I'm coming home. And listen, this probably sounds stupid, but when I get there...do you want to learn how to samba?"

The next morning, after donating a unit of blood for Aurora, I sat in the heart of CSJ headquarters in Katammu-Arc, in a much larger office than before. Field Marshal Lieutenant e-Loyolaan faced me across his desk and studied me for a while.

I was not out of the woods yet, not by any means. Everything up until now meant very little if it ended up with me in a CSJ interrogation cell facing some guy whose orders were, "Find out everything Naradnyo knows," and who did not share my aversion to traumatic interrogations. If they did that, they would find everything out eventually. I knew a lot of pretty incriminating stuff, and not just incriminating to me. Too many people would go down, most of them much better people than I was, so I figured I needed to do some pretty smart talking in the next ten minutes.

As before, e-Loyolaan's face didn't give much away. Finally he spoke.

"I sent four CSJ agents into Sookagrad and three were murdered."

"Murdered? They kidnapped a citizen without identifying themselves as CSJ. The legally constituted law enforcement authorities told them to surrender, and did not shoot them until they themselves opened fire. The locals did everything right and your men did everything wrong. If those men were murdered, the murderer is the one who ordered them to carry out that mission in that way."

"To what extent your gang of criminals and revolutionaries was legally constituted law enforcement is a matter of dispute, but also beside the point. I want the people who killed my agents."

If he felt any personal responsibility for that mess, he covered it well.

"Sift the ashes of Sookagrad. You'll find their bones."

He looked away for a while, his eyes on one of the identical blank walls, but unfocused, far away. Finally he looked back, his expression still unreadable.

"An interesting message sent with the survivor, Mr. Naradnyo: 'I have him and I know what he knows.' Were you disappointed when your sister transmitted the confession to the entire *Cottohazz* and stole your exclusive ownership of that knowledge?"

"Some things, it's too dangerous to be the only one who knows," I said.

"Ah, that is very true, Mr. Naradnyo. Very true. Of course, his confession implicating AZ Kagataan in his bioweapons research will have considerable repercussions, all of which will financially benefit your young ward, won't they?"

"Tweezaa e-Traak is not my ward. She's the adopted daughter of Arigapaa e-Lotonaa. My wife is her court-appointed fiduciary guardian until she reaches her majority, but my only formal relation to her is head of security. I keep her alive; I have no responsibility with respect to her inheritance."

"No responsibility, but your fortunes are tied to hers, yes?"

"I'm not on commission, if that's what you mean. I'm on straight salary, and she'd have to get a lot poorer for my paychecks not to clear."

I could tell he didn't believe me, but it was a lie he expected, one within his comfort zone. He stared at me and colored slightly, an ear twitched. I suddenly was certain he burned to ask whether my father's confession was *all* I knew, and that told me he knew the other part.

That was the first thing he had ever given away to me. The biggest secret, the biggest lie in the *Cottohazz*, and the head of CSJ knew it and guarded it, which figured. *Knowledge* was one of their three precepts, not *Truth*.

No matter what else happened, they were going to end up putting my father through the wringer and figure out what he'd told me. If e-Loyolaan was going to know that eventually, the question was how and when I wanted him to find out.

"There's something else you want to ask me," I said.

He shifted in his chair, the first time I think I'd ever seen any sign he was uncomfortable.

"I am always interested in the totality of one's knowledge," he said, "or at least what is relevant to the well-being of the *Cottohazz*. It is my responsibility."

"Sure. As far as that goes, I've told you everything I know. I've *heard* other things, but that's not the same as knowing."

He became very still and looked at me closely. "What is the difference between hearing and knowing, in your opinion?"

"Proof."

We sat there for a few seconds, studying each other, and I let him see as deep into me as he wanted. I wasn't hiding anything, at least on this point.

"One man's testimony can sometimes be considered an element of proof," he said.

"Not if he's already on record confessing to complicity in illegal bioweapons research, and that confession is everywhere on the float. Either he's a criminal or he's a liar. In either case, no one important's ever going to listen to him again."

"And is there a recording of this other conversation, the thing you *heard*?"

"Nope."

"I imagine that if there is, it is almost certainly in your sister's bio-recorder memory. I could simply bring her in and find out. She might not enjoy the experience."

"Probably not, but I think you would enjoy it even less. Maybe you haven't noticed, but she's the voice of Sookagrad, a heroine to everyone in the *Cottohazz* who watched this disaster unfold. Right now, this morning, the two hottest-trending topics on the float are which studio is going to get the holovid rights to pro- duce *Sookagrad Calling,* and who they're going to cast as Aurora. And you're going to snatch her off the street, pump her full of drugs, and do a surgical download of her recorder memory? If you do, you're finished as head of CSJ."

He actually frowned. Whatever else happened, I figured I could call this a win based just on making Field Marshal Lieutenant e-Loyolaan frown. He absently tapped his finger on the desk a few times and when its smart surface came to life he jumped a bit, looked annoyed, and immediately turned it off. I was careful not to react in any way.

"You will be leaving for Kootrin from here?" he asked finally.

"Yeah. Commissioner-designate Prayzaat, the acting commandant of the Sakkatto City Munies—he being a war buddy of mine and all—has lifted the material witness summons, so I'm free to travel. I have a couple things to do, but then I'm gone, as soon as I can arrange transport. Of course, things are still pretty snarled up."

"I believe I can expedite that. Under the circumstances, I think the sooner you leave Bakaa, the better for all concerned. But there is one more matter. Your father has been taken into custody and will almost certainly be remaining with us for...quite some time. He is in this complex. If you like, I can arrange for you to visit him before you leave."

I thought about it but shook my head.

"We're not really that close."

While e-Loyolaan worked on lining up my transportation, I checked in on Moshe in the Black Docks med center. The maglev was running again and I took it to Praha-Riz and then a local over to the Black Docks stop. A lot of the Varoki looked at me uncomfortably, some out of resentment, I guess for the humiliating invasion a Human enclave's troubles had brought down on the city, some out of guilt for why it had been necessary. No one said anything to me, though, possibly because of the Zack Mike trooper who stood at one end of the maglev car, glaring at the passengers between belches.

When I got to the med center Moshe already had a visitor, Dezi Zdravkova.

"Hey, Killer. That was a good move, holing up in Drak'zanaat Arcology."

She stood up and shook my hand, smiling. "I didn't think I'd see you again. I thought both of you were dead when I found out no one got past those gunsleds. I was up at the front of the column and didn't find out until later—too late."

"Nothing you could have done but get yourself killed," Moshe said from his bed. "Sasha, your sister told how you got out, through the storm sewers. That was good thinking."

"Yeah, we're all pretty smart," I said, "smart and good-looking."

And alive, unlike most of the others. The uBakai had not exempted the clinic from their no-surrender order so Doc Mahajan was dead along with all of her patients. Dolores Wu had been killed in the long running fight getting to Drak'zanaat Arcology. Billy Conklin had made it there but had died in the brutal room-to-room fighting on the lower levels along with Bogo Katranjiev. Bela Ripnick had disappeared somewhere in the chaos of Sookagrad's fall.

"What happened to Stal?" I asked.

"He got to Drak'zanaat and fought with us there," Zdravkova said, "but he and Ivanov disappeared once the Zacks showed up. That was something to see! Those Zack Mike troopers don't fool around, do they? Anyway, Stal slipped away. I think he wants to keep a low profile. I'm thinking I should do the same thing."

I shook my head. "That ship has sailed, Killer. You're going to be the real hero of Sookagrad, once all the dust settles, so you better get used to it."

I saw a look of genuine distress at the thought of it, and she looked around, as if for a way out. "There are things I have to do," she said.

"You still can, just in a different way," I said.

She looked at me, puzzled.

"You'll have a platform, and when it's time to speak you'll have an audience. Trust me, the time is coming."

She looked at me thoughtfully for a moment. "Is that all you'll tell me?"

"Yup," I said. "Except that I actually managed to find a bottle of locally distilled slivovitz." I pulled it out of my hip pocket, unscrewed the cap, and held it up. "To Sookagrad, and absent friends." I drank and passed it to Zdravkova.

"To Sookagrad," she whispered, eyes distant, and she drank. She looked at Moshe and smiled tenderly. "You're in no shape for this, dear. I'll do the honors for you."

"To Sookagrad," he said, and Zdravkova drank again. She held the bottle out to me but I waved it away.

"It's a present. Keep it. So Moshe, once you're up out of this bed, I'm betting there are any number of starship lines who'll be willing to hire the electrical genius of Sookagrad. You can probably name your price."

His eyes flicked to Zdravkova's and then he smiled wistfully. "Bah, I think maybe flying around isn't so good a life after all. You go from here to there to there and then back to where you started, and what have you got? All the repairs and new construction they'll be doing here...I think an electrician can do some good, and if I make a little money while I'm at it, that wouldn't kill me either."

I turned to Zdravkova. "So now that your blowing-up-stuff days are over, what are you going to do?"

She sat back down next to Moshe's bed and took his hand. "I suppose write political manifestos no one will read, and waste my time with this old fool."

"Old, young, all men are fools," Moshe said. "The young ones are just more trouble."

She smiled, raised the bottle in another toast, and drank.

Chapter Forty

I had one last errand to run in Sakkatto City. I talked Commissioner Prayzaat into a pass to see Elaamu Gaant in a private conference room, the ones counselors use and which are surveillance-free. He was being held in a Commonwealth detention facility pending trial on about twenty different charges, including high treason.

A guard brought Gaant in. Aside from the fresh bandage still covering part of the side of his head, he looked pretty good. This was the sort of detention facility where guys like him still got to wear suits.

As soon as he sat down across the conference table from me and we were alone, he said, "So, have you come to gloat?"

"Yeah, pretty much."

"It is exactly what I would expect from a Human."

"You know, Gaant, you've got bigot's disease."

He sat back and gave me a tight-lipped smile, eyes half closed. "You think I am a bigot because I recognize the truth which is plain for anyone to see?"

"Well that's part of bigot's disease right there. But the big thing is you think everyone in creation is as much a bigot as you are. You think they all share the same prejudices, the same fears and hatreds and sense of frustrated entitlement as you. You also think most of them deny it out of shame or fear. So you figure they have no right to feel superior to you, but you *are* morally superior to them, aren't you? By virtue of your courage in speaking what everyone else secretly believes but fears to say, and by your honesty in not taking part in their hypocrisy."

"That is not a disease," he said.

"Self-deception is always a disease."

"Self-deception!" He leaned forward across the table. "What would you call your own notion of reality, this absurd belief that somehow we are all the same deep down inside?"

"I don't believe that," I said, "just the opposite. I think we're all *different*. Every Varoki I know is as different from every other one as they are from every Human I know. You're the guy who thinks everyone is pretty much the same, at least in a couple big groups. All Humans basically the same, all Zacks, all Varoki.

"I've been thinking a lot about you, and I think my wife Marr nailed your biggest weakness way back before all this mess started: you're more glib than smart. You're better at selling your ideas than at really thinking them through, so you persuaded a lot of folks you were the smartest guy in the room, and then you let them persuade *you* they were right about that. It's the ultimate self-validating bullshit loop."

"A great many people would disagree with you about that," he said.

"Yeah, what did I just say?"

He scowled and sat back in his chair. "I did not come here to listen to some Human thug insult me. Are we finished?"

"Not quite. I actually came here to tell you a secret, something I'm pretty sure you never knew. I'm going to tell you because I don't like you very much, and this secret will eat at you for the rest of your life. It will poison you. It will undermine everything you believe about yourself and your entire notion of self-worth, and destroy every hope you have for the future.

"But here's my offer: if you are *afraid* that something a Human could tell you could actually have that effect, I'll stand up and leave right now and you can continue to live in self-deception. Or I can stay and tell you. Your call."

I waited, hands folded on the table. I could see the fear color his skin, see his ears trying to fold back and him fighting to make them stand out. He *was* afraid. But he'd have a lot of

time to stew here in detention, probably the rest of his life. He
didn't know for sure what my secret would really do to him,
but I think he did know that having to live with the knowledge
that he had given in to fear, and had been made to do so by a
Human, *would* destroy him.

"Tell me your pathetic secret," he said with an almost-convincing
look of contempt.

"First," I said, "I will tell you three facts which are widely
accepted as true and yet which cannot all be true at the same
time. All six known races have unique protein compositions.
Neurotoxins, as proteins, are specific to each major race and
affect no other. The jump drive components are guarded by a
neurotoxin which attacks all six races indiscriminately."

I paused and let him think about that. It didn't alarm him, of
course, but it puzzled him. He had probably heard most of those
facts at one time or another, in some form.

"One of those must be untrue," he said. "Is that the secret?"

"No, that's the clue.

"What hardly anyone knows is the neurotoxin which guards the
jump drive is not exactly a protein, but something like a protein.
It *functions* like a protein, but it has no DNA. It is RNA-based. I
don't know exactly what that means, but I gather it's a big deal.
Apparently no other life we know of is RNA-based."

Gaant shook his head. "So that explains the contradiction.
Why is this significant?"

"RNA-based life means it's from a different tree of life. It didn't
come from any of the biospheres of the six races of the *Cottohazz*,
or any other independently evolved tree of life we have found on
any other world. All of the life forms we know are DNA-based."

"Where did it come from?" he asked, his voice growing cautious.

"No one knows."

He frowned. "You mean one day it simply *appeared*, infecting
jump drives? Like some sort of interstellar virus?"

"No, it's always been there. You see, in a sense it *is* the jump
drive cortex itself. The controlling mechanism of the jump drive
is a bioengineered organism, or rather a colony of RNA-based
microscopic organisms. The cortex, I've been told, is layer after
layer of blank circuit boards. The organisms live there on the
circuit boards, feeding on electricity. They are some sort of
biological superconductors, and don't ask me how that works

because nobody's figured it out yet. But they move on the boards in response to stimulus through the control interface, forming different electrical circuits as they do, and then the jump actuators fire and you're someplace else. Like magic. When disturbed, they emit the toxin as a defense mechanism."

He shook his head again. "Ridiculous! I've never heard of Varoki doing any sort of bioengineering, let alone anything that sophisticated-sounding, let alone three hundred years ago. If we built the jump drive that way, why haven't we built other bioengineered devices since then?"

I said nothing. I just looked at him. The air circulation system made a faint whisper, the only thing that broke the silence for several long seconds. Gaant's expression shifted, curiosity beginning to supplant anger.

"You are saying we did not build it? Then where did it come from?"

"Apparently, and I only have bits and pieces of this, it came from a derelict alien ship, but I don't know where your guys found it—certainly somewhere here in your home star system, but it doesn't matter.

"The thing is the Varoki didn't invent the jump drive; they found it. But Varoki intellectual property covenants, the ones which formed the basis of the *Cottohazz* charter, cover invention, not found knowledge. So three hundred years ago Traak and Simkitik and Kagataan and those other two guys lied on the patent."

"How can no one know this?" he asked.

"For the last three hundred years the patent-holding houses have shared and protected the secret, no matter how bitter and violent the competition between them became, claiming the internal workings of the drive were proprietary knowledge. All that time they have been trying to reverse-engineer the process that originally created the jump drive, and understand the workings of the life form that makes it go. And you know what they've come up with? Nothing."

He stared at me for a while, then shook his head again. "I do not believe you. If this is true, where is your proof?"

"Oh, I don't have any. There isn't any, yet." I laughed. "That's probably all that kept me alive the last twenty-four hours. But here's my other secret."

I leaned forward and he did as well, almost involuntarily, and when our faces were close I spoke softly.

"I figured out how to prove it. It's going to take some time, a lot of work, and it may get a little dangerous, but I'm going to do it. And when I'm done, there won't be a big war, the *Cottohazz* will still be around, but the Varoki won't be on top anymore."

He licked his lips. "You would never do that. It will reduce the value of Tweezaa e-Traak's inheritance."

"She'll survive, and my responsibility is her survival, not protecting her money. Besides, when she finds this out, I know *exactly* what she will want us to do. What did you say when we first met? That we had corrupted her? In my experience, she is incorruptible, because her decisions are guided by her courage. Yours are driven by your fears."

He looked at me with eyes full of fear and hatred, all mixed up together. "You think Humans will replace us? You think you can take our place?"

I sat back in my chair. "I don't want *your* place! I don't want a galaxy where people think my son's something *more* because he's Human. I just want one where they don't think he's something *less*. And *that's* what I'm going to give him."

I stood up and looked down at Elaamu Gaant for the last time.

"You were right to be afraid of us, Gaant. One way or another, we were always going to be your undoing, but not for any of the reasons you thought. It's because we aren't who you imagine."

E-Loyolaan provided a very nice executive shuttle to get me out of town the next morning, ahead of almost everyone else looking for a ride. The weather had cleared and the shuttle rose out of blowing smoke from the residual fires and into a brilliant blue sky decorated sparingly with white accent clouds. As we banked over the city I caught a single flash of gold far, far to the south, reflected sunlight from the Old Tower needle. The devastation of Sakkatto City below surprised and shocked me. There had been many more fights than I had witnessed, and smoke still rose from the base of Drak'zanaat Arcology, where Zdravkova had made her last stand and a cohort of Zack Mike troopers had shot their way in to save her.

I'd had one other meeting before I left, with the new second governor of AZ Simki-Traak Trans-Stellar, a guy by the name of e-Drepaank. He wanted me to carry a personal message to The Honorable Arigapaa e-Lotonaa that the governors of the trading house had no further intention of interfering with Tweezaa e-Traak-Lotonaa's inheritance. The governors regretted the terrible consequences of the foolishness of his predecessor, the late Vandray e-Bomaan, but they assumed no collective liability for his disastrous miscalculations. They hoped to enjoy a constructive and profitable relationship in the future.

I asked about the e-Traak family and he said he could not speak for them, which meant the truce was only with corporate, not the family, and might only last until the family made another really good offer to them. So it was more a temporary ceasefire than a lasting peace, but it was better than nothing. I told him I'd pass along the sentiment. He thanked me.

The shuttle flew almost due north, over columns of uBakai Army units withdrawing back to their cantonments and bases. Sprawling urban strips along the maglev lines showed the lingering effects of conflict as well, and everywhere vehicle traffic filled the roads. People leaving. People going home. Army units returning to a very uncertain future. I wondered what would happen when loyalist units and rebel units returned now to share the same base. I wondered, but I didn't really care. Someone else could worry about that.

Soon the shuttle reached and started following the long deep blue coastline of the *Zhak Kakavaan*. After an hour we passed over the canyon which held The Valley House. I tried to pick it out and saw it, a spot of pink in the black and grey rocks below, but I felt nothing.

I'd last been there a lifetime ago, it seemed, but the span of a lifetime is negotiable. I'd left there to go to the reception in Katammu-Arc the evening of Day Four, Eight-Month Waning. Now it was Day Three, Nine-Month Waxing, nineteen days later. Nineteen days.

I'd stopped by the med center to say goodbye to Moshe and I'd told him about my post-death experience, how it had given me some sense of comfort when facing death since then, but no more, now that I understood it better. He'd shrugged.

"You know, you're in a spaceship falling into a really big black hole, you pass that event horizon and all of a sudden you and that ship are spread about one atom deep all over the surface of the superdense core, and nobody can tell which carbon atoms were from you and which from the ship, 'cause one carbon atom's like any other carbon atom."

"Yeah," I said, "that really cheers me up."

He chuckled.

"Well, another interesting thing about a supermassive black hole is the closer you get to it, the slower time goes. If it's massive enough, time slows down so much you die of old age in that ship before it collapses into the black hole, even though to someone outside looking in you're gone in an instant.

"So time is local, see? It's not universal. Who's to say those last things your mind makes up—that it conjures from the best of your memories and imaginings—*don't* last forever? Maybe forever depends on where you're standing."

Maybe.

I looked down through the shuttle window as we flew over more columns of military vehicles, these driving north, probably uKootrin forces withdrawing across the frontier. And then there were no more military vehicles, no more rising columns of smoke over cities and towns. The autumn noonday sun was not directly overhead, but slightly to the south, and so our shadow raced ahead of us, flashing over fields and forests and peaceful, intact towns, guiding our way to what would be my new home, because I did not think we would return to Bakaa, at least not to live, not for a very long time.

At some point we passed from Bakaa to Kootrin, from Gaisaana-la's country to *The'On's*, but I could not tell when. They looked the same to me.

Then we began shedding speed and altitude, the ground slowly rising and the grey stains of towns resolving into discrete pixels of buildings, then the buildings resolving into unique structures made distinct from one another by their sizes, colors, designs, but not the extent of their damage.

I saw the sprawling residential complex ahead and knew that must be our destination.

The shuttle settled on the yellow-painted foamstone landing pad. The small knot of people, so familiar, so precious, turned away and protected their eyes from the dust, then turned back, faces a mixture of anxiety and anticipation and love. The hatch hissed open, the boarding stairs unfolded to rest on the ground.

I came out into sunlight, the brightest, most beautiful day I can remember, and I can remember some beauts. In two long strides I was down the stairs and enfolded in Marr and Tweezaa's arms. After a long moment I found my voice and pulled back from them a little, turned and nodded to the hatchway and the other passenger.

"Marr, Tweezaa, *The'On*, I'd like you to meet my sister, *Avrochka*."

CHARACTERS

NOTE: *Characters with an asterisk first appeared in *How Dark The World Becomes*.

The prefix "e-" before a Varoki family name indicates membership in The Select, the Varoki aristocracy.

Sasha and Company

*e-Lotonaa, The Honorable Arigapa, aka *"The'On,"* aka "Gapa" aka "Boti-On" (Uncle *The'On*): Varoki high-ranking official in the *Cottohazz* diplomatic corps, close friend of Sasha, Marrissa, and Tweezaa.

*Marfoglia, Marrissa, aka "Marr," aka "Boti-Marr" (Aunt Marrissa): Sasha's wife. Human economist, and court-appointed guardian for Tweezaa e-Traak.

*Naradnyo, Aleksandr Sergeyevich, aka "Sasha" aka *"Boti-Sash"* (Uncle Sasha), aka "Xandinho": Human former gangster and current head of Tweezaa e-Traak's personal security detail.

*e-Traak, Barraki: (mentioned) Late brother of Tweezaa e-Traak.

*e-Traak, Sarro: (mentioned) Late father of Tweezaa e-Traak.

*e-Traak, Tweezaa: Varoki heiress to the largest fortune in the *Cottohazz*.

Employees and Associates

Ah-Quan, Baka: Zaschaan (or Zack) security guard assigned to protect Gaisaana-la.

Bonderovski, Gladys: Human, security guard.

*Borro (no other name given): Varoki personal bodyguard to Arigapaa e-Lotonaa.

Cartright, John: Human, security guard.

Darzi, Kamal: Human, shuttle pilot.

Gaisaana-la (no other name given): Varoki, Marrissa Marfoglia's senior executive assistant.

Huang (no other name given): Human, shuttle pilot.

Jutaant, Tita: Varoki, security guard, killed in the shuttle crash.

Lee, Hong: Human, security guard.

Mafengi (no other name given): Human, security guard, killed in the shuttle crash.

Ramirez, Norman: Human, security guard, killed in the shuttle crash.

Swanson (no other name given): Human, security guard, killed in the shuttle crash.

Tenryu, Iris: Human deputy head of Tweeza e-Traak's personal security detail.

Other Varoki of Note

e-Bomaan, Vandray: Second governor (equivalent of vice-chairman of the board of directors) of AZ Simki-Traak Trans-Stellar, the largest mercantile house in the *Cottohazz*.

e-Drepaank (no other name given): Replacement for e-Bomaan as Simki-Traak second governor.

Gaant, Elaamu: Motivational writer and speaker, head of a Varokist and anti-Humanist movement.

e-Kunin'gaatz, Rear Admiral Talv: officer in the uBakai Astro Navy, briefly president of the provisional government.

e-Loyolaan, Field Marshal Lieutenant Yignatu: Head of CSJ, the *Cottohazz* military provost corps.

Maganaan, Ita: Executive secretary of the Black Docks Citizens' Council.

Prayzaat, Captain Arkerro: mid-ranking official in the Sakkatto Municipal Police Force.

Rimcaant (no other name given): Counselor (lawyer) and vice-governor of the Good-Soul Counseling House.

e-Tomai, Captain (no other name given): Junior officer in CSJ.

Humans in the Black Docks
(a slum district in Sakkatto City)

Abílo (no other name given): Guard.

Constancio, Cristiano: Fisherman.

Ferraz, Cézar: Fisherman.

Pacifico, Joäo: Fisherman.

Socorro, Eduardo, aka "Dado": Fisherman.

Humans in Sookagrad
(a slum district in Sakkatto City)

Chernagorov, Corporal (no other name given): Soldier.

Conklin, William, aka "Billy": Building contractor.

Dhaliwa (no other name given): Explosives expert.

Greenwald, Moshe: Former starship electrician.

Ivanov, Petar: Criminal software specialist.

Jayaraman, Divya: Student.

Katranjiev, Bogomil, aka "RG," aka "Reasonable Guy," aka "Bogo": chairman of the Sookagrad Merchants' and Citizen's League.

Kalabratov, Andrei, aka "Andy": Construction worker.

Konstantine (no other name given), aka "Kostya": wounded refugee.

Krautmann (no other name given): Doctor.

Mahajan, Dr. Tanvi: Head of Sookagrad Human clinic.

Naradnyo, Avrora Sergeichnya, aka "Aurora", aka *"Avrochka"*: Journalist.

Naradnyo, Sergei Ramonovich: Biochemist.

Pablo (no other name given): Petty criminal.

Petrov, Boris: Doctor.

Ripnick, Bela, aka "Lefty": Petty criminal.

Stal, Nikolai: Prominent member of the criminal underworld.

Ted (no other name given): Video recording technician.

Wilson (no other name given): Soldier.

Wu, Dolores: Hydroponics technician.

Zaradavana, Yash: Laborer, becomes head of ammunition distribution.

Zdravkova, Desislava Bogdanovna, aka "Dragon Lady," aka "Dezi Oobiyets" aka "Killer": Leader of Human resistance group in Sookagrad.

Other Humans

Lorioli, Lieutenant Arturo: Officer in 10th *Bersaglieri Inserimento Meteorico*.

Massignani, Major (no other name given): Cohort commander, 10th *Bersaglieri Inserimento Meteorico*.